UNCOVERED

THE UNTANGLED SERIES
BOOK 3

IVY LAYNE

GINGER QUILL PRESS, LLC

Uncovered: The Untangled Series, Book Three

Copyright © 2019 by Ivy Layne

All rights reserved.

Find out more about the author and upcoming books online at www.ivylayne.com

Also By Ivy Layne

THE UNTANGLED SERIES

Unraveled
Undone
Uncovered

SCANDALS OF THE BAD BOY BILLIONAIRES

The Billionaire's Secret Heart (Novella)
The Billionaire's Secret Love (Novella)
The Billionaire's Pet
The Billionaire's Promise
The Rebel Billionaire
The Billionaire's Secret Kiss (Novella)
The Billionaire's Angel
Engaging the Billionaire
Compromising the Billionaire
The Counterfeit Billionaire
Series Extras: ivylayne.com/extras

THE ALPHA BILLIONAIRE CLUB

The Wedding Rescue
The Courtship Maneuver
The Temptation Trap

Chapter One

ALICE

IT STARTED WITH AN ORGASM.

No, that's not right.

It started long before Cooper Sinclair gave me the best orgasm of my life, but up until then, I did a good job of ignoring it.

There's something about life-changing pleasure that makes attraction to a man hard to ignore.

I couldn't ignore the man himself. Cooper Sinclair hadn't just given me the best orgasm of my life. He was my boss.

Oops.

Maybe I should rewind just a little. I work at Sinclair Security. I started nine years ago as the girl who answered the phones and made coffee. These days I pretty much run the front office, and Sinclair Security has grown into the premier security agency in the country.

I've worked side-by-side with Cooper Sinclair for years and nothing ever happened.

Nothing.

Not an inappropriate remark, not a touch that lingered a little too long. Cooper is bossy as hell, but he's a gentleman. For most of that time, I was married. My husband—well, he's another story—but I don't cheat. I went to work and busted my ass keeping the Sinclair team in line. Sure, I appreciated all the eye candy hanging around, but I never touched. I didn't even flirt.

Then a house exploded on top of me and everything changed.

The Sinclair team has been in any number of tight spots. Tight spots are their bread and butter. This wasn't their first explosion. Not me. I'm strictly behind the desk. I have basic training—Cooper's policy for all employees—but I never planned to use it.

It was supposed to be a quiet day. A chance to get out of the office and do something different. I volunteered to watch Knox Sinclair's girlfriend's son. Adam was five, a cute kid, no trouble at all. I figured we'd eat some PB&J's, check out his Legos, and before we knew it Knox and Lily would come home and I'd head back to the office. No big deal.

And it wasn't.

Not until I walked down the hall to see a pile of paper on the floor beneath the printer, every piece bearing the same chilling warning.

HOUSE SURROUNDED. GET TO SAFE ROOM.

We always wonder how we'll do in a crisis. When we're tested, will we pass or fall apart? If anything good came out of that day it's the knowledge that somewhere deep inside me all of Cooper's training paid off. That training saved our lives.

I saw the warning printed in stark letters and my brain clicked into a gear I didn't know it had. I didn't stop to wonder why they hadn't just called, or who was surrounding the house and why.

I strode to the kitchen, told Adam we were having a picnic in Knox's secret room, snagged some snacks from the pantry and a puzzle, led Adam to the basement safe room, and locked him inside.

I'd booked it back up the stairs and grabbed a weapon from the gun-safe, intending to lock the door to the safe room and sit tight.

I was trying to figure out how to hide the firearm from my young charge when feet thundered down the steps. A man with a gun. Not Cooper. Not anyone from our team. One of the men surrounding the house.

I don't know what I would have done if I'd stopped to think. There was no time to unlock the door to the safe room. No time to get to safety.

Deep inside all of us is an animal that wants to live. To survive. It doesn't care about conscience, about right and wrong. The animal inside me raised my arm, aimed, and fired a split second before the man on the stairs could do the same.

Before the echo of the shot faded, the house shook with a boom, the steps rolling under the intruder's feet, pitching him down the stairs and straight at me. Ears ringing, coughing from the dust in the air, I dove away from him. Something above me shifted and fell, whacking the back of my head with a sickening thud. The lights went out.

I don't think I was unconscious for that long. I remember Cooper's fingers on my throat, the ocean scent of him as he lifted me and ran. My eyelids weighed a ton. My mouth wouldn't work, and I drifted in and out, but I remember.

Cooper. Always Cooper. Holding me. Barking orders in the hospital. Brushing his fingers over the swollen lump on the side of my head.

3

I opened my eyes what felt like a lifetime later to see Cooper pacing at my bedside, his phone at his ear. I wiggled my fingers and toes and took a deep breath, verifying that I was in one piece. I felt okay except for a headache so bad it made my occasional migraines seem like a paper cut.

I must have made a sound. Cooper spun around, saw that I was awake, and ended his call. He stepped out of the room for half a second before he was back, demanding, "How's your head?"

Cooper is intense. I don't know if he knows how to relax. It was disconcerting to have all that intensity focused on me. Ice-blue eyes leveled on me, cheekbones sharp, lips tight. Only his dark hair softened him, thick and a little longer than usual. Cooper hadn't had time to get a haircut. I liked it like that, loved the annoyed flick of his head when it fell into his eyes.

"Alice," he said, those icy eyes narrowing.

"Uh-huh?"

"How does your head feel?"

"It's fine," I kind of lied. "What happened? Is everyone okay?"

"Everyone's fine. Everyone except for you. They're bringing you in for an MRI in a few minutes."

"An MRI? Why?" I didn't want an MRI. I wanted to go home and sleep off this headache.

"Because you have a goose egg on the side of your head and you were unconscious," he answered with strained patience, his weight balanced on the balls of his feet as if ready to catch me when I made a break for it. I knew better. If Cooper said I was getting an MRI, I was getting an MRI.

"I wasn't unconscious," I said, not entirely sure if that was true.

"No? Then why didn't you open your eyes? Why didn't you say something?"

I stared at him, speechless. Cooper wasn't angry, though a stranger might hear his tone and assume he was pissed. I knew him. Cooper didn't get pissed. He was cool and collected right up until he went nuclear. Pissed was somewhere in between. Cooper didn't do half measures.

No, Cooper wasn't angry. He was scared. I'd seen Cooper scared less than I'd seen him go nuclear. Only once. Why was he scared now? He'd said everyone was fine.

"It's just a bump on the head. It hurts, but it'll go away. You're sure everyone is okay? Adam?"

"Adam is swimming at Evers' house with Knox and Lily. He has no clue what happened."

"Knox?"

"Fine," Cooper bit out. "Not going to ask about me?"

"I can see you're okay."

Cooper's eyes flashed. Maybe he *was* pissed.

Maybe he had reason to be. I'd shot someone. I should ask what had happened. What was going to happen. My head hurt. I didn't want to think about it. Didn't want to think about anything.

"I shot him," I said in a low voice that wouldn't carry out of the room.

Cooper's eyes closed in a long blink. He shoved his hands in his pockets before he said, "Evers is explaining to Agent Holley. He'll want to talk to you."

"Okay." What else was there to say? Special Agent Holley was with the Atlanta division of the FBI. I'd met him more than once. He liked me. Hopefully enough that he wouldn't throw me in jail for murder.

"Alice." I rolled my head to look at Cooper, wincing at the movement. Cooper's face was soft. "You did good.

Adam is safe. Safe and clueless, just like he should be. The man you shot was one of Tsepov's. I don't want to think about what he would have done to you. You did good."

I let that sink in. Tsepov had been the obvious suspect, but I didn't want to jump to conclusions. Sinclair Security is a big operation. Andrei Tsepov wasn't their only enemy.

He wasn't their only enemy, but he was the only one who had it in for them personally. I knew who Tsepov was. Given everything that had been going on lately, it was impossible not to know about Andrei Tsepov.

Nephew to the former head of the Tsepov crime family with bases of operation in Las Vegas, Atlanta, and Chicago. Neck deep in all sorts of ugly shit. Running guns, drugs, human trafficking.

Former business partner to one Maxwell Sinclair.

Cooper's father.

Five years before, Maxwell's car had gone off a bridge with him inside. The medical examiner identified the body using dental records. Open and shut. His sons had grieved. His widow moved to Florida. Case closed.

It should have been. It was until Cooper learned that his father wasn't quite as dead as he'd thought. For the past few months, Cooper and his brothers had been scrambling to untangle the mess their father had left behind.

If that man in the basement was one of Tsepov's, then I was with Cooper. I didn't want to think about what he would have done to me either.

I wanted to ask what had happened. Who blew up Knox's house? Why? Why did they send the warning through the printer? What happened with Tsepov?

Before I could ask, a nurse came in pushing a wheelchair and took me off to my MRI. An hour later I learned I was concussion-free.

6

Discharge took way too long. Cooper stayed by my side for every second. I expected him to head out, to assign one of the other guys to get me home. Agent Holley would want to talk to him.

Cooper had better things to do than hang around the hospital watching me sign paperwork and wait for the discharge nurse. Every time I mentioned that he could leave he shot me a look and didn't respond. I didn't argue.

My head hurt like a bitch, I was bruised from hitting the floor, and I just wanted to go back to sleep. Finally, Cooper drove me back to Sinclair Security. Home. I was the only employee who lived in the building. Well, me and Cooper, but his place took up the entire top floor, nothing like my modest two-bedroom a floor below him.

Intended for clients in need of secure lodgings, the building had two of the small apartments. When our lease ran out six years ago and my husband forgot to sign the paperwork on our new place, Cooper offered us the smaller apartment until we found something else. I was still there.

Instead of hitting the button for the third floor, Cooper hit number four. I reached out to correct his mistake. His fingers closed around my wrist, leading my hand away from the panel.

"You need to rest. I'm taking you to my place where I can keep an eye on you. If I let you go home you'll find some project and you won't lay down and sleep."

I stared back at him, at a loss for words. I'd never been in Cooper's place before. I knew it had to be huge since it was the only thing on the fourth floor, and I knew it was nice because Cooper had expensive tastes. But I'd never been invited upstairs. Never had a reason to knock on his door.

That wasn't the only thing that stole my tongue. Cooper knew me too well. My head was throbbing. All I wanted was to crawl into bed and pass out. But if I couldn't find sleep? He was right. I'd be up, futzing around my apartment, looking for something to do. I'm not good at sitting still. I get restless too easily. For some people, a day on the couch with a movie or a book is heaven. Me? I always have at least five projects going at the same time.

That didn't mean I needed a babysitter. Especially not Cooper Sinclair. It looked like he wasn't giving me a choice. And maybe, just maybe, he had a point. Too tired to argue, I let him lead me into his apartment, barely registering the wide-open space, the gleam of stainless steel and black marble from the kitchen, the ridiculously huge flat screen mounted across the room.

Down a hall, around a corner, and I was in his bedroom. Floor-to-ceiling windows that looked out into downtown Atlanta and a bed the size of Georgia. Maybe Texas. Whatever, it was huge. The navy-blue upholstered headboard reached to the ceiling. It was neatly made in matching sheets under a crisp, white duvet.

My tired brain drifting, I wondered if Cooper had made his bed himself, tucking in his sheets so they were creased just so. Then he was pulling back the covers and nudging me between them.

"I'll be back with something to drink. You need to take the meds."

I hate pain meds. I hate all pills. I wasn't going to argue with Cooper. My head throbbed like a rotten tooth, pulsing so badly my vision felt like it swelled and contracted with every stab of pain. I just wanted to lay down and close my eyes. Being in an explosion hurts.

Then Cooper was there, pushing two chalky pills between my lips and handing me a glass of cold, sweet juice. I forced the pills down, sipped the juice and let Cooper lower me to the pillow. My eyes slid shut and I was out.

Chapter Two

ALICE

I WOKE SOMETIME IN THE NIGHT, BLINKING into the dark, instantly aware I was not in my own bed. I rolled to my side to find Cooper sleeping on top of the covers, an arm's length away.

I was in Cooper's bed. Cooper's apartment.

More importantly, *Cooper* was in Cooper's bed. With me. Not under the same covers, but still. What the hell?

I thought about getting up, sneaking out, and going down to my own place. As soon as the thought entered my mind, I pushed it away. I was warm and comfortable, except for the throb in my head and the ache in my shoulder and hip. My stomach churned from the pain pills. I wasn't fully nauseous, but if I got up—nope, not going to happen. I let sleep pull me under.

The morning sun speared my eyes as the mattress beside me depressed, and I rolled into a hard body. Squinting into the light, I realized my hand was on Cooper's thigh, my shoulder braced on his hip. He was sitting on the side of the bed next to me, and I was groping him. Crap.

I snatched my hand back and tried to sit up, pinned by the sheet Cooper sat on.

"Can you eat breakfast?"

I stopped trying to sit up and thought about it. My head still hurt. A lot. Enough that I might take another dose of the pain meds, and if I took the pills I'd need food in my stomach or I might throw them back up.

Like the creepy mind reader that he was, Cooper nodded before I spoke a single word. "You need breakfast so you can take the pain pills. Good you're not going to be a pain in the ass about it. I got one of the grunts to pick up takeout from Annabelle's. Breakfast sandwich, coffee, and a cookie if you behave yourself."

I thought about busting his chops for the *behave myself* comment, but if he had breakfast from Annabelle's I'd keep my mouth shut. Annabelle was a friend who owned a café. Everyone at Sinclair Security was a regular, even though there were closer options. While Annabelle was an artist with coffee, anything that came out of her kitchen was divine.

I sat up awkwardly and swung my feet to the side of the bed, sucking in a breath at the *woosh* of my empty stomach. Still queasy from the pills I'd taken the night before and the throb in my head, I let Cooper pull me to my feet and walk me across the room. He nudged me into the bathroom and left, calling out behind him, "If you're not out of there in five minutes, I'm coming in after you."

He would, too. That was okay. I didn't need five minutes to go to the bathroom and wash my hands and face. I tried not to look too closely in the mirror. I looked like crap and there was nothing I could do about it.

My usually neat bob was a mess, my black hair sticking out all over the place, bangs a disaster. Every shred of makeup from the day before was long gone. I looked about as good as someone who'd been through an explosion could expect to look.

At least all my parts were in the right place. At least I wasn't dead. I had a flash of the man coming down the stairs, of raising the gun and squeezing the trigger, his feet flying from the steps as the house bucked from the explosion.

I'd heard people with head injuries couldn't remember the things that happened when they got hurt. Too bad I wasn't one of them. I remembered squeezing the trigger with crystalline clarity.

I thought of the little boy in the safe room. Adam. Innocent and still alive because he had me between him and the bad guys. That was what I had to focus on.

Looking down, I caught what I was wearing and winced. An oversized Sinclair Security T-shirt and a pair of sweatpants cut off at the knee. Neither of them mine. I knew who they belonged to.

I'd seen them both often enough when Cooper stopped at the desk after a morning workout. Why was I wearing Cooper's clothes? He could get into my place. He proved that when I walked into the main room of the apartment to see a stack of my things on the kitchen island. A lightweight zip-up hoodie and matching tank. A pair of lace bikini panties and soft lounging pants that flared into ruffles just below the knee.

I was going to ignore the fact that Cooper had been in my underwear drawer. I hoped it was Cooper. "Please tell me you didn't send one of the grunts to root around in my underwear drawer."

Cooper shot me a wicked grin. My heart skipped a beat. "I got you some things I thought you'd need. Eat your breakfast before you change, or it will get cold."

A flash of relief at the knowledge that one of the junior employees hadn't been rifling through my underwear drawer, then heat hit my cheeks as I imagined Cooper at my dresser, taking in lacy wisps of nothing right next to my granny-panties, my laundry-day underwear, and the underwear I only wore when I had my period. Oh, great.

Deciding not to think about it, I picked up my still-warm breakfast sandwich, hoping the buttery croissant and smoky bacon would do something to dull the pain in my head. Cooper slid a to-go coffee cup with the logo of Annabelle's Café in front of me.

I knew it would be a skinny vanilla latte. That's what I drank, and Cooper knew everything. After nine years, he wouldn't get my coffee order wrong, even though I was the one who always ordered the coffee. Swallowing the bite of sandwich, my stomach grateful for food, I took a sip. Yep, skinny vanilla latte. Two white pain pills sat beside the cup. I took them without argument, washing them down with another sip of latte and another bite of sandwich. Maybe with food in my stomach they wouldn't make me so queasy. Cooper had thought of everything.

Just when I was feeling all warm and appreciative, Cooper had to open his mouth and ruin it. "I have to go to work. You're staying here. Rest. Watch TV or something. Just stay still."

"I can work," I insisted, though for once I didn't really want to. If something came up I could be there, but I wasn't sure I had it in me. Not with this headache.

Cooper didn't bother to reply. He shoved his phone in his pocket and turned to go. "I'll check in on you later, bring you lunch. When Agent Holley gets here, I'll bring him up."

I popped off of my stool, putting down my sandwich to follow him to the door. "You don't have to bring me lunch,

Cooper. I have food downstairs. As soon as I finish eating I
can go—"

"You're staying here," Cooper said again.

"Why?" I had to ask.

"Because I don't trust you in your place. You need to
rest. I want you where I can keep an eye on you."

I stalked behind him as he headed for the door, trying
to ignore the throb in my head with every step. I was still
staring at his back as the door closed behind him, the
deadbolt turning with a *snick*.

Wait a second, why would he lock the door from the outside? I could just... I reached out to flip the lock open. The
bolt refused to turn. It might as well have been welded in
place.

Did that bastard just lock me in?

I crossed my arms over my chest and stared at the door.
He had. Cooper Sinclair had locked me in.

I stood there, thinking. I could pitch a fit, call the office
and raise hell demanding he let me out. *I could*, but if I
went to war with Cooper, I wasn't sure I'd win. The guys
would have their hands full dealing with the aftermath of
the explosion and the man I'd shot.

Just this once, I'd stay put. Just this once. I didn't want
Cooper getting any ideas he could order me around when-
ever he wanted.

I finished my breakfast, leaving the cookie for later, and
brought my coffee to the huge L-shaped couch facing the
gigantic TV. Cooper's couch was more than big enough for
his tall frame. It swallowed me whole. Plumping up the
soft pillows and dragging a blanket over me, I grabbed the
remote and decided to channel surf.

That lasted less than an hour. Nothing against TV. I
binge-watched here and there, but not like this, just lying

on the couch doing nothing. I'd turn on the TV for company when I cooked or worked on one of my projects, but just sitting around? Even with the pain pills kicking in, I wasn't bored enough for that.

It's a vice or a virtue depending on your point of view, but that's me—if I'm not sleeping, I'm moving. I'm constitutionally incapable of vegging in front of the TV.

I changed the station to one with music and sat up, only a little woozy from the headache and the pain pills. Once my brain settled in my skull, I got up and looked around for something to do.

Cooper's place was decorated in a style I think of as *vintage bachelor*. Not a lot of knickknacks, only a handful of pictures—mostly him with his brothers and friends. The main room was flooded with light, one whole wall dominated by more of the floor-to-ceiling windows he had in his bedroom.

This part of Cooper's place was open plan, each space flowing into the next. The kitchen was all stainless steel and black granite, with breakfast counter and island beside a dining space with a long, dark, shiny table, gleaming in the morning sun. The lounging area with the couch and huge tv was opposite both.

What I could see from here was spacious, but Cooper's place covered the entire floor. There had to be a lot more than his bedroom and the open plan living area. What else did Cooper have up here?

I felt not a smidge of hesitation as I set out to explore. If he didn't want me to poke around he shouldn't have locked me in his apartment. He would reap what he'd sown.

He'd gone through my underwear drawer? I had all day to go through his.

Never mind the flutter in my chest at the thought of Cooper's underwear. *You have nothing to do with Cooper's underwear*, I reminded myself.

I wandered down the hall to Cooper's bedroom and discovered a laundry room with a massive washer and dryer, one whole wall neatly organized with a bench, hooks hung with jackets, cubbies filled with boots and running shoes.

That room led into another that was empty except for a padded floor. A tall wooden staff leaned against the wall, a few sets of free weights beside it. Why did Cooper have a home gym when he had the company gym downstairs? I took in the room again and realized he used it to practice his martial arts.

They had a sparring room downstairs, but I could see he might want privacy sometimes. Or just quiet. I didn't spend much time in the company gym. Despite the eye candy, it was weird being one of the only women with all those guys. Anyway, I liked to take classes. I couldn't imagine anyone on the team doing Zumba.

Further down the hall I passed Cooper's bedroom again and decided to save that for last. There were three more bedrooms, one filled with a bunch of boxes and an old desk. The other two were decorated in *generic guest room*.

The hall turned and I faced two doors—one an interior door that could have led anywhere. I wouldn't know because it was locked. The other door was painted to match the interior, but after a knock, I realized it was metal. Did it lead outside? Maybe that was the stairwell door. It, too, was locked.

I turned and headed back to Cooper's bedroom, swaying as I walked. I couldn't remember the last time I'd taken prescription pain meds. They hit me hard. Maybe it was a good thing I wasn't at work. I'd probably end up ordering five hundred reams of paper instead of five or fucking up the schedule.

Still, Cooper didn't have to lock me in. Grumbling under my breath about controlling asses, I went straight for Cooper's closet. What was good for the goose and all that.

Cooper's closet was as neat and organized as I'd expected. Everything hung just so, arranged by color and type. His sock drawer was the same. I had my hand on the pull for the drawer above, saw just enough to catch rows of neatly folded boxers, when from behind me I heard, "Snooping?"

I jumped, spinning to face him, and wobbled, the sudden motion sending a stab of pain through my head. Hands closed over my shoulders, gently steadying me. Cooper looked down, a smirk on his face. "Don't let me stop you. You want to look at my underwear, Alice?"

I glared up at him. Why was he so tall? My head swimming, I blurted out, "What are you doing up here?"

"I told you to stay put. You're supposed to be resting, not wandering all over the place."

His words trickled through my ears, into my brain, slowly assembling a picture that sent my temper skyrocketing.

He'd said he wanted me where he could keep an eye on me.

He knew I'd been wandering all over the place.

"You have cameras in here," I accused.

Cooper's icy blue eyes stared back, admitting nothing, but I didn't need the words. Cooper ran Sinclair Security. Surveillance was part of what they did, and they were damn good at it. I should know. I helped order the equipment, had been a guinea pig for testing. Most of the building was wired, except for the second-floor apartments and Cooper's place.

"When did you put in cameras?"

That smirk still curling his lips, Cooper said, "This morning. What do I have to do to get you to lay down and rest?"

Mulishly, I said, "Give me my laptop."

"No."

"Okay, then." I turned around and started to open his underwear drawer again. "You really like navy-blue, don't you? I don't know why I never noticed that. Maybe because everybody wears blue suits, and I'd never seen your bedroom, or your underwear—" Cooper reached around me and pushed the drawer shut.

"Fine, I'll bring you your laptop."

"And a phone."

"No fucking way. No phones. Just the laptop, and if you get sleepy you take a nap. Agreed?"

"Fine." I stalked back to the living room. Or, I tried to stalk. Between the effects of the pain pills and my headache, it was probably more like a shuffle. Cooper strode to the door.

"I'll be back with your laptop. Agent Holley will be here in an hour or two, so you might want to change. Or not. You look good in my T-shirt."

Chapter Three

ALICE

THE DOOR SWUNG SHUT BEHIND HIM AND I stared at it, jaw dropped.

Since when did Cooper notice what I looked like?

Since never. Cooper was everything appropriate in the workplace. He'd compliment me on a job well done, but he never mentioned my appearance.

He was the only one who didn't.

I have a style. People either like it or they don't get it. Rockabilly is fifties-inspired, with a dash of rock and roll whimsy. I put on my first rockabilly dress in college and I never looked back. Most of my dresses are vintage fifties, with a fitted bodice, nipped-in waist, and full, knee-length skirts. Both intensely feminine and modest, I've always felt like the line of the dresses and bright colors give my small stature more presence.

Over the years I've made the style my own, but I'll admit my look can be a little unexpected. Not unprofessional, but unexpected. Most of my dresses are fairly tame, but occasionally, when we don't have a client meeting, I'll bust out something more fun.

Cooper never said a word about the dress covered in lollipops or the one with miniature pieces of sushi, but he noticed me wearing his old T-shirt?

Maybe he was the one who got hit on the head. Or maybe the pain pills were hitting me harder than I thought. I looked at the pile of clothes on the kitchen island and realized Cooper could be back any second.

Moving as fast as I could without aggravating my head, I grabbed the clothes and went to his bathroom to change. He might have cameras in his place, but even Cooper wouldn't put them in the bathroom. He was controlling and overprotective, but he wasn't a perv.

I changed into the lounge pants and hoodie Cooper had picked out and looked through his drawers for a comb or brush. My vanity wanted to demand Cooper go downstairs and get my makeup so I didn't look like a sickly ghost when Agent Holley came to take my statement.

I pictured confessing to murder with my hair done and red lipstick on. Probably not the best idea. Wan and pathetic might be better.

I wasn't up to makeup anyway, much less trying to do something with my hair. This might be the one time in my life when leaving my armor behind and looking like crap was the best plan.

Cooper returned with my laptop, handing it to me with a strict warning to behave myself. I wouldn't put it past him to have keystroke tracking software installed or a second laptop on his desk so he could watch what I was doing, just to make sure I was following orders.

He didn't have to worry. The general email box had piled up since the afternoon before, and after two hours of dealing with that, I didn't have the energy to get into trouble. I closed the laptop, set it on the coffee table, and curled into Cooper's comfortable couch, my eyes sliding shut as soon as the throb in my head eased.

The sound of the door closing woke me. I sat up, still a little woozy but feeling much more myself. The pain meds from the morning had worked their way out of my system, and my head didn't throb as badly as before.

Cooper hadn't come alone. Beside him stood Agent Holley. A tall, lanky man with kind eyes, Agent Holley stared down at me with concern.

Cooper handed me another coffee, this one from the machine downstairs in the office. I moved to stand, but Agent Holley waved me back down.

"Don't get up, Alice. It's good to see you again. I just need you to take me through what happened yesterday."

I did, surprised when Agent Holley put his notebook away after asking only a few follow-up questions.

"That's it?"

"That's it," he confirmed, sharing a look with Cooper.

"Aren't you going to tell me not to leave town or something?" I had to ask.

Agent Holley gave me a rare smile. "Don't leave town, Alice. I can't formally let you off the hook yet. This is still an active investigation. But from everything you've told me and what I saw at the scene, it's clear that you were acting to defend not only yourself but Adam Spencer. There was a bullet in the wall opposite the stairs. Between your shot and the explosion you might have missed it, but Tsepov's man fired on you. Adam Spencer is lucky you were there."

My throat choked with useless fear at the thought of the bullet that could have killed me, a wave of relief washing the fear away. Agent Holley believed me. I wasn't going to jail. Good news.

I nodded and shook the hand Agent Holley held out. I heard Cooper say, "Hold up a sec, I'll walk you out," before turning back to me. "What do you want for dinner? Do you need another pill?"

"Maybe something over-the-counter if you have it. No more of the stuff from the doctor. My head's not that bad. I swear," I added when Cooper looked like he was about to protest.

He checked the time on his watch, judged it had been long enough since the pills this morning, and brought me a small red and white bottle from the top shelf of the pantry. I washed two of the tablets down with the coffee.

"So, dinner?" he prompted.

"I should go home, get out of your hair—"

"Had enough of me already?" Cooper asked, that smirk curving his lips again.

"No, I just... I just thought I should probably go home," I said, lamely.

Before, I'd wondered—was it the headache and pain pills throwing me off, or was Cooper being weird? Now the headache was manageable, the pain pills had worn off, and I knew for sure.

It wasn't me.

Cooper was being weird.

"Sushi, Thai, or Italian?" he prompted.

Without a thought, out popped, "Italian. Lasagna. I need lasagna." Lasagna was as good as chocolate or coffee when it came to smoothing away the rough edges of life. Melting cheese and pasta. Mmmm yeah, lasagna.

"Garlic knots?"

"Duh."

Another grin that was half wicked and half smirk. What was up with him? I wasn't surprised he knew my dinner order. Like the coffee, I was in charge of getting takeout most of the time, but Cooper knew what I ordered because he saw it on my desk. The Italian place we got food from had the best garlic knots on earth. I could make a meal just of their garlic knots.

"Lasagna with garlic knots it is. I'll be back in an hour or two. Try to stay out of trouble until then."

The lock turned on the door and I thought, *I can't help staying out of trouble when you keep locking me in.*

I was stir crazy by the time Cooper came back, his hands laden with bags of takeout fragrant with tomatoes and garlic. My mouth watered and I realized I was starving.

He came around to the couch where I'd been stretched out flipping through channels on the TV. Placing the take-out bags on the coffee table, he dropped a kiss on the top of my head and disappeared saying, "Can you unpack those? I'll be right back."

Had Cooper just kissed me on the top of the head? I was the one who'd been knocked out, but Cooper was acting like he'd had a personality transplant.

Maybe none of this was happening. Maybe I was unconscious in the hospital and this whole thing was just a coma delusion.

I unpacked the take-out containers, lining them up on the coffee table. Two orders of lasagna, garlic knots, and tiramisu. I grabbed a garlic knot and sank my teeth in the yeasty, buttery bread.

It had to be a coma delusion. That was the only thing that made sense. Otherwise, I couldn't think of any reason I'd be sitting in Cooper's apartment about to eat takeout with him. Nine years we'd worked together and I'd never been in his apartment, much less eaten dinner here. And Cooper had kissed me on the top of the head.

Coma delusion. Definitely.

He came back dressed in a T-shirt and cut-off sweats, dropping onto the couch beside me. Grabbing the remote and flicking on the TV, he asked, "This okay?"

I looked up to see a movie for rent, one we'd both talked about catching in the theaters and had missed.

"Sure." I dug into my dinner. The pain pills had completely worn off and my appetite had come roaring back. Normally, a serving of lasagna from this place would hold me for two meals, but I tore through every bite and my share of the garlic knots, fighting Cooper for forkfuls of the tiramisu.

When I stabbed his hand with the tines of my fork, he gave me an accusing look.

I shrugged. "You should have ordered two. You know I love tiramisu."

Stomach full, I leaned back into the couch to find Cooper's arm behind me. It closed around me, tugging me into his side. My appetite appeased, headache down to a dull roar, my eyelids drooped. Before I knew it, I was tucked into Cooper, my head resting on his chest. Cooper smelled of the ocean, of clean air and salt, and I breathed him in, the thump of his heart strong under my ear.

A flash of prickling panic shot through me, my heart kicking into a rapid beat as I realized where I was falling asleep. Laying against Cooper, his arm around me, my head on his chest.

What the hell? How did I end up here?

Coma delusion, I reminded myself. *None of this is real. I'm going to wake up in the hospital with a killer headache and Cooper will be his normal self. All business. Bossy and annoying. No kisses on the head. No bringing me dinner. Just Cooper.*

That thought should have been comforting. It would have been, but I liked my coma delusion. I liked the strength of his arm around me, his ocean scent in my lungs. If I'd been at home alone, I wouldn't be at peace, full and sleepy and safe. I would have been restless, remembering what had happened in Knox's basement, the feel of pulling the trigger, the roar of the blast, and everything going dark.

Not here. Not curled into Cooper, his heart beating under my ear, his arm holding me close. Cooper wouldn't let anything happen to me. Ever. On that thought, I fell asleep.

I woke to the flicker of the TV screen and the weightless sensation of swinging through the air. Cooper standing, lifting me in his arms, holding me close against his chest. Carrying me.

Carrying me?

My brain tangled in sleep, it fell back in time to the mad flight from Knox's house as I'd flickered in and out of consciousness aware only of Cooper's strong arms holding me close.

Reality slowly settled around me. There was no smoke here. Cooper wasn't running, just crossing the apartment in his normal stride. My eyes flicked open. I was in Cooper's apartment. I shouldn't be here. Coma delusion or not, it was time to go home.

I squirmed in his arms. "Cooper, put me down. Where are you taking me?"

"I'm taking you to bed."

No reason those words should send heat spiraling through my body. Cooper didn't mean it like that. Of course, he didn't. I pushed at his arm. "Cooper, put me down. I need to go home. I'm fine. I appreciate you taking care of me, bringing me dinner and everything, but my head is better. I'm not taking any pain pills. I need to go home."

"Why?"

Dumbfounded, I lost my train of thought.

Why? What did he mean, why?

Slowly, I said, "Because I live there."

Cooper ignored me and continued his path across the room.

"Cooper, seriously, put me down."

I'd never really thought before about the difference in our sizes other than to note that Cooper was tall, really tall, and he wore it well. Now, I was acutely aware that my small, slight frame had no chance against Cooper. He held me immobile with barely any effort. I would have liked it if it hadn't been so annoying.

Ignoring my insistence that I needed to go home, he said, "Your head doesn't hurt?"

Seizing on that excuse, I insisted, "No, I swear. It's much better. Barely hurts at all. I'm totally fine. Just let me down and I'll go home. If I need anything, I'll call. Promise."

Cooper stood in the shadowy darkness of the kitchen, eyes locked on my face. Again, he said, "Your head doesn't hurt? You feel okay?"

"I'm fine," I repeated, uneasy at his odd behavior. He should be ready to be rid of me by now. Shouldn't he?

Cooper turned, and instead of putting me down, he set me on the island, his arms still around me, my knees on either side of his hips. I looked up, confused. What was going through his head? I couldn't keep up.

Cooper cupped my chin in his fingers, tilting my head up. An odd, intent light in his pale eyes, he said, "I've been waiting for so long. Too long. I almost missed my chance. I won't make that mistake again."

I opened my mouth to tell him to stop being weird. For just a second, looking up at him in the near dark, I didn't recognize the man holding my face in his hands.

This was not the Cooper I knew.

This man wasn't all business, cool and driven. This man had molten blue fire in his eyes, his hands strong and gentle, his focus entirely on me. This man woke my body, left me needing something. Needing him.

"Cooper," I whispered, not sure what I planned to say next. It didn't matter. I wouldn't have gotten the words out anyway.

His name on my lips, his eyes liquid flame, Cooper dropped his head and kissed me.

Yep. Definitely a coma delusion.

Chapter Four

ALICE

I'D BEEN KISSED BEFORE. I'M THIRTY-THREE years old. I'd been married. Of course, I'd been kissed. A lot, if not in a while.

I'd never, ever been kissed like Cooper kissed me.

I handle Human Resources at Sinclair Security. I don't hire and fire, but if you want to know about health benefits or how to handle harassment, I'm your girl. If an employee came to me and said her boss kissed her I would have told her to remove herself from the situation, to tell him firmly that such behavior is inappropriate and immediately submit a written report.

That's what I would have said.

That was not what I did. Not at all.

At the touch of Cooper's mouth to mine, any thought that this was a coma delusion evaporated. No delusion felt this real, this warm and alive. This hungry. This needy. This passionate.

His breath hitched at the touch of our lips, igniting something in me that had smoldered for years. So many years.

Everything inside me ground to a halt at that touch, my very heart ceasing to beat for the longest moment—for an eternity—as the universe shifted on its axis.

I drew in a breath, and the world slammed back into place, shifting from a dead stop to high-speed in one lurching heartbeat.

I reached for Cooper, my fingers sinking into his hair, pulling his face to mine, kissing him, tasting him, driving my tongue into his mouth to stroke his.

Cooper.

Fucking hell, *Cooper*.

Who knew Cooper would taste so good? Would feel so right? He was too big, too distant, too much my boss. None of that mattered. He was right.

He pulled me against him, my breasts pressing to his chest, my throat vibrating with groans. His mouth fastened to mine, demanding and possessive.

I gave as good as I got, my hands wandering to yank at his T-shirt. I wanted his skin, the heat and strength of him. I wanted to touch, to taste.

I was barely aware of my arms flying over my head, cool air brushing my heated skin, the whisper of my camisole and hoodie hitting the kitchen island. Cooper's T-shirt followed, every rasp of his chest hair against my nipples sparking tiny explosions of bliss.

There was so much of him. I pressed myself against his chest until I thought our skin would meld together, wanting to suffuse myself with him. His taste. The ocean scent of him.

His arm going tight around my back, Cooper lowered me to the cool granite counter, settling my head on a makeshift pillow of our discarded clothes.

He protected my still-tender head from the unforgiving granite countertop even in his haze of desperate lust.

Cooper.

I was aware of it only in the most distant of ways, most of my attention on his hands, tugging at the fabric at my hips, stripping me, leaving me naked and spread out before him like a pagan offering.

His eyes locked on my body splayed before him, he groaned my name. "Alice. Fuck, Alice. So fucking beautiful."

I couldn't make words form in my head, much less come out of my mouth. Cooper stood naked between my legs, all muscle and smooth, tanned skin. Cooper, his ice-blue eyes molten hot and fixed on me. *Cooper.*

Then he was on me, his mouth on my breast, drawing on my nipple, kneading and molding my other breast with his long fingers.

I wrapped my legs around him, drawing him closer, the length of his erection pressed against my core, already slick with desire. Desperate. So fucking desperate, I rolled my hips into him, and he shuddered in my arms.

Lifting his head from my breast, his words were barely more than a rumble in his chest. "Alice. I need you to say it. Do you want this? Do you want me?"

"Cooper." That was all I could force out, his name a plea. He had to ask? He had to know how much I wanted him, had to feel my slick heat soaking his cock as it rubbed against me. I loved that he asked anyway. He rocked his hips into me before he spoke.

"Alice. I want to fuck you. To fill you with me. To mark you as mine. I need you to know that. I need you to tell me you want it too."

I spoke the truth of my body, though my brain was speechless. "Yes. Yes, Cooper. Please."

That was all he needed. His mouth took mine in a kiss of possession. Of triumph, of heat and need. His knuckles brushed the inside of my thigh as he moved his cock into position and thrust his hips forward.

At the stretch of his cock pushing inside me, I wrenched my lips from his, arching my back with a long deep moan. "Oh, God. Cooper. Cooper."

He froze, his lips a whisper against my neck. "Too much?"

"So good. So good, Cooper. Please. Please, Cooper. More. Oh, God, Cooper."

I couldn't seem to shut my mouth, couldn't stop babbling, everything in my brain and my body short-circuiting from the sheer bliss of his cock filling me up.

I'd been empty for so long. My whole life I'd been empty, and Cooper—his arms around me, his cock inside me— Cooper filled me up. Filled me to overflowing.

When I'd taken every inch of him, he circled his hips, grinding into my clit, splinters of pleasure slicing through my body, drawing another long, low groan from my lips.

His mouth at my ear, he rocked into me, murmuring nothing and everything. "Fuck, Alice, Alice, Alice. So good, Alice. I can't— I need you to come for me."

His mouth on mine, his hand slipped beneath me, tilting my hips, grinding into me as his tongue danced with mine. It was too much. It was everything.

I exploded, screaming into his kiss, my brain whiting out as his hips jerked against mine and he joined me in a release we'd been waiting for forever.

I came back to myself at that now-familiar sensation of floating, of swinging through the air. Cooper carrying me. Again. And this time, different.

This time, instead of cradling me against him, my legs were wrapped around his waist. This time I had no thought

32

of protest, no desire to walk by myself. I draped myself over him, my arms loose around his neck, my sweaty cheek glued to his shoulder. His cock was still half-hard inside of me, each step sending bolts of pleasure through my body.

Cooper carried me straight into his oversized, glassed-in shower, turning on the water, letting it wash away the sweat and the aftermath of sex. I tried to think, to say something. Anything.

No condom. That thought managed to slice through the cloud of lust and satisfaction in my brain. I had an IUD, got tested for everything after I'd left my husband, and hadn't slept with anyone since then.

I knew the guys all got regular physicals. I was the one who scheduled them and paid the bills. And I knew Cooper. He'd remembered to protect my head from the hard counter even as he'd been tearing off my clothes. He never would have skipped a condom if it would put me at risk.

Hell, he probably had my medical records, the sneaky bastard. Probably knew I was protected from pregnancy and safe to fuck bare. I didn't care except to be glad we didn't need to worry about condoms. Now that I'd felt him skin to skin, nothing else would do.

A small part of me tried to speak up. But what about—? What about *nothing*.

Sensible Alice could shut the hell up.

This felt too good for sensible Alice to get in the way.

Cooper's hands moved over me, his mouth at my neck, warm water raining over us. He still hadn't put me down. He lifted me off his cock, his hand moving between my legs, letting the water wash us clean, before he sat on the deep bench in the corner, still holding me in his arms.

Water streaming over us, he kissed me in endless, drugging kisses, his strong hands moving over my body until he lifted me, bringing me down onto his hard cock. My head spun as he dipped me back over his arm and feasted on my breasts, my hips rocking, orgasm washing through my body once, then again.

I was barely aware of him setting me on my feet, cleaning me, and turning off the water. We slid beneath the sheets of his bed and I passed out, my still-damp body draped over Cooper's, my mouth pressed to the pulse in his throat, his heartbeat lulling me to sleep.

Sometime later, my eyes opened in the dark, the glow of the moon barely penetrating the curtains.

Reality slammed into me like a freight train.

This was no coma delusion.

The soreness between my legs, the dull throb in my head, and Cooper's long body splayed beside mine were all too real.

What was I supposed to do now?

Did I stay?

Was this a thing now? Was I having sex with Cooper?

My body gave an involuntary shudder as those words formed in my head.

Sex with Cooper.

It sounded so dry and clinical. The act itself had been anything but. It had been hot and messy. Overwhelming and so fucking good.

In my most heated imaginings, I'd never dreamed of sex like that. But what was I supposed to do now? Roll over and go back to sleep? Sneak out and pretend nothing happened?

Lying there staring at the ceiling, option two seemed like the most sensible choice.

Okay, then. Sneak out and pretend nothing happened.

I rolled to my side, inching toward the edge of the bed, when a hard arm came down, dragging me back. Back to

Cooper. He rolled me, coming down on top of me, lacing his fingers with mine and holding them over my head, pinning me in place.

"Going somewhere?" he asked easily, a hot spark in his icy blue eyes.

Having no reasonable answer to that question, I wisely kept my mouth shut. Dropping his lips to graze my chin, he said, "I didn't think so."

Positioning my upturned palms carefully beneath my head, raising it so I wouldn't press the still tender lump into the pillows, he growled, "Don't move your hands."

Breathless, all I could manage was a whispered, "K."

He moved down my body, his mouth wet and hot against my fevered skin, nipping my breast, licking the line of my ribs, dipping into my belly button before planting a palm on each thigh and pushing my legs apart, baring me to his mouth.

I sucked in a gasp. Cooper worked his mouth over me, tasting every inch of my pussy, diving his tongue inside and filling me with his fingers while he sucked on my clit. My hips bucking beneath him, my mouth moved, babbling an endless refrain of lust-inspired nonsense that consisted mostly of *please, God, Cooper,* and formless, desperate groans.

I came twice before he rose over me, my knees automatically clamping to his sides, lifting for him as he filled me with that glorious cock, fucking into my oversensitive pussy until I screamed his name.

After, my legs no better than jelly, I passed out on top of him, our bodies sticky with sweat and sex. Neither of us cared. I'd think tomorrow. Tonight I wasn't going anywhere.

My eyes opened to sunshine and the tempting scent of bacon and fresh-squeezed orange juice. I rolled over, letting out a startled squeak at the sight of Cooper standing beside the bed wearing nothing but his cut-off sweatpants, that gorgeous body in full view.

Struggling to sit up, I held the sheet over my breasts, thoughts tumbling in my head. The smirk that curved the side of Cooper's mouth was satisfied. A little smug. "Hungry?"

I nodded. I *was* hungry. And eating would buy me some time while I figured out what to do next. My tender, over-used body perked awake at the sight of so much half-naked Cooper and slyly suggested, *Why do you have to do anything at all? Let's just have more sex with Cooper.*

Cooper slid in bed next to me and helped himself to a piece of toast from the tray he'd set over my lap. Content to eat in silence for the time being, I tried to get my thoughts in order.

Sensible Alice was telling me to bolt for the door, lock myself in my apartment, and not come out unless someone else was with me so I wouldn't be tempted to strip Cooper naked and jump him again.

Sensible Alice was a buzzkill.

Sensible Alice had stayed married to her ass of an ex-husband for way too long.

The Alice who'd just had multiple orgasms in twelve hours wasn't interested in being sensible. Knock on the head aside, I wasn't deluded enough to think this was anything more than sex.

Cooper wasn't just my boss—which made him untouchable enough—he was Cooper Sinclair, the oldest of the Sinclair brothers. Cooper was old Atlanta.

Cooper dated socialites. Models. He'd dated a movie star and the bass player in a famous all-female rock band. Cooper did not date quirky office managers. Especially not *his* quirky office manager.

I didn't know what madness had ended up with us naked on his kitchen island, but Cooper was too contained, too controlled to confuse sex with anything deeper.

I was convenient. When I thought of it that way, it was kind of a miracle he'd never tried to tap my ass before. I lived right downstairs, after all. *I was convenient.*

Before that ugly thought could worm a hole in my nice post-orgasm bubble, I snuck a glance at his sculpted chest, his broad shoulders, those strong hands currently peeling an orange that had lifted me so easily and dropped me down onto a long, thick cock...

And it occurred to me that *Cooper* was convenient.

Cooper was so contained, so controlled, I'd bet he could fuck me for fun and it would never touch our working relationship.

Why should it? We were both adults. We were both professional. We took the job seriously. I wouldn't be stupid enough to let sex mess up anything at work, and neither would Cooper.

This was just sex. Fucking amazing, mind-blowing, once-in-a-lifetime sex. I wasn't going to walk away because I was worried we couldn't handle it. I snuck another glance at the glory of half-naked Cooper and decided to stop being such a wimp.

"So, we're having sex now?"

Cooper handed me a slice of orange, his eyes impossible to read. "Right now, we're having breakfast."

"Smartass," I muttered, taking the orange. "After breakfast. And later. Is this a thing now? We have sex?"

Cool blue eyes slid to mine. "Do you want to stop?" His voice was so neutral I wasn't sure he cared about my answer.

"Not a chance," I said, instinct choosing my words before I could form them into something more graceful.

Cooper said nothing, just leaned over, lifted the tray from my lap and set it on the bedside table before pinning me to the mattress and taking my mouth with his. He tasted of oranges and coffee and everything good.

I wasn't walking away from this. No way.

Sensible Alice could take a hike.

I was going to take every bit of Cooper Sinclair I could before he lost interest and I lost my chance.

Chapter Five

COOPER

I KEPT ALICE IN MY BED UNTIL THE CLOCK ticked down to the very last second before she had to leave to get ready for work.

I wished I could cancel everything and keep her exactly where she was.

Under me.

Where she belonged.

I'd been waiting for her for so fucking long. Almost a decade. It felt like a lifetime. One weekend wasn't enough.

She slipped from my bed mumbling, blushing, yanking on her clothes and rushing through the door, leaving me hollow.

She'll be back, I reminded myself. No putting this genie back in the bottle. No fucking way.

Now that I knew how she tasted, the sound of her moan, the sexy, adorable way she babbled as I drove her to orgasm—no fucking way was I letting that go. Ever.

Alice was mine.

This wasn't the best time to turn our lives upside down.

It was probably the worst time. My father was still MIA, the Russian mob intent on hunting him down. We'd paid off Andrei Tsepov, secured his promise that he'd go after my father and leave the rest of the family out of their feud, but Andrei's word was worth nothing. He was still out there. Still a threat.

Scarier than the mob was my mother. My brother, Axel, and his wife, Emma, were bringing my mother to Atlanta. She'd left Florida to stay with Axel and Emma in Las Vegas when Andrei Tsepov had threatened to use her to get to my father.

Since then, Las Vegas had gotten too hot, Tsepov's empire beginning to fracture, with all of the collateral damage that implied. Axel ran the western division of Sinclair Security out of Vegas, and his team was top-notch, but he was spread too thin. The three of them would be safer in Atlanta for now.

Having Axel and Emma close was something to look forward to. Of the four of us, Axel had the least tolerance for my father's bullshit, and, like me, he'd wanted to run the show. As Sinclair Security had grown, it made sense for him to split off and head his own division. I was proud of him, but I missed having him around.

My mother was a different story. Only weeks after my father's car went off that bridge she'd put the house on the market and headed for Florida. Knox, Evers, and I had breathed a sigh of relief.

I love my mother. I want her safe and alive. I just don't want those things one flight of stairs away from me.

Not now, not when I wanted to spend every spare second buried in Alice.

Too much was up in the air, too many balls to juggle to do what I really wanted—tell Alice that things had changed. That she was mine. That we couldn't go back, and I wouldn't give her up.

If I'd had any doubt she wanted me as much as I wanted her, the last forty-eight hours had eradicated it completely. Whatever story she was spinning for herself right now, Alice didn't do casual sex.

She'd married her loser ex-husband and stuck with him until they finally divorced. Once she was done with him, when she might have gone out with girlfriends and let loose, she didn't. If she had, I would have figured out a way to stop her.

I'd waited, enough of an old-fashioned guy that I wasn't going to break up a marriage. Even a shitty one. Once Alice was free, I'd bided my time, giving her space to get over her divorce before I changed everything.

She might not realize it, and probably never thought of it in these terms, but I'd spent more time with her over the last nine years than her husband. She'd spent more time with me than any other woman on earth. She knew me inside and out.

No, I didn't have any doubts about Alice. Now all I had to do was make sure she didn't have any doubts about me.

She wasn't at work when I got there. That would have been a miracle. I was out of the shower and in a suit in fifteen minutes. Alice took that long just picking out a dress.

What would she choose after a debauched weekend of nonstop orgasms? I loved Alice's quirky style, her blunt bob, and her fifties dresses. She was so completely herself, tough and smartass, intelligent and sexy. I'd been hooked from the start.

I hit my office, sending one of the grunts to Annabelle's to get breakfast and coffee. By the time he was back, Alice was at her desk, the phone to her ear, her voice crisp and businesslike despite the blush that flooded her cheeks when her eyes caught mine.

She ended the call, jotting something on the notepad beside her hand, and stood, her head cocked slightly to the side. I held up the to-go cup of coffee and her eyes widened with pleasure.

Taking the cup from me, she sipped, her lipstick leaving a red imprint on the white lid. She wore a red dress with white nautical trim, the top a halter that tied around the back of her neck, a tiny white shrug sweater her defense against the chill of the air conditioning.

When she turned to move her chair, I spotted the flounce of white crinoline beneath the red skirt. If she had any idea how crazy those crinolines made me...

The crinoline wasn't big—sock-hop, not Scarlet O'Hara. It only added an extra few layers to the already-full skirt. But every time I caught sight of that froth of nothing fabric beneath her skirts, I was instantly obsessed with the way they lifted the skirt away from her legs, leaving no barrier between my hands and her body.

As styles go, fifties rockabilly is fairly demure. Barely any cleavage, and not a single skirt above the knee. I'd seen business suits that showed more skin. Didn't matter. On Alice, those dresses made me fucking crazy.

If I had a penny for every time I'd thought of bending her over her desk and sliding my hands under those fluffs of crinoline to get my hands on her legs I'd be able to retire to a private island and spend the rest of my life doing just that.

As it was, between the crinoline and the bow of the halter neck begging me to pull it free, it was all I could do not to drag her into the supply closet and lock the door.

Instead, I sipped my coffee and handed her the bag of baked goods. "Whatever you don't pick is mine," I said.

Alice rummaged through the bag, pulling out a flaky cinnamon roll and placing it neatly on a napkin on her desk. Her teeth sank into her full red bottom lip and she looked away from me, cheeks still pink.

Under her breath, she hissed, "Don't look at me like that."

"Like what? I'm not looking at you like anything." Yanking Alice's chain is my favorite hobby. I have to work at it. She knows me too well to make it easy.

Rolling her eyes to the ceiling, she said, "Go away, Cooper. I don't have time to deal with you. Your mother, Axel, and Emma will be here in a few hours. I need to leave the desk to give the apartment upstairs a final check before they get here."

"I'll send one of the grunts to cover the desk in half an hour. Give you time to drink your coffee. That work?" I asked, proving I could do business if she wanted to do business.

As long as she didn't forget the pleasure part.

Voice crisp, eyes cautious, Alice agreed. "That would be fine. Thanks for the coffee and the cinnamon roll."

A clear dismissal. Giving her a long, heated look that brought a flush back to her cheeks, I inclined my head and walked away.

My brothers aside, Alice was one of the few people in the office who busted my balls on a regular basis. From anyone else I would have shut that shit down, but Alice could bust my balls all day if she wanted to.

So many years I'd been wondering if that red lipstick was kiss-proof. Today, I planned to find out.

The phone rang when I got back to my office. A client with a problem. New day, same catastrophes. By the time I'd handled it, I judged Alice would be upstairs getting the safe house ready for my mother.

Alice, a bed, and a door with a lock. Perfect.

Pushing back from the desk, I strode down the hall to the back of the office and ducked into the emergency stairwell. I didn't need the grunt at the front desk seeing me leave while Alice was gone.

If it were up to me I'd shout to the world that Alice was mine, but I knew she was going to need more time.

Finesse. I could do finesse.

I found Alice in the bigger of the two bedrooms in the apartment, bending over as she smoothed the coverlet across the bed, that froth of white crinoline lifting in the back, exposing the barest hint of thigh.

Innocent, really. Innocent and so fucking alluring I did what I'd been dreaming of for years. Stepping up behind her, I leaned over and slid my fingers up the back of her legs, feeling the light, crisp crinoline pool around my hands, the heavier fabric of her dress sliding up, up, up.

Alice stilled for a moment before she went back to smoothing the coverlet. "That better be Cooper, or somebody's going to get his balls sliced off."

I don't know why her threats made me so hot. "You armed, Alice?"

"I have a letter opener at my desk."

Sliding my hand up to squeeze the curve of her ass, I said, "Anybody else touches you like this, I'll slice his balls off for you."

Alice laughed. I wasn't kidding. She stood and turned, her eyes hot and wary. "What are you doing here, Cooper?"

"What do you think?" Alice circled around me and backed up, giving the room one last glance before she edged through the doorway into the living room.

Pretending I hadn't just had my hands on her ass, she said, "I had groceries delivered, stocked the fridge with

44

everything your mother likes, coffee, her favorite wine, cheesecake."

I ignored her. "Where are you going, Alice?" I asked, stalking her as she backed across the living room. Another step and she bumped into the couch.

Realizing what she was doing, she stopped and propped her hands on her hips. "Cooper Sinclair, it's the middle of the workday. This is your mother's apartment. What do you think you're—"

I didn't care. I wrapped an arm around her waist, leaned down, and dropped my mouth to hers. Her lips tasted like cherries, her mouth of cinnamon and coffee and Alice.

She kissed me back, pulling on my shoulders to bring me closer, moaning in my arms. When I didn't think I could last a second longer without flipping those skirts up and burying myself between her legs, I lifted my mouth from hers.

"It *is* the middle of the workday, but the safe house is *my* apartment, not my mother's."

An eye-roll, less sarcastic than usual. Her kiss-swollen lips still parted, chest rising and falling as she tried to get her breath back, Alice flattened her hands on my chest. I wasn't sure if she was fending me off or feeling me up. When her fingertips dug in, I wondered if she knew either.

"Cooper. We can't do this at work. We— I don't want—"

"We're not at work," I countered to her fumbling protest.

I expected the hard slap to my chest. I deserved it. She had a point. She stepped back, her hands sliding down my chest before falling away.

I stayed where I was, watching with fascination as she ran her fingers through her hair, scraped a fingernail under her lip to correct the smudges to her lipstick, and resettled her skirts. A moment later she looked completely un-mussed except for the slight swell of her lower lip. She looked as if I hadn't just had my hands all over her which, perversely, made me want to kiss her again. And again.

"Cooper. I've been thinking."

I crossed my arms, braced for her to say, *We can't do this, it was a mistake, blah, blah*.

Alice surprised me.

"I like my job, Cooper. I don't want to lose it."

"You're not going to lose your job, Alice."

"Let me finish," she said, pulling her shoulders back as if to brace herself.

I nodded and kept my mouth shut, already preparing my rebuttal.

"I don't fool around at work. You know that," she said with such conviction that I was tempted to remind her of the one time she *had* fooled around at work.

But we'd never spoken of that. I'd spent nine years trying to erase it from my mind. It had nothing to do with me. With us.

Besides that single incident, Alice was right. She'd never fooled around at work. Never flirted. Never been anything but professional.

"I think it's important to keep business separate from my personal life," she went on. "I know it's different for you since you work with family—"

She trailed off and I wondered if Alice was losing her nerve. "But?" I prompted.

She sucked in a quick breath, her words streaming out in a rush. "But I've never had sex like that in my life." Her cheeks flared red. She looked away and gathered herself before going on, "I want to do it again."

The wave of relief was so great it almost crushed me.

"Good. So do I."

I was moving as the words left my mouth. Alice threw up a hand and I stopped.

Shit, she wasn't done. I should have known.

"I don't want anybody to know, okay? No messing around at work. When this is done, it's done. No hard feelings. Aside from my family, for the last nine years, you and the team, this job, have been the only constant in my life. The only *good* constant in my life," she corrected. "I won't ruin that over sex. Even amazing sex."

"I agree to your terms with one amendment."

"What?" she asked, rightfully suspicious.

"The office isn't off-limits as long as I can guarantee we won't get caught."

I wasn't going to agree to a complete hands-off policy at work. We all worked way too much. Sometimes around-the-clock. I wasn't boxing myself into a corner if I didn't have to. I waited for a snappy comeback or a counter-offer. Again, she surprised me.

"Cooper, if we get caught messing around everyone will look at me differently. I don't want that. Do you understand?"

"I promise, Alice. I won't do anything to compromise you at work."

Her mouth quirked as she caught my wording. "As long as you compromise me plenty at home."

"Exactly." I moved in, angling for another kiss, but she evaded me, slipping to the side and heading for the door. "I have to get downstairs. Too much to do before your mother gets here."

I let her go. I'd made progress. She'd agreed to an affair. I could work with that. I had my way in.

Sex.

Now I only had one goal: Get her so addicted to me she couldn't walk away. I could do that. I had to. Now that I'd had a taste of her, all I wanted was more.

Chapter Six

COOPER

AXEL, EMMA, AND MY MOTHER ARRIVED at lunchtime. With my brother, Knox, out of town with his girlfriend and my other brother, Evers, in the field for the day, it was up to me to greet them.

I hit the front office to find Alice standing behind the desk, her palms pressed flat to the dark wood. Her lips were a red line, her face set in an icily polite expression as my mother harangued her.

"It's not an appropriate way to dress in a business office. You should know better. I don't know what Maxwell was thinking hiring you in the first place. Go upstairs and—"

"Mother, drop it." Axel glared down at my mother, the flat look in his eyes telling me he was officially out of patience. My mother had been living with Axel and Emma for weeks. I imagined he'd been out of patience for a while.

Standing beside him was my sister-in-law, Emma, normally one of the kindest, friendliest people I knew. Giving my mother the same flat stare as Axel, she said, "I think Alice looks both professional and very pretty."

Turning her eyes to Alice, she smiled before rounding the desk and giving Alice a warm hug. She whispered something in Alice's ear that had Alice's eyes warming as she hugged Emma back.

Emma ran her hand down the arm of Alice's sweater. "I wish I could pull this off. You look fantastic. On me, it would be too much."

Emma was a beautiful woman in her own right, far taller than Alice, with full curves. She knew how to dress, her clothes elegant while making the most of her natural assets, but she was right.

Alice's look was perfectly suited to her more pixie-like frame. On Emma's rounded curves that dress would turn her into a bombshell. Despite her eye-catching red hair, or maybe because of it, Emma tended to go for understated vs. in-your-face.

My mother gave a disgruntled *harrumph*, smoothing a strand of her frosted blonde hair behind her ear. Her eyes only slightly bloodshot from the drinks I'm sure she'd consumed on the plane, she looked the picture of the society matron she was. Or had been before she left Atlanta for Florida.

I moved to stand behind Alice, putting a hand on her shoulder. "Mom, it's good to see you. I'm glad you're here, but I need to be clear. Alice is an essential part of this company. We wouldn't make it through a day without her. I happen to think, and everyone else agrees, that her work attire is perfectly appropriate.

"However, if she wanted to show up in her gym clothes or wearing a clown suit, none of us would give a damn as long as she kept doing her job as well as she does it now. If

I catch you talking to any member of our staff with anything other than appreciation and respect I will bar you from the office. Are we clear?"

I hated setting my mother down like that. If she hadn't asked for it, I never would have done it. But I knew her, knew her competitiveness with other women. Knew she'd always disliked Alice. If I didn't make myself clear she'd be unstoppable, bitching and complaining, digging at Alice when no one else was around.

Hell, she'd probably do it anyway, but at least it would be clear to Alice whose side I was on. I love my mother, but I know her.

If Lacey Sinclair excelled at one thing, it was being a bitch. A hard thing to have to admit about my mother, but I didn't get where I am in life by lying to myself.

The look she gave Alice was heavy with venom. As if the previous conversation had never happened, she said, "Is the apartment ready? I can't imagine none of my boys have room for me but—"

"Mom," Axel said on a sigh, "we've already explained. Emma and I are taking the only room at Evers' place. Knox's house exploded—"

"Only the garage," my mother cut in.

"It's not habitable," Axel went on, his temper barely leashed, "and Cooper doesn't have a guest room set up. Why would he when the on-site safe house is right here? We need you in the most secure location possible. The safe house is it."

The part about the guest room was a lie. A necessary one. My mother was not staying in my place when I had a perfectly secure apartment on site.

My mother held her hand out to Alice without a word. Alice placed the key in it just as silently. My mother turned on her heel, wobbling a little before regaining her balance and striding out the door.

It shut behind her with a decisive click. With a sad laugh, Emma said, "That went well."

I moved to give her a hug of welcome before doing the same for Axel.

"Good to see you, man."

Axel looked past me to Alice. "Sorry, Alice. That was way out of line."

"Don't worry about it, Axel. I've been around long enough. I know your mom."

Enough said. If I could have put my mom anywhere but in the apartment across from Alice's, I would have. Hell, if I could have talked Alice into moving in with me I would've done that, but there was no way.

One step at a time. Moving her in after one weekend of sex was too fast for her. *Patience*, I reminded myself.

"You guys had lunch?" I asked Axel and Emma.

"No, and I'm starving," Emma said. "Do you have to jump in to work right away? Can we go out or do we need to order in?"

She leaned around me to catch Alice's eye. "Can you come to lunch with us? I want to hang out while we're here. Everything is always so busy I never get to talk to you."

Alice's face fell with genuine regret. "I'd love to come to lunch, but I fell behind getting the apartment ready for Mrs. Sinclair and missing most of work on Friday. I have too much to do here. Rain check?"

With a grin, Emma confirmed, "Rain check. Definitely."

Unnecessarily, I said to Alice, "Call me if anything comes up while we're out."

"Will do, boss," she said, no hint things were anything other than business as usual.

That turned me on more than if she'd made a lascivious comment or winked. Alice. So fucking proper and efficient. I couldn't forget the feel of her under me, the spill of erotic, dirty, desperate words from her lips as I'd moved inside of her. The end of the day couldn't come fast enough.

As we left, Emma hooked her arm through mine, looking from me to her husband. "Except for the eyes, you two look so much alike, you could be twins. I don't know if it's scary, or hot, or both."

From behind us, Alice decisively stated, "Both," and Emma's laughter filled the room.

Lunch with my brother and his wife was almost enough to take my mind off my mother's arrival. Almost. She'd declined lunch but demanded we join her for dinner.

The evening meal was a roller coaster. The high of being with Axel and Emma as well as my youngest brother, Evers, and his girlfriend, Summer. Only Knox and Lily were missing, but they'd be home soon enough. Then all the Sinclair brothers would be together. I was proud of Axel and the job he was doing out in Vegas, but I liked having him home.

The low part of dinner was my mother. Watching her consume glass after glass of wine, ordering another bottle after Evers told the waiter we were done. The list of complaints about the safe house apartment, all bullshit considering we'd designed the place for high-end clients.

Unlike Alice's apartment, which was functional but basic, the apartment my mother was using was plush. From the thousand thread-count sheets and custom-designed furniture to the chef's kitchen and Italian marble bathroom, every inch of the place was designed to keep our top clients comfortable and entertained.

No one stayed there unless they were under a significant security threat, often unable to leave the building for days at a time, so we'd gone out of our way to make sure the apartment had a top-of-the-line entertainment system stocked with movies, books, music.

Everything but an open Internet connection. What there was, we kept strictly monitored. Bored clients can be trouble. After a few days in the apartment, sometimes they needed to be protected from themselves as much as any external threat.

I was good at tuning out my mother's complaints, but this time it was what she didn't say that dug under my skin. In all of her bitching, she never mentioned our dad.

Our dad, who'd cheated on her repeatedly, driving her deeper and deeper into the bottle. Our dad, who'd faked his own death five years before after stealing from the Russian mob.

Our father had been running a side business with that same Russian mob for years. A side business my mother hadn't been too surprised about. No, her relocation from her condo in Florida to Axel's place in Las Vegas and now back home to Atlanta—that was all *our* fault. We'd failed to clean up my father's mess for him. We were the fuckups, not dear old Dad.

Never mind that we didn't even know he was alive until six months ago. Never mind that he'd left us with nothing to go on, no clue what he'd been into until everything went to hell around us.

It blew my mind, her loyalty to a man who'd done more to ruin her life than any of her sons ever could have. We were the ones taking care of her, doing our best to keep her safe and comfortable.

Listening as she made a snide comment about Emma's career and the babies she hadn't given Axel, I wondered how my brother and his wife hadn't killed her in the last few weeks. Based on the set of Axel's chin and Emma's sigh, they'd come close.

Summer's eyes were wide at her first exposure to Lacey Sinclair. I'd met Summer's mother, knew she adored her daughter and was always there at the other end of the phone with love and support. She'd been here a few weeks before after Summer's father had been killed, another casualty of my dad's ties to the Russians.

After meeting Paisley Winters, I knew Summer wouldn't be prepared for the woman who would one day be her mother-in-law. Evers, as much to preempt criticism of Summer's career as to defend Emma, said, "Mom, maybe you got confused by Alice's outfit earlier, but this isn't actually the fifties. Emma worked her ass off to get her MBA, and now she's got the job she's always wanted. And they're not ready for kids, not that that's any of your business. Why don't you just lay off and enjoy the fact that your son is in love and happy and has a good marriage? That's a fucking miracle considering the example you and Dad gave us."

Shit. I'd love to blame Evers' outburst on too many drinks, but, like the rest of us, after watching my mother slide into the bottle none of us had a taste for alcohol. We'd have a beer or a glass of wine, maybe a mixed drink, but never enough to lose control.

Evers' outburst wasn't fueled by alcohol. It was fueled by stress and fear. We'd shielded my mother long enough. Way too long considering that, in all of this, her sympathy was with our dad.

She drained her glass and glared at her youngest child. "Don't you talk to me like that, Evers Sinclair. If it weren't for me—"

Summer closed her hand over Evers' and squeezed in support as Evers shot back, "If it weren't for you, what?

55

We wouldn't be here? True enough. Thank you, Mom, for giving birth to all four of us."

"Ev," I said, shaking my head at him. I wanted to tell him to lay off. Leave her alone.

I wouldn't. He'd almost lost Summer because of my father. After seeing Alice on the floor of Knox's basement in a pool of blood, I knew how he felt.

We were out of patience with my father's bullshit. With his crazy, co-dependent relationship with my mother, who'd stayed with the man even as he drove her to the bottle and then defended him over her own children.

I loved her with the helpless love of a child for his mother, a love tainted with hope. Hope that she would change. Hope that she'd give a shit about her children.

I couldn't help but love her, couldn't help but want to keep her safe, to hope that someday she'd want more from life than bitterness and her endless glasses of wine.

I could hope and I could love, but I was not going to put up with this bullshit.

I signaled the waiter for the check. I was done.

Emma exhaled in relief. Axel's tight jaw unlocked a fraction. Even Evers relaxed. Only my mother was annoyed the dinner was over. Why, I couldn't imagine. My mind was already racing ahead to home, and Alice.

I texted Alice after walking my mother to her door, my ears still ringing from her list of complaints about dinner. Ungrateful children. Inadequate lodgings. Etc, etc.

With another warning not to test the bounds of her security, I closed her door and knocked on Alice's.

56

Chapter Seven

COOPER

NO ANSWER. I KNEW SHE WAS HOME. AFTER the incident at Knox's place on Friday, I'd put a tracker in her purse. Paranoid, yes. But as we'd all learned the hard way, just because you're paranoid doesn't mean they aren't out to get you.

If any of Tsepov's men had seen my mad rush to get Alice to the hospital they knew they could get to me through her. I'd needed to know she was safe.

During dinner, my phone had beeped with an alert that her car had left the garage. I didn't need to track it to know she was headed to Zumba, or dance class, or one of the varied things she did to have fun and stay in shape. A second alert came an hour and a half later when her car had reentered the garage.

She might already be asleep. Neither of us had gotten much of that over the weekend. Just because I was half desperate to get inside her again didn't mean she couldn't

IVY LAYNE

use a break. She was probably sore. Exhausted. And I was a thoughtless asshole. One night away from her wouldn't kill me.

My cock insisting that a night away from her would definitely kill me, I went back upstairs to my place. I debated texting but couldn't think of anything to say that wouldn't sound desperate or stalker-ish.

I thought about watching a movie or going to bed early. Instead, I wandered my place, restless and out of sorts. I wanted Alice. Her smile. Her laugh. Her way of putting everything in perspective, so all of it—the dinner with my mother, problems with my father—didn't seem as overwhelming.

I picked up my phone and pulled up her name in the messaging app and stared at the screen. She might be asleep, but if she was awake, I just wanted to see her. I couldn't remember the last time I'd struggled with what to say to a woman. Junior high, maybe?

Alice wasn't just any woman. She was Alice. I knew her better than anyone. This should be easy.

As I deliberated, my phone vibrated in my hand. An alert from the tracker in Alice's purse. Her car had just pulled out of the garage.

What the fuck? It was almost eleven o'clock. Alice didn't go to bed early, but neither was she a night owl. Too many nights I'd come home late and her car was always tucked into the garage as it should be.

So what the fuck was she doing leaving at eleven o'clock at night?

All thoughts of not seeming like a stalker fled my mind as I hit her contact on the screen. When she answered, her voice was cautious. Careful. "Hey."

"What the hell are you doing? It's after eleven."

58

"Yeah, *Dad*, I know that. I have a clock on my dashboard."

"Cut the sarcasm, Alice. Where are you going at eleven o'clock at night? Until we know for sure that Tsepov has backed off, I don't want you out there on your own, especially this late at night."

"Are you going to send a guard with me to dance class?"

"I'm considering it," I admitted, "but there's a difference between dance class at six-thirty and heading out to—where the fuck are you going at eleven-fifteen at night?"

"Look, it's not a big deal. I'll be back before you know it."

"Alice," I ground out. "Talk."

A long exhalation before she said gently, "I ran into your mom in the hall. She asked me to go pick some stuff up for her. I knew you didn't want her driving around so—"

I didn't need Alice to explain. I already knew her story was a whitewashed version of the truth. She hadn't run into my mother in the hall. My mother had banged on her door and demanded that Alice go out, not to get her *stuff*, but to buy her alcohol. Because, apparently, the six bottles of wine in the pantry of her apartment weren't enough.

"You're going to the liquor store, aren't you?"

Another sigh. "Coop, it's okay. I know how she is."

"You're not an errand girl, Alice."

"I'm pretty sure that's actually part of my job description," she said, trying to infuse humor into the conversation. I wasn't in the mood.

My mother had been drinking all night. I didn't have to imagine the way she'd probably spoken to Alice, treating her like less than the dirt under her shoes. I knew why my mother hated Alice, even understood it, but that didn't mean I'd let her get away with it.

59

"I'll see you when you get back," I said. "Stay alert. So far, I think Tsepov is on the level and this is all about Dad now, but I don't want to take any chances."

"Got it, boss."

When she called me *boss* in that saucy tone it went straight to my cock.

The half-hour it took for her to hit the liquor store and get home stretched far too long. I went downstairs the second her car hit the garage. Alice walked out of the elevator, her arms loaded with two bulging brown paper bags. Seeing me, she stopped short. "Cooper. It's okay."

"It's not okay."

Striding ahead of her, I knocked lightly on my mother's door and stepped to the side, out of view. The door swung open so fast my mother must have been standing there, waiting. The look on her face sliced into my heart. Disdain at the sight of Alice. Relief at the heft of those brown paper bags.

"It took you long enough."

I could have guessed how she spoke to Alice when they were alone. Hearing it was worse than I'd imagined. I stepped into view and my mother blanched.

Angry words threatened to spill out of my mouth. I clenched my jaw and inhaled slowly before I said, "When you finish drinking all of that, let me know, and I'll send someone to restock. Do not ask Alice to run errands for you again. Understand?"

My mother jutted her chin in the air. "I don't see what the problem is. It's her job."

"It is very much *not* her job," I corrected. "Alice manages the office. She was kind enough to take time out of her day to stock your pantry and get the apartment ready, but keeping you in liquor is not on her list of responsibilities. If

60

you need something, call *me*. Not Alice. Tell me you understand, Mom."

My mother lifted her chin even higher, until, for a second, I thought she'd lose her balance and fall backward. Without a word, she walked back into the apartment, the door open behind her.

Relieving Alice of her burdens, I said, "Stay here."

I followed my mother into the apartment and set the paper bags on the kitchen counter.

Digging into my reserves of patience, I said, "Mom, we need to be careful. Tsepov said he'd leave us alone, but we can't trust him. I don't want anybody going out at night by themselves. Not you. Not Alice. We're trying to keep you safe. Please don't make it harder."

My mother didn't respond, too busy pulling out a bottle of gin, slicing a lime, and pouring tonic. Her drink assembled, she lifted it and took a long sip, giving me a cool, appraising glance.

"I never knew what your father saw in her. She's odd and not particularly pretty. Now she's got her hooks in you. Be smart, Cooper. If you want to be the head of this family, you can't get trapped by some nobody. Get what you want from her if you have to, but don't be a fool about it."

I stared down at my mother, my teeth clenched hard enough to crack, holding back the words I wanted to say. Words I couldn't speak to the woman who'd given birth to me.

Finally, I managed, "I *am* the head of the family. And who I get involved with is none of your business. I meant what I said before. Don't ever talk about Alice that way again."

My mother rolled her eyes in exasperation "This is what happens when I try to live a life of my own. I leave town and the next thing I know your brother's with a nobody who has a criminal for a father. Knox is off with some woman who has a child." She raised her eyes to the ceiling as if praying for the strength to deal with such an assault on the family honor.

Taking another sip and pinning me with her bloodshot eyes, she accused, "I don't know how you could have let that happen to Knox. That woman is not our kind. And now here *you* are, sleeping with the help. It's so trite, Cooper. I raised you better than this."

No, I wanted to say, *the nanny raised me. You were too busy being Maxwell Sinclair's wife to bother raising anyone.*

Instead, I said, "Sleep tight, Mom."

I left, shutting the door gently behind me. The hall was empty, but Alice's door was open a few inches. I found her in the kitchen stirring honey into a cup of herbal tea, her clothes discarded in favor of a fuzzy pink robe. She shoved the mug of tea in my hand when I walked in.

Before I could open my mouth, she said, "I'm sorry. I should have called. She was agitated. I figured dinner was rough and you needed a break. But I should've called."

I took a sip of the sweet, fragrant tea, the compassion in her eyes easing the knot in my chest. "No, *I'm* sorry. You shouldn't have to put up with that. The way she talks to you—"

"Cooper, you don't have to apologize for your mother." She turned to put away the honey and box of tea bags. "I don't know why she hates me so much, but it doesn't really matter. The list of people she likes is so short, I don't mind not being on it."

I stared at her back and wanted to ask, *How can you not know why she hates you?* More than anyone, Alice should know *exactly* why my mother hated her. The tone of her voice was so guileless, it was as if she really, truly had no clue.

It was so long ago, maybe she'd forgotten. God knows I'd decided to forget years ago. If it didn't matter to me, why should it matter to her? Except that it still clearly mattered to my mother. Either way— "She can't talk to you like that."

"Cooper," Alice slipped her arms around my waist, tipping her head to look up at me. "She's a lonely, bitter, unhappy woman. Should she be less of a bitch? Of course. No one should behave that way. I don't have the mental energy to hold it against her. She's never going to like me. That's fine. I don't particularly like her either."

I set the mug of half-finished tea on the counter and dropped my mouth to the top of her head, kissing her hair. I had no words. *Thank you* was inadequate. My chest was tight with a swirling mass of need, and affection, and something so big I wasn't ready to give it a name.

"How was class?" I asked.

"A little boring. I don't think I'm a ballet kind of girl. I might go back to Zumba. Or kickboxing. I liked kickboxing."

"I'll give you a kickboxing class," I offered, my mind latching onto the picture of Alice in tight workout gear, grappling with me on the mat.

Reading my mind, she laughed. "Somehow I don't think we'd end up doing much kickboxing."

"Maybe not," I agreed.

I slid my hands beneath her robe, trailing the backs of my fingers over the tops of her breasts, her soft skin warm against mine.

"Are you sore?" I hadn't needed Alice to tell me it'd been a long time since she'd had sex, never mind that much sex in two short days.

"A little. Pliés were not fun."

I slid my hand around to cup her ass, leaning over to reach down that far. I loved her size, but the difference in our heights was awkward when we were both standing. Wrapping an arm around her shoulders, I hooked the other beneath her legs and scooped her up.

"I can do something about that. But I'm going to have to take a closer look."

"Whatever you say, boss."

Yeah, my cock liked it when she called me *boss*. It liked it a lot.

Chapter Eight

COOPER

THE WEEK BEFORE LABOR DAY LASTED AN ETER-
nity. I called Knox in New Hampshire, where he
and Lily were visiting her family, and told him to
get his ass home. There were three of us in Atlanta,
but juggling my mother was turning into a full-time job.

We all owed Axel and Emma big time for the weeks
she'd spent with them in Vegas. Trapped in the apartment
with nothing to do, she was out of sorts, restless and irrita-
ble, and drinking more because of it. We tried to make sure
she had company for every meal. Emma stopped by once
a day, usually in the morning before my mother had more
than a few drinks in her.

The second the clock hit five on Friday afternoon, I
dragged Alice from her desk, locking her in my place and
doing every dirty, luscious thing I'd fantasized about. By
the time Monday night rolled around we were both sore
and exhausted but very well satisfied.

Which is why, when I strolled into the office Tuesday

morning, a satisfied grin on my face, I stopped short at the sight of the extravagant bouquet of flowers on the front desk.

Alice gave me a secret smile when she saw me, a smile I rarely saw in the office with so many other people around. I braced my elbows on the tall counter in front of the desk and leaned over, snagging a mini scone off the plate in front of Alice. I recognized those scones.

"Who went to Annabelle's?"

Before Alice had a chance to answer, I took a closer look at the flowers. Lilies and roses. The arrangement was huge, wild and gorgeous. "Who got the flowers?"

Shooting me a look I couldn't decipher, Alice said, "I did. Flowers and a gift box from Annabelle's."

Something sour washed through me. Was that jealousy? Was I jealous? Fuck. Yeah. I was jealous. Who the fuck was sending Alice flowers?

I spotted the card from the flower shop face down on the desk, but Alice anticipated me and snatched it up, tucking it behind her.

"Who sent you flowers?"

"None of your business," she said primly, a wicked tease sparkling in her sky-blue eyes.

I wanted to play the game, to let her tease me, to tease her back. That's what she expected. Another look at the flowers and all urge to tease dissolved in the sour pit of acid in my gut.

Whoever sent her those flowers knew Alice. *Knew her*. They weren't generic roses or a friendly pot of Gerbera daisies. These flowers were bright and wild, quirky and perfect. Whoever sent this arrangement knew my girl better than I wanted any man to know my girl.

"Show me the card," I said, trying to keep it light. Alice cocked her head to the side and studied me before glancing down the hall on either side of the reception area.

No one was in sight, but we could hear voices coming from both directions. We were very much not alone.

Alice grinned. "Don't worry about it, Coop. Play your cards right, and maybe I'll tell you later."

Her reassurance fell flat. *I'd* decide whether I wanted to worry about the fucker who was sending her flowers and a box of treats from Annabelle's.

I stole another scone, the taste dust in my mouth. I should have played her game, said something flirty and excused myself, then tracked down the delivery from my office if I had to know that badly.

I could beat Alice at this game any day, but instead of sending her a flirtatious grin and stealing the rest of her scones, I rounded the desk and reached for the envelope tucked securely between her lower back and her desk chair.

Alice let out a surprised screech and stood, the chair flying backward, the envelope falling to the ground. We both reached for it at the same time, Alice laughing, me anything but amused. My head *clunked* into her jaw.

"Cooper," she exclaimed, stepping back, the card clutched in her hand. Concern knitting her brow, she reached to smooth a finger across my forehead where I'd hit her jaw. I stood, pulling away from her hand, and glared down at her like a sulky child.

"Let me see the card," I demanded, holding my hand out imperiously.

Stepping back slowly, the realization that I wasn't playing dawning at last, Alice shook her head. Her voice barely audible, she said, "Get it together, Cooper. You're being weird."

I closed the space between us, reaching behind her to get the envelope. She gave it up without a fight, her eyes flaring with alarm as I wrapped my arm around her back and pulled her flush to me right there at the front desk.

Dropping my head to her ear I murmured, "You want flowers? I'll send you flowers. I'll send you fucking flowers three times a day. Me. No one else."

The heel of Alice's wedge sandal came down on my instep in one quick stomp. Between my dress shoe and the dull sole of her sandal, it wasn't enough to hurt. It was exactly enough to shake loose the inner Neanderthal currently in control of my brain.

I dropped my forehead to hers. "Alice, I'm sorry. I don't know what—"

"Cooper—"

The sound of a familiar voice had us both jumping back as if scalded. I straightened, trying to pretend I hadn't just had Alice in my arms, my mouth inches from hers.

"Well, isn't this interesting."

I turned, my body blocking Alice from view, to narrow my eyes on Griffen. One of my senior employees and a friend so close he might as well have been another brother, Griffen Sawyer was one of the few people who knew I had more than a professional interest in Alice. He also knew how to keep his mouth shut. I stepped away from our office manager anyway.

"There's nothing interesting here," I said. "I was just joking around with Alice, that's all."

"Since when do you joke around in the office?"

"Since never," Alice said, acerbically. "He was trying something new, but he's not going to do it again because it's weird and irritating."

I wanted nothing more than to claim her in front of Griffen, to end this secrecy, the farce that this was a fling, but doing that in front of a co-worker would make me the world's biggest asshole.

I handed Alice back the card without opening it. All these years I'd wanted her, and still, I'd kept my shit together. I never got distracted at work, never did anything inappropriate.

I'm Cooper Sinclair. I don't fuck up, and I don't fuck around.

Two weeks into making my fantasy a reality and I was fucking up right and left. Distracted. Losing my touch. How had I let fucking Griffen sneak up on me?

My situational awareness had gone to hell. *Everything* had gone to hell, my need for Alice expanding until it filled every space inside me, pushing everything else aside.

With a curt nod to both of them, I walked away. Behind me, Griffen asked, "Who sent you flowers?"

I slowed, waiting for Alice's answer. To Griffen, she gave it easily. "Knox. A thank you for hooking him and Lily up with that hotel suite when they were in Maine."

Relief bloomed in my chest. Knox. My fucking brother. Of course, he would send Alice flowers. Partly because she deserved them, and partly to yank my chain.

I'd been a dick about Knox hooking up with Lily. I can admit it. It wasn't personal. I like Lily. I like her kid. I like her with Knox, but when they first started up, she was a client and a target.

Lily was off-limits on two fronts and possibly mixed up with our dad *and* the Russian mob. We already knew her dead husband had been involved up to his neck. It wasn't reaching to think Lily was as well.

I hadn't liked the way my little brother headed up to investigate and ended up falling head over heels. So, I was an asshole, not that it did any good. Alice, annoyed and exasperated by my attitude, booked them in an expensive suite on the company account to push my buttons. Knox had dropped a few hundred bucks on flowers and treats to do the same.

Wouldn't he be amused to know his shot hit the bull's-eye? I sent him an annoyed text telling him to stop giving Alice presents and get his ass home. He set back a laughing emoji, bright blue tears of hilarity streaming from the smiling yellow face.

Brothers. Assholes, every single one. Me most of all.

My phone chimed with a text a minute later. I picked it up, thinking it was Knox yanking my chain again. Not Knox.

Alice.

> That can't happen again. Please. If we can't keep it quiet we can't do this anymore.

The simple words were a blade in my heart, stealing my breath.

No. I wouldn't give her up now. I *couldn't* give her up now.

I knew Alice had reasons she wanted to keep her behavior in the office circumspect. My father's inability to keep his fucking mouth shut nine years ago had made her first months at Sinclair Security difficult. I wasn't the only one who'd given her a wide berth back then.

She'd settled in, mostly because she was fucking excellent at her job. Efficient, a creative problem solver, and always, *always* focused on work. After she turned down the first few propositions, no one bothered her. I understood why she didn't want me to ruin that. I did.

We didn't have an official policy against intra-office dating. Our team tipped heavily towards men, but we had women on staff. Almost half of Lucas Jackson's hacker division was female. We had some female bodyguards who kicked ass.

I wouldn't tell my people who they could date, but we did have an ironclad policy against harassment. No suggestive comments. No flirting. It could be hard blending mixed-gender teams, way harder if my employees had to be on guard against each other.

I'd been out of line earlier. I owed Alice an apology. I had to think of something to say to salvage this. Something better than just *I'm sorry*. I started with that anyway.

> *I'm sorry.*

I thought about what else to say, considered making an excuse, hiding behind sarcasm, or flirting. If Alice wanted to keep this undercover, fine. I'd give her that for now. I could hide from everyone else, but I wasn't going to hide from her.

Feeling a little sick at being so exposed, I told her the truth.

> *I was jealous. I don't want anyone sending you flowers but me. I'm a caveman and I overreacted. I won't let it happen again.*

Nothing. Not even a read notice. I set my phone on my desk, trying not to stare at it, waiting for those three dots that would tell me she was typing a reply.

Nothing.

With every second that passed without a response, I grew more distracted. I didn't have time for this. Too much was in play. I needed to stay sharp.

Special Agent Holley was coming in next week to discuss our options if we found my father. My brothers and I needed to come up with a game plan before then. The more information we could put together, the better off we'd be.

Andrei Tsepov was still out there, hunting our father. Tsepov had promised he wouldn't come after us, but he was a liar and a criminal.

On top of all of that, I still had a business to run, clients who had their own problems and depended on me to solve them.

I didn't have time to be distracted.

There was a part of me that didn't fucking care.

For once in my goddamn life, I wanted what *I* wanted.

Alice.

Something had broken loose inside me at the sight of her splayed on that basement floor, blood pooled under her head.

In that moment, I'd realized I might have lost her before I ever had her. Standing over her, her eyes closed, body so still, I'd watched a dream die.

For years I told myself we had time.

Between one breath and the next, time ran out.

I'd buried the part of me that wanted her. Needed her. Now that it had broken free, I couldn't put it back. I didn't want to.

I was so close to having everything I'd ever wanted.

So close, and right on the edge of seeing all of it slip through my fingers.

Chapter Nine

ALICE

INCE THE DAY KNOX'S FLOWERS ARRIVED, Cooper had been the model of good behavior. In the office, he treated me just as always, maybe a shade cooler and more abrupt. That coolness might have made me worry if he hadn't been at my door every night backing me into my apartment, hauling me against him and fucking me until I could barely walk. In the mornings he set the alarm early and woke me with his mouth and hands, leaving me limp and breathless.

Cooper said morning sex was better than any cup of coffee. I had to agree. I didn't need caffeine. I was on a Cooper high.

I don't know if it was all the orgasms or the fulfillment of such a long crush, but two weeks into this thing with Cooper and I was reeling. He wanted to tell people. I couldn't get my head around that. If we told everyone, this wouldn't be a fling. It wouldn't be temporary. I'd never known Cooper to do anything *but* temporary.

If he'd wanted more with me, he'd had years. Except he hadn't. Not really.

I'd been married until six months ago, and Cooper—unlike his father—was a man of honor. He'd hated my husband, but he'd respected our marriage. Every time I considered the idea that Cooper might have been interested in me all these years, my brain veered away from the thought.

Wishful thinking, Alice.

This is the man who dated an Oscar winner. Who *dumped* a pop star because she was too high-maintenance. After those two relationships, Cooper had sworn off women he met through his work. He seemed to have sworn off relationships entirely in the past few years. Why would I be any different?

I trusted Cooper when he said this thing between us wouldn't affect our jobs. The way he'd acted at work this week proved he could compartmentalize. He'd be fine when it ended.

And it *would* end. I had to keep reminding myself of that.

One day, probably far sooner than I wanted, Cooper would move on. My brain veered away from that thought, too. It had to, defense against the fractures in my heart every time I thought about the day Cooper would leave my bed—and me—behind.

Until then, I was going to enjoy every minute, every second, that I could get. This was temporary, and no matter how much Cooper pushed, it was going to stay a secret. I wasn't going to sit at that desk every day knowing everyone pitied me. Sad-sack Alice, who hooked up with the boss and ended up dumped, just like every other woman who'd spun dreams of landing Cooper Sinclair. At least I'd be in good company.

I wouldn't be an object of pity. If we told everyone we were together, I'd have to leave the company when Cooper moved on. I loved my job. I didn't want to leave.

I never bothered to consider that I'd end things before Cooper. I'd told him the truth. I'd never had sex like that in my life. I'm not a fool. The thing between Cooper and me? That wasn't about his skills in bed, it was about Cooper.

There would be someone after him. I didn't want to spend the rest of my life alone, but no one would ever be the same. There was only one Cooper Sinclair. I was going to keep him as long as I could. Maybe, just maybe, if we could keep playing it cool at work, I could keep him long enough to get over my crush.

Fat chance, I thought, trying to focus on the order form in front of me. I could have millennia and I wouldn't get over my crush on Cooper Sinclair. Still, crush or not, there was work to be done. On top of their normally heavy caseload, the guys had the situation with Maxwell to deal with.

Knox was back from New Hampshire, and the brothers had been holed up for two days hammering out a plan to present to Special Agent Holley. Eventually, someone would run Maxwell to ground. Despite everything he'd done, no one wanted that person to be Andrei Tsepov. If Tsepov found Maxwell first, Maxwell Sinclair would end up dead.

Maxwell's boys might be furious with him, but they'd prefer a living father on whom to vent their rage. Cooper had confided that they'd all agreed their best chance to keep their dad alive was to work with Agent Holley, even if that meant their father would end up in jail. At least in jail, he'd be alive.

In honor of the FBI's visit, I dressed more conservatively than usual in a navy-blue dress with matching navy crinoline beneath. The boat neck of the dress showed my collarbone and little else, dropping into long sleeves tight at the wrist.

When Cooper strode to the front of the office to greet Agent Holley, I wasn't surprised to see we matched, his navy-blue suit the perfect foil for those icy eyes. His glance flicked over me. I was the only one who saw the message in those frozen depths. *Later*, he promised.

I hoped no one else could read him. Griffen had given me a few long looks since the day with the flowers but hadn't said a word.

Agent Holley was joined by two agents I didn't recognize. I gave them all a cool smile. "Refreshments are in the main conference room. Let me know if you need anything."

Cooper nodded in thanks and turned down the hall, the agents I didn't know tight on his heels. Agent Holley stopped at the desk and gave me a considering look. "You doing okay, Alice?"

My eyes slid away from his before I dragged them back and forced a smile. "I'm okay." It was the truth, kind of.

Another long look. "If that changes, make sure you have Cooper set you up with someone to talk to."

"I will. I promise."

With another nod, Agent Holley made his way to the conference room. He'd been here before, didn't need me to lead him, so I sat at my desk and watched him go.

I hadn't lied. I was doing okay, only waking in the night here and there with flashes of memory. The gun jerking in my hand. Tsepov's man raising his own. In my nightmares, he loomed closer and closer, my own weapon awkward and heavy.

In reality, I'd raised my gun and fired smoothly, as if I did it every day. Cooper had a point about muscle memory. He made all of us train as if we'd have to fire that gun at any moment. I always thought it was overkill for the support staff, but it was a part of my job so I did it without complaint.

Now I understood why. He drilled me so many times a part of my brain I never acknowledged saw the threat and handled it before I could process. Those drills had saved my life. Saved Adam's life. In my dreams, those drills had done nothing. When I slept, I remembered being a disaster with the gun.

Over and over, I saw Tsepov's man, saw the gun in his hand, and I was slow. Too slow. In my dreams, I couldn't get my weapon up in time. It was too heavy, my fingers sweaty. Clumsy.

In my dreams, I didn't get hit from something falling in the explosion. In my dreams, I took a bullet to the chest, and I died. In my dreams, I didn't save Adam's life. In my dreams, everything went to hell.

I hadn't told Cooper yet. I would if they didn't go away. However bad the dreams were, they must have been quiet because he never woke, never knew how often that scene replayed in my mind with a different ending.

I'm not stupid. I've set up enough appointments for our own people after a job went sideways to know none of us should handle this stuff on our own. Counseling was mandatory when there was loss of life on a job. I wasn't an exception, but since I made the appointments, it was easy to slip through the cracks.

Things were just so busy in the office. I'd deal with it. I would. Once everything calmed down. Anyway, the dreams would probably go away by the time that happened.

Agent Holley had been through the scene and all the evidence. He'd assured me I'd acted in self-defense. Cooper had told me I'd done the right thing. *I* knew I'd done the right thing.

What was there to stress about?

Nothing, that's what.

The office was unnaturally quiet as Cooper and his brothers hashed things out with the FBI. They had no interest in trying to get their father off the hook. Maxwell had caused too much damage to too many lives. The Sinclair brothers had honor. They understood justice.

That said, there are layers to guilt once you hit the legal system. Maxwell had access to information the FBI could use to take down the Tsepov organization.

No one was in that conference room arguing in favor of Maxwell's innocence, but there was room to negotiate once they'd all agreed he was guilty as hell.

My heart hurt for Cooper. For all of them. Maxwell was an asshole. I'd known Maxwell was an asshole when he hired me, propositioning me pretty much the second I accepted the job despite knowing that I was married. My husband had been the one who'd sent me Maxwell's way, the two friendly through some connection that had disappeared in the mists of time.

I'd turned him down firmly, expecting the job offer to be withdrawn, but he'd simply sneered and said he'd see me Monday. That was the first asshole move I'd witnessed, and it wouldn't be the last. Not by a long shot.

I didn't like Lacey Sinclair, but I felt for any woman who'd tied her life to Maxwell. I'd paid too many hotel bills with itemized lists of champagne and pornography, seen too many charges at lingerie stores I knew Lacey would never patronize.

Maxwell cheated on her flagrantly and often. If he didn't bother to hide it from me, I doubted he bothered to hide it from his wife. She was a bitch, but no woman deserves that.

My own parents had been married since their early twenties, and while they might bicker occasionally, I still turned the corner and caught them making out like teenagers. They backed each other up, presenting a united front to the world. Sometimes I marveled at the men the Sinclair brothers had grown into, knowing their parents as well as I did.

As if my mind had conjured her up, Lacey Sinclair pulled open the door to the office.

Crap. I'd planned for everything this morning—except for Lacey Sinclair.

Chapter Ten

ALICE

LACEY HAD SHOWN HER FACE IN THE OFFICE once or twice when one of her boys took her to lunch, but for the most part, she'd avoided me, and I'd avoided her.

Today, it appeared our mutual détente was over. Her frosted blonde hair perfectly arranged, diamonds at her ears and pearls around her neck, she stormed to the front desk wearing a cream linen suit more suitable for lunch at the club than hanging around her apartment.

I knew she wasn't cleared to leave the building since all of her available escorts were currently meeting with the FBI. I like to dress up—obviously, since I did it every day of the week—but even I didn't go full makeup, heels, and stockings when I wasn't going anywhere.

Lacey turned a hard right in front of the desk and headed down the hall for the conference room. Bolting out of my chair, I dashed to block her, propping my hands on my hips to take up as much space as I could. Lacey isn't a big woman, but almost everyone is bigger than me, and the Sinclair boys came by their height honestly. Neither of their parents was short. Lacey towered over me, clearly thinking she could use her height to intimidate me. Not likely. I had a crew of badasses to corral every day. I'd long gotten over feeling small just because I was small.

"Get out of my way, slut," Lacey hissed, only loud enough for me to hear. The scent of lime and gin hit my face. Lovely. Not long after noon, and Lacey had already sucked back her first gin and tonic. Given the open use of her pet name for me, I'd bet more than one.

Where she got off calling me a slut, I didn't know. I was married for eleven years and I never once stepped out on my husband. I'd been tempted, sure, especially when we'd stopped sleeping together, but I'd never so much as kissed another man since the day we'd met. Not until Cooper, and that was more than six months after my long-overdue divorce.

I tried to let the slur roll off. This was Lacey, after all. She wasn't one to let the truth get in the way of a good insult.

She darted to my left, trying to slide by. I blocked her, putting my hands up to grab her shoulders and hold her back. How a woman who lived on cocktails could be so strong, I didn't know. I was fit, dammit. Okay, maybe I wasn't cross-training every day, but I was at the gym three or four nights a week. Dancing, not pumping iron, but still.

The alcohol Lacey had consumed worked against her and she lost her balance. I pushed her back, setting her on her feet before propping my hands on my hips again and giving her my best glare.

"Mrs. Sinclair, go back upstairs. I'll have Cooper or one of the guys come see you when they're out of their meeting.

You're not cleared to go past the front desk. Cooper told you that."

My words couldn't penetrate Lacey's haze of gin. Shoving her shoulder into mine she tried to push past me again, sneering when I sidestepped her and kept her from making her way down the hall.

"I know they're in a meeting, you idiot. That's why I'm here."

In a burst of strength fueled by alcohol and rage, Lacey threw her body into mine, knocking me against the wall. I stumbled and she was off like a shot, headed straight for the conference room.

Dammit. *Dammit.* The last thing they needed was Lacey butting into that meeting. She reached the door ahead of me and yanked it open, bolting through and trying to tug it closed behind her before I caught up.

Gin slowed her hands and I managed to slip in behind her, already apologizing to the room. No one heard me under Lacey's irate shout.

"I don't know what you boys think you're doing, but this meeting is canceled," she announced. "You can't make any agreements on your father's behalf. None. You might as well just pack it up and go home."

Agent Holley pushed his chair back but didn't stand, narrowing calculating eyes on Lacey.

"Mrs. Sinclair. Nice to see you. Saves us a trip. So, you're aware that Maxwell is alive, yes?"

"I'm not aware of anything," she protested, blustering.

Agent Holley raised an eyebrow. "If that's the case, then you're free to excuse yourself. If you don't know anything you're of no use in this meeting."

I could have kissed Agent Holley for that. He looked unassuming in his brown suit, the cut ill-fitting on his tall, lanky frame. The kind eyes I was used to were nowhere in sight as he examined Lacey Sinclair like a bug under a microscope.

"Mrs. Sinclair, you're interrupting. If you have nothing to add, then your presence here is unnecessary. Do I need to have one of my agents remove you?"

"You have no right—"

"I have every right," Agent Holley said smoothly, "and if I learn that you have knowledge of your husband's whereabouts, knew that he faked his death, you can be charged as an accessory. At the least with obstruction of justice. Do you understand that?"

Lacey did what she always did when faced with something she didn't like. She ignored it. Turning her attention to her sons, she spat out, "After all he did for you, you betray your father like this. You should stand by him. You should back him up. Instead, you're throwing him to the wolves, treating him like a common criminal—"

"He is a common criminal," Knox said, his eyes hard.

Knox never had much to say to his mother. As long as I've known him, he was the one brother who never played his mother's game, never let her get away with anything. He was a good man, a good friend, and a good brother, but he lacked his siblings' charm. Knox didn't talk unless he had something to say, and he always cut straight to the bone. This was no exception.

Lacey's face went white. "How could you say something like that? He is your father! Your job is to protect him—"

Knox stared her down, his eyes black granite. "—and what, Mom? Should we go to jail for him? Take responsibility for his crimes and do his time in prison? Is that what you're saying? Just so we're clear."

Knox appeared impervious, but deep in Cooper's ice-blue eyes, I saw agony. The pain of a child betrayed again. Betrayed by one of the two people on this planet who should put him first and never had. His finger tapped on the surface of the conference table, the burn of pain in his eyes turning them to blue fire. That tapping finger... Cooper was about to lose it.

I snapped.

That's the best way I can describe it. I just fucking snapped. My hand shot out, grabbing Lacey's upper arm. Using moves I hadn't practiced in months, not since my last mandatory training session, I wrenched Lacey's arm behind her back, pulling her hand up between her shoulder blades until it twisted her arm in the socket enough to drag a yelp of pain from her lips.

Unable to look at Cooper, I met Knox's eyes. I could have sworn I saw a glint of ironic amusement in their black depths as I said, "Please excuse us, gentlemen."

Using my leverage on her arm, I turned Lacey around and frog-marched her out of the room. Her shoulder was going to hurt like hell later. I couldn't find it in me to care.

She'd hurt Cooper enough. Hurt all of them enough. Lacey swore at me, calling me every name in the book. I closed my ears as I shoved her through the office door to the elevator. Every time she tried to squirm out of my grip, I wrenched her arm higher until she squeaked with pain.

I didn't enjoy it, I swear. If I thought there was any way I could have gotten her out of the room without man-handling her, I would have done it. The elevator took an eternity, the ride to the floor above just as long.

I pushed her through the door of her apartment, watching impassively as she stumbled into the kitchen counter.

She had the loose limbs of a habitual drunk, and while her arm might hurt tomorrow, the rest of her would be fine.

She spun to face me, and the sound of her voice came into focus.

"You little whore. You think because my son is fucking you that makes you special? Who gives you the right to lay your hands on me? Your days here are numbered. When my husband gets back—"

"When your husband gets back," I interrupted, "he's going to prison. Unless Tsepov kills him first. I doubt staffing is going to be on his list of concerns."

"We'll see about that," she flung back.

"You know, this is hard for your sons. They love Maxwell, despite everything. And he put all of you at risk. He put the business at risk. They're doing everything they can to keep you safe and save what they've built. They need you to back them up. Them, not Maxwell."

"You're so fucking high and mighty, aren't you?" Lacey sneered. "Since the day you showed up all you wanted is to get your claws in a Sinclair. I know your game. I know why he hired you, you little slut. You bided your time when he was done with you. Now you think you have Cooper, but you'll never keep him. He knows what you are. Just another whore."

I was used to bitchiness from Lacey, even some light name-calling, but this was over the top. Was it stress? Too many gin and tonics?

I won't deny I've had a crush on Cooper since the first day I saw him, but I never, ever did anything about it. Not until that day two weeks ago when he'd kissed me. I'd never been interested in any other Sinclair, and I'd never laid a finger on one, much less indicated I wanted to.

Let it go, I told myself. *She's drunk and she's freaking out. Just lock her in and get back to the desk.*

I took my own advice, turning my back on Lacey and bolting for the door before she could beat me to it. She didn't bother, leaning against the counter and staring at me with hate.

She's a lonely, bitter, unhappy woman, I reminded myself. *Feel pity, but don't let her hurt your feelings.*

I pulled the door shut and typed the code into the keypad that would lock the door from the outside. We rarely had to use that code, but all of us knew it. Our job is to keep our clients safe, even if that meant keeping them safe from themselves. This definitely qualified as one of those times.

Whatever trouble Lacey could get into in that apartment, it couldn't be as bad as what she'd get up to if I let her out.

It wouldn't be long before I learned how very wrong I was about that.

Chapter Eleven

ALICE

*I*PULLED ON MY DRESS, PLEASED AT THE REFLEC-
tion in the mirror. The fabric shimmered in the
light, shifting from emerald to a green so deep it
was almost black.

I'd purchased the party dress on a whim over a year
before with no idea where I would wear it. At the time, I
hadn't cared. It had been on sale and so perfect I couldn't
resist.

The pleated wrap bodice dipped to a V between my
modest breasts showing a lot more cleavage than I usually bared. Classy cleavage, but cleavage all the same. I'd
pulled out my secret weapon for dresses like this, a black
lace push-up bustier that turned my less-than-impressive
breasts into a whole lot more.

I grinned at the thought of Cooper's eyes bugging out of
his head when he caught sight of me. With a tight waist,
a matching V at my back, and a full skirt held out by two
black crinolines, the dress made the most of my assets.

Smoothing on lipstick, I gave my reflection one last look. Sky-high heels, sheer black stockings, knockout dress, and red lipstick. I'm no supermodel, but my best is pretty damn good.

I was lucky I had the dress in my closet since I hadn't planned for the party tonight. None of us had. Earlier that afternoon, just as we were all packing up, Lacey had swanned into the office handing out invitations.

Squares of cream linen bearing our names in calligraphy on the front. Confused, I'd opened mine and pulled out a card. I was cordially invited to an engagement party for Evers Sinclair and Summer Winters.

What was this? My eyes had popped up to see disbelief on Cooper's face, anger on Evers'. Evers held the card out to his mother.

"What the fuck, Mom?"

"Language, Evers," she chided. Evers had set his jaw and glared.

Lacey shrugged a shoulder and tossed her hair, somewhere between dismissive and defiant. "You boys locked me in that apartment with nothing to do. Wouldn't let me see my friends, wouldn't let me go out to lunch, and we have an engagement to celebrate. So, I took it upon myself to throw a party."

The Sinclair brothers stared at each other, dumbfounded. How the hell had she planned a party? When he got over his shock, Cooper protested, "Mom, Jacob Winters' wedding is next weekend. We can't throw an engagement party the weekend before. It's rude."

Lacey waved a hand in the air, shooing away Cooper's concerns. "Jacob won't mind. I've known that boy since he was born. He'll be happy to celebrate. In fact, he's already RSVP'd."

"Summer wanted to plan the party," Evers said, his voice flat. "This fall, after Jacob's wedding, when things with Dad were resolved. She told you that. You know she's been looking forward to it."

Lacey rolled her eyes, unconcerned. "I'm her mother-in-law. It's not up to her."

Knox asked the only relevant question. "How many of these invitations did you send out?"

Lacey beamed. "Only a hundred. And most of them said yes."

Cooper, staring at the invitation in his hand, said only, "Fuck me."

Every available and qualified employee had been roped into handling security. Lacey didn't seem to mind forcing so many people to cancel their Friday night plans with no notice.

Cooper minded. A lot. He promised them all a bonus for putting up with his mother's thoughtless planning. Jacob and Abigail had, of course, assured him that they weren't the least bit offended Lacey had decided to throw Evers and Summer an engagement party the weekend before their wedding. Not only were the Winters and Sinclairs practically family, Jacob knew Lacey. He knew this party hadn't been anyone's idea but hers.

The boys were dreading it. I understood that. I kind of was, too. Still, I had this gorgeous dress and hadn't had an excuse to wear it. Even if Cooper and I weren't official, even if I didn't have any idea what we were really doing, and no one would know, I loved the idea of dressing up for him. This dress would drive him crazy. Especially when he found out what I was wearing beneath it.

As I left my apartment and locked the door behind me, I was struck by the fleeting wish that this thing with Cooper was real. That he'd pick me up at my door and escort me to the party on his arm instead of picking me up with his mother and giving me a ride because he was my boss and we lived in the same building.

I hoped for a moment alone with him, but Lacey's door opened as mine closed. She met me in the hall, her cold eyes scanning my dress. I silently dared her to say something about it.

Technically, it fit with the rest of my clothes, but the wrap bodice and full skirt were classic. In fact, I'd found it on the rack at a department store at the mall. It was absolutely appropriate for the party, and, as I'd suspected, Lacey couldn't find anything to insult.

Instead, she turned her face away from mine, chin in the air, and tapped her foot with impatience. Scanning her from the corner of my eye, I realized that while she looked as she normally did, her hair and makeup perfect, she was steady, not wobbling the slightest bit. Was it possible Lacey was actually sober? Or maybe just *not drunk*. She didn't even seem tipsy.

Maybe tonight wouldn't be a total disaster. It was possible.

The hum of the elevator drew my eyes. Cooper stepped out, his eyes skimming past his mother to land on me. They traced the neckline of my dress, dipping between my breasts. Knowing his mother was watching, his only response was a quick flare of his eyes before his jaw went hard. He tapped the button for the elevator. "Let's get this over with, shall we?"

Lacey strode past me, looping her arm through her son's and beaming up at him. "Don't be such a party pooper. This is going to be fun. I have a surprise waiting for you at the club."

Cooper let out a huff of exasperation. "Is it a surprise that means we'll get through the evening without any incidents and go home early?"

Lacey's laugh was a crystalline tinkle of sound, each giggle splintering to deadly shards as it landed. Cooper's jaw flexed as he clenched his teeth. I moved to his other side and set a hand on his arm.

"Don't worry, it'll be fun," I tried to reassure.

Lacey leaned across Cooper, the venomous glee in her smile driving me back. "Oh, yes," she agreed, "it will be fun."

I followed them into the elevator, suddenly uneasy.

There was a line of cars at the valet stand when we pulled up, despite being early. Not surprising.

All of Atlanta—the part that mattered to Lacey Sinclair—was eager to turn out for her last-minute engagement party. The drama of the rush was part of the draw. Everyone would be examining Summer for a baby bump, studying the family for signs of discord, gossip moving like wildfire as the guests tried to figure out why a Sinclair would throw such an important event with only a few days' notice.

Lacey didn't care. If she had, she would have left well enough alone. I followed Cooper and his mother into the country club, ignoring the curious stares of guests who hadn't entered yet. Cooper did the same, fending off several approaches with an abrupt wave of his hand.

Cooper kept his cool, but he was perilously close to losing it. Lacey didn't care about that either.

I'd gotten dressed thinking I'd make the most of this, try to find the fun in a potential disaster. As I entered the ballroom and laid eyes on Evers and Summer, all thoughts of a silver lining evaporated.

Summer's usually bright smile was dim as she shook hands and hugged people she barely knew. We'd only met a few times, weren't close enough for me to offer any real comfort, but when I greeted her, I gave her a tight hug. "You okay?" I murmured.

She hitched her shoulder and gave me a brave smile.

"Trying not to kill my future mother-in-law," she murmured through gritted teeth.

"If you want, I'll do it for you," I offered, only half-kidding.

Summer's blue eyes went dark. Ominously, she said, "Oh, you're not going to do it for *me*."

She passed me to Evers, who was so pissed he practically vibrated with rage, though the only outward sign was the tick in his jaw. Giving me a hug, he said in a low voice, "Don't be mad at him, he didn't know."

Who didn't know what? I wanted to ask, but the line of partygoers waiting to see Evers and Summer had piled up behind me.

I was strolling in the direction of the bar, a glass of champagne in my future, when I spotted Cooper standing beside his mother, his arms around a tall blonde in a strapless pink gown.

Placing an enthusiastic kiss on his cheek, she practically bubbled as she slipped her arm through his and smiled up at him.

Chapter Twelve

ALICE

ACEY RADIATED SMUG HAPPINESS CUT ONLY by the triumphant glance she sent in my direction.

I stumbled, catching myself before I could do a header into the polished hardwood floor. It didn't take me long to put the pieces together. Lacey had ordered Cooper a date.

Seriously?

Cooper was thirty-eight years old. He didn't need his mother to set him up.

The woman on his arm was tall and gorgeous and blonde. Taking in the sparkle of diamonds at her ears, neck, and wrists, I could guess she was a member of the club like the Sinclairs. Exactly the kind of woman his mother would choose for him.

Catching the faint apology in Cooper's eyes as they met mine, the sight of the blonde princess holding onto his arm cut a hole in my heart.

This was who he'd leave me for. Maybe not her exactly, but someone like her. Glamorous and wealthy, with the right pedigree.

Someone who was *someone*.

Not a divorced office manager from a normal middle-class family. I sipped at my champagne and tried to disappear into a potted palm on the side of the room, wondering if I'd need an excuse to leave early.

There would be no sneaking away for stolen kisses tonight. Not when Cooper already had a date. The dress and the black lace underwear felt stupid.

I wasn't Cooper's girlfriend.

He was my boss.

My boss and my temporary hookup. That was it.

The blonde glued to Cooper's side offered him an hors d'oeuvre from a plate, her fingertips brushing his lips as she fed it to him.

I felt his eyes on me and studiously avoided them, examining the guests of honor across the room, hoping for their sake the receiving line would end soon. Evers looked like he was about to snap. Summer was miserable beneath her polite smile.

Lacey Sinclair was a fucking bitch.

An arm slid around my shoulders, a familiar voice in my ear. "Smile at me like I'm Cooper and kiss me on the cheek. It'll drive Lacey bat-shit crazy."

I glanced up to see Griffen looking down at me with a spark of mischief in his eye. Like me, he wasn't a fan of Lacey Sinclair. He'd spent too many years watching her make his best friends miserable.

Feeling Lacey's eyes on us, I gave Griffen my most radiant smile and kissed him on the cheek. He turned his face, bringing us so close our lips almost touched.

Devastating in a dark suit, his sandy blond hair cut short to reveal perfect bone structure, Griffen's sea-green eyes were filled with mischief.

"Nice job. Try not to look so miserable, and we might pull this off."

"What are you doing? I thought you were coordinating security."

Griffen led me away from the bar, taking a position by the French doors to the gardens, still on the side of the room but far more visible than I would have liked. Lacey's triumph had melted into confused anger.

A flick of my eyes to the man standing beside her and I saw that Cooper wasn't confused, he was furious. His eyes were arctic, the vein in his temple pulsing red.

Answering my question, Griffen said, "I delegated. There's not much to manage now that all the guests are here. And I'm not leaving you alone while Cooper has that harpy on his arm."

Griffen wasn't talking about Lacey, he meant the woman feeding Cooper another hors d'oeuvre. What was her deal? He wasn't a toddler. He could feed himself.

Don't be a bitch, I chided myself. "Just because Lacey set this up doesn't mean she's a harpy."

"I know Heather Spencer, and she *is* a harpy. She's been engaged three times. She's holding out for the big score."

Not knowing why I was defending the woman who was currently hanging all over my not-actually-a-boyfriend, I argued, "Charlie Winters was engaged three times."

Griffen just laughed, snagging another glass of champagne off the tray of a passing waiter and shoving it in my hand, taking my empty one.

When did I finish my champagne?

"Charlie dumped three gold-digging assholes. Not the same thing. Heather traded up each time. Cooper is exactly what she's looking for."

"Why would Lacey do that to him? Doesn't she want him to be happy?" The moment the words left my mouth I heard my own foolishness. Lacey hadn't given Cooper's happiness a single thought.

If she thought about her children's happiness she never would have ruined Evers and Summer's engagement celebration this way.

If she thought about their happiness she wouldn't have done a lot of things.

The strains of music began, couples drifting to the dance floor. Cooper's date tried to tug him in that direction, but he was unmovable.

Griffen smirked. "Want to dance?"

I sucked back a slug of champagne and tried not to sigh. "No. I want to go home," I said, honestly. "I think I'll just call for a ride and—"

"No fucking way," Griffen said, his arm tightening around me. "You two are being dumbasses, you know that?"

"Can we not talk about this?"

"Nope. If you don't want to talk, you can listen. This is stupid. You're both adults."

"Exactly." I emptied my champagne and shoved the glass in Griffen's hand, aggravated that he was butting into something that was none of his damn business. "We're adults, and what we do outside work is nobody else's business."

"You're outside of work right now. So why are you over here with me while he has Heather Spencer on his arm? It's a fucking waste of that dress, for one thing."

My righteous indignation deflated. It *was* a waste of this dress. I should have saved it for something else.

For what? It's not like Cooper was ever going to take me to a party. The champagne turned sour in my stomach. "I don't want work to get weird when this whole thing fizzles out."

"What makes you think it's going to fizzle out?"

I leaned back and stared up at Griffen, uncomprehending. He had an equally disbelieving expression on his face.

"Griffen. Don't be an idiot. Look at her," I tilted my chin in Cooper and Heather's direction, "and then look at me. There's a reason he's at the party with her and not me."

"Yeah, because his mother is a raging bitch. And I'm not the one who's an idiot."

"Are you calling me an idiot?" I demanded, champagne bubbling through my brain, muddling the emotions swirling through me until I couldn't tell if I was mad, or depressed, or indignant.

I was something, and it wasn't happy. Griffen shoved a mushroom tart in my mouth to shut me up.

"I call it how I see it, kid. You two are dumbasses. Life is short. You're wasting it playing a stupid, fucking game."

I chewed as fast as I could, swallowing so I could fire off the uninspired retort of, "It's not a game."

"Exactly my point," Griffen agreed. He slid another glass in my hand and tightened his arm around me. "Heads up. Incoming."

I sipped to wash down the remains of the mushroom tart. I was drinking too much, and I didn't really care. When I looked up, Cooper loomed over us, his mother and his date nowhere in sight.

"What the fuck do you think you're doing?" he growled at Griffen.

"I'm Alice's date," he said, easily. "I'm sure you don't mind, considering you have your own."

The vein in Cooper's temple pulsed harder. I took another sip, murmuring, "Griffen—", not sure what I was going to say but knowing I had to say something or Cooper was going to hit Griffen and this whole thing would go to hell.

The band struck up a slow song. Griffen plucked the champagne glass from my fingers and shoved it at Cooper with an amused, "Excuse us."

He steered me to the dance floor, leaving Cooper glowering after us in frustrated silence.

Chapter Thirteen

COOPER

I WATCHED GRIFFEN LEAD ALICE TO THE DANCE floor and drew in a slow breath, one last effort to get my temper under control. It didn't work.

This whole fucking night had been a fucking disaster, starting with my mother and those goddamn fucking party invitations. I'd known she had something up her sleeve when we left for the party, but I hadn't imagined it was Heather Spencer.

Heather wasn't all bad, but she was very much not my type. I was going crazy standing there with Heather hanging all over me while the only woman I wanted was across the room.

My chest had ached at Alice's haunted, bruised eyes as she watched Heather push a tart between my lips. I'd resisted the urge to smack Heather's hand away. It wasn't her fault my mother had shoved her so publicly between me and Alice.

Setting me up with Heather explained why my mother

had invited Alice when she hated her so much. The moment Lacey handed Alice her invitation I should have known Lacey had something like this up her sleeve.

I wouldn't humiliate Heather even if I didn't like her, but I wasn't above lying to get her out of the room for a while. She and my mother distracted by a story about a friend who was looking for them, I was on borrowed time, wasting it watching Griffen and Alice dance.

Griffen slid his arms around Alice, pulling her close. Way too fucking close. His fingertips grazed the creamy skin exposed by the V at the back of her dress. I was going to fucking kill him.

The fact that Griffen and Alice were only friends, that she would never cheat on me, that he would never go after my girl—it all meant nothing as I watched Griffen lead her in smooth arcs around the dance floor.

He was fucking with me. I knew it and it didn't matter. I was still going to fucking kill him.

The low voice beside me barely penetrated the rage flooding my brain. "You going to let that go?" Knox asked, his arms crossed over his chest and a knowing look in his eyes.

"What the fuck do you want me to do about it?" I ground out.

"If anyone danced with Lily like that I'd rip his fucking head off," Knox said in such a calm, even tone I had no doubt he spoke the truth.

Griffen swung Alice in a circle, dipping her over his arm, the arch of her back pressing her ripe cleavage into the bodice of her gown.

My vision went red.

If he looked down at her breasts—

Shooting a knowing glance at me, Griffen did exactly that, his eyes hot and appreciative, his glance lingering.

He might be Alice's friend, but he was a man. Every inch of Alice was sexy on her worst day, but in that dress, her breasts were fucking spectacular.

"You keep grinding your teeth like that you're going to crack one," Knox said blandly.

"Shut the fuck up." That was the best I could come up with. Every part of my brain was wrapped up trying to leash the caveman inside me.

The caveman didn't give a shit about promises or good manners. He wanted Alice.

That's it. Alice.

Maybe the caveman also wanted to throw a punch right into Griffen's perfect jaw for daring to touch her.

Alice was mine. Mine.

Don't make a scene at your brother's engagement party, I lectured myself.

The party he didn't even want, the devil on my shoulder whispered.

Alice wants to keep things a secret at work.

Because she's afraid you're going to dump her, the devil countered. *But that's not going to happen, is it?*

I knew it even if Alice didn't.

You promised you wouldn't compromise her, but since you're keeping her, letting everyone know wouldn't be compromising her, would it?

Fuck, the devil on my shoulder had a convincing argument.

Griffen led Alice into another spin. She stumbled and he caught her, pulling her even closer, his mouth dropping to her ear, the words he whispered just for her. Alice tipped her head back and laughed, eyes bright.

Griffen's face hovered above hers, his mouth a breath from kissing her.

I shoved Alice's discarded champagne glass in Knox's hands as the devil on my shoulder joined forces with the caveman inside me.

I was done being reasonable. Done looking out for other people.

Done with my mother.

Done with Heather.

Done with this whole fucking disaster of a party.

I strode across the ballroom, bumping into another couple without apology. Alice saw me coming, her eyes flashing wide in alarm.

My hand closed on Griffen's shoulder and wheeled him around. When his eyes met mine, they weren't surprised. They were wickedly amused.

Without a word, I hauled my arm back and swung.

Griffen wasn't some drunk asshole. He was one of my top guys and he hadn't had a sip of alcohol. He shifted at the last second, and my fist missed his nose, connecting with the side of his jaw. The impact was muted, but still enough to send him down hard. He stayed there, splayed on the ballroom floor, grinning up at me.

My obstacle taken care of, I closed my hands around Alice's waist and tossed her over my shoulder, clamping an arm over the back of her thighs to keep her dress from flipping up.

I was almost at the door, the murmurs of the party guests a wave of sound rising behind us before Alice started to squirm. Beating her fists against my back she demanded, "Cooper, put me down. What are you doing?"

I strode through the doors of the club, keeping my mouth shut. Hitting Griffen was bad enough. I wouldn't spit out words in anger that I couldn't take back later.

Shifting Alice, I reached inside my jacket and pulled out the valet ticket. The valet, a wizened old man who'd been at the club for decades, didn't so much as blink as he took the ticket and nodded.

"One moment, Mr. Sinclair."

Alice growled, her voice drifting up from behind me. "Put me down, Cooper."

I only tightened my arm. If I put her down she'd try to run. Then I'd have to chase her, and this whole thing would be more embarrassing. For her.

I wasn't the least bit embarrassed. The devil on my shoulder had been right.

Claiming Alice publicly felt better than anything I'd done since I'd kissed her two weeks before.

My car was there two minutes later. I'd driven my Aston Martin, and the valet staff always put it at the front so the other members could admire its sleek lines. I didn't give a shit who saw the car, but the convenience was an advantage when I had a furious woman thrown over my shoulder. Not that this was a common occurrence.

I deposited Alice in the passenger seat, leaning in to fasten her seatbelt, warning, "Don't even think about getting out."

She ignored me, arms crossed over her chest, chin jutting up, eyes fixed on the window. Not a word passed between us on the short drive back to the Sinclair Security building.

I should have been worried that she was pissed. I wasn't.

Every moment I'd pretended there was nothing between us had felt wrong. Acting like she was just another woman was a betrayal of everything I felt for her. A betrayal of everything I wanted from her.

She was pissed. She had a right to be. Yet again, I'd acted like a fucking caveman. I'd gone against her wishes, not only claiming her but making her into a spectacle.

All my darker impulses knew I'd made the only choice she'd left me. That caveman inside me, the devil on my shoulder, they knew if I waited for Alice to give me permission we'd still be dancing around each other a year from now. Two years from now.

She didn't believe in me.

If I waited for her to get there on her own, I'd be waiting for eternity.

We were safely locked behind the door of my place before Alice acknowledged my presence. Stepping out of her sky-high heels, she picked up one delicate shoe and hurled it at my face.

I dodged it easily.

Her control snapped.

"How could you do that to me? Everyone we work with was there. Everybody knows."

"He had his hands all over you," I said, thinking that was explanation enough. From Alice's uncomprehending stare, I knew it wasn't.

"It was Griffen," she said. "*Griffen*. You know, your best friend?"

"He was about to kiss you."

Alice threw her hands in the air as she stepped out of the other shoe, turning it in her fingers and looking at me as if considering whether she should throw that one, too. "Are you nuts? He was *not* going to kiss me."

"Trust me, he was."

Griffen had absolutely been about to kiss Alice. I knew that just as I knew he'd been pushing my buttons the whole time. I fucking knew it and it didn't matter. Griffen had been sure I'd stop him before his lips touched hers.

Later, I'd probably regret the bruise I'd left on his jaw. Later, but not yet.

Alice stomped her small foot and winged her other shoe at my head. My hand snapped up and caught it. Smiling, I met Alice's furious eyes, the clear blue of the summer sky. Even furious she was the most beautiful woman I'd ever seen.

I tossed her shoe behind me, crossing the room until I stood before her.

Chapter Fourteen

COOPER

*Y*OU LOOK BEAUTIFUL."

Tucking a gleaming strand of dark hair behind her ear, I traced my finger over the line of her jaw and down her neck, lingering in the hollow of her collarbone before dropping between her temptingly-plump breasts.

She quivered beneath the featherlight touch as if about to take flight, but her feet stayed where they were. Staring up at me, those sky-blue eyes I loved were torn between fear and desire.

Her voice was barely a whisper, anguished and raw. "You said you wouldn't."

"I said I wouldn't compromise you. I won't. I didn't."

"But—"

Cupping her face in my palms, I tilted her head up to mine. "You're not my dirty little secret, Alice. You're mine. Today. Tomorrow. Next week. Next year. You're mine."

Her voice shook as she said, "I don't understand."

"I know you don't, but you will."

Her lips parted beneath mine, her mouth tasting of champagne. I deepened the kiss, my hand pressed to the bare skin of her back, her heart thumping, wild beneath my touch.

When I straightened, she swayed, still staring up at me, her eyes clouded with confusion.

"I told you, Alice, you're mine. Don't you want to be? Mine?"

She nodded, her mouth open, words stuck in her throat. All she got out was, "But, I— You—"

"I'm done waiting. I wanted you, but you were married, and I waited. Finally, you divorced him, and still, I waited. I wanted to give you time, but that time is up. I'm done waiting, Alice. I'm not going to pretend this is less than it is."

"What is it?" she asked, breathless, light filling her eyes, chasing away the clouds. She needed me to say the words. I could give her that. I'd been waiting to give her that for years.

"It's you and me, Alice. Together. At work. At home. This isn't a fling. Not for me."

"This is real?"

"As real as it gets," I promised. Sliding my arms around her, pulling her flush to my body, I looked down into her wide, wide eyes. "Doesn't it feel real?"

She swallowed hard and nodded.

"If you want out, now's your chance. I'll let you walk out that door. You can come to work on Monday, and we'll pretend nothing happened."

It might kill me, but if that was what she needed, I'd do it.

Fear opened a chasm in my heart, but I forced out the words I needed to say. "If this is just sex for you, tell me now and I'll let you go."

Alice stroked her fingertips across my cheek in a touch so light it sent shivers down my spine. "It could never be just sex with you, Cooper. It's only this good because it *is* you."

"Because it's *us*," I said, the chasm in my heart filling with a light that shoved out all the dark. My mother's manipulations, my father's betrayals. None of it mattered. Not in this moment. Not with her.

I couldn't remember the last time I felt this free. A grin stretched across my mouth as I closed my hands around Alice's small waist and lifted her, tossing her over my shoulder for the second time that night.

She shrieked, the sound dissolving into laughter. Instead of battering me with her fists, this time she reached down and closed a hand over my ass, squeezing appreciatively.

I strode down the hall to my bedroom like the victor in a bloody battle. Alice was my prize and I planned to enjoy her. Thoroughly.

In my bedroom, I set her on her feet. Not on the floor, but on a trunk at the foot of my bed. I couldn't remember what was in there—the decorator had chosen it—but it was sturdy, and it put Alice six inches taller than me.

Stepping back, I took in every inch of her, from the gleam of her dark hair to the painted toenails hidden by dark stockings. "Are you going to show me what you have under that dress?"

Alice's lips quirked, and she reached behind her for the zipper. She drew it down slowly, so slowly I thought I'd die of unfulfilled lust by the time she got to the bottom.

One smooth shoulder dipped, dark green taffeta sliding down her arm. She dipped the other and the whole dress fell mere inches, revealing two narrow black straps and a hint of lace at her breasts.

My cock was a steel bar. I needed more.

Alice drew in a sharp breath and pressed her hands to her chest, halting the dress's slide. With a toss of her short hair, she looked down her nose at me, suddenly imperious.

"Lose the jacket."

Only a fool would argue with a half-naked woman telling him to take off his clothes.

I'm no fool.

My jacket hit the chair behind me. I looked back at her, expectant.

"And the tie."

The tie was gone.

"Now you," I countered.

Alice moved her hands, the weight of the dress pulling it down two more slow inches. The tops of her breasts came into view, framed by a wide strip of black lace.

"That's all you get until I see some skin," she said.

My hands busy on the buttons of my shirt, I freed them and stripped it off, tossing it behind me.

Alice narrowed her eyes on me, assessing, before cocking her head to the side. "You can't touch me until you're naked."

"Agreed." The words left my lips without thought, the promise an easy one to make. Naked was my plan.

Trusting my word, Alice let go of the dress. The taffeta fell to her feet in a rustle, leaving her standing there in nothing but yards of frothy black tulle and a black lace bustier.

My mouth went dry. My fingers itched to touch. I took a step forward, dazed.

Alice shook her head, wagging a finger at me. "No, no. You promised."

The easiest promise I'd ever made. My hands at my belt, I worked fast, lowering my zipper, stripping off the rest of my clothes in a heartbeat.

The caveman who'd thrown Alice over his shoulder wanted to toss her on the bed and feast on her body.

The caveman wasn't in charge anymore.

Naked, I closed the distance between us and came to a halt standing before her, for once looking up into her perfect, lovely face.

I reached for her shoulders, cupped them in my palms before running my hands down her arms, feeling every inch of her soft, soft skin.

My fingers tangled with hers, pulling her arms wide, my eyes eating up the sight of all that black lace against her creamy skin.

"Alice. You're so beautiful."

She only stared back, her breath hitching in her chest as she took in the tension coiling in my body, the eager thrust of my erection.

Releasing her hands, I hooked my fingers in the waistband of her crinoline and pulled it down slowly, inch by inch. It slid over her hips and I let go, the fabric pooling at her feet, my mind wiped blank at the vision of her pussy framed by a thong so tiny and sheer it somehow made her more naked than if she'd only been wearing her skin.

I stroked my fingers over the curve of her ass. "So fucking beautiful," I breathed, leaning in to press my mouth to the curve of her breast, pushed high by all that black lace.

I pressed a kiss to one breast, then the other, nuzzling between them, all that soft flesh surrounding me. She smelled like heaven, sweet and spicy, of flowers and fruit and Alice.

The scent of her arousal reached my nose and my restraint broke. A flick of my fingers unhooked all that lace. Another and the thong joined the dress and crinoline on the floor.

Then I was lifting her, tossing her on her back, clambering over the trunk to rise above her, spreading her legs, dipping my fingers between them to find her wet and ready.

She lifted her knees, her arms opening in welcome. Cock in hand, I guided myself inside her heat, sinking deep. Alice clasped her body around mine, legs hooked around my back, her arms around my neck.

I filled her, stopping when I was buried to the root inside Alice. Her skin pressed to mine, breath ragged, she held on.

"Does this feel real to you?" I ground my body into hers, moving my hips in a circle as she shuddered beneath me.

"Yes. Yes, Cooper," she said, her voice splintering with pleasure.

"You're mine," I said again.

I couldn't say it enough. Maybe if I kept saying it she'd finally believe I meant it. To the core of my soul, I meant it.

She was mine. I moved inside her, driving her to the peak and over, feeling her tight heat clasp around me, her cries filling my ear.

It wasn't enough. I drove her up again and again until I couldn't take it anymore and spilled inside her, a long-vacant piece of my soul complete, knowing that Alice, at long last, finally belonged to me.

Chapter Fifteen

COOPER

I WOKE TO AN EMPTY BED, COMING FULLY ALERT in a blink.

Alice. Where was Alice?

A glance at the clock told me it was later than either of us usually slept. Not a surprise given that we hadn't found sleep until well after midnight. Add in the champagne she'd drunk, and I had to wonder—why the hell was Alice up at all?

I caught the rustle of taffeta somewhere outside my room. The hallway? Rolling to my feet, I yanked on my discarded boxers as I strode to the door.

All I could think about was Alice. Find Alice and bring her back to bed. That was where my critical analysis began and ended.

She froze when I entered the living room, her dress on and mostly zipped, crinolines bundled under her arm in a cloud of black tulle. Her face bare of makeup, hair tangled, she looked impossibly young. And exhausted.

Dark circles marred her eyes, the usually clear blue dull, bloodshot. She should be in bed.

"Alice, what are you doing?"

She winced at the sound of my voice. "Nothing. Nothing, Cooper. Go back to bed. I'm just—I just have to go home and take a shower. Change. You know."

No, I didn't know. I had a perfectly good shower here. I opened my mouth to tell her that, and stopped, really seeing her. The fragility in the set of her shoulders. The way she squinted against the bright light flooding through the floor-to-ceiling windows. The vulnerable bend of her neck, her head tilting forward as if it weighed too much to hold up.

"What's wrong?" I asked, my voice low. "Too much champagne?"

"No. A little, maybe. I just—" She wrapped her arm tighter around her front, squeezing the mass of crinolines against her, brow furrowed. The more I watched her, the more I realized something was wrong.

She wasn't just tired. This wasn't just too much champagne. Was she still angry?

Thinking about the way I'd punched Griffen and thrown her over my shoulder in the middle of the ballroom, I was the one who winced. It had all seemed like a great idea at the time.

That's what I got for letting the devil on my shoulder and the caveman in my gut conspire against me. I knew better. Alice asked me to keep things quiet, and I deliberately sabotaged her in the most public way possible.

Fuck. I thought she'd forgiven me. Maybe I was wrong.

Alice bent slowly and picked up one of her shoes from beneath the couch. Eyes half-closed, she tucked it into the bundle in her arms.

"I just want to go lay down. Can you help me find my other shoe?"

I joined her in the search, trying to remember what had happened to it. One shoe she'd thrown at my head, the other I'd caught. I didn't know which one she'd already found.

I needed to find that shoe before she did, needed it as leverage to keep her here long enough to find out what was going on.

This wounded, fragile Alice wasn't the woman I'd made love to the night before, the woman who'd imperiously demanded I strip for her, who'd squeezed my ass as I carried her down the hall.

For that matter, she wasn't the woman who'd winged her high heels at my head either. I didn't recognize this Alice, but I needed to. If I was the reason behind it, I had to know so I could fix it.

I spotted a spike heel sticking out from beneath a console table and snagged it. "Got it."

Alice took a step, reaching for it, but I held it above her head, examining her tired, drawn face.

"Not yet," I said. When she dropped her hand at her side without so much as a scowl, I knew something was very wrong.

Wanting to pull her into my arms, I asked softly, "Are you angry? About last night?"

Bracing, I waited. Alice started to shake her head and froze abruptly, wincing again. "I should be," she muttered, "but I'm not. I think you fucked the mad out of me."

A surprised laugh burst from my lips. Alice winced again at the sound. I couldn't stop the grin that spread across my face. "Good to know that works. I'll keep it in mind for the next time I piss you off."

"I like how you assume there'll be a next time," she said, reaching for her shoe again. I held it behind my back.

"Just playing the odds."

She gave a harrumph, but that was it. This was not my Alice.

Changing tactics, I handed her the shoe. Before she could step away, I was there, closing my arms around her and tucking her into my chest, the pile of fabric and shoes between us.

Now that I knew she wasn't pissed at me, I didn't have to worry she'd drive that spike heel in my eye. Alice pushed back, and reluctantly, I loosened my hold. The shoes and crinolines fell to the floor and Alice melted into me, pressing her forehead against my chest.

The skin of her back was warm and silky, her forehead cold and clammy. Bending, my lips brushed the top of her hair.

"Baby, what's wrong? If you're not pissed at me—how many glasses of champagne did you have last night? I counted four. A lot for a pixie like you, but not enough to make you this miserable."

"I'm not a pixie," she argued. Her disgruntled response was heartening. I think she secretly liked it, but Alice always got annoyed when I called her a pixie. With her blunt cut bob and small frame, the name was a perfect fit.

I tightened my arms around her. "You're my pixie. Tell me what's wrong."

Hiding her face, she mumbled something, her lips moving against my skin, her words inaudible.

"Alice, come on, just tell me what's wrong so I can fix it."

Louder, more clearly, "You can't fix this."

"Then tell me who I have to kill to make it better."

I was mostly kidding. Mostly.

Alice sighed. Lifting her face, her eyes oddly shy for my brazen girl, she said, "I have cramps and a migraine, and I just want to curl up and die, okay?"

Fuck. I hate problems I can't solve.

Now that the truth was out, Alice leaned back, trying to break my hold. Fuck that. I couldn't get rid of the migraine or the cramps, but that didn't mean I couldn't do anything to help.

I kept my arms around her, rubbing a thumb up and down her spine. "Poor Alice. What do you need?"

Mulishly, she said, "I need to go home."

Leaning back to see her face, I asked, "Do you need to go home to get stuff? Or do you need to go home because you feel like shit and you just want to curl up in bed until you feel better?"

"Both," she said, her chin still set in that stubborn line.

"What do you take? Do you have a prescription for the migraines?"

"No. They're not bad enough to need a prescription. I don't have to lock myself in a dark closet or anything. It just hurts like a bitch and it's harder to handle when they come with the cramps."

"Ibuprofen? Do you need a heating pad?"

Alice stared up at me dumbfounded. "When I get them both together I take over-the-counter migraine stuff. I have some downstairs. No heating pad."

Stepping over the bundle of clothes on the floor, I turned her, gently shoving her back toward my bedroom. "Bath or shower?"

"Cooper, I—"

"Bath or shower?"

"Shower," she said, finally.

Arriving in my bathroom, I turned on the shower.

"What do you need from downstairs?"

Alice let out a long breath, finally realizing I wasn't giving up. "Clothes, I guess. The migraine pills from the cabinet in my kitchen. Next to where I keep the Band-Aids. And there's a bag under my sink with daisies on it—" An embarrassed slide of her eyes to the side. "It has all the, uh, stuff I need."

Kissing her on the forehead, I said, "Take a shower. I'll be back before you're out."

I left Alice in the steamy bathroom and headed for her apartment after a quick pit stop in my bedroom to pull on something other than boxers.

I found the migraine medicine exactly where she'd said it would be. Ditto for the cloth bag covered in daisies. I grabbed a gym bag from her closet and threw them in, along with a bottle of lotion from her bathroom counter, her face cream, hairbrush, a stick of deodorant, and a few changes of clothes. Comfortable stuff she could curl up in.

She was still in the shower when I got back. I cracked the door, setting the bag on the counter, not at all reassured by her weak, "Thanks."

Shit. Alice was a whirlwind, a bundle of energy. I knew she suffered from bad headaches occasionally, even knew they were related to her cycle. We'd worked together for nine years, and I'm an observant guy. Particularly where Alice is concerned. Eventually, I'd figured it out.

They weren't usually this bad. Then again, most of the time the headache wasn't on top of too little sleep and too much champagne.

Leaving Alice in peace for the moment, I pulled up a food delivery app on my phone. If she wasn't hungry now, she would be eventually. It would take a while, but I ordered from Annabelle's. Breakfast sandwiches, pastries, and a mocha.

I'd never noticed her avoiding caffeine when she had headaches, and chocolate seemed like a good call when she felt like shit. Eventually, she emerged from the bathroom smelling like fresh fruit, her hair combed straight, skin shining from the face cream, but still too pale.

Chapter Sixteen

COOPER

THE BOTTLE OF MIGRAINE MEDS IN HAND, SHE headed for the kitchen. I stopped her and pointed her in the direction of the couch.

"I ordered breakfast. Coffee. You don't have to eat it until you're ready. Do you want juice to wash down those pills?"

"Please," she said in a near whisper, sinking into the couch. Even recovering from that bump on the head she hadn't been this weak. Loopy from the pain pills, but not like this. Her skin looked paper-thin, her voice hollow.

I got the juice and sat beside her on the couch, propping my feet on the coffee table. When she set down the empty glass, I pulled her into me. She let out a sigh, tension leaking from her body as she relaxed.

Pressing the balls of my thumbs to her temples, I rubbed. "Better or worse?"

With a throaty groan, the first sound she'd made that sounded like her, she said, "Better."

"Just close your eyes. Go to sleep if you want. Food will be here soon."

She curled into me, burrowing her head into my chest, her arm thrown around my waist. I settled a blanket over us, combing my fingers through her wet hair, watching as she fell asleep, the knot in my gut loosening as the line between her brows smoothed away. The migraine pills must be working.

Was it this bad every month? If it was, she'd be taking the day off from now on.

She'd argue, but I wouldn't listen. Alice was tough. She was a smartass who gave as good as she got. It didn't take much to imagine her in this kind of pain, hiding it so no one would know, going home alone to an empty apartment with no one to take care of her.

Even when she'd been married her husband had been gone most of the time, an airline pilot who made no effort to arrange his schedule so he could be with the wife he barely noticed. Since her divorce, there'd been no one.

Now she had me, and I would do everything in my power to keep Alice from ever feeling pain again.

She slept hard, not waking until I eased out from under her to answer the door for our food delivery. Blinking up at me, her blue eyes adorably misted with sleep, I saw the dark circles had faded some, her skin less pale and drawn.

"How's your head?" I asked, handing her a croissant breakfast sandwich loaded with bacon, eggs, and melting cheese. She took the sandwich eagerly, taking a bite, letting out a moan that had my cock stirring. She waited to speak until she'd swallowed. "Better. Not gone, but better."

"Cramps?" I asked, raising an eyebrow at her flush. I knew she didn't want me to ask, but I did it anyway, partly because I wanted to know how she was feeling, but mostly because it was hard to fluster Alice. I loved the pink in her cheeks when she was embarrassed and annoyed at the same time.

With a huff, she said, "Those are better, too. They were early. Took me by surprise. I guess I should be glad. Early is better than late, right?"

I laughed. "I won't argue that. Where periods are concerned, early is better than late."

Just like that my brain threw me a twist.

What if late was better? What if we wanted her to be late? *Slow down, Coop,* I told myself. *One thing at a time.*

A shrug of her shoulder. "I wasn't expecting it, and then the champagne and the headache... Normally I'm on top of this stuff, but somebody's been distracting me lately." She shot a smirk in my direction and took another bite of the breakfast sandwich.

I'd take Alice any way she came, but it was better to see her getting her spirit back. We finished our late breakfast. I cleared the trash away while Alice pulled up a movie on the TV, and we settled into the couch the way we'd been before, Alice curled into me, my fingers sifting through her hair.

As the opening music of the movie filled the room, Alice looked up at me, ignoring the screen. "So, everybody knows about us now?"

"Yes. Everybody knows."

"And this is a thing. A serious thing. Like, we're together?" She wrinkled her nose up at me. "I feel too old to say boyfriend."

I knew what she meant. We weren't in high school. The words *boyfriend* and *girlfriend* were too light. Insubstantial. Transient.

I told her the truth. "What you are is mine. And I'm yours. That's all anybody needs to know. All you need to know."

She said nothing to this, just stared at me so hard I imagined I could see the wheels turning behind her eyes. "You know if this doesn't work out I can't stay at the company. You know that, right?"

"I know. And since I don't think we can run the place without you, that should tell you how serious I am."

"Yeah," she said, "I guess it does."

I thought about making the offer I had last night, to let things go back to how they'd been before.

I was almost positive she wouldn't take me up on it.

I still couldn't make myself say the words.

She'd had her chance to walk. I wouldn't give her another.

Alice must have agreed because that was the end of the conversation. She snuggled into me, her hand on my leg, her head on my chest, and we watched the movie. Later, we ordered dinner, Alice falling asleep in my arms as I watched a game on TV. If I could have erased her pain and added sex, it would have been the perfect day. As it was, it was pretty damn close.

The next week unfolded like a dream. Sunday we spent curled up on the couch, watching movies and talking. For once I didn't so much as open my laptop. Nothing in the office was more interesting than having Alice all to myself.

After nine years working together, you'd think we would have run out of things to say. Not a chance.

My mother called repeatedly. I sent every call to voicemail. She'd knocked on the door early Sunday morning. Alice and I pretended we didn't hear it. Whatever she had to say about that scene in the ballroom, I didn't want to hear it.

It was none of her business, and that was how it would stay.

I managed to behave myself in the office. Mostly. Word about my carrying Alice away from the party had spread to the few employees who'd missed it. Everyone was watching to see what would happen next.

I wasn't going to push my luck. Once everyone realized there'd be no fireworks in the front office, they lost interest. Thursday morning, I woke before my alarm, pulled from a dream of fucking Alice to the reality of her hot, wet mouth on my cock.

When she climbed on top of me naked, her eyes sparkling and her breasts swaying, it felt like my birthday and Christmas all rolled up into one. My hands closed over her hips. As she stroked her wet heat over me, I managed to gasp, "It's over?"

She gave me a wicked grin. "It's over. And I missed this." Her hand closed around my cock, guiding me inside her as she sank down and rocked me inside.

I filled my hands with her breasts, teasing her nipples, thrusting up into her, my eyes absorbing everything. The arch of her back. Her teeth sinking into her lip. The flush of her skin.

The sound of her crying out my name as she came on my cock was enough to shove me over the edge.

Alice collapsed on top of me, breathing hard, her mouth against my neck, and I thought my life couldn't possibly get any better.

That should have been the sign right there.

Just when I thought my life was perfect, I should have known everything was about to go straight to hell.

Chapter Seventeen

ALICE

CHAMPAGNE, AGAIN.

I took a sip, a small one, noting that this was much better than the champagne at Lacey's party. But then, Jacob Winters seemed determined to mark his marriage with the best of everything, a reflection of the way he felt about his bride.

From across the room, I watched as they stood arm in arm, both glowing with happiness, the smile on Jacob's face so wide I thought his cheeks must hurt. Every once in a while, his eyes dropped to Abigail's face, and I knew there was no treasure in the world he valued so much as her.

I didn't know Jacob Winters that well, only from his visits to the office, but he'd been friends with the Sinclairs since birth. In all the years since I'd met him, I'd never seen him like this.

Jacob was known as a shark: icy, determined, and ruthless. None of that was evident on his wedding day.

Taking in the crowded room, my arm looped through Cooper's, I teetered between happiness and nerves. This was our first public outing since he'd hauled me out of the engagement party only a week before. So far, no one had brought up the incident. Everyone was acting like Cooper and I had been together forever. Everyone except for Lacey, who shot me vicious looks but otherwise kept her distance.

The music kicked up and Cooper led me out on the dance floor, swinging me into his arms. I'd known him for nine years and had no idea he knew how to dance.

"You know what you're doing," I commented as he spun me out and reeled me back in. I couldn't remember ever seeing Cooper wearing that carefree smile before. He winked at me—another surprise—and said, "Dance class. Way too many years of dance class."

I should have known. Of course, Lacey had sent all the boys to dance class. Pushing away the thought of Cooper's mother, I said, "It paid off."

"How did you know *I* could dance?" I asked as the song ended, easing into something with a slower rhythm.

Cooper pulled me into his arms, leading me in a slow foxtrot. "Alice, I don't think there's anything about you I don't know."

"I'm not sure if that's romantic or creepy," I said.

"Maybe a little of both," Cooper admitted without remorse. "But if you're on the line, I'd go with romantic."

I made a noncommittal noise in my throat. Secretly, I agreed, but I wasn't going to let him off the hook that easily. He glanced over at Jacob, now dancing with his new bride. "It was a nice wedding."

Nice was an understatement. The wedding was at Château du Jardin, a vineyard and resort about an hour outside of Atlanta. Luxurious didn't even begin to describe the place. Jacob had reserved all the available rooms for family and friends, but most of the five hundred guests had made the trek from the city. No one was going to miss the wedding of the decade.

Jacob and Abigail had been married in the atrium at sunset, the pink and gold rays streaming through the glass roof, the light gilding Abigail as she strode down the aisle. As beautiful as the setting had been, I found myself getting a little weepy at the devotion in the bride and groom's eyes as they said their vows.

Weddings always got to me. My own had been a rushed affair, my husband and I two kids too stupid to slow down and think things through, in too much of a hurry to have a proper ceremony.

My mom hadn't mentioned it in years, but I knew there was a part of her that still hadn't forgiven me for depriving her of a wedding. I was her only daughter, and if my brother Pete's wedding was anything to go by, she had more rehearsal dinners in her future, but not much else.

Even though my own marriage had ended in disappointment, I wasn't a cynic. It had been a privilege to watch two people so deeply in love pledge their lives to one another.

The excellent food and fantastic champagne didn't hurt either. Cooper had a room in the resort, and we'd arrived early, spending most of the day at the pool.

After the spectacle Cooper had made of us the weekend before, I was taking it easy on the champagne. Most of the guests had been partaking since well before the wedding and formal dinner. By now, everyone was loose and happy, exactly the way they should be at a wedding.

The rest of the Sinclair siblings were clustered on the far side of the dance floor with some of the Winters. When the music stopped, I expected Cooper to guide us in that direction. Instead, he led me to a quiet corner.

Angling his body to block me from view, he dipped his head and brushed his lips across mine. "You're making me crazy in that dress." Lifting a finger, he tapped it against my lower lip, painted a deep, vibrant red. "All I want to do is pin you against the wall and kiss you."

I felt my eyes flare with alarm. If Cooper kissed me my lipstick would tell the tale to every single one of the five hundred guests surrounding us.

"I know I can't," he said, reading my mind, "And that's making me even crazier."

Bending, he pressed his lips to the side of my neck just below the hollow of my ear. Heat speared through me, and I wobbled on my heels. His lips brushing my ear, Cooper murmured, "You need to carry around a step stool. I can't reach all the places I want to put my mouth. You're too short."

"You're too tall," I shot back. "It's not my fault you're so big."

"At least I'm in proportion."

I knew exactly what he meant. He *was* in proportion. Cooper Sinclair was big everywhere. "Anyway," he went on, "I like you small. Makes it easy to pick you up and put you where I want you."

He rested his mouth at my temple before straightening. "But not in the middle of the wedding reception. One scene was enough for now. We can make another scene later."

"How about we not make any more scenes at all?" I asked, expecting Cooper to agree. Cooper wasn't exactly known as the wild man of the family. If one of them was going to make a scene it would be Evers, or maybe Axel. Not Cooper.

Defying expectations, he sent me a heated glance. "Oh,

I can guarantee we'll make another scene. Too many more parties like this and I won't be able to resist throwing you over my shoulder again."

I rolled my eyes, but I didn't mean it. At the time, I'd been pissed as hell that he'd kidnapped me from the middle of the party, but now, looking back? Yeah, I wouldn't mind if he threw me over his shoulder again. That had been hot.

I leaned into him, the hard length of his body warm against my side. "You can put me anywhere you want when we get back to the room."

"I plan to."

Heat spiraled through me. We weren't staying late at the reception. Not with that plush hotel room upstairs.

"You want another glass of champagne?" Cooper asked. "Or something else?"

"Champagne," I said. "I think they're going to cut the cake soon."

Cooper eyed the bar closest to us. People crowded around, the bartenders moving at top speed, the path between packed with people.

"Stay here. I'll be right back." Cooper disappeared into the crowd.

The ballroom of Château du Jardin was massive and filled to capacity. I didn't recognize most of the wedding guests. The Winters family ran in very different circles than a lowly office manager. I spotted Evers across the room with Summer, standing beside Axel and Emma. I thought about going to join them once Cooper came back when a familiar figure stepped into my view.

Lacey.

She moved into my space, standing so close she loomed over me. I resisted the urge to retreat. I wasn't going to let Lacey intimidate me.

Unlike her impromptu engagement party the week before, Lacey hadn't bothered to stay sober for this party. Her eyes were red and bleary, her body loose and uncoordinated as she threw her hands wide and hissed down at me, "You got what you wanted, didn't you, you little slut."

Oh, fuck this. I wasn't putting up with this bullshit tonight.

This was one of those *retreat is the better part of valor* situations, because letting Lacey Sinclair hurl invectives at me was not on my to-do list.

Have fun.

Dance.

Get Cooper naked.

Those were my priorities. Not humoring his bitter, drunk mother. I glanced over her shoulder for Cooper and stepped to the side, trying for a clean getaway.

Lacey was having none of it. Her hand shot out and closed over my wrist.

It was stop or fall.

I stopped.

"What do you want with me?" I asked, suddenly so very done with Lacey's bizarre vendetta against me. "I have never done anything to you, Lacey. *Anything.* I have no idea why you hate me so much, but I'm sick to death of—"

"Oh, you know. You pretend you're so innocent, but you know."

Chapter Eighteen

ALICE

I WRENCHED MY ARM OUT OF HER GRIP AND stared at her. I was missing a piece of the puzzle. I *didn't* know. I had no clue why Lacey hated me so much, but it was becoming very clear that Lacey thought she had a reason.

As far as I'd seen, Lacey didn't like anyone, but her hatred for me was personal.

"Lacey, I really don't know. If I've done something, if there's some reason you dislike me so much, please, just tell me so I can apologize and we can move on."

Her laugh was brittle. Sharp. "You think you can just apologize for fucking my husband? That's rich. Maybe wedding vows don't mean anything to you—"

She looked down her nose at me as if I were a piece of trash she'd scraped off her shoe. "—but if you thought you could seduce him into hiring you, fuck him while he signed your paycheck, and no one would blink an eye, then you're a lot stupider than I thought. Everyone knows what a whore you are. *Everyone.* Maxwell wasn't going to leave me for you. I'm his *wife.*"

The word came out on a hiss, her face less than an inch from mine. I was too stunned to flinch.

What the hell was she talking about? *Me? And Maxwell?* Was she insane?

She closed a bony hand around my upper arm, shaking me hard enough to make me wobble on my heels. "You're just another of his sluts. He should have fired you when he was done with you. And now you have your claws in my son? You think I'm going to let that go? You're trash."

My mouth fell open in shock. My brain was blank. Later I'd wish I'd had a snappy comeback, but in that moment, I was utterly without words. Why would she think I'd slept with Maxwell? *Gross.*

Maxwell was an asshole and a letch. He propositioned me once when he hired me. I shut him down, and that was it. End of story.

And what did she mean *everyone knows*?

Cooper's voice barely penetrated my shock. "Mom, drop it," he said, the words falling like stones. "It's ancient history. Alice was hardly the first woman Dad seduced, and she sure as hell wasn't the last. It ended almost a decade ago. It doesn't mean anything. I don't understand why you blame her when you sure as hell don't blame him."

Horror curdled in my gut.

What the fuck?

Cooper, too? Cooper thought I'd slept with Maxwell? Did *everyone* think I'd slept with Maxwell?

Oh, my God, that's what Lacey meant by *everyone knows.* They *all* thought I'd slept with Maxwell.

My mind raced, putting it together. I thought back to those first few months at Sinclair. The guys who'd propositioned me. The way Cooper and his brothers had been distant and unfriendly.

Oh, God. They all thought I'd been sleeping with Maxwell. That I'd cheated on my husband with their father. The rich dinner and glass of champagne turned rancid in my stomach. Saliva flooded my mouth, and for a terrible moment, I thought I was going to throw up right there in the middle of the wedding reception.

I turned, desperate to flee the crowd, to let this new reality sink in somewhere private.

My world was upside down. In a split second, everything I knew had changed. *I* was still the same, but the person everyone saw when they looked at me—she was a stranger.

They thought I'd slept my way into the job. That I'd had an affair with my married boss, and now I was sleeping with his son.

I was going to throw up.

Cooper's hand closed around my arm yanking me to a stop. "Where are you going? Don't listen to my mother—"

Pain sliced through my heart. Cooper thought I'd slept with his father. He thought I was capable of showing up to work every day with a smile on my face after spending my nights in his father's bed. That I could so easily betray my husband and ignore his father's wife. All this time, Cooper thought that's who I was.

I couldn't stand it a second longer.

"You think I slept with your father?"

Cooper's eyes locked on mine as if he were trying to read my soul. In his own eyes, I saw the absolute truth. He did. He really did think I'd slept with his father, that I'd betrayed my vows. That my moral compass was so askew I'd been able to hop from my husband's bed to his father's and to my desk without a hitch.

Finally, he said, "Alice, it was a long time ago—"

I wrenched my arm back, but his grip was iron. Deciding something, Cooper turned, striding toward the door and pulling me along with him. Fine. I'd said I didn't want another scene, and I meant it.

I didn't want to think, didn't want to put these pieces together all the way. Didn't want to understand what this meant. He came to a stop in the hall outside the ballroom. Pulling me beside a stack of chairs that had been tucked behind the side curtain, he looked down at me, concern clouding his icy blue eyes.

"Alice, I don't understand why you're so upset. I know. I've always known. I forgave you a long time ago. I don't care anymore. Like I told my mom, it's ancient history."

"Why do you think I slept with Maxwell?" I demanded, cutting him off.

He forgave me?

The presumed generosity—like he was doing me a favor—broke through my shock like shards of glass in an open wound.

Cooper was finally getting that something was wrong because he took a step back and said slowly, "My father told me. When he hired you."

"What exactly did he say?" I asked, my words clipped and quiet.

Cooper shifted, crossing his arms over his chest. He opened his mouth to speak, then closed it for a moment, appearing to reorder his thoughts before he said simply, "That he was sleeping with you when he hired you, and a few months after that, he said it was over."

Yeah, right. I knew Maxwell. I'd worked with him for four years before he'd disappeared. I was absolutely sure whatever Maxwell had said about me hadn't been that generous or appropriate.

Considering the names Lacey had called me, and knowing Maxwell's vocabulary, I could only imagine what he'd told his son.

Bile rose in my throat. My heart thumped in my chest, bruised and aching. I couldn't look at Cooper, couldn't see that forgiveness for my sins in his eyes.

My chest so tight I could barely draw a breath, my words came out propelled by little more than sheer will. Looking past him at the wall, I said, "It would have been nice if someone had asked me. I never slept with your father, Cooper."

"Alice—" Cooper reached for me, but I dodged to the side, looking over my shoulder and seeing the door to the ladies' room.

"Just... Give me a minute, Cooper. I just need a minute, okay?"

I lurched across the hall, pushing through the door, barely hearing him say, "I'll be right here," before it shut behind me.

Women crowded the generous space, sitting at the vanity tables touching up their hair and makeup, gossiping about the other guests. No one spared me a glance. I was a nobody.

Heartsick and numb with shock, I wove through the crowd, taking the large handicapped stall at the end and locking the door behind me. I closed the seat on the toilet and sat, bracing my elbows on my knees, holding my head in my hands.

I couldn't go back out there, couldn't look Cooper in the eye. Forget about the rest of them. Axel, Evers, Knox. Emma. Oh, God, did Emma think I'd slept with Maxwell?

Everyone knows.

My heart turned to ice at the thought. They'd all believed Maxwell's story. I couldn't go back out there. Not now. Maybe not ever. All I wanted was escape. To hide. To get away from the ugly truth I'd never suspected.

The moment that thought surfaced, I knew what I had to do.

Run.

Run fast and far, before Cooper could figure out what I'd done. Once I was alone, really alone, I could stop and think about what to do next.

I sat up, pushing aside my pain and humiliation, forcing myself to think. And then I saw it.

My one stroke of good luck.

The bathroom had a window. And I had my way out.

Chapter Nineteen

COOPER

I STARED AT THE DOOR OF THE WOMEN'S restroom, still as a statue, my brain turning over on itself. I couldn't get my bearings.

Was it possible I'd been wrong all this time?

Thinking of my father with Alice had been unrelenting torture. It ate at me for so long, eventually, I'd had to find a way to make peace with it. The only other choice was to avoid Alice, which would have meant firing her.

Firing Alice wasn't an option for so many reasons. The most important being that I couldn't live without her. When I'd realized I needed to see Alice every day more than I needed to hang on to the past, I'd forced myself to let it go. Mostly.

I couldn't let it go completely, couldn't forget that the woman I wanted had been his first. That she'd let him touch her. She'd had him inside her.

It was wrong to want her, but I did. I couldn't help myself. I'd been telling myself to get over it for years. Years.

Alice could never be mine.

Even if she left her loser of a husband, she couldn't be mine because she'd been his first.

One day I'd walked into the office after a job gone bad, feeling like the world was crashing on my head, and Alice had smiled at me. She'd looked up from her computer, handed me the coffee she'd had waiting, and smiled at me.

A smile overflowing with her heart, with care and compassion, with friendship and concern.

A smile that was just for me. All at once, I'd known.

I was never going to get over Alice.

Never.

I'd never stop wanting her.

Because Alice was worth wanting. She was worth waiting for. The past didn't matter.

I didn't want to be defined by choices I'd made years ago. Why should I hold Alice to the same standard? Whatever she'd done with my father, there hadn't been anyone else since.

She'd been faithful to her jackass of a husband even though he didn't deserve it. That one fling with my father aside, she'd been everything that was loyal and honest.

She was Alice, and I didn't fucking care that she'd slept with my dad once upon a time.

I told myself that, and it was mostly true. It was also a lie.

I'd never forget the day I found out. Alice had been new at the company, and even knowing she was married, I'd been interested.

I wasn't going to make a move. I wouldn't do that, but I liked her. She sparked like a live wire, dangerous and enticing. I couldn't stay away.

Watching me linger at the front desk for yet another bull-shit reason, my dad had pulled me aside. "Don't get any ideas, kid. She looks like she's sweet as pie, and she is—" A lascivious wink that turned my stomach to a lead weight. "Sweet and spicy. A real firecracker. But you don't want my leftovers, and the husband's jealous. A pain in the ass. She's not worth the trouble. Find your pussy elsewhere, Son, not in the office."

With that, he'd strolled off, probably patting himself on the back for a good father-son talk.

My nascent attraction to Alice died in a burst of excruciating humiliation. I'd barely spoken to her for months after that, angry at him, at her, at myself for caring.

She was married. It's not like I could have her anyway. I put it aside, and slowly, over the years, something else grew in the place of that first spark.

Something bigger. Deeper. Something I couldn't put aside. Something so big it pushed out everything else, including the thing with my dad.

I'd been living with the story of Alice and my father for so long.

And now—that look on her face.

Sheer horror.

Horror because I knew and she was trying to cover?

No. No, not Alice. If Alice had done it, she would have assumed I knew. Would have brazened it out, told me to mind my own business.

No. That horror was because she'd never slept with my father.

Horror because he'd lied, and I'd believed him. Horror that she was sleeping with a man who believed she was the kind of woman who'd fuck around on her husband. Who'd sleep with her married boss.

I rubbed my chest with the heel of my palm, trying to soothe the hollow ache that grew worse every time I remembered the look in Alice's eyes.

After a few minutes, a new worry joined the others.

She'd been in the restroom for too long. What was she doing in there? From the stream of women in and out I knew she didn't have any privacy.

Alice wasn't shy, but she wasn't going to share personal business in a room full of the biggest gossips in town. So why hadn't she come back?

Uneasy, I shifted my weight back on my heels and shoved my hands in my pockets, trying to pretend everything was fine.

No problem here.

Okay, we'd had a misunderstanding. It wasn't a big deal. I'd explain and apologize. It was a long time ago. I already told her it didn't matter. I didn't care. If I didn't care, why should she?

A flash of familiar red hair caught my eye. Relief blooming in my hollow chest, I grabbed onto it like a lifeline. "Emma," I called out. She turned, her smile filled with light.

"Cooper. Where have you been? Wasn't that the most beautiful wedding?" She sighed, not waiting for an answer.

Trying to play it cool, I said, "Yeah, it was. Hey, listen, were you headed for the bathroom?"

She cocked her head to the side and gave me a curious look. "I was, why?"

"Could you look around and see if you see Alice in there? She went in a few minutes ago. She wasn't feeling well, and I just want to make sure she's okay."

Emma gave me a long look, trying to read something in my face I didn't want her to see. I gave her my best blank slate. Her expression told me I wasn't pulling it off. If I was that obvious, I was in more trouble than I thought. I wasn't sure I cared. I just wanted to talk to Alice.

Emma reached out and squeezed my arm. "I'll check on her, Cooper. Be right back."

I waited impatiently, rocking from my heels to my toes, shoving my hands in my pockets and pulling them out again.

Where the fuck was Alice?

The minutes stretched into an eternity. The bathroom was crowded. I had to be patient.

Impossible. A lifetime later Emma came out, her brows knitted in concern.

I already knew what she was going to say before she opened her mouth. "She's not there. I checked every stall. Cooper, are you sure you saw her go into that bathroom?"

Fuck.

My thoughts splintered in a thousand directions. Alice was gone. I'd fucked up and hurt her. Hurt her so badly she'd run. Alice, who didn't run from anything.

Goddammit. I sucked in a breath, trying to force my scattered thoughts in order.

I had to find her. As those words passed through my mind, focus returned in a rush, every disparate thought narrowing into a single goal.

I had to find Alice.

Forgetting Emma, forgetting the wedding and the crowd of guests, I took off, pushing through the crowd, not hearing the gasps of outrage at my heedless flight. The stairs in sight, I put on a burst of speed as a hand closed around my arm, dragging me to a stop.

I turned and swung, not caring who I hit. I just wanted to go. I had to go. I had to find Alice.

Axel's dark eyes looked at me in implacable concern. Fuck.

"What happened?" he asked, his fingers a steel cuff around my bicep. "Is it Dad? Tsepov?"

I yanked at my arm. There was no give in Axel's hold. The pounding need to get to Alice fell back. I'd get rid of Axel, then I could find her.

"It's not Dad. Alice took off. I have to find her."

"Shit. Is she okay? You're sure it's not Tsepov?"

"It's not," I insisted, pulling on my arm again. "Let me go."

Axel tightened his grip, pulling me into the dark corner of the stairwell, out of sight of the rest of the wedding guests. "If it's not Tsepov why did she take off? What did you do?"

"Why do you assume I did anything?"

"Because I know Alice, and I know you."

"What's that supposed to mean?" I shot out. He was my brother. What happened to benefit of the doubt?

"I saw Mom talking to Alice right before you two left the ballroom."

Under my breath, I muttered, "I'm going to kill our mother."

Axel rolled his eyes to the ceiling in exasperation. "You're going to have to get in line for that. Right now, Evers and Summer have dibs."

"Yeah? Well, I just went to the front of the fucking line."

"Tell me what happened with Alice," Axel ground out, his eyes black with temper. "What did Mom say to her?"

"She threw the thing with Dad in her face. I got her away from Mom, told her it was ancient history. She went into the bathroom and now she's gone."

As summaries go, it wasn't great, but it covered the basics. Axel said nothing, his eyes flat, his face a wall. His voice was dangerously quiet when he said, "What thing with our father, Cooper?"

"You don't know?" The ground tilted under my feet as I took in his expression, felt the weight in his words. Slowly, I said, "The thing with Dad. That she was sleeping with him when he hired her, and it ended a few months later?"

I heard a gasp from behind Axel. Emma. Shit. Alice wouldn't want her to know.

Axel shook his head, staring at me as if I were the worst kind of idiot. "Alice never slept with Dad, Cooper."

Chapter Twenty

COOPER

AXEL'S WORDS FELL WITH SUCH ABSOLUTE certainty I knew he was telling the truth. When Alice was hired, Axel hadn't yet opened the Las Vegas office. He'd still been working out of Atlanta, side-by-side with our father most days. He knew more about what Maxwell had been up to during that time than anyone.

The world I knew turning inside out, I said, helplessly, "Dad told me about it. About them."

"And you believed him? What kind of moron are you?" Axel raised one eyebrow in a look so familiar I might have been staring into a mirror. Fuck, that was annoying. Did I look this smug and arrogant when I stared people down? Probably.

I opened my mouth to respond, to say something, anything, but no words came out. I tried again. "He— I was— You don't understand," I finished, lamely.

Emma's voice cut through my protests, her eyes narrowed on me in supreme displeasure. "Let me get this straight. You just accused Alice of sleeping with your father? With Maxwell?"

"No! Hell, Emma, I'd never do that to her. My mother cornered her. I told her it didn't matter. That I didn't care."

"Oh, that's so much better. So, you told her you don't care that she was sleeping with your dad? I'm sure that made her feel wonderful."

"The sarcasm isn't helping, Emma," I muttered.

"I'm not sure I want to help you, Cooper."

Axel dropped a kiss on his wife's temple. He loved Emma's spirit. Usually, I liked her attitude almost as much as he did. Not today. Today I just wanted her to shut up. The magnitude of my fuck-up was dawning piece by piece.

Alice's horrified eyes kept flashing in my memory, over and over, each time twisting my insides tighter.

How could everything have gone so wrong so fast?

"I have to find her," I said.

Emma looked around, her eyes taking in the crowded hallway, people moving in and out of the ballroom, headed for the bathroom or the bar. "She's not going to be down here. If she didn't leave the bathroom by the door, she must have gone out the window."

"We'll check this floor," Axel said, "just in case. You head to your room. She's probably there."

"Yeah, packing," Emma added. Her words arrowed through my shock, galvanizing me into action.

I didn't wait for Emma to finish, turning and sprinting up the stairs to the fourth floor, cursing myself all the way. I jammed the key card in the door and threw it open.

The room stared back at me.

Empty.

Alice wasn't here. Her things were gone.

Not all of them. A tube of lipstick lay on the counter. A hairpin was forgotten in the sink. Her hangers in the closet were empty, her overnight bag missing. It wouldn't have taken her long to pack.

An image of Alice invaded my mind, her racing through the room like a whirlwind, shoving her things in the bag and going— Where?

Her purse and phone were gone. I unlocked my own phone and opened the tracker app. With a few taps on the screen, I knew exactly where Alice was. On the road back to Atlanta.

The door opened behind me. I ignored it, my eyes locked on her blinking red dot on the screen as it moved millimeter by millimeter down the line of the highway, taking her further away from me.

Axel shut the door behind him, coming to look over my shoulder. "She's not here?"

"Her purse is on the way home. I'm assuming she's with it." I said, my voice flat, dead. A thought occurred to me, and I strode across the suite to check the dresser in the bedroom. The top was strewn with my wallet and loose change.

My car keys were missing.

"I need to borrow your car," I said, turning to Axel. "Alice took mine."

Axel stared at me with assessing eyes, probably trying to decide how much shit he could give me. My misery must have been apparent, too deep for brotherly ribbing.

"Follow me. Emma and I will get a ride back with someone else." Under his breath, I caught his mutter. "Fucking asshole."

"I heard that," I said without heat. I *was* a fucking asshole. Why had I believed my father? Back then, sure. I didn't know Alice, and it wasn't unlike my dad to cheat on my mom. But later, once I'd gotten to know Alice, why had I still believed him?

Because believing made it easier not to have her, a voice whispered in the back of my mind.

I pushed the voice away. It didn't matter now. All that mattered was finding Alice.

The drive to Atlanta was endless. I'd been in any number of tight spots over the years, times when every second stretched to an eternity, when my life hung in the balance, and with every heartbeat, I saw another way it could end.

None of it was as bad as that trip back to Atlanta.

Alice's phone was turned off. Every call went straight to voicemail. I thought about calling the emergency line at the office, telling whoever was on duty to restrain her when she got back to the building.

No. That would cross every line. I'd promised I wouldn't humiliate her at work. If I had her locked up by one of her coworkers... Even in my desperate state, I knew that wasn't an option. Fuck.

Finally—fucking finally—I pulled into the garage at Sinclair Security, relieved to see my Aston Martin parked neatly in its space.

The elevator crawled up. One flight. Two. Why was it so fucking slow?

I reached her door and knocked. Waited. Knocked again.

The misery and fear in my chest pushed at me and I caved, using my key to let myself in.

What was a little breaking and entering on top of everything else?

The lights were off, her apartment empty. She'd been here. I caught a faint whiff of the perfume she'd been wearing, but that wasn't how I knew.

Her purse and cell phone sat on the kitchen counter.
Fuck.

Such a simple thing, the purse and cell phone. She'd left them lined up, side by side, a message for me. Alice didn't want to be found.

A stab of agony in my chest. Alice wasn't going to give me a chance to explain. I'd pushed her into this thing with me, knowing she was worried about her job, knowing she'd been unsure, arrogantly assuming that I could make everything all right.

Now she was gone.

Knowing it was useless, I checked her place anyway. Her driver's license was the only thing obviously missing from her purse. Her dress from the wedding hung in the closet, the hanger tilted at an awkward angle. I straightened it, settling the dress properly, trying not to think about how beautiful she'd looked in it only hours before. When she'd still been mine.

Beneath the dress, her heels were tossed on their sides. A pair of Converse high tops were missing from the shoe rack, along with a backpack.

Where was she? It was close to midnight. I pulled up the security cameras on my phone. Her car was parked in the garage. Wherever she'd gone, someone else had given her a ride.

The next few hours flew by in a fruitless search. Alice was nowhere in the building. The camera showed her leaving on foot a mere ten minutes before I'd pulled into the garage.

She'd walked out the front door, turned right, and disappeared from view. According to her phone, she hadn't called for a ride. Hadn't called or communicated with anyone since a quick text to Emma that morning. Alice didn't have a landline, and her email was equally devoid of clues.

She'd simply packed a bag, walked out the front door, and gone *poof*.

The sun was rising by the time I fell asleep on my couch, my laptop open on my chest, showing nothing useful.

I was going to miss Jacob's wedding breakfast. I knew he'd understand. I couldn't go back to the resort and risk missing Alice if she changed her mind and came home. I worked the keyboard most of the night, trying to find some trace of her.

I was rusty. There'd been a time when my hacking skills could rival our best guy, but these days I spent too much time wooing clients, more busy running the business than handling cases.

Credit card and phone records gave me nothing. Traffic cameras didn't cover the block where Alice had vanished.

She might have used a ride share service, but hacking into those was a step beyond my current abilities. The head of our tech division could get into them in a blink. That was Lucas's job, after all. But Lucas was with his wife, Charlie Winters, Jacob's cousin, at Château du Jardin.

As much as finding Alice felt like the most important thing in the universe, I wasn't enough of an asshole to screw up Jacob's wedding any more than I already had.

My heart screamed that Alice was out there on her own. It wasn't safe. Tsepov could get to her. I needed to apologize, to make things right. I needed her back. I needed to fix this.

My head told my heart to shut the fuck up. My heart had caused enough trouble already. Alice wasn't stupid. She was furious with me—and rightfully so—but she wasn't stupid.

Wherever she'd gone when she'd walked out the door, she wasn't wandering around the streets of Atlanta with

a big sign saying *Kidnap Me*. If I couldn't find her Tsepov
would be out of luck, too.

I didn't want to wait for Lucas to get back. I forced
myself to do it anyway, obsessively checking her credit cards
in case I'd missed something. Nothing, nothing, and more
nothing. Like I said, Alice isn't stupid.

She'd left her purse and phone behind for a reason. Alice
didn't want to be found. If Alice didn't want to be found
she sure as hell wouldn't do something as obvious as use
her credit cards.

I cursed myself for including admin staff in training.
Always have an exit plan. Back-up. Cash, transportation.

I tried to put myself in Alice's place, to figure out what
she would have done. Maybe she'd stopped on the way
back to Atlanta and bought a burner phone. Called one of
her friends. Or her family. I thought about hunting them
down, one by one. Her family would be easy. They were all
in the D.C. area.

Stalker much?

And that was the problem. Alice is an adult. She was in
her right mind. She wasn't in danger. I didn't have the right
to stake out her friends to see if she was holed up at one of
their houses. If Alice found out I'd gone to those lengths to
find her, she'd be even more pissed at me than she already
was.

The ruthless, hungry part of me didn't give a damn.
That part would do anything to find her, to bring her back
to me where she belonged.

No. I was on thin ice as it was.

If I wanted Alice back, it wasn't enough to be ruthless,
I'd have to be smart enough not to make this whole fucking
disaster worse before I found her.

Chapter Twenty-One

COOPER

THAT HORRIFIED LOOK IN ALICE'S EYES FLASHED IN my mind again. Yeah, thin fucking ice. The last thing I needed was to make Alice think I was an out-of-control stalker who couldn't let her have a few days to herself when she was pissed at me.

Some women might find it romantic to be chased all over town. Alice would not be one of them. The last thing I needed was to give her another reason to push me away.

I forced myself through a semi-normal Sunday. Nothing like the Sundays I'd had since Alice had been with me. Spending the day alone only reminded me how much I needed her back. My place was too quiet without Alice. Empty. Everything was empty.

I put in a punishing workout when the quiet got to be too much, stopping only to take a quick call from Axel. "She turn up yet?"

"No. Left her purse and phone."

"Doesn't want to be found, then," he commented. Axel

might work in Vegas, but he knew Alice almost as well as I did.

"Yeah."

"Everyone is still here, hanging at the pool. No one but Emma knows what happened. Didn't want to fuck up the wedding. Maybe she'll turn up at work tomorrow."

I could only hope.

The only other interruption in my miserable Sunday came in the form of my mother, who showed up in the early evening, banging on my door. I ignored her for a while, tuning out the relentless pounding until my phone rang with call after call. When she hit the limit of my tolerance, I strode to my door and yanked it open, looking down into bloodshot, tear-filled eyes.

"Cooper. Finally." She pushed in past me and headed for the small wet bar at the end of the kitchen. After pouring herself a hefty slosh of gin, she took a sip and turned to face me. The sight of the glass in her hand, the red streaking her eyes, her mere presence in my house after everything she'd done to Alice—all of it was enough to freeze me in place. I reminded myself that this woman was my mother. No matter what she'd done, she was still my mother. I couldn't throw her out of my home. I owed her that much.

"What are you doing here, Mom?"

"I came to make sure you're all right," she said as if it were obvious. "You and that woman left the wedding early. Everyone noticed you were gone, and then you never came back. I was afraid she was here with you, but I can see that she's not."

"Don't call her *that woman*. Her name is Alice."

"I know what her name is," she snapped at me. "And it's time this ridiculous farce was over. The scene at your brother's engagement party was bad enough. If I'd known you were going to bring her to Jacob Winters' wedding... Everyone saw you together. Everyone! How could you be so cruel to me?"

"I wasn't aware that my personal life had anything to do with you," I said evenly, knowing it was a lie. When she bothered to pay attention to her sons, my mother took everything about our lives personally.

She waved her hand in the air as if wiping my words away. "Cooper, don't be a fool. Everyone knows who that woman is. You look like an idiot parading her around on your arm."

"What do you mean, '*Everyone knows who that woman is?*' What lies are you spreading?"

My mother took another sip of gin and lifted her nose in the air, ignoring my question. "Tell me it's over with her. Tell me you're done and you fired her."

"I won't tell you that. I won't fire her, and I won't ever be done with her." She refused to meet my eyes and I officially hit my limit. I'd never be done with Alice, but I was more than done humoring my mother. "You know she never slept with Dad, right?"

"Oh, Cooper, don't tell me you're that naïve. Of course, she slept with your father."

"Why are you so sure? Because you caught them? Or because he told you?"

"He told me. He tells me everything. I know you've never understood our marriage, but your father doesn't lie to me."

I choked on the laugh that tore from my throat. The alcohol had pickled her brain.

"If that's the case," I said dryly, "then you're an accessory to a number of felonies. Should I call Agent Holley so you can make a statement?"

My mother refused to acknowledge my comment. Typical. If it didn't fit her world-view, it didn't exist. I pressed on.

"You never caught him with Alice. You only have Dad's word for it."

"I don't need anyone else's word for it. He's my husband, and you should have more respect for your father."

Talking in circles with her was going to make me lose my mind. With Alice missing I was hanging on by a thread as it was. I didn't need a trip to crazy-town.

"I honestly don't know what to say to you, Mom. I love you, but you're delusional. What I really don't get is how Dad cheated and you're blaming Alice. He's the one who made vows to you. He's the one who broke them. But she's the only guilty party? It's her name you're smearing all over town?"

"Don't be such a child, Cooper. Your father strays. So what? Men stray. He didn't marry any of those women, did he? He's married to me. He's given me a good life and I've tried to be a good wife. You're the one who's delusional. You think marriage is fairytales and true love. You need to get your head out of a storybook and into the real world. I hope you're not considering anything serious with that woman."

I stared at my mother, at her arms crossed over her chest, fingers gripping the crystal glass, now almost empty of gin.

She was never going to change.

She was never going to listen to reason.

She would cling to the reality she wanted to believe until her last breath and nothing I could say would make a difference.

I could play along, or I could make a stand. Thinking of the horror in Alice's eyes, put there by my parents' lies and my trust in them, I did the only thing I could.

"Mom, I need to make something clear to you," I said, a piece of my heart crumbling at the words leaving my mouth. "If you ever speak disrespectfully about Alice again, I will cut you off. Alice has earned my loyalty. My trust. I will choose her over you. Every single time."

My mother drew back in shock, her mouth falling open before she rallied and shrieked, "How could you pick that woman over your own mother?"

"You've been picking Dad over us for years. Always, you choose him. He's a liar and a criminal, and still, you choose him. We're busting our asses to build up Sinclair Security—which, by the way, pays for the lifestyle you like so much—and when he puts the company at risk, you *still* choose him.

"I'm just learning from your example. I found someone who deserves my loyalty. I'm not going to throw that away because you and Dad want to drag us all down with you. We're doing what we can to help Dad and keep you safe, but don't push me. Don't make me choose between you and Alice. You won't win."

My mother's stare stretched into eternity, her eyes icing over until they carried no trace of affection for me, her oldest son. Turning in a neat pivot, barely wobbling despite the alcohol, she pitched the crystal glass into the sink with all the furious power in her thin arm, watching with a satisfied glint in her eye as it exploded into glittering shards.

In the silence that fell, she speared me with a cold look before she stormed to the door and let herself out. Numb, I went to my laptop and pulled up the security cameras, tracking her progress from my door to her safe house a floor below.

I half expected her to pack her bags and leave, but she didn't, instead filling a wine glass to the brim and settling in front of the television as if nothing had happened.

Maybe, in her mind, nothing had. I couldn't underestimate her ability to rewrite history.

Closing the cameras, I cleaned up the shattered glass and put my mother out of my mind. She'd made her choices. And I'd made mine.

Alice. Alice was my choice. Every time.

Chapter Twenty-Two

ALICE

I WAS GOING STIR CRAZY. THE NEXT TIME I FLEE from my home in the middle of the night, I need to remember to pack better. Hidden away in a cabin on a small lake in North Carolina, I was concealed from Cooper—for now—but I had nothing to do but brood. I am not a brooding kind of girl. I hadn't even thought to bring a book or a bathing suit.

There were games in the shelves beside the fireplace—useless for a person alone. I could only play so much solitaire. The stack of dog-eared westerns weren't my thing, but if I was here any longer, I might be forced to crack one open. Anything to keep my mind off the reason I was here.

The cabin belonged to my sister-in-law Kristi's family. I owed her one. Big time. I owed both Kristi and my brother, Pete. I love all my brothers, but nothing matched my relief when I'd called Pete on Saturday night and he'd said in a sleepy voice, "Take a deep breath, honey, and tell me what I can do."

I'd been fine until I got to my apartment. Well, not fine. I'd been a mess. While my heart had shattered, my brain worked double time. I'd seen that window in the bathroom and known exactly what I had to do.

Fortunately, it wasn't far off the ground. I'd been smart enough to toss my heels out first, landing barefoot in the mulch. Clutching my shoes in one hand, I'd sprinted around the side of the building and gone in through the front door as if there was nothing odd about a barefoot wedding guest strolling through the lobby.

The second I'd been out of sight I'd bolted for the stairwell, my only thought to get to our room. Fortunately, I hadn't unpacked, more interested in spending the day at the pool than hanging up my clothes. It only took a minute to dump everything in my overnight bag, grab Cooper's keys, and run back down the stairs. I was out the side door and unlocking Cooper's car while he was probably still standing by the bathroom, waiting for me to come out.

I drove through the gates of the resort, wondering how long it would take Cooper to realize I was gone. I had no doubt he'd be in pursuit once he figured it out.

I know, I know, running out on Cooper was not the most mature thing to do.

I should have stayed and had a rational, adult conversation about his father's lies and his mother's vicious name-calling. A calm discussion about how Cooper had believed all of it.

I should have, but it wasn't going to happen. A sick ball of humiliation festered in my stomach, growing bigger every time I remembered Cooper's placating voice telling me *it was a long time ago and he didn't care anymore.*

It was okay, he *forgave me* for cheating on my husband with his married father.

I couldn't get my head around the level of asshole Maxwell was to have spread that story behind my back. It explained so much about my first few months at the company.

Cooper's coldness.

The gross propositions from other team members.

I'd almost quit a few times, but my husband had encouraged me to stay and the salary and benefits were off the charts. I'd loved the challenge of the job itself, but the work environment had left much to be desired. Then everything had gotten better, almost overnight.

No more propositions. Cooper's ice had thawed until he was, if not friendly, not openly *un*-friendly. Cooper, Evers, Knox, and Axel had gradually taken over running the day-to-day business and the work environment became just as appealing as the pay and benefits package. I'd forgotten about those first few months until Lacey's accusation.

Remembering her words, another stab of anguish stole my breath.

How could Cooper have thought—?

By the time I got back to Atlanta, I'd managed to put my humiliation on ice and think clearly. Part of our training at work included exit strategies. Always have a plan.

I'm an office manager. I know how to order bullets, not pack them in a bug-out bag. But, just for fun, I'd figured it out years ago. How would I get away from the building if I didn't want to be tracked?

The first part was easy. I stopped at a gas station on the outskirts of Atlanta and withdrew the maximum the ATM would allow, spending some of it on a burner phone. I'd have to leave my own phone behind, along with all my credit cards.

Knowing how the guys searched for people helped, but some cash and a burner phone weren't enough. Sinclair

Security is the best. I wouldn't be able to hide from them for long. I didn't even want to. I just needed a little space. Time to think.

I was mad and hurt, and the thought of staying put until Cooper came through the door made me feel like giving in to the tears prickling the backs of my eyes. I couldn't even consider the idea of walking into work on Monday knowing what everyone thought of me. I needed to get my head straight, and I couldn't do that anywhere near Cooper.

I'd parked Cooper's car in the garage, leaving the keys inside, and took the elevator to my apartment.

Once I was safe in my place, out of the reach of Cooper's cameras, I called the one person I knew would always, always be there for me. My big brother, Pete. I had to call three times. The burner number was an unknown. Pete probably looked at his phone and figured it was a mis-dial. Finally, he answered with a sleepy, "What?"

"Pete, it's Alice. Sorry to wake you up, but I have a problem, and I really need my big brother."

I heard the rustle of him sitting up in bed, the murmur of Kristi beside him. "What happened? Are you okay?"

I didn't have time for a full explanation. Cooper would be right behind me, the last person I wanted to see. Not now. Not yet. Not until I'd had time to sort this out on my own.

"I'm okay. I'm safe. I just... There's no time to explain, but I need to get away from here and I don't want my boss to be able to find me. Could you call me a car to take me to the airport and rent a car for me? I can't use my phone or my cards or he'll know exactly where I am."

"Those fucking guys," Pete swore under his breath. "I knew working for them would get you into trouble eventually."

166

"Pete, you can yell at me about my job later. For now, can you just help me?"

"I've got you, honey. I'll deal with the Sinclairs once we get you somewhere safe. Do you have a plan? Where are you going to go when you get the car?"

"I don't know. I haven't figured that part out yet."

"I'm on it. You get ready to go. I'll call you back in a few minutes."

"Thanks, Pete. Tell Kristi I'm sorry for waking you up."

Pete hung up, already focused on the task at hand. I left my regular phone and purse on the counter where Cooper would find them later. I didn't feel like writing a note, but when he saw the phone and the purse, he'd know.

In my bedroom, I threw my dress on a hanger and changed into a t-shirt, shorts, and a hoodie, shoving my feet in an old pair of high-tops, about as far as I could get from my wedding finery.

Grabbing a backpack, I stuffed it full, transferring my toiletries bag from my suitcase to the backpack. I took my driver's license from my wallet, leaving the wallet itself and everything inside.

Pete called back as I was jogging down the steps to the front door of the building. "Your ride is going to pick you up the next block over. I'm looking at the app, and he'll be there in three minutes. That good?"

"Perfect. You're the best big brother ever."

"I know. I want an explanation once we get you out of there."

"I'll tell you everything. I promise. Tomorrow. For now, I just have to move before he gets here."

"Yeah, I got it. The ride is going to take you to the car rental counter at the airport. Kristi put the ride on her work account. I billed the rental to my company. Should make it harder to trace. Call me when you're in the rental and I'll give you directions. "

"Directions where?" I asked.

"Kristi's family's cabin. It's in Blowing Rock. It's a hike, about five hours from Atlanta, but no one's using it this weekend or next week, and it's not rented. I can give you the code to get the key. No one will look for you there. Kristi manages the rental schedule for the family, but all the paperwork and the deed are in a trust from her maternal grandfather. Should be a few layers removed from her and definitely hard to trace to you. You can hide out there for at least a week."

"Pete, that sounds perfect. Thank you." I pushed out the front door and turned right, heading to the next block over.

"Your ride is a light blue sedan. Do you see it?" Pete asked. I watched as a light blue sedan pulled up to the curb fifty feet ahead.

"Did I mention you're the best big brother in the world?" I asked, reading him the license plate on the car and getting confirmation before I slid into the back seat.

"I know I am. I expect you to pay me back in babysitting once this kid is born," he said. Kristi was six months pregnant. Theirs would be my parents' first grandchild, my first niece or nephew. All of us were beyond excited to have a baby to cuddle.

"You know it."

"I'll text you the address. If you have any trouble plugging it into the GPS in the car, let me know."

"Roger that," I said.

"Get some coffee in you so you don't fall asleep and call me when you get there."

"I promise. I'll be careful. Thank you, Pete. And tell Kristi thank you, too."

"Love you, Allie. Stay safe." Pete hung up. I hoped he wouldn't have any trouble getting back to sleep.

I didn't see my family as much as I'd like. Work kept me busy, and they were all up in the DC area. I made it home for the weekend every few months, but it still wasn't enough. I was tight with my mom and dad and close to my other brothers, but growing up, Pete and I had always been partners in crime. We were almost the same age while our other two brothers were five and seven years older.

Pete and I had caused trouble together and been grounded together. No matter what, we'd always had each other's backs. Distance had grown between us during my marriage to Steve. My fault, really. Steve and Pete hated each other. Steve hated Pete because we were so close, and Pete despised my husband because his asshole radar was much better than mine.

Pete's close marriage to Kristi had made it worse. I adore Kristi, have since the first time Pete shyly introduced us. She was sweet and feisty and absolutely devoted to my brother. What more could I ask for in a sister-in-law? But it was hard sometimes, seeing them so happy, knowing my marriage was missing so much and having no idea how to fix it.

When I called Pete to tell him I was getting a divorce, he'd said, "*Thank God*," and left it at that. My first weekend home after my announcement, my brothers took me out to get drunk, never mentioning Steve or my disaster of a marriage. They were the best.

Pete hadn't demanded an explanation about the end of my marriage, probably because he was so grateful it was over he didn't want to jinx it. I wouldn't be so lucky this time. He let me off the hook while he helped me get out of Atlanta, but that wouldn't last.

I didn't care. I'd tell Pete everything once I was out of Cooper's reach. If he caught up with me... It wasn't that I thought he'd lock me up or force me to stay. Cooper isn't a monster.

I was furious and hurt, but he was still Cooper, one of the best men I've ever known. That's what I was afraid of. I needed space, needed to think.

If he asked me to stay with his heart in those striking ice-blue eyes, I might give in. I might give him everything he wanted. And I might hate myself for it later.

The transition from my ride to the car Pete had reserved was seamless. Forty-five minutes after I'd left the Sinclair Security building I was on the road to North Carolina. The drive was uneventful. I grabbed a coffee, but I didn't need it. I was too wired on adrenaline to need caffeine. For five hours I sped through the night, ignoring the speed limit and doing my best to think of anything but Cooper.

I found the cabin in the dim light of the rising sun, the key exactly where Kristi's text message said it would be. The place was small and basic, the air stale from disuse, but it had air conditioning. I locked the doors behind me, clicked on the AC, and texted my brother to let him know I'd arrived safely. Once that was done, I collapsed into one of the beds, not even bothering to put on sheets, too tired and heartsick to deal with anything.

Waking after a few hours of restless sleep, I found coffee and a loaf of bread in the freezer. I could have tracked down a grocery store, but I couldn't seem to muster the energy. My chest ached, and I wanted to crawl back in bed, shove my head under the pillow and shut out the world.

Every time I closed my eyes I heard Lacey's accusations echo in my ears, Cooper telling me he forgave me, and tears would flood my eyes.

How could he have thought—

No. I couldn't process it yet. Maybe it would have been easier if Maxwell hadn't been such a creep, if I hadn't stayed faithful to my husband all those years despite finding out later that he'd been cheating on me the whole time.

But there I was, honest and loyal while the men in my life thought nothing of sleeping with anything in a skirt, and I was the one accused of being a whore.

The injustice of it burned in my gut, in my heart, a conflagration that my feelings for Cooper couldn't extinguish.

The whole thing got to me deep down, bringing back the sense of failure that had haunted the end of my marriage. I thought I was so smart. Life had proven I was anything but. Steve had been cheating on me practically from the honeymoon and I'd had no clue. Maxwell lied about me to everyone I worked with and I was none the wiser.

I wasn't who I thought I was. I'd never be the person I wanted to be. Now I was sleeping with my boss, and he thought I was the slut his mother called me.

Cooper had pulled the rug out from under my feet, and I'd landed smack on my ass with no clue what to do next.

He said he didn't care anymore that I'd slept with his father.

He didn't care *anymore*, which meant that for years he *had* cared.

For years he'd looked at me and seen a woman who'd thrown out her wedding vows to sleep with her boss. Who was sleeping with her boss *again*.

A small voice in the back of my head piped up to point out that if Cooper thought I'd slept with his father I should have been forever off-limits. If he'd gotten past it enough to pursue me, he must want me an awful lot. It wasn't like Cooper was desperate. He could have anyone.

I wasn't ready to absorb that part of it. His desire for me felt like a tainted consolation prize after the hit of finding out he thought I'd been sleeping with his father.

I spent Sunday morning curled up on the couch, sipping on endless cups of stale coffee, nibbling on toast, and feeling sorry for myself. Around mid-afternoon, just when my stomach was starting to demand real food, the crunch of tires sounded on the gravel outside, scaring the living daylights out of me.

No. I wasn't ready.

Chapter Twenty-Three

ALICE

I BOLTED TO MY FEET, NOT SURE WHERE I WAS going to run, when I glanced through the front windows and saw Pete emerge from a familiar gray sedan. He came through the door bearing a brown paper sack, Kristi behind him.

"What are you doing here?" I asked, staring at him in shock. "It has to be a six-hour drive from D.C."

Pete enfolded me in a hug, the paper sack crinkling between us, my mouth watering at the scent of grease and salt.

"Seven, but who's counting? We stopped in town for lunch. Kristi figured there wouldn't be any food here."

I buried my face in his shoulder. Pete handed the bag to Kristi and closed his arms around me, ruffling my hair. Like everyone else in the world, Pete was much taller than me, though not as tall as Cooper.

He'd settled into his thirties with a few extra pounds gently rounding his midsection and a set of very appealing laugh lines around his mouth. He worked hard, played hard, and loved his wife the hardest.

"Pete," I said in a watery warble, "you shouldn't have come. It's too far. You're crazy."

"Are you kidding?" He hugged me tighter. "When was the last time you asked for help, Allie? Never. You take care of everyone. Those ungrateful assholes you work for. Your friends. Hell, you pitch in for Mom and Dad and the rest of us when you come up for the weekend. If things are bad enough that you call me at midnight, you think I'm not going to make sure you're okay?"

"You shouldn't have driven all this way with Kristi pregnant," I protested, grateful they'd done it anyway.

Kristi came over to pry me away from Pete for her own hug, her pregnant belly pressing into me as her arms squeezed me tight. "Oh, please. Like you wouldn't have done the same for us in a heartbeat."

She had me there. If Pete or Kristi had called me with a problem in the middle of the night I would have sped to their sides the second I could.

Setting the paper sack on the table, Pete said, "Let's eat and you can tell us what's going on."

Over piping hot subs and fries, I spilled the details. When I got to the part at the wedding, Pete's affable expression was replaced with something dark and forbidding. He swore under his breath, pushing away from the table to pace into the kitchen.

Giving her husband a sideways glance, Kristi took advantage of his absence to lean across the table. "He's amazing in bed, right? He has to be because there's no way you'd screw around with your boss unless you had a really good reason."

Giving my brother a sideways glance to make sure he was out of earshot, I whispered back, "He's beyond amazing. Cooper is—" His name caught in my throat, and I couldn't finish. Swallowing hard, I forced myself to be honest.

"It would be easier if it was just that. But it's more."

If it hadn't been *more* I never would have touched Cooper in the first place. If it hadn't been *more* this wouldn't hurt so much.

Kristi leveled a worried look on me, tucking a lock of straight brown hair behind her ear. "I saw a picture of him when he was dating that drummer. He's smokin' hot, babe, but he's a little scary. Intense. Did you take off because you needed space to think or because you're afraid of him?"

Afraid of Cooper? Never.

Afraid of getting my heart broken? Of falling for him and then having to leave my job, my home, when he moved on? Absolutely.

Afraid of Cooper? No way.

Before I could reassure her, Pete came back to the table. "I'm taking you home. I never liked you working for those guys. They're dangerous. They think they're above the law. Come back to D.C. and stay with us while you get settled. Forget about the Sinclairs and Atlanta. You need a fresh start."

I stared at Pete, dumbfounded. My job isn't dangerous. I spend all day at a desk. Then again, considering Tsepov and whatever Maxwell was mixed up in, Pete might have a point. That didn't mean I wanted to leave.

Even if I did, Cooper would never let me go. Not like this, walking out without a word. No matter what he'd believed about me, I couldn't do that to him.

"Pete," I said gently, "I can't leave Sinclair Security."

"Why the hell not? You don't owe them anything. They let their father lie about you, their mother treat you like shit, and now this thing with your boss. You deserve better."

I couldn't argue with that. I did deserve better than Maxwell's lies and Lacey's slurs.

But did I deserve better than Cooper?

Was there anyone better than Cooper?

You know there isn't, my traitorous heart whispered, *No one is better than Cooper.*

"I can't just quit," I protested.

"Why not?" Pete threw back.

I thought about Cooper's icy stare. "Cooper won't let me leave," I said without thinking.

"You're here, aren't you? He doesn't own you, and I can't believe you're okay with him controlling you like that."

"He's not controlling me." Pete didn't get it and I wasn't sure how to explain. "I don't know that I want to leave, I just needed some time to think."

"Then come home with us and we'll stash you someplace more secure. Somewhere you can be alone until you figure out what you want."

"Pete, there isn't anywhere I can go that Cooper won't find me."

Pete leaned across the table and took my hands in his. "Do you not hear how creepy that sounds, honey?"

"It's not like that." I pulled my hands back and wrapped my arms around my chest, unsettled.

It wasn't like that. Cooper wasn't the villain here.

I was mad at him, sure. Angry. Embarrassed. Humiliated. But that didn't make him the bad guy. I was fine with Maxwell and Lacey being the bad guys, but not Cooper.

"Pete," I said softly, trying to make him push aside his big-brother protectiveness and listen, "I didn't run because I'm scared of Cooper. Cooper would never hurt me, never let anything hurt me."

176

"Except his family. He stood by and let them hurt you."

I bit my lip to hold back the instinctive protest. Pete wasn't wrong. Maxwell and Lacey had hurt me. Badly. By believing them, so had Cooper.

Sensing his advantage, Pete pressed on. "If you're not scared of him, why are you hiding? Why the subterfuge to get away?"

"Because she's hurt and embarrassed, you sweet idiot," Kristi cut in. Pete tried to be annoyed at her interruption, but his eyes went soft when they fell on his wife. She reached out to take his hand, squeezing his fingers.

Sending me a look, she asked, "Am I right? You're not done with him. And you don't want him to be done with you. You just need some time alone. And Cooper Sinclair is way too used to being in charge to give it to you."

I smiled gratefully at my sister-in-law. "Yeah. Pretty much. And I'm not sure I can face going back to work, knowing what everyone thinks of me."

"Which is why you should come home with us," Pete said again. "If you're so sure Sinclair will come after you, make him follow you home. He can deal with you on your turf."

I *could* do that, but... Pete's words didn't fit. D.C. hadn't been home for a long time.

Atlanta was home.

Cooper was home.

Well, shit. Was there any way I could go back to Atlanta and not have to face everyone at work? Just the thought of looking them all in the eye, knowing they thought I'd been with Maxwell, made me sick.

"Alice," Pete grumbled, "I've half a mind to go down there and tell him to leave you the hell alone."

"No, Pete, don't do that."

I love my big brother. He's the best, and he's not weak, but Cooper is a head taller and solid muscle. Pete hadn't seen a push-up in a few years. If he and Cooper got in a fight, I had no illusions about who would win. It would be over before I could blink, my teddy bear of a big brother face-down on the floor.

To his credit, Pete didn't insist he could handle Cooper. "Alice, I'm not going to let him walk all over you. You put up with enough from Steve. If you want this guy, fine, but don't let him get away with this shit."

The outrage went out of me and I sank back into my chair, deflated. "I know. I'm so pissed at him. How could he have thought I cheated on my husband? And with his father? His father?! Maxwell was such a man-whore! Not that I would have cheated, but at the least, I would have had better taste!"

A growling rumble of frustration erupted from my throat and I glared at the scarred top of the kitchen table. Every time I thought I was moving past it, I remembered Cooper telling me he *forgave me. Forgave me!* Like *I* was the one who needed forgiveness in this clusterfuck of a situation. He should be begging *me* for forgiveness. They all should.

Clearly, one day away was not enough time for me to calm down and get my head straight. In the midst of this whole mess, that was the only thing I knew for sure. I was still too turned upside down to make any decisions.

"What do you want to do?" Kristi asked gently.

"I don't know," I said on a moan of sheer frustration. "I'm still too mad to think. Is it okay if I stay here for a few days?"

"Of course, you can," she said immediately. "The place isn't booked until Friday, so you've got some time."

I nodded, tracing one finger over a gouge in the tabletop.

"Are you going to go back to work?" Kristi prompted.

Just the thought of it had a voice in my head shouting a vehement, *No freaking way*. I pictured myself walking through the door, everyone's eyes on me, knowing they thought I'd slept with Maxwell, that he'd hired me because I'd been in his bed—

No freaking way.

But what did that mean? Was I going to leave Sinclair Security? Walk away from my job? From Cooper?

An equally strong voice from my heart said, *No. Not from Cooper. Never from Cooper.*

Being with Cooper was— I pressed my palms into my closed eyelids until my vision exploded in white stars, trying to settle my thoughts.

I wanted to run.

I wanted to stay.

I never wanted to see anyone from work again.

I wanted Cooper.

I wanted to go home.

And I was pissed as hell at Lacey and Maxwell and Cooper for putting me in this horrible situation at first place.

I was in no state to make any decisions.

I didn't know anything else, but I did know that.

Kristi shoved the sub and fries in front of me. "Eat. Stop thinking so hard. You can stay here until you settle a little. You don't need to figure it out right now."

Pete let out a sigh of defeat, reaching for the plastic-wrapped cookie Kristi slid across the table at him. "Thanks, honey."

He took a bite and chewed, thinking, before he said, "We'll take the rental with us. Knowing this guy, he'll find you before you're ready to leave anyway. If he doesn't, we'll get you home. If we leave the car, it'll be too easy for him to trace the car to the cabin once they figure out how you got out of Atlanta."

"Thanks, Pete. I owe you guys, big time."

"You can make it up to us in babysitting."

Kristi nudged my shoulder. "Do you mind if we hang around until tomorrow? Get in some lake time, let Pete drop a line in the water?"

"Of course not. This is your place, and you drove all the way here."

My eyes got wet at the thought that these two people had dropped their plans and hauled themselves on a seven-hour drive just to make sure I was okay. Whatever else was messed up in my life, I was lucky to be so loved.

Kristi bumped her shoulder into mine again, an affectionate smile on her pretty face. "Don't get all weepy on me, Allie. I'll start thinking we have an invasion of the body snatchers thing going on."

I couldn't help it, giving her a watery smile, my bruised heart aching with love. Slinging an arm around her shoulder, I hugged her close. "I'm so glad my brother married you."

Kristi leaned her head against mine. "Me too, babe, me too."

Chapter Twenty-Four

COOPER

WALKED INTO THE OFFICE MONDAY MORNING unaware of how desperately I'd needed to see Alice sitting behind the desk, her red lips quirked in a sardonic smile, a teasing look in her eyes. Hell, I'd be fine with frost. With rage. With anything but her absence.

Her chair was empty. Maybe I was just early. When the phone rang through to my desk an hour later, I knew Alice wasn't coming in.

I dealt with the call and forwarded the main line to an intern's desk, telling him Alice was out for the day. Then I tried to focus on work, telling myself she'd come back when she was ready. I tried to resist the urge to track her down, but with every moment that passed, my reasons for giving her space fell apart.

When I realized I'd spent two hours on a job proposal that should have taken me forty-five minutes, I was ready to toss everything to the side and—

Do what? What did I think I was going to do? Find her and force her to come home?

Finding Alice and forcing her to come home was starting to sound like a good idea. I already had enough to apologize for. What was one more thing? I forced myself to stay at my desk, growing more restless with each minute that passed.

Not long after lunch, Evers strolled into my office, dropping into one of the chairs opposite my desk. "Got a call from Agent Holley," he said. "Possible sighting of Dad in Texas. No word on Tsepov's location, but things in Vegas seem to have shifted. His guys have scattered, and it looks like a rival crew picked up the slack. Still, I think Axel and Emma should stay here until we find Dad."

"Yeah, that's good," I said, my eyes staring blindly at the proposal on my screen.

"Coop? Did you hear me?"

"Yeah, I heard you. Dad might be in Texas. Tsepov lost Vegas. Axel and Emma should stay. Got it. You can go now."

Evers didn't go. He sat there, ankle propped on his knee, and leaned back into his chair, obviously prepared to hang out for a while. I waited, knowing he wouldn't be able to keep his mouth shut. Between the two of us, I always won the quiet game.

"Where's Alice, Cooper?"

"Not here," I answered.

"She upstairs? Is she sick?"

"No."

I did not want to tell Evers what had happened. I love my brother. I love all my brothers, but the last thing I needed was to bring them into my fuck-up.

Unfortunately, Alice had a point about mixing work and our personal lives. Outsiders would see her as just the receptionist, but Alice was more than a cog in the wheel.

Alice was the linchpin. She facilitated communications from all the various teams, ordered supplies, handled the schedule. We could do without her for a day or two, longer if we'd planned for her absence, but every minute she wasn't here the entire office noticed.

I hadn't just fucked up my personal life, I'd fucked up everyone else's workflow. There was no way I could hide that. Especially not since Axel already knew what was going on.

He'd kept quiet through the weekend so he didn't spoil the celebration, but the wedding was over. The newlyweds were off on their honeymoon and everyone was back to normal.

Everyone except for me and Alice.

I pushed back from my desk and crossed the room to the wet bar in the corner. I used it mostly for coffee but kept a small working bar for the occasional client who needed extra fortification.

Clients came to us for all sorts of reasons, some of them under a lot of emotional stress. Every now and then, a drink was exactly what they needed. I couldn't remember the last time I'd had one myself during work hours. When I poured a healthy slug of whiskey and sat back down, Evers knew the shit had hit the fan.

"What the fuck, Cooper? Where the hell is Alice? What did you do?"

"Why does everyone always assume it's me?"

"Because I've seen Alice show up to work when she's half-dead from the flu. When she has a migraine. The day after her grandfather's funeral. You two disappeared before the cake was cut on Saturday night and didn't show all day Sunday. So, what the fuck happened? Is she okay?"

"Not interested if I'm okay?" I asked, sardonically.

Evers eyed the amber liquid in my crystal highball glass. "No. You're clearly a fucking mess."

Not waiting for my answer, Evers looked down at his phone and typed out a message.

"Who are you texting?" I demanded.

He didn't answer my question, just inclined his head toward my glass. "Am I going to need one of those?"

I ignored him, already knowing who'd been on the other end of that text. My guess was proved right when Axel and Knox walked in less than a minute later.

Axel took in my bleary eyes, the whiskey in my hand, and laughed. "Shit, man, she fucking destroyed you, didn't she? Still haven't found her?" He dropped into the chair beside Evers.

"Obviously not," I said.

Knox closed the door behind him. "Cooper drinking during the day? Fuck, what happened? Is Alice okay?" He dragged a smaller chair over and angled it by the corner of my desk, dropping into it and waiting.

"I don't know," I admitted. "She left the wedding Saturday night. Took my car, drove back here, ditched her purse and phone, and disappeared."

"It must have been bad," Evers added, talking to Knox and Axel and ignoring me, "because I could see Alice freezing him out, but to walk out on the office? She knows she keeps this place running. She wouldn't ditch us unless Coop here screwed the pooch big time. So, what did you do?"

I opened my mouth to answer, but Axel got there first. "Mom cornered her at the reception. Threw Dad's bullshit about them having an affair in her face. And Cooper told Alice that it was a long time ago and he forgives her."

"That's not what I fucking said," I protested, but Evers and Knox drowned me out.

"Are you fucking kidding me?" Evers gave me a look of such disgust I sank back into my chair. "What the fuck do you mean *it was a long time ago and you forgive her*? Don't tell me you fucking believed that bullshit? Dad told me once and I fucking shut it down. I didn't even have to know Alice to know it was a lie."

"I didn't know, okay?" The protest sounded weak, even to me. "He pulled me aside and told me they had a thing and she was hot, but her husband was jealous and I should keep my distance."

"And you bought that?" Evers asked. I had to wonder what he'd seen that I hadn't.

"If I'd known you fell for his shit, I would've said something," Knox said, gravely. "He lied, Coop."

"He lied about fucking women all the time," Evers tossed out.

"Yeah, he did, but this was different," Knox said. He shook his head at me. "I'm sorry, Coop."

"Are you saying this was more than his random bragging? He made it up for a reason?" Axel asked.

"It was a couple weeks after Alice started working for us. One of the guys—Jason, not with us anymore—he hit on her. Was a real asshole about it. When I pulled him aside and told him to can it or get out, he told me that if Dad was fucking her then he might as well make a run at her, too. I shut that shit down and went to Dad."

"It's a good thing Jason's gone or I'd fucking kill him," I muttered.

Knox shook his head at me. "Dad told me that you were getting all googley-eyed over the new receptionist. He didn't give a shit that she was married, but he said you were too young to settle down. He didn't like the way you were looking at her, so he made up that bullshit story about sleeping with her to scare you off."

"Why the fuck didn't you tell me?" I demanded, jerking forward, almost knocking over what was left of my whiskey.

Evers slid it out of my way before cocking his head to the side and parroting my question. "Yeah, why didn't you tell us that?"

Knox looked up at the ceiling for a moment. "I wish I had. Cooper had to go out of town for something, I can't remember what, and I had a job that kept me out of the office. By the time we were both back, everything seemed normal. Alice had settled in, Dad dropped his bullshit story, and everything was fine. There didn't seem to be much of a reason to bring it up."

"You should have told me," I said, sick at the idea that my father had seen through me so easily that he'd sought to poison my feelings for Alice by lying about her.

"It's not like you could have made a play for her anyway. She was fucking married, or am I the only one who remembers that?" Knox shot back.

"I remember," I growled.

"Alice never cheated on that bastard of a husband," Evers said, his voice as low and rough as my own. "Jesus, I can't believe you accused her of sleeping with Dad. No wonder she took off."

"I didn't accuse her of anything," I ground out through gritted teeth. "That was Mom. I tried to tell her it didn't matter."

"Yeah, that went over well," Evers muttered.

"She could have talked to me," I protested.

"See it from her side," Knox interrupted. "Not only does she find out that you think she committed adultery, twice over, and she slept with her boss, she probably thinks the rest of us think the same thing. I wouldn't want to walk into work today either."

Fuck.

"She's not going to come back, is she?" I asked the room, not needing an answer.

I'd been so focused on what was going on with Alice and me I hadn't thought about that part of it. I'd just about convinced myself to give her time, to let her come back on her own, but if she thought the entire office believed she'd been sleeping with my father, Alice might never come back.

"I have to find her," I said. "She's not using her cards, didn't fly, take the train, or a bus. Didn't rent a car as far as I can track. I ran into a wall."

Closest to the phone on my desk, Axel leaned forward and grabbed the handset, flipping the base around to punch in a few numbers. A second later he said, "Jackson, Cooper's office."

Evers asked, "No trackers? She left her car?"

I nodded. "Cameras show her walking out of the building at eleven-thirty Saturday night and turning right. Then she disappears. I thought about checking out her friends, her family, but going full-on stalker didn't seem like a good way to get her back."

"Normally, I'd agree with you," Axel said, "but after the way Mom's been treating her and Alice thinking everyone at the office believes she was fucking Dad, I think going full-on stalker is your only option. If you leave her to her own devices, there's a good chance she might not come back."

Axel was right. Alice loved her job, but she didn't need it. She made a healthy salary and had low living expenses. She'd been smart enough to parlay that into a very robust investment account. She couldn't retire at thirty-three, but she wasn't under any pressure to pick up her paycheck on Friday.

She wasn't alone in the world, either. Alice had friends. She had a sprawling family who adored her. If she wanted to walk away from her life and start new somewhere else, she could do it. If she wanted to hide out and avoid all of us for months, she could probably do that, too.

Time to stop being patient and bring in the big guns.

Lucas Jackson strolled through the door, his eyes falling on me. "Want me to find Alice for you?"

Fucking Lucas Jackson. He had his ear to the ground. Lucas knew everything that happened in the office. Fuck, he knew everything that happened in Atlanta. He ran what we jokingly called our *Hacker Division*. His title was Director of Information Technology.

Innocuous enough, it sounded like he worked on networks and fixed the printer. Instead, Lucas was the guy who got us information. He could get into any system, no matter how secure, and he had the skills to work in the field. His team moved seamlessly between the worlds of zeros and ones and flesh and blood. He could do almost anything with a keyboard and was equally able to handle any field work we threw at him.

Lucas was a little scary. If he wanted to know something about you, he knew it. And if anyone could find Alice, it was Lucas. I just had to hope she'd forgive me if I let him loose on her.

I'd find a way to make things right.

I'd grovel.

I'd beg.

If Lucas could tell me where Alice was, I'd do anything to get her back.

Chapter Twenty-Five

ALICE

KRISTI AND PETE STAYED THE NIGHT. Unlike me, Kristi remembered to bring a bathing suit. She floated in the cool water, a blissful smile on her face at finally being weightless after carrying around her pregnant belly in the heat of early fall.

Pete pulled a kayak from the shed and paddled off with his fishing pole, giving us plenty of time to catch up on family gossip and baby plans. He returned with a smile and no fish a few hours later, ready to fire up the charcoal grill and toss on the steaks he'd bought in town when they'd stopped for lunch.

They left the next morning after a late breakfast, Pete driving the rental and Kristi behind the wheel of their sedan. My big brother had hugged me tight before he left, his voice gruff as he promised, "If that guy doesn't make this right, you tell me. I'll come get you and bring you home."

I'd squeezed him back just as tight. "Love you, Petey."

"Love you too, Allie."

Then they were gone, and I was alone with my thoughts. I tried distracting myself with Pete's leftover worms and fishing pole, dangling the line off the end of the dock and pulling in tiny sunfish and baby bass. I threw them back, one after another, until the worms were gone and the sun was sliding down the horizon.

Dangling my feet in the cool lake water, I watched the setting sun streak vibrant red across the darkly glittering surface. It was too quiet. I was lonely.

Maybe being by myself to think hadn't been the best plan. I was still going in circles in my head, angry and heartbroken, sad and indignant, wanting to rage at Cooper and missing his arms around me.

I hadn't realized how much I'd come to rely on him until he was the last person I wanted to see. This is why friends shouldn't sleep together. Because when things went wrong, who did I have to talk to? I knew I could call Kristi or one of my friends. I could talk to my mom.

Perversely, I didn't want any of them. I wanted Cooper. And Cooper was the last person I could talk about this with. I already knew what he would say.

I watched the sun disappear into the lake and I forced myself to think. It wouldn't be long before Cooper tracked me down. I was no criminal mastermind. Cooper knew Pete and Kristi, knew where they worked. Now that the weekend was over and everyone was back from the wedding, he'd have everything—everyone—he might need to run me to ground.

I had to decide what I wanted before he did.

Out of nowhere, it occurred to me that I was absolutely positive Cooper was coming for me. Absolutely positive that despite what he believed about me and his father, Cooper still wanted me.

I had a right to be angry at Lacey and Maxwell, but why was I so mad at Cooper?

I'd been a stranger when Cooper met me. Maxwell was his father. Of course, he'd believed Maxwell. By the time Cooper knew me well enough to judge, Maxwell's story about our affair was buried in the past. Ancient history, just as Cooper had said.

Watching the lake as evening turned into night, I realized that while I was furious with Lacey and Maxwell, when it came to Cooper what I felt was more about embarrassment than anger.

I couldn't bear the idea of facing him. It was irrational. I hadn't done anything wrong. He was the one who should be too humiliated to look me in the eye.

So why was it the other way around? Why did I cringe every time I replayed his voice telling me he forgave me for sleeping with his father?

I thought about my desk at Sinclair Security, sitting empty all day. In almost ten years I'd never missed a day of work without notice. Never. Even when I was sick, I still covered email and the phones. As much as a part of me wanted to turn tail and run, Sinclair Security was my place, too.

The boys had rescued the family company from their father not long after Maxwell hired me, turning it from the most successful security agency in the Southeast to the best in North America. I knew how much they'd billed when Maxwell had been at the helm and that number was nothing compared to the business they did now.

I'd been there every step of the way. Was I just going to leave it all behind?

Not showing up to work would cause problems for more than just Cooper. The angry, embarrassed part of me didn't give a crap. The part of me that had worked her tail off for almost a decade, who took pride in the job she did—that part cared.

It wasn't everyone else's fault that Maxwell was an asshole and Cooper was a dumbass. Most of the office hadn't even been around back then. They didn't deserve to suffer for Maxwell and Cooper's mistakes.

And I made a killer salary with great benefits, including an on-site apartment that was practically free. On the other hand, getting free rent for so many years, I'd socked away a heck of an investment portfolio. If I didn't want to go back to Sinclair Security, I didn't have to. I needed to work, but I had enough saved to give me time to make other plans.

I missed my family. There were plenty of companies in D.C. that would love to get their hands on someone with my specific skill set. I could move home and see my family more often. I could be there when Kristi and Pete's baby was born.

I'd always wanted to start a family, but I'd held off, knowing my marriage had cracks long before our divorce. I tried to ignore the tick of my biological clock, but it was still there. I was self-aware enough to understand why I was so excited about my niece- or nephew-to-be. Even if I'd screwed up yet another relationship, I could be there for Pete and Kristi's kid.

The idea of going home floated in my head as a hazy, unformed potential. It was possible but held very little concrete appeal. I loved D.C. as the home of my childhood, but it wasn't my place anymore. I loved and missed my family, but if I left, I'd miss the family I'd made in Atlanta.

I lay in bed Monday night, tossing and turning as I tried to sleep, my tangled emotions slowly sorting themselves out.

I wanted to kill Maxwell.

I could happily never see Lacey Sinclair again.

And I missed Cooper like a hole in my heart.

I was standing at the kitchen counter watching the coffee maker work on yet another pot of crappy coffee when the door to the cabin opened behind me. I whirled in alarm, my fear quickly replaced by the sense of fate asserting itself.

Fate or Cooper Sinclair. Sometimes I thought they might be the same thing.

Cooper stepped through the door and everything inside me stopped. Like a clock wound too tight, I was frozen in time for an endless moment, staring at Cooper, my soul drinking in every inch of him.

Slowly, I became aware of the beat of my heart, the breath in my lungs. Of Cooper waiting at the door, an unfamiliar hesitancy holding him back.

I expected my stored-up anger to sweep in and bring me back to life, but my rage was nowhere to be seen. All I felt was sweet, cool relief, a balm to my soul.

Cooper was here.

I'd run from him because I'd needed space to think, only to find that without Cooper I couldn't untangle the emotions in my heart. Why he should be the answer to a problem he'd helped cause, I didn't know.

I stayed where I was, eyes burning with unshed tears, and waited.

Cooper hovered at the door, a white bag in one hand, his other still closed over the knob. Was he nervous? Kristi had taken one look and said he was hot but scary. I was so used to the scary I took it for granted most of the time.

Watching him stand there, waiting, I realized that I wasn't the only one who'd been messed up by Maxwell's lies. I'd thought of Cooper as an adversary, as coming after me because that was what he did. Because it was about ego and him being in charge.

Seeing uncertainty in his eyes, the pale blue a flame instead of ice, my heart thawed. I'd been hurt by Maxwell's lies, but so had Cooper.

When he stayed where he was, didn't barrel in demanding he get his way, a tight knot inside me relaxed. I opened my mouth, not sure what I planned to say but knowing instinctively that Cooper needed words.

Out came, "You're late."

Cooper let out a bark of a laugh, tinged with relief. "I would have been here yesterday, but I didn't want to break up the wedding celebration to track you down."

I focused on the bag in his hand. "What's that?"

"I wanted to bring you Annabelle's, but it's a long drive. The place in town isn't as good, but I brought you breakfast."

"Coffee?" I asked with a raised eyebrow.

"That I did bring from Annabelle's," Cooper said, pulling a vacuum-sealed thermos from the bag. "Skinny vanilla latte."

I took the coffee and retreated, leaving a few feet between us. I sipped, savoring the scent, the taste of rich bitter coffee, sweet vanilla, and cream.

Maybe I needed coffee to reboot my brain. Maybe all I needed was Cooper. He opened his mouth and my hand shot up to stop him.

"Before you say anything, I have to ask you a question and I need the truth. No matter what. It won't change anything, even if it isn't what I want to hear, but I have to know."

Lips pressed in a thin line, Cooper nodded.

"I know you said you want this thing with us to be real, but when it first started, was it because of what your father told you? Did you think since I was finally divorced I'd be up for a fling with my boss? Was I just convenient?"

"No!" Cooper barked out the word so fast I couldn't doubt its truth. His tan skin faded to an ashen gray, and he took a step forward before forcing himself to stop, every muscle in his body locked tight, his eyes aflame with an emotion I was afraid to read.

"No, Alice," he finally choked out. "It was never a fling. Not for me. My father had nothing to do with it. I swear."

"Why did you believe him?" I asked, realizing that was the only question that mattered. Why had Cooper believed Maxwell's lies? How could he have thought so little of me?

Cooper shifted the bag in his arms, his eyes never leaving mine, seeming to weigh his words before he spoke. Finally, he said, "My dad made up the whole story because he knew I had a thing for you. I wasn't going to do anything about it, you were married, and, unlike my dad, I respect that. But he knew. He didn't want any of us to get involved with any woman beyond sex, said it was a trap. He made up the story about sleeping with you to scare me off."

"How do you know?"

"He admitted it to Knox. Apparently, I'm the only asshole who fell for Dad's story. Knox, Evers, and Axel all knew it was bullshit."

I tightened my fingers around the thermos, shock chasing words from my brain. Cooper had feelings for me way back then? He was so cool, so remote, I never would have guessed. Not in a million years.

Cooper drew in a deep breath and let it out slowly. "I should have known he was lying. Maybe I would have, but I was trying to talk myself out of wanting you. You were married. There was no chance. Ever since you took off, I've been asking myself— *Why*? Why couldn't I see through his lies like everyone else? I think it's because I needed to put you out of reach. Just like he planned, my dad gave me the perfect excuse to convince myself to walk away. To stop pining."

I was a statue, unable to move, mouth hanging open, eyes wide, breath trapped in my lungs.

What. The. Fuck?

Cooper had pined for me?

Cooper had wanted me so much he couldn't convince himself to stay away?

He waited for me to say something. Anything. I had nothing. Of all the things I'd imagined he'd say, this was nowhere on the list.

He'd pined for me?

I was going to melt into a puddle. *Pined* for me?

All those years I watched him in the office, admiring him from afar, knowing I'd never act on my crush—

He was my boss. I was married.

All that time reminding myself he'd never have looked at me even if I'd been free, and he was *pining*? My brain couldn't fit around that idea.

I must have looked like a fish out of water, gaping at him, my mouth open to speak only for the words to dissolve before they reached my tongue.

Done with waiting for me to get it together, Cooper closed the distance between us, setting the paper bag he still held on the kitchen table, taking the coffee from my hands and putting it beside the bag.

I stared up at him, my heart an erratic drumbeat in my chest, still soaring with hope, diving into confusion, leaving me utterly without words.

Cooper's hands closed over my shoulders, and the heat of his palms spread through me, thawing me, bringing me back to life.

Chapter Twenty-Six

ALICE

"I'M SORRY," HE SAID, HIS EYES FIXED ON MINE. "I'm sorry I believed my father. I'm sorry I let my mother get anywhere near you. I'm sorry I hurt you. It's always been you, Alice. Only you. Since the day you walked through my door.

"Even when I thought there was no chance, it was you. These last few weeks have been perfect. Because of you. All I want is this. Us, together. Tell me what I need to do, and I'll do it."

And just like that, I found my voice. "I'm sorry I ran. I was so embarrassed I couldn't face you."

Cooper smoothed my hair off my face, pressing his lips to my forehead and murmuring, "No, no, Alice. You have nothing to be embarrassed about. I'm the one who fucked up."

"Cooper." That was all I could say. *Cooper.* It was enough. "Will you come home with me?"

I nodded, my throat tight, body loose with relief. Home.

With Cooper. That was what I wanted. To go home with Cooper.

Because home *was* Cooper.

D.C.

Atlanta.

It didn't matter as long as Cooper was there.

I leaned into him, winding my arms around him, ready to stay like that, his heart beating under my ear, my body pressed to his, forever. A face invaded my mind and I jerked back, knowing it wasn't this easy.

Taking a careful step in retreat, I looked up into Cooper's wary eyes.

"What is it? What's wrong?"

"I want to go home with you, but there's something we have to get clear first. About Lacey."

"Alice, you don't have to—"

I shot up my hand, and like he had before, Cooper stopped and waited. Too bad that little trick wouldn't last beyond today. Cooper was way too headstrong to be shut up so easily under normal circumstances.

"She's your mother, so I've always tried to be polite. Respectful. I'm not putting up with her anymore. The name-calling. Her snide comments. I know she's unhappy, but I'm done with her throwing her misery at everyone but your father when he's the only one who deserves it. I'm not going to be a bitch, but if she comes after me, I'm not going to take it. Not anymore."

Cooper pulled me back into his arms, resting his cheek on the top of my head. "I fucked up there, too. I didn't realize how bad it was or I would have put a stop to it before this. I talked to her before I came up here, told her if I have to choose between you two, I choose you. You, Alice. I'll choose you."

Silence as I digested what he'd said. "Did you really tell her that?"

"I did. And I meant it."

"Did she lose her shit?" I shouldn't have enjoyed that picture in my head, but I did. I enjoyed it a lot.

A wry chuckle from Cooper, his arms tightening around me. "She did, but then she went back to her apartment and poured herself half a bottle of wine. That was after the gin she had at my place. She probably doesn't remember the conversation, but that just means we'll have it again. And again. As many times as it takes."

My satisfaction fell away as I pictured Cooper's part in that scene. Watching his mother erase him with alcohol, knowing he'd have to relive the painful ultimatum over and over because the one person who should put him first never would.

"Oh, Cooper. I'm sorry."

"You're not the one who should be sorry," he said darkly. "She'll learn. Eventually. And if she comes after you in the meantime, I'll handle it."

"We'll handle it," I corrected. I wasn't leaving him alone to deal with Lacey. Not when she'd hurt him like this.

"Is the office a mess?" I asked, wanting his mind off his mother.

"Don't care," Cooper growled, his hands running down my back, pausing as they registered the lack of a bra strap under my t-shirt.

"I'm sorry—"

He stopped me with a finger on my lips, leaning back to meet my eyes. "I mean it, Alice. I don't care. Come back to work or don't, as long as you come home with me. I want you to be happy, and I want you with me. That's all I care about." He rubbed his finger against my lower lip. "Though you should know, no one else believed Dad. I'm the only idiot."

"A few people did, back then—"

"Any of the assholes who bothered you still with us?"

I thought about it. "No. They've all left or been fired."

"Everyone else who was around back then knew Dad was lying. And if anyone says shit to you, I want to know. I choose you, Alice. Over my mother, over the company. Don't ever question that."

"But you'd be okay if I didn't come back to Sinclair Security?" I wasn't thinking about leaving my job. Not really. I was just trying to get my head around the new reality Cooper had laid before me.

"Not if you don't want to. But we'd all miss the hell out of you. I'd never hear the end of it."

"I like working with you," I said quietly, thinking of Cooper in his suits, the masterful way he strode around the office. A tendril of heat curled through me. "I used to feel guilty for the way I looked at you. I was married. I wasn't going to do anything about it, but I looked. I thought about you. I shouldn't have, but I did."

His mouth brushed the corner of my lips, caressing my skin as he murmured, "You can look all you want now. You can even take me back to my office and lock the door and tell me all the things you've been thinking about."

"I think we've done all the things I was thinking about."

"Then we can do them again. Or you can think of more." Cooper dropped his head to press his lips to the skin behind my ear, sucking lightly, sending heat shooting through me in fireworks of lust.

"I like the idea of you sitting at your desk making secret plans for my body."

Hands closing over my ass, he hauled me up, bringing my mouth even with his. I lunged, my lips on his, drinking in his taste, his scent, every cell in my body parched for Cooper.

My legs went around his waist, holding tight as he strode down the hall in search of the bedroom. Laying me down on the mattress and covering me with his long body, his mouth ghosting over my cheek, my jaw, my neck, his words spilled into my ears.

"I missed you so much, Alice. Home was empty without you. Don't walk out on me again. Promise me. If things go wrong, if I fuck up, don't walk away. Promise me, Alice."

Cooper lit a fire everywhere he touched me. I couldn't string together my thoughts, except to give him the vow he'd asked for. "I promise, Cooper. I promise."

Then just his name. *Cooper*. Every time his mouth grazed my skin. *Cooper. Cooper.*

I pulled at his clothes, dragging them off, tugging on his buttons, baring his warm, smooth skin to my touch. His mouth was everywhere, tasting my breasts, his tongue dipping into my belly button, across my hipbone, licking my folds, closing around my clit with a hard suck.

I arched off the mattress, my mind splintering, all the scattered pieces of my life—my worries and hopes and fears—coalescing into one bright ball of pleasure, of joy.

I came against his tongue, sobbing his name, tugging on his hair to pull him up until he covered me, filled me with his cock. Legs locked to his sides, I rocked up into him, giving him everything.

It had been two days and felt like an eternity. Everything was empty without Cooper. My body. My heart. With him I was complete.

He filled me over and over, taking me with hard, claiming thrusts that threw me into another orgasm, my body claiming his in tight pulses, drawing him into release along with me.

After, draped over his chest, sticky with sweat and sex, I flicked out my tongue to taste his skin and imagined all of this contained in one of his formal business suits. It hit me and I burst out laughing.

"What?" Cooper asked, a hand dropping to close over my ass.

I tried to talk, and a snort burst from my nose. That just made me laugh harder. Cooper's chest moved under me as he chuckled at my oh-so-unsexy snort.

I kept seeing him in my mind, so cool and contained in his suits, his eyes giving away nothing as he secretly imagined bending me over my desk.

I'd had no clue. Not one.

Sitting at that very desk every day, pretending to be all business while I secretly wondered what his hand would feel like exactly where it was, those long fingers curving over my skin, dipping down to skate between my thighs.

"Are you going to tell me what's so funny?" he asked, his voice still lazy from orgasm, though his fingers were anything but. A gasp cut through my giggles and I squirmed, aroused and still laughing, not sure how to balance the two.

"It's just—I had no idea. We were thinking the same thing and neither of us had a clue. Griffen was right, we are dumbasses. You put on a good front, Cooper Sinclair."

"Leave Griffen out of it," Cooper grumbled, voice sharp, all his post-orgasm laziness gone. He sat up, pulling me with him so I ended up straddling his hips, looking into his intense ice-blue eyes.

"I don't want to put on a front anymore. I want you to move in with me. At least for a trial run. You can keep the apartment downstairs as long as you want, I don't care. I want to go to bed with you at night and wake up with you in the morning. I want you with me all the time. I want us to be together."

"I want that, too," I whispered.

Cooper went still, hands tight on my hips, eyes searching mine. "You'll move in with me?"

"I'll move in with you, Cooper." It felt like another vow.

His lips took mine, moving away only long enough to whisper, "Finally." Then he leaned me back over his arm, his mouth closing over a nipple, and he didn't say another word for a long time.

Later, after we'd jumped in the lake—me in a t-shirt and Cooper gloriously naked—after we'd squeezed into the small shower and thrown on clothes, after we'd eaten the breakfast Cooper brought with him, he asked, "Do you want to go home or stay here another day?"

"I want to go home, but you were driving all morning. Unless—did you fly here?"

"We needed the plane for a client, and all the flights were sold out, so I drove."

I did some quick math, realized how early he must have gotten up to be at my door by breakfast. "We should stay."

"There's plenty of time to take a nap and drive home tonight. I want to fuck you in my bed. In our bed."

In *our* bed. My heart did a little swoon at the way that sounded. *Our* bed.

"Then let's take a nap and drive home later. I want you to fuck me in our bed, too."

Cooper carried me to the bedroom, where we tried to make sense of the tangled sheets. Pulling me into his side, he stretched out, letting his eyes slide shut.

"Cooper?" I asked, sleepy and sated, my mind wandering in circuitous paths.

"Hmm?" His fingers traced up and down my arm.

"I call half the closet," I murmured, a little drunk from the salt and man scent of him, the heat of his skin against mine.

"Done." Rolling to his side, Cooper wrapped himself around me, one leg over my hip, his arm keeping me close. I should have felt smushed given my small size and the pounds of muscle he carried on his long frame. I didn't. He held me as if I were the most precious thing in his heart. Cherished. Protected. His.

I was his. With that thought steadying me, I fell asleep.

I woke hours later to find myself alone. Cooper was in the kitchen, placing the clean coffee pot on the rack. While I'd dozed, he'd cleaned up, the cabin as neat as it had been when I'd opened the door early Sunday morning.

"You really want to get home," I said, bemused at the sight of him so domestic.

Turning from the sink, he crossed the room to pull me into his arms. "I really want to get *you* home. Are you ready?"

"Just let me grab my things."

I texted Kristi once we were on the road, letting her know all was good, that we'd straightened up the cabin and put the key back where it belonged.

> Thanks, babe. Call Pete tomorrow or his head will explode.

> Tell him to cool his jets. I'll call tomorrow.

I laughed as I hit send.

"What's so funny this time?" Cooper asked.

"Nothing. Pete wants to kill you."

A smirk. "He can try."

"You're not mad?"

"That he was looking out for his sister? Hell, no. I'd think there was something wrong with him if he didn't want to kill me."

"I can look out for myself," I said, a little peeved that Cooper and Pete thought I needed looking after. Never mind that Pete was involved because I'd needed his help. That wasn't the point.

"If you had a little sister you wouldn't look out for her?" he asked, sending me an arch look. I didn't bother to answer. Instead, I reached out and threaded my fingers through his. I wasn't going to argue about my overprotective brother.

I was too happy to be annoyed at anyone. I was going home with Cooper. We were moving in together.

I was still on edge about going to work, about facing Lacey, but Cooper's hand holding mine was an anchor. I could handle the rest of it with Cooper at my back. Of that, I had no doubt.

If I'd known what *the rest of it* would entail, I would have grabbed Cooper's hand and taken off for a bunker in the desert. But at that moment, speeding toward home, it felt like the rest of my life was spread before me, filled only with possibilities and happy endings.

It was too easy to forget that real life awaited.

Tsepov. Maxwell. The FBI's investigation.

Cocooned in Cooper's car, our tires eating up the miles between North Carolina and Georgia, real life seemed far away.

Too bad it didn't stay that way for long.

Chapter Twenty-Seven

COOPER

I WASN'T READY FOR THE SOUND WHEN IT CAME.

Bang.

Bang.

A fist pounding on my door.

I looked at the woman in bed beside me, her nearly-black hair a sharp contrast to the white of the pillow. Even in the dim light of the room her lips were red, her lashes dark fans on her cheeks.

If whoever was banging on the door woke her up I was going to kill them. If she woke up, she might remember where she was. She might leave. I wouldn't let that happen.

I liked her right where she was. Asleep in my bed. I preferred her in my arms, where she'd been a moment before the asshole at the door interrupted.

Pulling on a pair of pants, I grabbed my weapon from the bedside table and strode through my apartment. With a stab of my finger at the panel, I woke up the screen to see the face of the man I was about to kill for disturbing my sleep.

I had to blink at the image that flicked into view.

Are you fucking kidding me?

It couldn't be.

I had to be hallucinating.

As a teenager, his betrayal had sparked a flicker of rage in my heart. Nearly a year ago that spark ignited, the flames growing hotter day by day. I saw his face on the screen and those flames erupted into a raging inferno.

In an instant, my control evaporated. All I could see was red.

I was going to fucking kill him.

I wrenched open the door and stared into the ice-blue eyes of Maxwell Sinclair. My father.

My father who'd faked his death five years before, leaving us to grieve with no answers.

My father who'd stolen money from the mob, making his family and the people we loved into targets.

My father who had broken so many laws I couldn't keep count.

My father who moved through life thinking only of himself, leaving destruction in his wake.

My father who stood at my door, wearing the cocky grin I'd learned to hate.

I did the only thing I could, the thing I'd dreamed of doing for far too long.

Lunging at him, I swung, my fist connecting with his jaw in a solid thunk, sending a shockwave ricocheting up my arm.

My father flew back to sprawl on the carpet in the hallway, his head lolling to the side, blood trickling from his mouth.

My chest heaved, lungs tight with adrenaline and rage.

A slender yet strong arm slid around my waist. Sky-blue eyes looked up at me, concern and amusement battling in their depths.

"I think you knocked him out," was all she said.

We both froze at the rustle of feet on the carpet. A small figure came into view.

She looked up at me with a familiar pair of ice-blue eyes, then down at Maxwell and said, "Daddy?"

From beside me, Alice muttered, "Oh, shit."

Exactly.

The small figure in front of me dropped to her knees beside my father, shaking him with frantic desperation, her little fingers curled into his rumpled button-down.

Her light, clear voice was so fast the words spilled over themselves, but I thought she was saying *Daddy, Daddy, Daddy,* the sound slightly accented in tones that brought to mind Eastern Europe.

What. The. Fuck?

My father groaned and rolled his head to the side. Dramatic. Typical.

Alice broke through her shock before I did, diving forward to scoop up the little girl and take her into the apartment.

I heard sobs and Alice's voice, gentle and low, asking if she liked ice cream. That was one problem solved.

Glad I didn't have any nosy neighbors, I leaned over and wrapped my hand around my father's arm, hauling him to his feet. I didn't regret hitting him. I regretted not hitting him harder.

"Fucking asshole," I muttered under my breath as I shoved him into my place, pushing him past the kitchen to the living room, where he dropped on to my couch with a groan.

"Hell of a way to greet your old man, kid."

"Don't even start with me. I'm not in the mood for your bullshit, Dad."

"When you can't go anywhere else, you go home, right? Isn't that the saying?"

"You've worn out your welcome everywhere else. Did you know Mom's downstairs in the safe house?"

My father had the grace to look away for a second before meeting my eyes with his trademark combination of disregard and defiance, seasoned liberally with charm. "I figured she would be. Always stuck by me, your mother. She's a good woman."

I didn't know what to say to that. Neither of them was good people. The list of reasons why was so long I had no clue where to start. I was tempted to toss my father out on the street and be done with it. I couldn't.

So many reasons I couldn't kick him out, that list almost as long as the list of reasons why he was an asshole.

We needed to convince him to help the FBI nail Tsepov or the company would go down with him, my brothers and I along with it. We'd worked too hard to let that happen. I wasn't going to let Maxwell destroy everything we'd built despite his best efforts to sabotage us.

And then there was that little girl. Based on those familiar ice-blue eyes, I had to believe she was a Sinclair. Someone had to look out for her. I doubted that someone was my father.

Raising my chin toward where the girl sat at the kitchen counter with Alice, I asked, "She's yours?"

My father let out a deep sigh, his chest rising, then falling, sinking, like a balloon losing air until he looked deflated. Defeated. To my utter shock, tears swam in his eyes. He pressed the heels of his palms against them, wiping the moisture away and nodding his head.

His voice low—I would've said repentant if I didn't know better—he said "Petra. Her name is Petra."

"Where's her mother?"

My father shook his head, his eyes opaque with something that looked like grief. I couldn't figure out if he was putting on an act. He looked over his shoulder at Petra, her mouth open as Alice fed her a spoonful of ice cream.

His face twisted with pain, he said, "She looks just like you at that age. That hair. Her eyes. But her smile is her mother's. Mila."

"And where is Mila?" I pressed.

"Dead. She's dead."

"Who was she?"

"She was one of Tsepov's."

My stomach clenched as I watched Mila's daughter swallow a bite of ice cream and give Alice a sweet, shy smile. *One of Tsepov's.* I knew what that meant. One of the women he trafficked. Essentially a sex slave. Probably taken from her home at a young age and moved here and there for profit.

Knowing that was bad enough. Worse was knowing how my father had met Petra's mother. He hadn't been there to save her. She'd been a job, just one of many women Maxwell had helped Tsepov hurt.

That little girl was my sister. I owed her more than to turn away from my father's crimes. I owed her dead mother more.

"What happened?" I asked, wishing I didn't have to know. I couldn't think of many things I wanted to hear less than the story of how Maxwell had met Petra's mother.

Maxwell looked past me. "Can I get a drink?"

"Fuck, no. Tell me what happened and then I'll think about giving you a drink."

"Asshole," he muttered. The feeling was mutual. All signs of grief wiped away, he let out a huff before he started to talk.

"I was moving some girls for Tsepov. Mila was from Croatia. The Russian branch of the Tsepovs had problems with her family. They owed him money. A lot of money. They sold her to him to write off some of their debt. She'd been with Tsepov for two years when I picked her up with the others. I don't know why she was different. She just was. She was Mila. I looked at her and—"

"—you fell in love?" I asked, not bothering to hide my sarcasm.

My father's head sagged, eyes wet and broken. I wasn't child enough to believe his fictions. Maybe he'd fallen in love with Mila. And maybe she'd been a beautiful young woman at his mercy and he'd convinced himself he was doing her a favor. She was dead. All I had was his word for it.

"Please, tell me she wasn't a minor."

He shot me a look of wounded disgust. "Of course not."

"How old was she?"

"Twenty-two," he admitted, his eyes on the wall across the room.

Only forty years younger than him. Maxwell looked good for his age, but no matter how I twisted it around in my head, I couldn't turn it into a pretty picture.

Maybe Maxwell had been in love with Mila, maybe he'd convinced himself she was in love with him, but my guess was Mila wanted to get away from Tsepov and was willing to sleep with Maxwell for the promise of safety.

Yeah, there was no way to sell this that made my father anything but a user and a creep.

"Look," he said, dodging my eyes, "I know I always told you boys love was for pussies. Don't let a woman tie you down. I was wrong. I didn't know. I met Mila and everything changed. Everything. I was supposed to deliver her to a man in Rome and I— I couldn't do it. I stashed her somewhere safe, delivered the other girls and then—" He cut off and glanced over his shoulder at Petra again.

I could put the pieces together well enough, and I wanted to punch him all over again. *He'd delivered the other girls.* Clearly, falling in love hadn't given him a crisis of conscience over his fucking job.

"She's why, isn't she? This girl. Mila. She's why you faked your death and took off. We grieved for you, you asshole."

"I know. I know. I'm sorry. But you didn't need me. None of you boys needed me. Your mother does fine on her own as long as her credit card works. You don't know what it's like. For the first time in my life, I was in love. I lost my head. There was no way Tsepov would let me have her, and I couldn't live without her. I had no choice, Cooper. No choice."

Responses swirled in my head. I didn't know what it was like to be head over heels in love? I fucking damn well did. And I knew that the woman I loved wouldn't want me to burn down the world just so we could be together.

I didn't blame Mila. She'd been a victim. I knew who deserved the blame, and he was sitting right in front of me.

"So, you fell in love, you faked your death, and you and Mila took off, lived on the run. *After* you stole millions from Andrei Tsepov. Or did you forget that part?"

"That was probably a mistake," Maxwell conceded in the understatement of the century. I would deal with the missing money in a minute. First, I wanted to know about my little sister.

"Did you marry her? Mila? Because Mom is still alive."

"Don't be a smartass, Cooper. I know your mother's alive. This has nothing to do with her."

I couldn't hold back the snort of laughter at his absurdity. He ran off with a girl he stole from a Russian mob boss leaving my mother to mourn his supposed death, but this had nothing to do with Lacey. Sure. Only in Maxwell Sinclair's world did that make sense.

Chapter Twenty-Eight

COOPER

SO, WHAT WAS YOUR PLAN? WERE YOU AND Mila going to run forever?"

"I didn't have a plan. I took the money and we headed to a small village in Thailand. Lived quiet. Simple. Then she got pregnant. I was working all the time when you boys were born. I was there, but I wasn't there. Mila was so excited. Wanted to name her after her grandmother. Petra. When the doctor put my daughter in my arms, I knew I had to do better. I had to keep them both safe.

"I had my side stuff going, popped over to the States here and there to deal with Leanne Gates and Trey Spencer. A dollar still goes a long way in Thailand." He looked down at his feet, his fists clenched at his side.

"I got cocky. Careless. He found us. One night, Tsepov's men broke in. Slit Mila's throat. Tried to take Petra."

He swallowed hard as if struggling to go on, and I almost believed his grief was real. I wanted to believe it, wanted to believe my father was human, that he had a heart, as misguided as it was.

I looked at the little girl who'd climbed into Alice's lap, a bedraggled stuffed rabbit clutched under one arm, face smeared with strawberry ice cream. For her sake, I wished my father had loved her mother, but wishes were a waste of time.

"How long ago?"

"Six months. Since then, we've been hopping all over the globe. Staying one step ahead of Tsepov. He's almost had us a few times."

A chill spread through my gut, up my spine, and into my brain, icing me over with cold calculation.

He'd almost had them a few times?

I looked at my little sister, at Petra, taking in that dark hair and her Sinclair eyes, the bow of her red mouth and her soft child's skin. She was so small, even compared to Alice.

I shuddered to think of what would happen to her if she fell into Tsepov's hands. Knowing Maxwell, her mother had undoubtedly been beautiful. Petra sleepily rested her head on Alice's shoulder, eyelids drooping. She was so vulnerable. Defenseless. And for six months, she'd had only my father to keep her safe.

Except my fucking father—*her* fucking father—had put her in danger in the first place. Whatever happened tonight, he wasn't taking Petra with him.

Taking in the hard line of my jaw, the anger in my eyes, Maxwell looked for a diversion. Surging to his feet, the charm back in full force, he turned to watch Alice wipe Petra's sticky face with a wet towel.

"Alice will put you to bed, sweetheart," he said to Petra. Alice stiffened.

Oh, fuck no.

Maxwell was not giving orders to Alice.

Not to my Alice.

He could go fuck himself first.

He didn't run the company anymore. Alice wasn't his employee, she was my woman. I crossed the room to stand beside her.

"Alice doesn't work for you, and she isn't the nanny. You can put Petra to bed in the guest room. Then we'll talk."

Maxwell's eyes narrowed on me, flicked to Alice and back to me. Without a word, he strode forward and took Petra from Alice's arms. Petra reached for him. "Sleepy, Daddy."

To Alice, I said, "Will you follow them to the guest room? See if he needs anything to put her down while I secure the exits and call the control room? When you're done, meet me in the kitchen."

"On it, boss." She rose to her toes and pressed a kiss to the side of my jaw before following Maxwell down the hall. I was right behind them, headed not to the guest room but to the fire door that led from the back of the apartment to the roof and the back stairwell.

I dialed the control room in the office as I checked to make sure the lock was secure from the inside. Without the code or a key, Maxwell wouldn't be able to open it. He was trapped with me until I was done with him.

The control room was staffed twenty-four hours a day, ready to handle anything that came up after hours. Lindsey, one of our newer recruits to Lucas's hacker team, picked up on the first ring.

"Cooper? Everything okay?"

"My father turned up. He's in my place for now, but he'll be staying with my mother on the second floor. Make sure all the exits are covered. Bring in extra staff if you need to. I want everyone carrying a Taser along with their weapon. Go for a stun before a shot, but if he tries to run, stop him any way necessary."

"Understood. Do you want me to update your brothers?"

"Yes. Loop in Griffen, too."

Lindsey hung up and I headed back down the hall past the guest room. Alice had already left Maxwell with Petra. The low rumble of his voice and Petra's answering words were muffled through the door as I passed it.

Alice waited in the kitchen, running a towel under cold water.

"Come here. Let me see your fingers. You tore a knuckle when you hit him."

I raised my hand. She was right. I hadn't even noticed. I let her clean the blood off my skin, absorbing the feel of her soft, strong hands, so much smaller than mine, yet just as capable.

"You okay?" I asked. Alice laughed.

"The question is are *you* okay? That was a hell of a lot to get hit with in the middle of the night."

"Yeah, well, that's Maxwell. Could you hear his story from the kitchen?"

"I heard enough. He never said what he's doing here."

"I can guess," I said. "He's run out of options. And maybe, possibly, he's thinking about somebody other than himself."

"You have a little sister," Alice said with wonder in her voice. She dropped the wet towel on the counter, and I pulled her into my arms, needing the comfort of her body against me.

"I have a little sister." The thought left me reeling. "We just have to figure out what we're going to do with her."

"Before that," Alice said, "we have to figure out what we're going to do with Maxwell."

Maxwell strode back in, the grief wiped from his eyes, his smile all charm. "So, you two. Wondered how long that would take."

Alice stiffened but said nothing, giving him her stoniest stare. I followed her lead and ignored him. I wanted to take another swing at him for daring to comment after all he'd done to keep us apart, but I stayed where I was, my arm firmly around Alice.

The silence grew more uncomfortable with every passing second. Maxwell shifted his weight and opened his mouth, but I got there first.

"Petra asleep?"

"It's been a long day," he said in answer.

"I bet. Do you want a beer? Whiskey?"

"Whiskey," Maxwell said with another flash of that charming smile. His charm had worn off on me long ago.

"Sit. I'll get you a drink and we'll talk." I raised an eyebrow at Alice, and she answered with a quiet, "Yes, please."

Maxwell sat in the middle of the couch, knees spread wide, taking up as much space as possible. He should know better than to think his power plays would do any good here. He'd raised me with this crap.

Alice perched on the arm of the chair opposite the couch, waiting for me. I delivered my father's whiskey and sat, handing Alice her own glass. Her free hand closed over my shoulder, a show of solidarity.

Taking a sip of my whiskey, I gave my father an assessing stare. "What's your plan? I know you didn't come back here without one."

"Things are a little hot right now. Petra needs to stay with you. Here. Where she's safe. I can't lose her like I did her mother."

If that was a bid for sympathy, Maxwell had the wrong audience.

"Petra can stay as long as she wants. You're staying, too."

Maxwell lifted his chin, a hard look in his eyes. Just as I'd guessed. He wasn't planning to stick around, just wanted to dump his kid and run. I had no issue with keeping Petra. Hell, if he tried to take her, I'd stop him.

That little girl was my sister. She deserved better than to be dragged all over the world fleeing the man who'd killed her mother.

"It's time to stop running, Maxwell," I said.

My father stared back, nonplussed, his impermeable veneer undamaged as if my words had bounced right off.

He shook his head with a wry smile I knew was an act, as was the smooth sip of whiskey before he spoke. "I can't come back, Cooper. Surely, you can see that. I'm sure as hell not going to spend the rest of my life sitting behind a desk."

I barked out a laugh, the amusement taking me by surprise. "Agreed. You're not coming back to the company. Ever. There's no place for you at Sinclair Security."

I expected to feel something as the words left my mouth. Guilt. Pain. I felt a twinge of regret, but that was it. Maxwell had made his choices. Much like our mother, Maxwell's family had never been on his list of priorities. Not really. Like Lacey, he only cared about us when we served his interests.

We'd busted our asses to make the company what it was today, and now his bullshit with Andrei Tsepov put everything we'd built at risk. If it came out that Maxwell Sinclair

was the subject of an FBI investigation into his ties to a
mob boss we'd lose every one of our high-profile clients.

We needed to work with the FBI or we'd lose everything.
My father didn't give a shit about that. I didn't care. He was
going to cooperate whether he liked it or not.

"I'd argue with you, boy, but I'm done with the company.
You can buy me out and have the whole thing. I just need
you to keep an eye on your sister while I settle things with
Andrei." He slugged back the rest of his whiskey and made
to stand.

"I don't think so," I said putting my own glass on the
side table. Alice's hand fell on my shoulder and squeezed,
a silent message of support. I leaned into her for a second
before bracing my forearms on my knees.

"Move one inch, and I'll put you on the ground."

Maxwell froze for a second before settling back into the
cushions as if he'd never intended to get up. Time to lay out
some truths.

"First, we will not be buying you out of Sinclair Security.
You're dead. Your ownership share was divided among the
four of us as directed in your will. Unless you want to go
through the legal process of coming back to life. I'm sure
Agent Holley can help with that."

His face blanched as the ramifications of being dead
hit home. There was no way he could take that risk unless
he cooperated. Not that we'd give him back the company
even if he did cooperate with the FBI. I'd see him in court
first.

"My father founded that company," he protested.

"And you almost destroyed it. You still might. Who
do you think Grandpa would want in charge? You or his
grandsons?" I barely paused. We both knew the answer to
that question, and it wasn't Maxwell.

"Here's what's going to happen now, Dad. You're going downstairs to the safe house with Mom. The whole building is secured and under guard. No one gets in and no one gets out without my approval. Everyone on guard is authorized to use force on anyone who moves without clearance. In the morning, we're going to call Agent Holley. You will work out an arrangement with him that is satisfactory."

"Satisfactory? For who? Me or the FBI?"

"For the FBI," I answered, inwardly shaking my head. I reiterated, "Satisfactory for the FBI. And in case you don't understand, satisfactory means that the FBI will not be pressing charges against me, Axel, Knox, Evers, or Mom as accessories to your long history of criminal behavior in coordination with the Tsepov empire. You will give them whatever you need to to get the rest of us off the hook. Do you understand?"

"You might as well pin a target on my back, Cooper."

"That's not my problem."

"You'd throw your old man to the wolves like that? You're asking me to inform to the FBI, to hand them Tsepov. You might as well put a gun to my head."

"What do you think you did to us when you stole his money and ran? You took your girlfriend and you left us at the mercy of the fucking mob. You left *Mom* at the mercy of the mob. Did you know they broke into her condo? Took pictures of her sleeping to scare us into getting their money back?

"And Andrei is a fucking moron. At least when his uncle was in charge we were dealing with a professional. He almost killed Alice and Adam at Knox's house by accident. He shot Smokey Winters and left him to bleed to death.

"This whole shit-storm is your fault, and not only could you take down the business, we could all end up in jail as accessories."

"Holley knows you boys aren't involved," my father said in a weak protest.

"That doesn't matter," I shot back. "He might believe us, but you used the company to run protection for Tsepov's deliveries which makes us accessories anyway. But you don't give a shit about that. I guess we should count ourselves lucky you care enough about our little sister to get her somewhere safe before you take off again."

I hated the anger in my voice. I wanted to be cold, ruthless and unemotional. I wanted to be ice. Instead, that pure rage was back, the flames burning hot.

"You're my son," Maxwell blustered. "You don't get to tell me what to do."

"Where's the money, Dad?"

"What money?"

I gritted my teeth, losing patience. My hand fisted at my side. If not for Alice's presence beside me, her fingers curled over my shoulder, I might have launched myself out of the chair and planted my fist in his smug face.

"Don't fuck with me, Dad. Where's the goddamn money?"

My father looked at me through eyes I knew as well as my own. I could see the calculation there as he weighed and measured his answer before he said, "It's gone."

"Bullshit. That's bullshit, but fine."

Maxwell and I stared at each other, the silence in the room a lead weight. I knew exactly what he was thinking, knew he was already working out a plan to make a clean getaway from his family, the FBI, and Andrei Tsepov. Then he could ride off into the sunset, his pockets stuffed with his stolen cash and the rest of us holding the bag.

Not this time.

He must have read me right, must have known I wasn't going to let him go anywhere because he sat back, all charming smiles again. "Okay. Okay, kid, we'll play it your way. I'll go downstairs and make nice with your mom. We'll see about tomorrow. But listen, don't tell your mom about Petra."

Disgusted, I agreed. At the thought of how my mother would react if she found out my father's love child was stashed one floor above— Nope, not going there.

Petra was three. My mother was confined to her apartment. How hard could it be to keep them apart?

Chapter Twenty-Nine

ALICE

E WERE JUST FINISHING BREAKFAST WHEN Cooper's phone rang. He looked at the screen, his jaw going tight before he stabbed at the answer button and said, "Hey, man. You're on speaker. Alice is here."

"Hate to bug you so early," came Griffen's familiar voice, "but we just nabbed your dad trying to leave the building. I hit him with the Taser—clean shot in the leg. I've got him in the holding room. What do you want me to do with him?"

"Fuck," Cooper swore, but it was halfhearted. I didn't have to ask to know he'd been expecting this. "Keep him there. I already messaged Agent Holley. I was going to call him as soon as we finish breakfast. Do me a favor?"

"Anything, Coop."

"Call my brothers and tell them to meet me in the conference room in an hour and thirty."

"On it. Anything else?"

"Yeah, how do you feel about doing a little shopping?" Cooper looked up at me, the lighthearted glint in his eye warming me from the inside.

"Shopping for what?" Griffen asked warily.

"My dad didn't come alone."

"Shit. Who did he bring?"

"My little sister."

A long pause. "Holeeee shit. How old?"

"Three. And typical of Dad, she showed up with her pajamas, a stuffed rabbit, and not much else. I don't know what the fuck we're going to do with Maxwell, but he's not taking off with my sister. Not with Tsepov on his trail."

Cooper looked up at me in question. "Do you mind, Alice? Can you go with Griffen and get her sorted out?"

I answered, "Of course," at the same time Griffen offered, "Let me call Lily, see if she can come with us. If anybody knows what a little kid needs, it's Lily. Better than the rest of us."

"Great idea," I said in relief. I was happy to hit the stores and set Petra up with whatever she needed, but beyond clothes, I had no clue.

Knox's girlfriend Lily was mom to five-year-old Adam, the boy I'd shot Tsepov's man to protect. Lily was great— not a surprise since Knox was too cool to hook up with anyone who wasn't. Lily would know exactly what we needed for Petra.

As Cooper nailed down the details and got off the phone with Griffen, the subject of our conversation came wandering into the kitchen clutching her bedraggled stuffed rabbit. Petra looked lost and confused, but not scared. Not yet.

Her eyes landed on Cooper and she picked up speed, her little feet covering the distance between the hallway and the kitchen faster than I would have guessed. She was small and slight, but she was quick.

Petra reached Cooper and closed her small hand around the fine wool of his suit pants. She tugged, lifting her other arm to reach for him, the bunny dangling from her tightly clenched fingers.

Neither of us had any experience with kids, but her request was unmistakable. Cooper leaned down and picked her up, settling her on his hip. Her eyes drooping, still half-asleep, she laid her head on his shoulder. In her light, clear voice she asked, "Daddy?"

Cooper rubbed a hand over her back in comfort. "Your daddy had to go to work. Alice and I are here. Do you want to go out with Alice? Get some clothes and toys?"

Petra's dark eyebrows raised at the mention of toys, but she snuggled deeper into Cooper's shoulder. "Hungry," she mumbled, her eyes still only half-open.

"We'll make you breakfast," he promised, moving his hand over her back. Her eyes slid shut, and I thought she might have fallen back to sleep.

Cooper's voice low, he said, "I'll give you my credit card. Get whatever she needs. Long-term, not just for the next week or so."

I looked at the little girl holding on to Cooper, my heart melting and twisting with worry at the same time. What was it about a tough guy holding a little kid that was so sexy? If I could have blinked Petra back into her bedroom, I might have jumped him right there.

Sexiness aside, did he really know what *long-term* meant? I thought he did. He'd said he wasn't letting Maxwell put Petra in danger. Knowing Maxwell, I couldn't imagine he was truly interested in being a parent to this little girl. Not now that he'd dumped her on Cooper.

Regardless, Cooper didn't look like he planned to let her go.

"Are you sure?" I asked, aware that Petra looked asleep but might be listening to every word.

Cooper reached out with his free hand and wove his fingers through mine, pulling me to his side. His eyes fixed on me, a question lurking in their depths, he said, "She's my sister. I'm sure. Are you okay with that? We haven't talked about—"

"I'm okay with it." The words shot out before I could think, but I didn't regret them.

I knew she was Maxwell's daughter, but seeing her in Cooper's arms, her dark head tucked against his shoulder, she might have been his. In the secret part of my heart, I'd imagined a little girl that looked like Cooper, and here she was, flesh and blood.

The logical part of my brain protested. This little girl was going to need full-time care. She needed parents. Is that what we wanted? Cooper was a workaholic. So was I. I had my classes and my friends. Cooper traveled for work.

I'd always pictured a life with children, but that was the fuzzy, distant future. Petra was here now.

I took in the curve of her cheek, flushed with sleep, the fan of dark lashes against her skin. So innocent. Far too vulnerable.

Was I going to tell this little girl she was inconvenient? That she wasn't part of my plans?

Were children ever convenient? Even when you'd planned for them?

I had a feeling the answer was *No*.

I decided to worry about all of that later. For now, Petra needed a sense of stability. She needed affection and care. Food and clean clothes. I may not know what *long-term* meant, not yet, but I'd happily handle affection and care.

Cooper glanced at the clock over the stove. "I have to get downstairs. Are you okay with her this morning? I can—"

"I'm good. Give her to me. I'll get her some breakfast. When you get downstairs, check with Maxwell and see if he has a bag for her. I can take her shopping in her pajamas but—"

Something occurred to me, and I reached up to tug at the back of her pajama pants. As I'd expected, she was wearing a diaper or a pull-up or something. Not potty-trained.

"At the least, she probably needs a new pull-up or whatever before we go out."

Cooper transferred the sleeping toddler from his arms to mine, and she resettled herself against me, nestling her head in the hollow between my neck and collarbone, eyes open but still drowsy.

Cooper pressed a soft kiss to my mouth, both of us aware of Petra taking it all in. He reached out to run the back of a finger up and down her soft cheek before promising, "I'll see you later, Petra, okay?"

She nodded, reaching out to tap his chin with her fingertip. "Look like Daddy."

Something burned in Cooper's eyes as he caught her finger in his and shook it in a jiggling motion that made her giggle. "I look like your daddy because I'm your big brother. And you're my little sister."

Petra looked up at him, uncomprehending. There was a sweetness to her that was a miracle considering Maxwell had been her primary caregiver for the last six months. I had to wonder about the poor girl who'd been her mother.

My bet was that Mila had loved her little girl, had given her as much as she could in the short time they had together. Cooper pressed a quick kiss to her forehead, dropped another on my cheek, and left.

I wished he could stay. I had no idea what I was doing with a three-year-old, but whatever happened with Petra, it was going to be better than what Cooper was walking into.

He and his brothers may have found Maxwell, but holding onto him was another matter altogether.

Petra patted my cheek with her open palm to get my attention. When I looked down into those familiar ice-blue eyes, she said, "Hungry. Beffast?"

Breakfast I could do. "Eggs? Toast?"

Thankfully, Petra nodded. I settled her into my chair at the bar, suddenly aware how high it was off the hardwood floor. I slid my plate of half-finished eggs and slice of toast in front of her and she tucked in.

The food was cold, but she ate with such appetite and lack of complaint I had to wonder when Maxwell had last fed her.

When she was halfway finished, my phone beeped with a text.

Griffen's on his way up with Petra's bag.

So, she did have a bag. That was something. Griffen let himself in, a good thing since I was Petra's seatbelt for the tall chair at the kitchen bar where she was eating. She needed a high chair. Another thing to put on the list.

I hoped Lily was coming with us. I knew Petra needed clothes and pull-ups or diapers or whatever she was wearing. Hopefully, Lily would be able to tell me the difference. A high chair. What else?

Griffen stopped in front of us, his green eyes soft as they landed on Petra. In a low voice, he said, "She's the spitting image of Maxwell and the rest of them, isn't she?"

"She is," I agreed. "Is that her bag?"

"What there is of it," he said, handing me a beat-up gym bag, disdain for Maxwell heavy in his voice.

As I unzipped the bag and rooted through it, Griffen went on, "I heard from Lily. She and Adam are going to come with us. We'll swing by and pick them up on the way."

I looked up in relief. "That would be great. Doesn't Adam have kindergarten?"

"Lily said he can miss a day. She thought he'd want to meet Petra, and Petra might feel better with another little kid around."

"Good thinking," I mumbled, sorting through Petra's meager possessions.

There wasn't much. A few changes of clothes, most of them well-worn, and half of a package of pull-ups size 2T – 3T. I took a quick picture of the package with my phone so I'd know what to get at the store. Checking the tags in the clothes, I found they were a mix between 2T and 3T.

When Petra was done eating, I coaxed her into trying on both sizes, quickly determining that the 2T was a close fit and the 3T was better, if a little too big. I added to the list I'd started on my phone. There weren't any shoes in the bag, and she hadn't been wearing any the night before.

I added shoes. We'd figure out her size at the store. She also had nothing in the way of grooming supplies. No hairbrush, no ponytail holders or barrettes. No toothbrush or toothpaste. I added those, too, and gave Petra's hair a quick brush with my own, glad that despite its length her hair wasn't too tangled and felt clean. At least Maxwell had bathed her recently.

Thinking about the way she'd devoured the cold eggs, I wondered if she'd been eating enough. The idea that she hadn't, that Maxwell hadn't been taking care of her basic needs—I didn't want to think about it.

Was she slight because that was her natural build or because she was hungry? When things settled down, we'd have to find her a pediatrician. On our way out the door I grabbed a small orange and some soft granola bars from the pantry in case she got hungry again.

In the garage we piled into Knox's SUV, Griffen explaining, "We don't have a car seat for her, but Knox has a booster for Adam. That'll have to do until we can buy her the kind she needs at the store."

I added Car Seat to the list. Once we were settled, Petra clutching my hand, Griffen pulled out on the street, sending me a quick look through the rearview mirror. "You okay with all this?"

"Weirdly, yeah," I said honestly. "I mean, surprised. Worried for Cooper. He's, it's—" I glanced at Petra, who was staring out the window. I wasn't going to say Maxwell's name in front of her. I didn't need to.

"You still mad at him?"

"At Cooper? Nope, not mad at Cooper."

"Yeah, I get you." Griffen knew exactly who I was mad at, and it wasn't Cooper. Now I had a whole new reason I could happily kill Maxwell.

Chapter Thirty

ALICE

IT WAS A SHORT DRIVE TO KNOX'S HOUSE. I hadn't been there since the day Tsepov had blown up the garage with Adam and me in the basement. Most of the house had escaped damage, a good thing since it was a work of art. In a million years I never would have guessed big, tough, silent Knox would have a house that looked like a fairy-tale cottage.

With its steeply peaked roof, diamond-paned windows, and flower boxes overflowing with blooms, Knox's house was too gorgeous to be real.

Fortunately, only the garage had been damaged, and Knox was using the repairs as an excuse to turn the two-car garage into three, with a bonus room above and an extra guest room on the back, tucked behind the kitchen. It sounded like Knox and Lily were already making plans to expand their ready-made family.

Lily and Adam opened the front door as soon as we pulled to a stop, Adam holding Lily's hand and tugging her along, the sun gleaming off his white-blonde hair. He looked nothing like his mother with her cloud of dark curls and tawny brown skin, but the bond between them was unmistakable even from a distance. Lily smiled down at her son and said something, probably telling him to slow down.

Using the extra booster seat she'd brought with her, Lily got Adam settled in the backseat, asking me, "You okay sitting between these two?"

"I'm good." Squeezing Petra's hand, I said, "This is Lily and her son, Adam. Guys, this is Petra."

Lily gave Petra a warm smile and said hello before closing Adam's door and getting in the front seat.

Adam leaned around me to catch Petra's eye. "I'm Adam." Petra said nothing, her face serious, her eyes wide. Adam was undaunted. Lily's boy had a sunny disposition and he'd never met a friend he didn't like.

Looking at me, he said, "Hi, Alice!" before leaning forward further to get a good look at Petra. "I'm five. I'm in kindergarten now. How old are you? Do you go to school?"

Petra's hand squeezed mine as she pressed into my side, getting closer to Adam while keeping me between them. Scared but curious. Rubbing my thumb over her fingers in comfort, I said, "It's okay, honey. Adam is a friend of Cooper's. Of your brother's."

Petra looked at me and back at Adam, still uncertain. "Can you show him how old you are?" I prompted. Another long look at me, another hesitant look at Adam, and she transferred her stuffed rabbit to her lap before holding up three fingers.

Adam grinned and started to tell her all about kindergarten, his enthusiasm undiminished by her lack of verbal response. Her eyes were bright with interest despite her silence. Brave girl. This must be overwhelming, on her own with so many new people, but Petra was hanging in there.

Everything was fine as I grabbed a cart built for two kids and settled Adam and Petra side-by-side. I must have looked taken aback when Lily grabbed a second shopping cart. She grinned and shook her head. "You're going to need it."

When I thought about my list, I realized she was right. A high chair and two car seats—one for Cooper's car and one for mine—would fill a cart and a half on their own, and Petra needed everything.

We started at the front of the store, stocking up on sippy cups and a plastic dish set, then bath toys and no-tears shampoo, a thermometer, hairbrush and toothbrush—pretty much everything we'd need to keep a toddler fed and clean.

Next up were high chairs. I was grateful Lily was with us when she grabbed a circular plastic mat and tossed it in the cart, explaining, "It helps keep the floor clean. She's not a baby, so you might not need it but..."

Adam broke off his chattering to Petra to give me a very adult look. "You'll need it. I loved to throw food when I was three."

Lily bit her lip to hold back the laugh. Adam was taking his role as Petra's companion seriously, gracefully accepting her offer of the stuffed bunny and examining it closely, nodding in approval before handing it back and telling her it was really cool.

Petra was quiet, smiling hesitantly at Adam here and there, but not speaking. When she wasn't looking at Adam, her eyes were fixed on me. I didn't think anything of it until I stepped away from the cart, going around the corner at the end of the aisle in search of the upgraded version of the high chair I liked.

The second I disappeared from Petra's view, a high-pitched shriek filled our corner of the store, the sound rising to an ear-grating crescendo before fading as she gasped in breath for another scream.

I forgot all about high chairs and bolted back to the cart. Petra wailed her heart out, tears streaking her cheeks. Griffen and Lily tried to comfort her, but she batted their hands away, shrieking in panicked fear.

"Petra," I cried, reaching for her, "Petra, honey, it's okay. Everything's okay."

Her hands locked onto mine and she lunged for me, the seatbelt of the cart jerking her back. Lily fumbled for the snap, opening it just in time for Petra to throw herself into my arms so hard she almost knocked me over.

Her arms locked around me, her wet face pressed into my neck, her body shuddering under my hands. I rocked her back and forth, rubbing her back, crooning, "It's okay, honey. It's okay."

After endless minutes of weeping, she quieted. I craned my head to look into her teary eyes. "Did you get scared because you couldn't see me?"

She nodded, sobs still hiccupping in her chest. Tears pricked my eyes and I dropped my head to press a kiss to her hair.

"Okay, honey, okay. I won't leave you. I promise. Everything's going to be okay. I won't leave you."

I pressed the side of my cheek to the top of her head, the tears that prickled my eyes falling hot against my cheeks, my heart breaking. She'd been so composed, so quiet, I hadn't realized how scared she was.

It was a good thing Maxwell was locked in the holding room because if he was in front of me I would have torn him to pieces.

I'm sure he'd swear he'd done his best by Petra, but this was his fault. He'd dragged her all over the globe, running from the man who'd killed her mother, and then he'd ditched her at the first opportunity. He'd had plenty of time that morning to ask about his daughter, but Cooper hadn't gotten so much as a short text to see if she'd slept well. Nothing.

I didn't know exactly how Cooper and I were going to work a toddler into our lives, but I would not be one more person who abandoned this little girl.

I don't know how long I stood there rocking Petra in my arms, waiting for her sobs to quiet. I was aware of Griffen and Lily taking the cart to the front of the store, returning with an empty one, leaving and coming back as they filled it with various odds and ends. A few packages of pull-ups. The high chair I'd been looking for.

When Petra was quiet, her little body limp in my arms, I moved to set her back in the seat of the cart beside Adam. The moment her feet hit the plastic she tensed and began to wail again.

"Okay, honey. Okay, Petra. You want me to carry you?"

She lifted her face to look up at me, those ice-blue eyes so like Cooper's swimming with tears, shadowed with deeply-held fear. My chest burned with impotent fury at Maxwell. At Tsepov for taking Petra's mother. A toddler shouldn't know fear like this, shouldn't be terrified she'd be abandoned.

I smoothed Petra's hair back off her face and pressed a kiss to her forehead. "I'll carry you, honey. I won't put you down, I promise."

As much as I meant my vow to carry Petra, I regretted it ten minutes later. Her little body sat in my arms like a lead weight, straining muscles I didn't know I had. I shifted her from one hip to the other, wincing a little. Lily caught the movement out of the corner of her eye.

"Arms killing you?"

I shook my head and lied. "I'm good."

Her eyes narrowed for a second. "Stay there." She disappeared back toward the section where we'd already grabbed an umbrella stroller. I watched her doubtfully. If Petra wouldn't let me put her in the cart I didn't think she'd tolerate a stroller.

Lily returned, walking so fast she was almost at a jog, her arms laden with bundles of cardboard-wrapped fabric. She lay them out across the shelf beside me. Baby carriers.

"You're brilliant," I breathed. "I'm so glad you came with us."

Lily smiled. "Me too. She's probably close to the top weight limit for some of these, but even if she can't use it for too much longer it's worth it." She quickly read the backs of the carriers she'd grabbed, choosing one and tearing off the packaging.

"Stand still," she said. "It's been a while since I put one of these on, but if you hold her just like that I can strap it around you. This one was my favorite when Adam was her age. He'd snuggle right in and fall asleep." Turning to Adam she said, "Do you remember?"

Adam bounced a little in the cart. "It can go on your back too, Alice. It's fun for walks for when my legs used to get tired. And it has a hood thing you can pull up so your head's in the shade."

Lily moved around me, looping the straps over my arms, buckling the carrier around my waist, and pulling the whole thing tight. Finally, she said, "Okay, move your arms and let's see how this thing fits."

I did as she said and Petra settled into the carrier in the same position I'd been holding her—her head against my shoulder, her knees on either side of my ribs. Now, instead of pulling my arms from their sockets, the carrier distributed her weight over my shoulders and around my waist. Petra raised her face, her dark eyebrows knitted together.

"You okay?" Brushing her hair off her face, I cupped her cheek in my hand. She looked uncertain for a moment before giving me a tentative nod.

"Bubba. Bubba." She reached an arm out, grasping.

Lily, Griffen, and I looked at each other in confusion. Adam knew exactly what Petra wanted and leaned down to pick up the rabbit she'd dropped, handing it to her with a cheerful, "Here you go, Petra."

Petra grabbed her Bubba and tucked the stuffed rabbit under her chin, giving Adam a shy, grateful smile.

My heart pounded with adrenaline as we carried on with our shopping expedition, Petra cradled against me, calm now that there was no chance I'd walk away and leave her behind.

What the hell was happening? How did I end up with a toddler strapped to my body when twenty-four hours before I'd had no clue she existed?

More than that, why the hell did I want to keep her exactly where she was?

I had no business getting attached. None. She was Cooper's sister. Maxwell's daughter. Petra was nothing to me.

Everything inside me rebelled at that thought. Petra was Cooper's baby sister. It didn't matter that he'd never laid eyes on her until last night. She was his family and she needed him. She needed *us*. I had every reason to get attached. If she was Cooper's, she was mine.

241

My head was spinning, arguments for and against Petra raging in my mind as I carefully chose toys and books, rubbing her back as we moved from aisle to aisle.

Cooper and I were brand new. There wasn't room for a child in our relationship.

We weren't new at all. We'd known each other almost a decade, had been friends for years.

My brain wanted to pick apart the Petra problem, to find a reasonable and logical solution.

My heart didn't care about reason and logic. My heart wanted to keep this little girl wrapped in my arms where she was safe, to hold her and love her until that fathomless fear of being abandoned was gone from her eyes.

My heart wanted to do battle with anyone who might harm her, wanted to kill Maxwell for his obvious neglect. My heart wanted to do right by the young woman who'd been Petra's mother and wasn't here to see her daughter grow up.

My brain wasn't sure what was going on, but my heart had already decided. I was keeping Cooper, and together, we were keeping Petra. I could only hope Cooper was on board.

You know he is, my heart whispered, far more confident than my brain.

Lily watched us quietly, taking in the way Petra clung to me with innocent trust. As we tried different sizes of shoes on her feet, Lily murmured, "She's going to be okay, Alice. You're both going to be okay."

I wanted to believe her. Not just for me. For Petra. For Cooper. Head spinning with too much change too fast, I turned my attention to a smocked dress in hot pink embroidered with daisies. I might not know what I was doing with a toddler, but I knew fashion, and that dress was ridiculously adorable. It wasn't fair that the girl's department was three times the size of the boy's, but I wasn't going to complain. I was going to take advantage.

Beside me, Lily said, "I need a little girl just for all these cute clothes."

"I know, right?" I held up a package of daisy-shaped barrettes next to Petra's dark hair. She spotted them and reached out, taking them from my hand for a closer look.

"Do you like them?" I asked gently.

Petra rubbed her finger over the bright flower on the barrette. "Pretty."

Good enough for me. The dress and barrettes went in the cart. Adam made a sound of disgust. I caught him and Griffen rolling their eyes, bored now that we were looking at girl's clothes.

I stuck my tongue out at Adam and made a face. "Hold tight, cowboy, we'll go back to the toy section in a few minutes, but I need to do some damage here first."

Hoping Cooper wouldn't mind what I was doing to his credit card, I shopped to my heart's content. New clothes and toys wouldn't fix the hole in Petra's heart, but they wouldn't hurt either. She'd need this stuff no matter what, and if shopping helped me put my topsy-turvy world to rights, just for a little while, I'd take it. I needed all the help I could get.

Chapter Thirty-One

COOPER

MY FATHER SAUNTERED INTO THE CONFERENCE room and splayed out in the chair at the foot of the table, as relaxed as a guy meeting buddies for a beer after work. The two armed guards who'd escorted him might not have existed for all the attention he gave them.

At my nod, they took up positions on either side of the door. If Maxwell tried to bolt, they'd stop him. He might have run the company after Granddad retired, but he'd been gone a long time, and he hadn't exactly been beloved while he was here. The men on the door were mine, not his.

I sat opposite my father at the head of the long, polished conference table, in the chair that used to be his. Evers, Knox, and Axel were arranged in between us, their eyes grim. Resigned.

None of us wanted to be here. Hell, I wanted to be in Griffen's place, with Alice, shopping for Petra. That said a lot considering I hate shopping. But remembering Petra's faded pajamas, the way she'd reached for me—I wanted to be with her. With Alice.

Too bad. Agent Holley was out of town, chasing down a lead on Tsepov, but he'd be here the next day. Either he'd secure Maxwell's cooperation or he'd toss Maxwell in jail where he'd suffocate under a mountain of charges. Charges that would drag Sinclair Security down with him. I couldn't let that happen.

I had a plan, and it hinged on one thing. Me being as good a liar as my father.

Maxwell lounged back in his chair, legs spread wide, arms crossed over his chest as if he hadn't a care in the world, his eyebrow raised in a cocky smirk.

"What? No coffee? No *hello* for your old man? It's been what, five years?"

"Not the best opening, Dad," Axel said, his eyes frigid. "I guess I should be glad you're back from the dead, but considering the mess you left us..." Axel left the rest unspoken. Maxwell refused to let the words wound him, turning away from Axel as if he hadn't spoken.

I lifted my chin in the direction of the single-serve coffee maker on the cart in the corner. "Help yourself if you want coffee, but do it now. I'd like to get this over with."

"Alice not serving coffee?" he asked in a silky, dangerous tone.

I restrained the urge to knock him unconscious. One punch hadn't been enough. Not even close.

"Alice is out buying supplies for your daughter, who not only didn't have clothes that fit, she didn't even have a toothbrush. Even if Alice were here at her desk, she would not be doing anything for you. Ever. Not transferring phone calls, not making copies, and absolutely not getting you a cup of coffee."

"Hell, she doesn't even get me a cup of coffee," Evers said.

With a glare at my younger brother, I reminded him, "That's because getting coffee isn't Alice's job."

Mug in hand, my father returned to his seat, giving me an annoyed look. "You've got a bug up your ass. You need to get laid. I figured she'd at least do her job in the sack."

I was moving before I thought about it, stopped only by Axel's hand clamping down on my shoulder, pinning me in my seat.

"You need to shut the fuck up, Dad," he said.

Maxwell rolled his eyes at Evers and Knox. If he was looking for allies there, he was disappointed.

"What are you doing here, Dad?" Evers asked, not bothering to hide his anger. "Why now, after five years? I know it's not because you give a shit about your family, so what do you want?"

Maxwell reared back in exaggerated offense. It was mostly an act. I saw him think about going for indignant, then deciding it wasn't going to fly with this audience.

Maybe he saw the wisdom in saving us some time because he took a long sip of coffee before placing the mug on the table. After a dramatic pause, he said, his voice low, almost theatrical, "Tsepov is closer than you think. Petra and I barely made it out of Prague. If I want to stay ahead of him, I need cash, firepower, and clean papers."

Knox laughed, shocking the hell out of me. Of all of us, Knox excelled at stony silence. Our father's sudden reappearance had knocked all of us off our stride.

"You've got to be fucking kidding me," Knox said, words heavy with disgust. "You show up five years after your funeral, after stealing millions from the mob, and hit us up for cash and guns? Not going to happen. And we're sure as hell not going to help you get clean fucking papers. You think we'd burn one of our contacts by dragging them into this clusterfuck?"

"I'm your goddamn father," Maxwell erupted. "Everything you have is because of me. If I ask you to give me some cash and the fucking guns, you'll goddamn well do it."

There was the good old Dad I knew and loved. It didn't take him long to get to the point. Of course, he wanted money. What else would he want? Forgiveness? To come home to his family? Not Maxwell.

"And Petra?" I asked. "What's your plan for our little sister? Are you going to drag her along while you keep running? Do you even care about what Tsepov will do with her if he catches up to you?"

Maxwell squirmed in his seat, his eyes on the steam drifting from his mug of coffee.

Before he could answer, Evers kicked in. "I wasn't sure your shitty parenting could get worse, but here you are, proving me wrong again."

"Shut the fuck up," my father shot back. "Just shut up. You have no fucking clue what you're talking about—"

His words cut off abruptly, and the grief in his face left me speechless. He was a good actor, an even better bullshit artist, but the raw pain in his eyes, the tremble to his chin—those were real.

Fucking hell. He'd loved that girl.

Just as I started to feel sorry for my father, I remembered the sound of Knox's house exploding with Alice trapped inside. Every drop of my sympathy for my father drained away.

I'd never forget the way my heart had stopped as the ground shook beneath my feet. Never forget running through the smoke to find Alice on the floor in a pool of blood.

I'd never forget how close I'd come to losing her. Or whose fault it was. Forcing the heat of emotion from my voice, I pressed harder. "You got Mila killed. You almost got Alice and Summer killed. So, tell me, what are you going to do about Petra? Can you live with her death on your conscience?"

Maxwell studied his half-empty coffee as if the answer to all his problems was written on the side of the mug. Avoiding all of our eyes, he finally said, "I thought I'd leave Petra here with you."

I leveled ice-cold eyes on Maxwell, silent, letting him squirm at my apparent lack of concern. Evers didn't bother to play it cool. "What a shock. You're interested in making children, but not raising them. You aren't here to make things right. You aren't here to clean up your mess. You're here to dump your kid so you can go off and do whatever the fuck you want. Find another young girl to knock up. Steal another fortune from the mob. Do I have that right? You're here to talk us into funding your next adventure while you grease the wheels for a clean getaway. Am I missing anything?"

Easy-going Evers was as angry as I'd ever seen him. Then again, he'd almost lost Summer because of our father and Tsepov. Evers had endured endless hours tied to a chair, watching Summer's father bleed to death, terrified Summer would suffer the same fate—or worse—at Tsepov's hands. Evers had had plenty of time to think about how fucking pissed he was at our father.

Marshaling the indignation he seemed to thrive on, Maxwell retorted, "I can't take Petra with me. It's too dangerous. She's your sister. Your responsibility—"

"Oh, that's rich," Axel said. "How the hell is she our responsibility? And what are we supposed to tell Mom? Have you thought about that?"

Maxwell didn't acknowledge the problem of Petra and our mother. "Look, I thought I would do a better job this time. When Mila was alive and the three of us were together, I thought this time I'd get it right. A new start. And then it all went to hell, and you're right, I'm a shitty father. Any one of you could do better than me with your eyes closed. I'm asking you to try. To keep her safe and give her the life I can't give her."

Evers leaned forward, ready with another sarcastic comment. I held up my hand and he restrained himself.

Doing my best to sound unaffected, disinterested, I laid it out for Maxwell. "Here's how this is going to go. I want two things from you. If you give them to me, I'll keep Petra and raise her like she's my own. I'll give her everything you never gave us. Love. Attention. I'll give her my time. A happy home. I'll give her a mother who gives a shit about her. The best of everything."

Maxwell's face lightened with relief, and he leaned forward. "You won't regret this Cooper, I—"

I held up my hand again, stopping him in his tracks. He shifted with unease as he finally registered my frigid tone.

"You didn't let me finish." Each word fell into the room like a block of ice, leaving a brittle tension in its wake.

Maxwell's eyes locked on mine, fear overriding his relief. Good. He should be afraid.

"Two things, Maxwell. If you don't give me what I want, I'll throw both of you out on the street."

"You wouldn't." There was no conviction in his shaking voice as he processed the thought that maybe I would.

"I absolutely will," I threatened, knowing I had to play

this part so well Maxwell believed I was as ruthless as he was.

In truth, I was exactly as ruthless as Maxwell. It was only my priorities that were different.

"The rest of us have been through enough. We're done with you and the problems you've caused. You give me these two things, and I'll take the kid and give you whatever cash you need."

"Fine." Maxwell slumped back in defeat. The wounded look in his eyes caused the tiniest twinge of remorse, gone so fast I barely felt it. My father was an adult. He could suffer his own consequences. He didn't deserve my loyalty. My baby sister did.

"What do you want?" Maxwell asked on a sigh.

"Dave Price is drawing up documents to voluntarily terminate your parental rights and give me guardianship of Petra. You will sign them. That's number one."

"Fine. If you're going to take her, that makes sense anyway," he said, not looking too cut up over losing all rights to his daughter. "And the other thing?"

"You help Agent Holley nail Tsepov."

"You've got to be out of your goddamn mind," he blustered, shooting to his feet, the chair rolling behind him until it bumped into the wall. He started to pace, ranting at me. Something about me being a Judas, ungrateful, whatever.

I tuned him out, turning to Knox. "Do you still have Tsepov's number? I doubt he'll answer, but I have a feeling if I leave a voicemail telling him we can hand him Maxwell, he'll call us back. That would save time. I doubt we'll need those custody papers signed if he's dead. We're Petra's next of kin anyway."

His voice just as cold as my own, Knox said, "It's programmed in my phone. I'll make the call."

I nodded in approval, watching Maxwell from the corner of my eye as Knox pulled his phone from his pocket and started tapping the screen. Knox wasn't fucking around. He *did* have Andrei Tsepov in his contacts, and he didn't hesitate before he hit the number and lifted the phone to his ear.

Maxwell froze mid-stride, finally realizing no one was listening to him. His eyes locked on Knox, watching with narrowed eyes as Knox shrugged a shoulder. "Voicemail. I'll just let him know he can have Dad—"

Maxwell flew across the room, knocking the phone from Knox's hand. It hit the floor and skidded, Maxwell diving after it, stabbing frantically at the screen, desperate to end the call before any of our voices were captured on Tsepov's voicemail.

The second he terminated the call, Maxwell pitched the phone into the wall, not satisfied until it exploded in pieces. "What the fuck were you thinking? I'm your father—"

"No, you're not," Knox roared, striding toward Maxwell, his usually stony face twisted with rage. "You're a fucking sperm donor who walked away from us years before you left. *I'm* a goddamned father, and I'll do anything to keep my family safe. Anything. Including hand you over to Tsepov. Do you get me?"

Shit. I thought my bluff would scare Maxwell enough to get what we needed, and maybe it would have, but seeing Knox lose control so completely shoved our father right over the edge.

Just in case the message hadn't gotten through, I summarized, my demeanor as calm as Knox's was enraged.

"I think we've made it clear. You're only useful to us alive if you're going to help the FBI. Otherwise, the best way to deal with you is to hand you over to Tsepov. Axel? Evers? Any objections? Either of you want to plead Dad's case?"

The silence that fell on the room was deafening. Maxwell stood on shaky legs, his eyes landing on Evers, then Axel, waiting for one of them to say something. They stared back, eyes hard.

For the first time in our lives, Maxwell saw us for who we were instead of as tools to serve his interests.

What he saw was pure, unyielding resolve.

Resolve to salvage everything we'd worked for.

Resolve to protect our own.

In the face of that resolve, his shoulders slumped. He made his way back to his chair, falling into it with a resigned thud.

"Fine, you win. I'll help Agent Holley, and I'll sign your goddamn papers. As long as you don't make that call to Tsepov."

"Agreed."

If only everything were that simple.

Chapter Thirty-Two

COOPER

I DITCHED THE OFFICE SHORTLY AFTER MAXWELL was secured in the apartment with our mother. There was nothing at work that couldn't wait, and I needed to see Alice. I wasn't ready to talk about the confrontation with my father. I just needed her. Her arms around me. Her smile.

I found her in the guest room we'd given to Petra, standing in front of the dresser, quietly folding and putting away a pile of brightly-colored clothes.

Eyes solemn, she turned a pink dress in her hands, studying the embroidery on the front before the sound of my entry registered and she looked up.

The smile that spread across her face when she saw me went a long way to lightening the cloud around my heart. Still holding the dress, she crossed the room and hugged me, her warmth sinking in, driving away the chill of the last few hours.

"Where's Petra?" I asked, keeping my voice down.

"Napping in our bed. We bought some books at the store. I read to her then she just dropped off. It's been a long day."

Alice snuggled her forehead against my chest and let out a long sigh. "She's so scared, Cooper. I walked away for a second at the store and she lost it, even though Lily and Griffen were standing right there with Adam. She screamed and screamed until I picked her up."

Her arms tightened around me as she let out a gust of a sigh. "He hasn't even asked about her, has he?"

"No." He hadn't. Asked us to keep her so he could take off, but he hadn't asked how she was. If she'd slept well. Eaten breakfast. If she missed him. Needed him. "He wants to leave her here."

"Here in Atlanta? Or here with us?"

"I don't think he cares."

"He's such an asshole," Alice said into my shirt.

"You've got that right," I agreed.

I should have asked Alice what *she* wanted.

Could she see herself being a parent to Petra? Fitting her into our lives? Or was she just making the best of the situation?

I should have asked, but I didn't. Later. We could get into it later. Instead, I asked the other thing that had been preying on my mind while she'd been out with Griffen and I'd been stuck in the office dealing with Maxwell.

"I know you've had Petra all day, but did you get a chance to move any of your things up here?"

Her eyes shuttered so completely I could feel her withdraw even though she didn't move away. One shoulder hitched up in a shrug, her eyes dropping to the dress still in her hand. "I'll do it later. I haven't had time."

"I'm here with Petra if you want to go down and get some things together."

"It's fine. I'll get to it later."

Later.

It didn't sound so bad when I'd said it to myself. From Alice, it felt like what it was. Avoidance. Distance. I hated it.

She pulled away and looked back at the pile of bags on the bed. "I want to get the rest of this put away while she's sleeping. You might pass out when you see your credit card bill."

"I don't care how much you spent, Alice. Did you get everything she needs?"

Alice gestured to the mountain of bags on the bed and laughed. "For now."

It looked like she'd bought half the store. As if seeing the room through my eyes, she added apologetically, "This isn't all of it. There are two car seats in the kitchen. One for your car and one for mine. And a high chair."

Two car seats. That had to be a good sign. If Alice didn't want Petra in her life, why get her an extra car seat? I wanted to ask, and I was afraid to push.

So much was at stake, my entire future suddenly balanced on a razor's edge. One wrong move might send it all crashing down.

I didn't like that Alice wasn't moved in. I wanted to see her dresses hanging in my closet, her shoes left haphazardly by the door, her makeup strewn across the bathroom counter. I wanted her *here*, not just spending the night.

Was she avoiding the issue because she was focused on Petra, or was she using Petra to put me off?

I didn't know and couldn't tell.

It shouldn't have mattered. Twenty-four hours before, I wouldn't have blinked at her procrastination. We were busy. Moving is a pain in the ass.

Petra's arrival had turned everything inside out.

I wanted too much, and for the first time in my life, I was afraid to ask for it. Afraid the answer would be something I didn't want to hear.

I wanted Alice. I'd wanted Alice for so long, the need for her felt like a part of me.

For one shining moment I'd had what I wanted, and now I needed more.

Petra.

I'd always imagined having kids. I'd never dreamed I had a little sister, much less that she'd be dumped in my lap. I barely knew the kid, so how had she sunk her hooks so deeply into my heart? Why did I look into her eyes and feel like she was mine?

Was it just biology? We look alike. Maybe my instinct to protect her was only because she was so familiar, with her Sinclair blue eyes and dark hair so much like my own. Maybe she'd only connected with me because I resemble our father so much.

Did it matter? That little girl was my family. My sister. Life had dealt her a shitty hand, mostly due to our asshole of a father. I had the power to make it better. I couldn't live with making it worse.

The idea of stepping up made a pretty picture, but that was a far cry from the reality of becoming a parent overnight. I work too much. I wanted time alone with Alice now that I finally had her.

A toddler was a bomb dropped in the middle of my life. A great big inconvenience. Was I really going to turn my life upside down for Petra? How could I expect Alice to do the same?

I hated the idea that Petra might scare Alice away, hated it with everything I had.

I wasn't willing to give either of them up.

I might not have a choice.

Would I still want Petra if she ended up being the wedge that drove Alice and me apart? Could I love my little sister the way she deserved if she cost me Alice?

I wasn't Petra's only brother. Knox and Lily already had Adam. What was one more kid? And there was Evers or Axel. I wasn't the only option.

I pictured Petra's eyes, so like my own, the way she'd reached for me that morning with such pure, innocent trust. The way she'd done the same with Alice when she'd panicked at the store.

I didn't want to push Petra off on one of my brothers.

I wanted my father, Tsepov, and Agent Holley out of our lives. I wanted Petra settled and happy. I wanted Alice with me. In my arms. In my bed. In my life.

What were the odds I could have all of that, exactly the way I wanted it?

Just ask Alice what she wants, my conscience urged. Or maybe it wasn't my conscience, maybe it was my balls. Throw me in a dangerous situation at work and I'm all confidence. Not so much when I'm faced with losing the woman I love.

I kept my questions to myself and helped Alice put away Petra's things. I hauled empty shopping bags stuffed with packaging material to the front door over and over until the guest room was slowly transformed into a little girl's bedroom.

Standing side-by-side, we looked at the queen-sized bed, now bracketed by safety railings on either side. "Does she need a kid's bed?" I asked. "Something smaller?"

"This is probably okay for now."

For now.

What did that mean? *For now*, as in *we'll get her a new bed later*? Or *for now*, as in *she isn't staying so why worry about it*?

Everything Alice had purchased could be packed up and moved. A bed was permanent.

I was making myself crazy. I opened my mouth to ask Alice what she was thinking. "Alice—"

"Hmm?" she asked, rearranging the books on the nightstand.

I lost my nerve. "I invited everyone over for dinner tonight. Evers and Summer are going to bring takeout."

Alice checked her watch. "Good idea. We should have time to put that high chair together before Petra wakes up."

"Yeah, that sounds like a plan," I said, as full of shit as I'd ever been.

I'd faced down my father, forced him to give in to all of my demands, and ended up with everything I wanted.

I'd have to find the courage to do the same with Alice before it was too late.

Chapter Thirty-Three

ALICE

DINNER WAS NICE BUT WEIRD. THIS WASN'T the first time I'd eaten with Cooper, his siblings, and their women, though it was the first since Knox had brought Lily into our lives. Conversation was easy, touching on things like the repair and remodel at Knox's house and Emma's plans at her job when she was back home in Las Vegas. Stuff we might have talked about anytime. Normal.

It would have been great if anything in our lives had been remotely normal. Instead, everything was inside out and upside down, and the longer we went without discussing the elephants in the room, the more on edge I became.

Elephant number one, Petra, sat on Cooper's big couch with Adam, snuggling her stuffed rabbit and watching a movie.

Despite her long nap she still seemed tired. Maybe she was exhausted, or it could be the giant dinner she'd eaten. Every time I put food in front of the kid she inhaled it.

Either Maxwell had been starving her or she was going through a growth spurt.

She'd devoured her breakfast, eaten every bite of the snacks I'd brought along for the shopping trip as well as a peanut butter and jelly sandwich for lunch, and she'd dived into her plate of macaroni and cheese at dinner like she hadn't seen food in weeks.

I always heard people talk about how picky kids could be, but Petra ate whatever I put in front of her until every scrap was gone. Don't get me wrong, I'm glad she was eating, but even Lily seemed unsettled by her appetite.

I don't think Maxwell was intentionally withholding food from his daughter, but he wasn't the kind of guy who thought about other people's needs before his own. I doubted a kid's meal schedule would be the same as an adult's. I skipped meals all the time and made up for it later, but I didn't think you could do that with kids. Then again, what I knew about kids would barely fill a postcard.

Not talking about Petra was one thing, but it was also odd that no one had mentioned Maxwell. Conversation flowed from topic to topic, all of them mundane, as the tension inside me wound tighter and tighter. Cooper sensed it, sending me worried glances as we ate dinner.

I wanted to reassure him, but I didn't know what to say. I couldn't bring myself to say I was fine. I wasn't fine. I was stressed and freaked out. I was worried about Petra, about Cooper having to deal with Maxwell, about the changes in my life, so fast and so huge.

We were sipping on coffee and after-dinner drinks, finishing the crumbs of the cake Axel and Emma had picked up from Annabelle's, when out of nowhere, Knox said, "Dave Price sent over the paperwork."

Beside me, Cooper went solid, every muscle in his body locked tight. I leaned closer, my own muscles going stiff with tension when I realized he wouldn't meet my eyes. What paperwork?

Fortunately, Summer asked for me. "What paperwork? What did you need Dave for?"

Dave Price was their family lawyer. All at once I knew, before Evers answered his girlfriend's question. "Cooper strong-armed Dad into agreeing to sign papers terminating his parental rights to Petra."

I glanced over my shoulder to make sure the kids weren't listening, even though I knew the surround sound speakers would drown out any conversation from this side of the room.

My head spun. Maxwell agreed to sign papers terminating his parental rights. Evers hadn't said who would get custody of Petra. Somehow, in all my mental back and forth about Petra, it hadn't occurred to me that Cooper had three brothers, one of whom was currently raising a child not much older than Petra.

It hadn't occurred to me that she might not end up with us.

My stomach clutched. My heart ached with a stabbing pain. I didn't know what I was getting into, didn't know if I was ready, didn't know if I'd be any good at this, but the thought of packing up that bedroom, of handing Petra over to someone else, sent panic arcing through me.

I bit my lip to keep my mouth shut, wanting to shout into the room, *No! She's ours.*

I couldn't do that. She wasn't my little sister. I hadn't even talked to Cooper about it. Cooper wasn't meeting my eyes. Had he decided Petra was better off with one of his brothers? What if none of them wanted her? Were we just going to give her away, abandon her like her father had?

No, of all the things to worry about, that wasn't one. I knew these men. They would not abandon that little girl. No way.

I wanted her. I had no right, but that was how I felt. I saw Lily and Knox looking at each other, having a silent conversation, and my heart kicked up in another rush of panic.

They were going to offer to take Petra. I knew it. I shouldn't even argue. Lily was already a mother. She knew what she was doing. Wouldn't Petra be better off with Lily and Knox?

In desperation, I looked at Cooper. He was watching me, his eyes wary yet hopeful. He raised an eyebrow and my heart leapt. In a low voice that no one else could hear, he said, "Do we want her?"

The shortest of questions, but there was no time for anything else. I'd already cataloged all my doubts, all the reasons to say no.

I did the only thing I could. I said, "Yes."

Cooper's eyes lit with incandescent joy. He reached to take my hand, squeezing it hard, pulling it to rest on his leg, his fingers wrapped around mine as he said to his siblings, "We want her to stay with us. Alice and I want custody."

Surprised expressions from everyone at the table but Lily. My heart still pounding, Cooper's hand the only thing anchoring me in place, I barely heard Evers when he said, "How's that going to work? Is Alice going to quit? Alice can't quit. We had three days without you this week," he said to me, "and the place is about to fall apart. I don't want to be an ass—" a quick glance at the kids on the couch and he lowered his voice. "I don't want to be an asshole but—"

I rode a roller coaster from joy to dismay. I wanted Petra. Cooper wanted Petra. We wanted to give her a home, love, and safety. But I didn't want to quit my job. Cooper couldn't. He ran the company.

It's not that I have anything against staying home with kids, but I love what I do. And Evers was right, my leaving would affect a whole lot more than just Cooper, myself, and Petra.

I looked at Cooper to see his eyebrows knitted together with worry. He squeezed my hand again and said to the table, "We'll figure it out. Alice doesn't want to leave her job, and we need her there, but we can get creative. Before we know it, Petra will be ready for preschool, and maybe at that point, we can look into a nanny. With everything she's been through, I don't feel right putting her with strangers during the day. Not for a while."

"Then what?" Knox asked.

"We could do half days," Cooper offered. "I can scale back, you guys can pick up some of my client work and team management so Alice and I can switch off, one of us working in the mornings and the other in the afternoon. Part-time with both of us is better than one of us leaving."

Lily leaned forward, and everyone looked in her direction. Quietly, looking a little nervous now that the entire table was staring at her, she said, "I'll watch Petra during the day. I think you're right, for the next few weeks maybe both of you doing half-time or figuring out how to take some days off would be best. That scene at the store today—"

Lily shook her head, her eyes dark with concern. "It was bad. She needs time to settle in. I can come over during the day here and there while she gets comfortable, and once she's ready she can spend the days with me."

Relief was sunshine in my heart. Lily was a great mom, and once she married Knox she'd officially be Petra's family.

Still, Adam had just started kindergarten and she was still getting used to a new city. Full-time childcare is a huge commitment.

"Are you sure?" I asked.

"Unless anyone can think of a reason that wouldn't work—" Lily waited for an objection.

Knox kissed the side of her mouth before saying, "I think it's a great idea."

With more confidence, Lily went on, "To be honest, the house is a little empty—a lot empty—now that Adam is in kindergarten. Knox and I decided—" Lily sent a questioning look at Knox, who gave her a reassuring smile.

"We're not ready to start trying for another child until Adam's had more time to adjust to the last year. He's doing great, but losing his dad and then moving...it's a lot all at once and he's only five. We have time to add to our family, and by then Petra should be starting school herself."

Lily looked at Cooper and me. "Just because you guys are taking custody doesn't mean we all shouldn't pitch in. She has four brothers, you know?"

I let out the breath I'd been holding. If Lily would watch Petra, if we could do what she suggested and ease her in so she was comfortable with everyone before Cooper and I went back to work full time... That solution would be just about perfect. I leaned forward to catch Lily's eye. "You really wouldn't mind? It's a lot to ask."

"We're family, aren't we? This is what families do. That little girl is attached to you. I saw it today. She didn't want me, she didn't want Griffen. She wanted you. I've already seen her with Cooper tonight. You both genuinely want her, and she clearly wants you.

"And honestly, I'm at loose ends right now. I don't want to get a job I don't really need just to fill the time. I love kids, loved being with Adam when he was Petra's age, but I don't want to take care of a stranger's kids. This is different. If it doesn't work out, I'll tell you and we'll find another solution."

"If you really don't mind," Evers said, "you'd be a life-saver, Lily. Because seriously, if we don't have Alice at the office we'll all end up killing each other."

"What about me?" Cooper cut in with mock offense. "You can't live without Alice, but you can live without me?"

"Exactly," Knox rumbled, his face straight but the gleam of humor in his eye. "But seriously, Evers and I can fill in for you if we have to. Alice? No way. The interns and new hires do their best, but they fuck up half the stuff we throw at them."

"A few suggestions," Axel interrupted. All eyes turned to him. "Alice needs an assistant. You have room in the budget, and it would mean that if she has to take off work the office has coverage and Alice isn't coming back to a mess. Knox and Evers can cover for Cooper, but you don't have anyone to cover for Alice. My office manager has an assistant and it's worked out for everyone."

Cooper turned serious eyes on me. "That's a good idea. Do you want an assistant?"

My knee jerk response was to insist I could handle it all on my own. Then I thought about the days I'd worked through being sick, and how I couldn't do that when it was Petra who was sick. Or had a doctor's appointment. Or Lily had something going on and couldn't watch her. Cooper would handle some of those, but if he had commitments he couldn't reschedule...

"I want to sit in on interviews and have veto power on whoever you hire," I said.

"Obviously," Evers said with a grin. "Can you imagine if we hired someone you didn't like? You'd eat him for breakfast."

"Another thing," Axel interrupted, "You might want to touch base with Vance and Maggie Winters. Their Rosie is almost three, and they're still on the search for a new nanny. The girls might like playing together, and bringing in a nanny would give Lily some relief when she needs it."

Cooper let go of my hand and wound his arm around my shoulder. I scooted my chair closer and leaned into him, content despite the challenges we had yet to face.

Not one person sitting at this table was perfect, but they didn't have to be. This was family, pitching in together to make things work. This is what Maxwell and Lacey didn't get. Family was everything, and we were going to give this to Petra.

We couldn't erase her past or give her back everything she'd lost, but we could give her something good. Something real. And we would. I thought again of Petra's mother, dead far too young, and silently promised, *We're going to do right by your daughter. I swear we will.*

Petra didn't want to go to bed after everyone had left. She asked for Maxwell, crying, "Daddy, where Daddy?" until Cooper's jaw was tight and I wanted to march downstairs and bitch-slap Maxwell for abandoning his daughter.

If he was going to continue the life he'd been living, then leaving Petra with us was the right choice, but for now, he was just an elevator ride away. How could he bear to ignore her, knowing she had to be scared in a new place?

Cooper and I finally got her down by lying on either side of her, me rubbing her back and Cooper telling story after story until the rumble of his voice lulled her to sleep. We crept out, hoping she'd stay asleep, and made our way to Cooper's room.

Torn by conflicting needs, I turned apologetic eyes on Cooper. "Just so you know, I totally want to have sex with you."

"But..."

"But I feel weird about locking the door when she had such a hard time falling asleep."

Cooper closed his fingers around my wrist, pulling me into the circle of his arms. His mouth dropped to mine in a long, sweet kiss that left me lightheaded by the time he straightened. "I don't know, you wore me out between the cabin and last night. I think I need a day off to recover."

"Like I believe that." I smacked the back of my hand against his rock-hard abs and had second thoughts about locking the door. It would be okay for a little while, right?

"Will you move your things in tomorrow?" Cooper asked, changing the subject. He'd asked me that earlier, but I'd been thinking about Petra and her freak-out at the store and hadn't really paid attention.

"It's important to you, isn't it?"

"It is. I want you here, Alice. I want to know you're staying, that you're in this with me."

Winding my arms around his waist, I leaned back to look up at him, hoping he could see my heart in my eyes. "I'm in this with you, Cooper. All the way. I didn't think moving my things was that important, but if it means something to you, I'll start bringing stuff up."

"I'll make room in the closet," Cooper said, brushing my hair back from my face.

I'd figure it out the next day, I decided, as I got ready for bed and climbed in beside Cooper. The meeting with Agent Holley was set for late morning, but Cooper could stay with Petra while I went down to my place before heading into the office for a few hours. Maybe I'd get up early.

Getting up early didn't happen. Sometime after midnight, I woke to the alien sensation of the bed moving under a small weight. I came awake in a panic to see Petra climbing up from the foot of the bed. Sitting up, I reached for her. "Are you okay, honey? Did you have a bad dream?"

She didn't answer, instead burrowing into the sliver of space my sitting up had created between Cooper and me. Squished between us, Petra closed her eyes and appeared to go to sleep.

"I guess it's a good thing we didn't have sex," Cooper whispered over her sleeping head.

I stifled a laugh. I don't think I'd ever bothered to put on nightclothes after having sex. Just one of the many habits that would have to change now that we had a toddler in the house. Fortunately, Cooper was wearing boxers, and I had on one of his t-shirts.

I lay down beside Petra, a warm glow settling inside me as her little body relaxed into mine. Such pure trust, to sleep with us when she was scared. I'd do anything to be worthy of that trust.

My thoughts weren't so generous after three hours of being kicked awake by a restless toddler. Petra slept on, but she was an active sleeper. She turned, stretched, and resettled herself at least every fifteen minutes, shoving Cooper and me out of her way as she did.

I never would have guessed elbows could be a deadly weapon. When six o'clock rolled around, I was cranky, bleary-eyed, bruised, and definitely not going to fall back to sleep.

Propping myself up on one elbow, I saw Petra sleeping peacefully, no hint of the whirling dervish in sight. How could she look so placid when I knew for a fact she was going to pop up at any moment and roll over, leading with her sharp little elbows?

Cooper opened his eyes, his smile so content, so right, I forgot about my bruises and wished I could start every day exactly like this.

A glance at the clock and I said, "Hey, since I'm up, I'm going to leave you with elbows here and go downstairs to grab some things from my closet."

The light in his eyes nearly brought me to my knees. If I'd realized filling the other half of his closet would make him this happy, I would have done it already.

"Works for me," he said. "Leave anything you don't need right away by your front door and I'll carry it up for you later."

I kissed Petra's temple, then Cooper's lips, lingering there for a long moment, seriously considering falling back into the bed. Sleep. I needed more sleep.

I could sleep later. For now, I was going to grab as much of my closet as I could cram into my few suitcases and start moving in with Cooper.

Chapter Thirty-Four

COOPER

ALICE SNAGGED MY CUT-OFF SWEATS FROM the floor, sliding them on under the borrowed T-shirt she'd slept in, and headed out the door with a whispered, "Be back soon."

I rolled out of bed as carefully as I could, giving Petra a wary look. Man, the kid had some elbows on her. And knees. And a hard head. I wasn't a restless sleeper. Once I was out, I was out.

Alice, on the other hand, moved around in the night, rolling into me, then away, star-fishing on her stomach before flipping to her back, but she kept her elbows to herself.

Petra rotated around the bed like the arms of a clock. At one point I'd woken to a big toe poking me in the nose, its owner splayed on top of the covers, her other foot resting beside Alice's head. I pushed her foot away and watched in surprise as she sat bolt upright, eyes still closed, turned ninety degrees, and flopped back down, her head on Alice's back and her feet almost turning me into a eunuch.

At least she'd slept. I made a mental note to talk to Alice about finding a child therapist. I wasn't sure if three years old was too young for therapy, but losing her mother and then being abandoned by her father six months later was a lot for anyone to handle.

Alice and I would love Petra, give her security and attention. Keep her safe. But at the end of the day, I didn't think either of us was equipped to give her the tools she'd need to process losing both of her parents. Especially when one of those parents had abandoned her voluntarily.

I was under no illusion that my father would show up when she got older, interested in being her parent. He'd objected to the idea of working with the FBI, but he hadn't put up a fight over terminating his parental rights.

Watching Petra as she shifted restlessly under the covers, her lashes dark fans across cheeks flushed with sleep, I couldn't understand. How could he just walk away from his own kid? I knew she was going to turn our lives upside down. I wasn't sure I was ready for it, but this was life. It wasn't always easy, but that wasn't going to stop me from doing the right thing.

I wouldn't waste any more of my morning wondering what the fuck was wrong with my father. He was going to eat up enough of my day once Agent Holley showed up to negotiate the terms that would keep Maxwell out of jail.

I'd think about Maxwell later. Instead, I went to my closet, surveying the neatly arranged space to figure out how to make room for Alice. It wouldn't be hard. While I had a more than adequate wardrobe, I'm not into clothes. I have what I need, maybe a little extra, but not enough to fill the entire closet. Not even close.

I rearranged things, emptying drawers, finally using the empty baskets my decorator had added when I moved in and consolidating my suits and shirts to free up hanging space.

Alice had a lot of dresses. She probably thought I didn't know how many, but I had a good idea. And those crinolines... She'd need room.

I'd made decent progress by the time Petra woke up, padding into the closet in her cartoon nightgown, her bare feet peeping out beneath the hem, eyes bleary.

She walked to my side, pulled on my T-shirt, and raised her arms, bunny clutched in one hand. "Up, Coop. Up."

I lifted her, and she lay her head on my shoulder. *Coop.* Fuck, the sound of my name in her clear, light voice. I'd heard her call Alice *'Lis*, but so far she hadn't said my name.

Damn. I was proud, like I'd had anything to do with it. I guess proud that I got in there enough for her to call me by name. Petra wasn't exactly a talker. I had no idea how much of a vocabulary was normal for a three-year-old. Maybe it depended on the kid, but every word she said was precious.

"Breakfast?"

That sweet smile. She patted my chest with the flat of her hand bouncing a little on my arm. "Beffast, beffast!"

Lily was an angel for going shopping with Alice. She'd dropped hints as they went on the best ways to handle this and that, gleaned from her years in the trenches with Adam. Thanks to her, I knew to give Petra a handful of cereal to munch on after I put her in the high chair and rolled her into the kitchen where she could watch me while I cooked.

She devoured the cereal, then another handful, pretending to feed every other piece to bunny before popping it in her mouth. It was probably weird, but I almost hoped she turned into a pickier eater when she relaxed with us. I didn't like the idea that she'd been hungry with my dad. Didn't like the idea he hadn't been taking care of her.

My brothers and I may not have gotten the attention we'd needed, but our material needs had always been covered. A nice place to live, great education, food in our stomachs. Far more than the basics. Petra had barely had clothes and she attacked every meal like it would be her last.

I pushed back the rising tide of rage at my father. *Not the time*, I reminded myself. Get through the next few days, help the FBI nail Tsepov, and Maxwell will walk away, Lacey along with him. Then life could go back to normal.

Or, rather, Alice, Petra, and I would find a new normal. I was making Petra scrambled eggs to go with the cinnamon raisin toast I'd already put on her tray when the front door opened and Alice walked in, carrying a duffel bag.

In a light blue and white polka dot dress with a boat neck that showed her collarbones and slender neck, she looked almost like the Alice I was used to seeing at work, right down the hint of white crinoline beneath her full skirt. Her hair was a sleek dark fall to just below her chin, but her lips were bare of color, and she was barefoot.

I love the way Alice looks when she's fully turned out for work, but I found I loved this half-finished Alice even more. This was the secret Alice, an Alice only I got to see.

"I'm just going to go put this stuff away. I left some other bags by my door for later. Be right back."

"Take your time, we're good."

She turned and her skirt flared, showing her knees and a flash of frothy white under her skirt. My cock came to life. When was the next time I'd get her to myself? Better not ask that. I might not like the answer.

Alice was back a few minutes later.

Still barefoot and without lipstick, she helped herself to a cup of coffee and came to join us at the breakfast counter where I'd wheeled Petra's high chair so we could both eat.

"I made you a plate," I said.

"I see that." She stood beside me, nuzzling my neck for a long blissful moment. "Thanks for making me room in the closet."

"Anytime. Let me know if it isn't enough."

"You know I will." She laughed and straightened, climbing onto her own bar stool. "Did Petra eat breakfast?"

"And then some." We shared a look of concern.

"You want more toast?" I asked Petra, who nodded and said something I thought might be toast. Or roast. Or ghost. Or maybe nothing. I stood, carrying my dirty plate and put it in the sink, grabbing the plate I'd put together for Alice. "Ready for your eggs?"

"Thanks, I'm starving."

I added two slices of cinnamon raisin bread to the toaster before getting Alice her eggs. "I can handle her toast if you want to go take a shower."

"I was just about to ask. I won't be long."

I can't describe the ridiculous sense of satisfaction I got from walking into my closet after a quick shower to see a row of Alice's brightly-colored dresses hung beside my suits.

It's possible I felt the prickle of tears behind my eyes. I'd wanted this exact thing for so long. Now, here she was, moving in with me. More than that, more than just moving in, I'd been hit with something life-changing, and Alice stuck.

I didn't have any illusions. It was one thing when I was on my own. Now I was a package deal, a ready-made family. I wouldn't have blamed her if she decided to back off. But she hadn't; she'd brought up a load of dresses and hung them in the closet.

Lost in satisfied thoughts about my life finally coming together, I spent a minute too long getting dressed. I emerged from my room to hear shouts coming down the hall.

Not Alice. Not Petra. My fucking mother.

I really wanted to go with that whole thing of honoring your mother, but Lacey was making it pretty goddamn hard. I sprinted down the hall to find them at the front door, Lacey with her foot over the threshold, pushing her way in, yelling my name.

"Cooper! Cooper!" And then shoving at Alice, almost growling, "Get your hands off me!" Alice spared me a quick glance of apology.

"I'm so sorry. I shouldn't have opened the door. She just, I thought—" Alice changed her grip on my mother's arms, pushing her wrists above her head, shoving her off balance enough that Lacey couldn't kick her shins anymore. "For some insane reason, I thought she'd behave if I told her you'd be out in a minute."

"Cooper, where the hell have you been? Tell this slu—"

"Not another word. I thought I made it clear what would happen if you talked about Alice like that. Don't fucking test me."

Lacey gave me a wounded look, dropping her arms and seeming to shrink into herself. Alice let out a sigh of annoyance and stepped back now that Lacey had stopped fighting her.

Shit, my mother had her act down to perfection. How could she go from a raging lunatic to this wounded, fragile woman in the blink of an eye?

"It's just that you have us locked up in there," she sobbed, crocodile tears spilling down her cheeks. "You won't even come see us. Your father is beside himself. He's getting older, you know, you can't let him handle this on his own. You can't just throw him to the FBI and expect them to look out for him. They want to throw him in jail, Cooper."

I crossed my arms over my chest. "That's because he broke the law, Mom. A lot. I have a feeling he's going to be serving time one way or another, but if you don't want it to be for the rest of his natural life, you should be encouraging him to work with the FBI."

As usual, my mother ignored what I'd said and went on with her rant. "You have to stop this. Call that Agent Holley and tell him he can't come today. Tell him that we'll figure something else out. Or just let us go. Maxwell and I will leave. If you don't have us, the FBI can't use us to get Andrei."

"Andrei, is it?" A horrifying thought occurred to me. "Andrei? Mom? How involved are you with Dad's business? Maybe Dad's not the reason you don't want this meeting with the FBI, huh? Maybe you're just watching out for your own ass."

She drew back, splaying her fingers across her chest, the perfect picture of refined affront. "Oh, Cooper! How could you say such a thing to me? I am your mother."

Fed up, I rolled my eyes at Alice. "That's what she says every time I don't tell her what she wants to hear."

Alice's eyes met mine, and I could practically feel her straining not to look back toward the kitchen. To Petra.

Shit, for a second, I'd forgotten. Petra was in the kitchen. We had to get rid of my mother. I wasn't going to hide Petra from her forever, but this didn't seem like the ideal moment to reveal that we had my father's love child stashed in our apartment.

My mother pulled herself together, sensing that outrage and plaintive entreaty weren't going to work. She moved on to calm reason. This was a new look for her. I would have liked it if I hadn't known she was trying to manipulate me.

"Cooper, surely you can't think I'd be involved with your father's dirty business. I understand that you want this situation cleared up, but your father can handle it. The FBI is only going to make everything more complicated. If you don't want to openly let us go, just distract the guards for a little while. Put them on something else and we'll slip away. It won't be your fault, and we can go solve this problem ourselves."

"It would be my fault. I'm not going to lie to the FBI, Mom. You need to turn around and go back downstairs. Tell Dad your little ploy didn't work, and I'll have him escorted to the conference room at ten forty-five. Agent Holley will be here at eleven."

"Cooper—" she tried again.

Alice had had enough. "Mrs. Sinclair, do you realize that if Maxwell runs out on the FBI Agent Holley will probably press charges against your sons as accessories? Maxwell left them on the hook by using the company, and Agent Holley has all the evidence he needs. Do you even care about that? Because you should. We're talking about your children. They'll lose everything they've worked for. How can you not understand that?"

My mother said nothing, setting her jaw and crossing her arms over her chest, glaring at Alice. At least she'd paid attention to my warnings about Alice. Not that I expected it to last. That would be too good to be true.

"Fine. Your father is not going to be happy, but I'll go down there and try to explain to him how his sons want to send him to prison—"

A high-pitched cry of distress echoed from the kitchen. All three of us froze.

Another cry and Alice whirled on her bare foot and took off, Lacey hot on her heels. I followed them both, cursing my mother for hanging around a second too long.

Chapter Thirty-Five

COOPER

I CAUGHT UP TO THEM TO SEE ALICE HANDING bunny back to a crying Petra. My mother stood in the middle of the kitchen, staring at Petra with a combination of horror and revulsion.

"What is this? You have a child with this...this...this... woman?" Lacey struggled mightily to hold back the word she wanted to call Alice, but the way she said *woman* was more epithet than anything else.

Alice unbuckled Petra and pulled her out of the high chair, holding her tight, the bunny sandwiched between them. She turned, hiding Petra from sight. My mother's face was growing increasingly red, her eyes wide as she shook with indignation and rage.

We saw the eruption coming and there was nothing we could do to stop it.

"You fucking whore. I told you to stay away from my son. I'm going to make you pay—"

Petra started to wail, set off by the vitriol in my mother's tone as her shouts filled the room. Clinging to Alice, Petra sobbed, "Daddy. Daddy. Where Daddy? Where Daddy?"

Unable to stand her panicked distress, I crossed the room to take Petra from Alice. My little sister burrowed her head into my neck, clutching the front of my shirt, still crying, "Where Daddy? Where Daddy?"

In that moment, I would have gladly killed both my parents. Lacey for setting her off and Maxwell for walking out and leaving her confused and abandoned.

Lacey fell silent, her brain trying to process through the cocktails she'd probably consumed with breakfast, but finally, she ended up in the right place.

When she spoke, her voice was hard as stone. "She's not yours, is she?"

"She is now," I said, cradling Petra against me, rubbing her back to soothe her sobs. "That's all you need to know. She's mine now. Mine and Alice's."

"Is this why you've turned on your father? You want him out of the way so you can claim her? I don't understand why you'd even want her. If you have to have a child, you can't take your father's leavings. For God's sake, think about how it will look! Just get rid of her, and your father and I will leave. Everything can go back to normal. That's your only option."

"Listen up, crazy lady," Alice cut in.

I knew that tone. Alice was done. So was I. If my mother's voice was stone, Alice's was adamantine. I'd never seen her sky-blue eyes so coldly furious.

"Cooper is going to take you back downstairs and lock you in the safe house. You are going to stay there until he decides to let you go. You can keep your bullshit opinions to yourself. He doesn't care what you have to say. I don't care what you have to say. And you have nothing to do with this little girl.

"If you'd lay off drinking for a few days, your brain might un-pickle itself and you'd see that you're throwing away everything worth having in your life to cling to a man who doesn't give a shit about you. But that's your problem. I'm not going to let you make it ours."

Alice strode across the kitchen and took Petra from my arms, passing Lacey without a backward glance. "I'm going to get her calmed down and give her a bath. Cooper, could you take out the trash?"

I shouldn't have enjoyed the outrage splashed across my mother's face at Alice's pithy comment, but I did. I enjoyed it a lot.

My mother transformed again after Alice disappeared, meekly allowing me to escort her back downstairs. I followed her into the safe house to find my father lounging on the couch, reading the newspaper, a steaming cup of coffee in hand. With wary eyes, he took in Lacey's lack of expression and my hard jaw.

"Whatever you two are cooking up, it's not going to work," I told him, tired of beating around the bush. "At ten forty-five, someone will bring you to the conference room. Agent Holley is arriving at eleven. Understood?"

"I'll be there, boy," he said easily. Too easily.

I looked from his relaxed smile to my mother's utter lack of expression. I couldn't shake the feeling that they were up to something. I tried to convince myself it was nothing.

For one thing, my father was way too clever to trust anything important to my mother considering the amount of alcohol she consumed in a given day. She was not what I would call a reliable partner in crime.

She was, however, infinitely persuadable if offered any of her weaknesses. My father had said she was happy as long as her credit cards were paid off. I wished I could say he was wrong.

After I got to my office, I texted Alice to check on Petra. She responded after a short delay with a picture of Petra, covered to her neck in white bubbles, a dot of bubbles on the tip of her nose. She was smiling and looked like she was playing with some kind of bath toy.

The idea had been for Alice to hit her desk for a few hours this morning while I watched Petra, but things had turned around since then. I texted,

I'll switch with you once we're done with Holley.

Works for me.

We definitely needed to get her an assistant. I rescheduled some meetings, reviewed the paperwork Dave Price had sent over, and made a short list of current employees who might be interested in the assistant job. It sounded like a junior position, but only to someone who didn't realize that Alice was a whole lot more than an office manager.

Ten forty-five rolled around way too fast. Evers, Axel, and Knox joined me in the conference room, sitting on either side of the seat we'd saved for Dad, leaving the far side of the table for the FBI.

Right on schedule, two of my men escorted my father into the conference room. As if he wasn't the flight risk we all knew he was, Maxwell ignored his guards, striding ahead of them with his most charming smile plastered on his face.

When he was seated, I slapped the termination papers in front of him and handed him a pen. He signed, muttering,

UNCOVERED

"Your mother about chewed my head off. That woman is
pissed."

I met Agent Holley at the door at exactly eleven o'clock.
He'd showed accompanied by three of the bureau's attorneys. All male, and all dressed in identical ill-fitting
charcoal grey suits, they observed my handshake with
Agent Holley without expression.

Holley's greeting was friendly, but as we walked back to
the conference room, neither of us mentioned the reason
for our meeting. I liked Agent Holley. Respected him. I
wished I could say I was entirely on his side. Until I was
sure he wouldn't toss me in prison along with my father, I'd
keep my own counsel. I had to.

My father greeted Holley as if they were old golf buddies,
shaking his hand and patting him on the shoulder with an
affable smile. Holley allowed him his pretense but didn't return
it, taking a seat at the head of the table opposite Maxwell.

Maxwell's jaw hardened at Holley's assumption of
authority, but he was smart enough to keep his mouth shut.
Then Agent Holley started to talk. He listed the charges
against my father, referencing the incontrovertible evidence
they had for the majority of them.

Some of it was small-time, most of it was firmly in
felony territory. When he was done, Maxwell sat back,
crossed his arms over his chest, and said easily, "You'll
never make all that stick."

"I don't have to make all of it stick, Mr. Sinclair. In
truth, any one of these charges would put you in jail for at
least ten to fifteen years. Maybe you can skate on some of
them, but do you really think you can shake them all?"

"I have evidence, too," my father replied, eyes narrowed
in something that almost looked like satisfaction, his head
cocked to the side as he studied Agent Holley. "You've been

287

running around like busy little bees building a case against the Tsepovs, but you have no idea what I've got tucked away. I could make your career."

Agent Holley didn't react in the slightest. Looking down at his pad, he wrote something without acknowledging Maxwell's statement, reminding me of a psychiatrist calmly taking notes while his patient ranted and raved.

My father probably expected Agent Holley to surge forward, salivating for more, and beg him to cooperate. He hid his disappointment when Holley shared a glance with the FBI counsel before he said, "No matter what you think you have, Mr. Sinclair, it's unavoidable that you'll spend some time in prison."

"I don't know about that," Maxwell cajoled, "you don't know what I have."

"No, but I know what I have. We don't need your evidence. It would be helpful, but it's not necessary. I'm here to give you a single opportunity to cooperate in exchange for a reduced sentence. If you can assist us in bringing in Andrei Tsepov we're willing to talk. Anything less than that and the deal is off the table."

"Listen, you boys can't expect me to hand you Tsepov. Information? That I can deal with."

"We don't want information, Mr. Sinclair. We want Andrei Tsepov."

"I'm not putting my ass on the line to draw Andrei out. You're crazy if you think it'll be that easy."

Agent Holley tapped the back of his pen on the desk to retract the point and closed his notebook. Unfolding from the chair to his full height, he loomed over the table.

"We're done here. I'm sorry we couldn't come to an agreement. I need you to stand and put your hands behind your head."

Pulling a shiny set of handcuffs from his suit pocket, Agent Holley looked from one side of the table to the other, meeting the eyes of the attorneys he'd brought with him. "Gentlemen?" All three rose in unison.

For the first time, Maxwell's façade of charm cracked. He didn't stand, but he did lean forward, bracing his elbows on the conference table.

"Hey, let's not be hasty. I don't want to go to jail. I want to do the right thing as much as anyone—"

Lie. Such a fucking lie, and we all knew it.

But Maxwell wasn't done. "You can't expect me to be the one to bring him in. I may not want to go to jail, but more than that, I don't want to die. Andrei is not like his uncle. He's a fuck-up, and a nut-case, and he's more dangerous than Sergey ever was. If Andrei thinks I've betrayed him, he'll shoot me without a second thought."

"Prison or cooperation, Mr. Sinclair. Those are your choices." Agent Holley laid it out and waited.

Maxwell sat back and dropped his hands in his lap, staring at the floor between his feet. Finally, he let out the breath he'd been holding. "I'll cooperate. You keep me alive and I'll cooperate."

With another shared glance, the FBI agents sat back down. Agent Holley re-opened his notebook and clicked his pen open.

"I suggest we hammer out a plan, Mr. Sinclair. Between your own people and ours, we'll do everything we can to keep you alive, assuming you follow our directions. Your only other option is prison. Am I clear?"

Maxwell nodded.

I'd kept my mouth shut through their initial negotiations, but as they began to work out a way for Maxwell to draw Tsepov out into the open, I chimed in along with Evers, Knox, and Axel.

I didn't want my father to go to jail. He was an asshole and a shitty dad, but he was still my father.

I definitely did not want him to die. Tsepov had taken too much from too many people. Petra's mother. Summer's father. Lily's husband. Every single woman and child whose life he'd destroyed.

Helping the FBI bring Tsepov in was a risk, but even my father had to admit it was worth it if it would keep him out of jail for the rest of his life.

If Maxwell was going to put himself in the line of fire, my brothers and I would do everything we could to make sure he came out of it in one piece. We could protect him from Tsepov. We couldn't protect him from himself.

Chapter Thirty-Six

ALICE

I WOKE TO THE SENSATION OF SOMETHING VITAL slipping through my fingers. Of something I desperately needed being dragged away as my hand closed on air.

In those first foggy seconds as sleep receded, I thought it was a dream.

A cry broke through the fog and I knew. The heat of Petra's small body beside me was gone, the sheets moving around me. Another plaintive cry and a vicious swear.

That was all it took.

I was painfully awake, panic spiking through my limbs, firing up my brain.

Petra.

My skirt tangling around my legs, I lunged to the end of the bed, my hand reaching to catch Petra's arm. Lacey stood there, a manic look in her eyes, her hands closed around Petra's leg, pulling with all her strength.

Lacey?

What was Lacey doing here? How had she even gotten in? Everything was on lockdown. Cooper's front door required a handprint, and there were cameras everywhere.

I lunged again, wrapping my arms around Petra's chest and kicking out at Lacey to make her let go. Her fingers around Petra's ankle were a steel manacle.

Hacking at her arm with the side of my hand, I tried to break her grip.

She was impervious, just drunk enough that she felt no pain but not so drunk that she was going to give up and go away. Dangerous.

Holding Petra to me with one arm, I closed my fingers around Lacey's wrist and twisted hard. Nothing, her fingers were still locked around Petra's small leg in a bruising grip.

Shifting my attack, I grabbed Lacey's thumb and yanked hard. With a shriek of pain, her hand fell off Petra and I whirled, shoving the little girl behind me.

Lacey dove around me. I shot out one arm to block her, sending her flying back. This wasn't the first time I'd been grateful for my training, but it was the first that I wished I'd had more.

"What are you doing here?" I asked, trying to stall her. "What do you want?"

Lacey's eyes fixed on me, the lines of red snaking through whites less bloodshot than usual. She was feral. Focused. She wanted my girl and she'd go through me to get her.

I shoved Petra further behind me, not taking my eyes off Lacey. I didn't want Petra within arm's reach as Lacey steadily advanced. We were trapped in Petra's bedroom, Lacey blocking our only exit.

I couldn't let her close enough to grab Petra again. She might be drunk, but she was oddly strong. Determined.

We needed help.

I'd fallen asleep in Petra's room not long after lunch. For a kid who'd tossed and turned all night, she slept like an angel when she napped. I only meant to stay until she was out, but she'd been so warm tucked into my side and I was so tired. I'd drifted off right beside her.

I don't know how long we slept. It didn't matter. No one would come to our rescue unless they knew we needed help. There was no phone here. No alarm panel.

We had to get out of Petra's room.

I backed slowly away from Lacey, moving deeper into the room to put space between us before changing my path to an arc, trying to get Lacey to clear the doorway. With each step to the side, Lacey mirrored me, gradually taking a position on the far side of the door. She was closer to us, almost within grabbing distance, but she no longer blocked our way out.

Lacey was strong and determined, but she was still a little drunk and not very smart. Not realizing she'd open up an avenue for our escape, Lacey advanced, hand outstretched.

"Just give me the girl," Lacey cajoled, her voice a terrifying singsong. "You said she's not yours. Why do you even care? I just need to get rid of her. Once I hand her over to Andrei, he'll make her disappear. Then Maxwell will forget her slut of a mother and everything can go back to normal."

"Do you really think he'll forgive you for that?" I took a slow step sideways, closer to the door, hoping Lacey would again mirror my movement. She did, coming closer, but setting herself deeper into the room. Almost...

"You don't want her anyway," Lacey crooned. "You and Cooper want to be alone, don't you? Why would you want a child? Sticky and messy. So demanding. Just give her to me. I'll make her go away. Then you and Cooper can be happy. Maxwell will come home. Everything will be the way it's supposed to be."

Lacey's utter lack of conscience was chilling. She couldn't figure out how to get rid of me, so she found a way to convince herself that Petra was the source of all of her problems.

Get rid of Petra and Maxwell would forget about the girl he claimed he'd loved? Forget about their child?

Considering Maxwell, I could kind of see Lacey's point. He probably would forget about Petra once she was out of sight. But to give her to Andrei, knowing what he did with women and children? Lacey was a monster.

No matter what, she wasn't going to touch Petra.

Swallowing the bile rising in my throat, I made a quick quarter turn and snatched up Petra, bundling her into my arms as I barreled through the open door and into the hall. Lacey lurched after me, hands clawing, nails digging into my arm. With a burst of speed, I tore through her grip and down the hall.

Cursing my short legs, I sprinted for the front door. Too far. It was too far. Lacey was gaining on me way too fast for an out-of-shape drunk woman twice my age.

I wasn't going to make it. Her fingers closed on the back of my dress, yanking so hard I rocked back on my heels, almost going down. With a lunge, I broke free and veered right at the end of the hall.

On the wall opposite the windows was a panic button discreetly placed beside the light switches. I slammed my hand on it the second I was close enough, the faint *click* of it activating filling me with relief.

I'd reached the panic button but sacrificed my escape route.

I bumped into the side of the couch as Lacey emerged from the hall. A triumphant smile spreading across her face, she came to a stop directly between us and the front door.

Lacey studied Petra and me as if we were bugs under a microscope, assessing her options. Sidling ever closer, she stopped again at the side of the couch, right next to the light switches. Lacey didn't seem to notice the panic button pushed flush with the wall.

No, her attention was on the table beneath the switches and the tall, black, iron lamp in the center.

Shit.

Two feet tall, with the circumference of a baseball bat, the lamp made for a hell of a weapon. Why hadn't I thought to grab it?

Lacey ripped the cord from the wall with one wide swing of her arm, brandishing the lamp above her head, a hungry gleam in her eyes.

She was fucking insane. I juggled Petra in my arms, raising her until my mouth was level with her ear. "Hide behind the couch. Do you understand? Nod if you understand. Hide behind the couch."

For an endless second, Petra remained still, no response to my whispered order.

Please, please sweetie. Please understand.

I could try to fight off Lacey, but not while holding Petra in my arms. The panic button would bring help, but every second passing was an eternity. Lacey could do a hell of a lot of damage with that lamp in the few minutes it would take to mobilize a rescue.

After an endless moment, Petra gave a slow nod, whispering back, "Hide."

I kissed her temple. "That's right, baby. Hide. Hide for me, okay?"

I set her on her feet. She took off like a shot, scrambling around the glass coffee table and behind the short side of the L-shaped couch. Pushed up against the wall of windows, the slanted back created a narrow tunnel. Far too small for an adult, it was the perfect hiding place for a wiggly three-year-old.

Even if Lacey took me down, she'd have a bitch of a time getting to Petra before help arrived. Lacey was strong, but the couch weighed a ton. The worst of my fear retreated now that Petra wasn't seconds away from being bashed in the head with two feet of iron.

Petra was safe, but me? I was in some trouble.

Lacey howled with rage as her quarry disappeared behind the bulk of the black leather couch.

"Why do you always get in my way?" she demanded with a petulant whine.

Advancing on me, she adjusted her grip so she held the narrow base of the lamp with two hands, cocking it back over her shoulder in a decent imitation of a batter's stance.

Fucking hell.

I dodged, staying between Lacey and the end of the couch where Petra had disappeared. The lamp grazed my arm as Lacey swung.

Too close.

Lacey swung the lamp again. I slid to the right, slamming my shin into the edge of the heavy glass coffee table. Fuck, that hurt. The lamp struck the side of my arm, and the pain in my leg was knocked right out of my head.

How the hell was a sixty-something-year-old alcoholic strong enough to swing that fucking lamp?

My left arm went numb from the blow.

I watched with horror as Lacey stepped forward and raised the lamp over her head, her thin arms shaking from the strain.

Lacey advanced, the lamp beginning its slow arc down to split open my skull. My right arm flew up over my head. My left hung useless by my side.

Fuck. Why did I have to be so goddamn short? My arm was no match for the iron length of the lamp.

Defense wasn't going to work.

Offense was all I had.

I dove straight at Lacey, ducking under the arc of the lamp, driving the top of my head into the center of her chest and taking her off her feet. We tumbled to the ground, rolling in a tangle of limbs, Lacey's hand still tightly gripping the lamp.

I didn't have the weight to pin her down. She rolled, pushing me off. Instead of trying to pin her, I gripped the lamp with both hands, trying to wrench it from her fingers. I only ended up dragging her to her feet as I gained mine.

My left arm screaming with pain now that the numbness had faded, we wrestled for control of the lamp, Lacey gaining ground with each step, driven by alcohol-fueled rage. I dug in my heels as my calves hit smooth, cool leather.

This was it. I was out of time. We were only inches away from where Petra hid. I had to neutralize Lacey now.

How long since I'd hit the panic button? It felt like an hour. It could have been less than a minute.

Not enough time.

Definitely not enough while Lacey still had that fucking lamp.

Closing both hands over the length of metal, I twisted hard, managing to loosen her hold. With another sharp tug, I got it free.

It was long and heavy, throwing me off balance as Lacey let go. Stumbling back, I tried to get a better hold on its length, to put space between us.

The couch behind me, there was no room to move. Lacey came at me in a dive, leading with her long, sharp fingernails.

Falling back into the couch, I swung out of desperate instinct. The lamp cracked her hard in the ribs, sending her flying to her left, her eyes wide with surprise, mouth open in a shocked *O*.

Chapter Thirty-Seven

ALICE

LACEY LANDED SMACK IN THE MIDDLE OF THE coffee table, crashing through it in an explosion of glass shards. I froze for a split second, my heart thundering in my chest, lungs tight, gasping for breath.

Lacey didn't move. Blood seeped through cuts on her arms, across her chest and face, striping her with jagged lines of red. Seconds passed, her blood flowing freely, faster with each heartbeat, dripping from her skin to stain the carpet in a pool of red.

Still, she didn't move.

I bolted to the other side of the couch, away from Lacey and the trap of the seating area. Dropping the lamp, I knelt by the corner of the couch where it met the wall, peering into the narrow, dark tunnel for Petra. "Petra? Come on baby, we gotta run. We gotta run now."

Petra squirmed through the tight space and popped out on the other side, straight into my arms. My left arm was working again, but it sagged at her weight. I had to get to the front door. I had to get Petra out of here before Lacey got up.

Just because she was down didn't mean she was out. I'd seen way too many horror movies to believe we were safe.

The door swung open as I reached for the handle. I screamed at the top of my lungs, all reason gone in a haze of terror.

Griffen's green eyes fell on Petra clutched in my arms, turning to hard, cold emerald when they focused on the floor behind me.

A shiver of fresh horror ran through me as I imagined Lacey, back on her feet, wielding the iron lamp with fresh rage. I turned to see a path of bloody footprints leading from the couch to where I stood at the door. My footprints. I must have stepped in the glass from the coffee table.

My feet didn't hurt. Nothing hurt. Not anymore. Not as long as Griffen was here and Petra was safe.

"Status?" Griffen asked, the emotion in his voice tightly leashed.

"Lacey. We woke up and Lacey was trying to take Petra, going to give her to Tsepov. She— I— She tried to hit me with the lamp, and I swung and... And I hit her, and she fell on the coffee table."

"Okay, Alice. Take a deep breath for me, okay? Why are you bleeding?"

I did as Griffen asked, trying to calm down. Why was I bleeding?

Oh, the glass. The glass.

My heart wouldn't slow, pounding so hard in my chest I couldn't breathe. I clutched Petra tighter.

"Glass. Coffee table. She broke the coffee table. I ran for Petra. Must have cut my feet."

"Are you hurt anywhere else?"

"No. Yes. My leg. My arm. I'm okay, but she's not moving, Griffen."

Griffen wrapped his arm around my shoulder, pulling Petra and me into his solid strength.

"I need you to hold it together for a few more minutes, okay? Cooper is on his way. He'll be here soon."

Cooper was on his way. That meant he wasn't in the building. Okay. I could hang on. Griffen let go and crossed the room, walking to the other side of the couch to check on Lacey. A moment later, I heard him speaking into his phone. I couldn't make out everything, but it was enough to figure out he was calling the paramedics.

I thought I should go over there and see. I couldn't make my feet move. I stood by the door, clutching a silent, shaking Petra, too terrified to do anything, afraid my next choice would make everything worse.

Eventually, Griffen came back. "I need to get you off your feet. Hold tight to Petra, okay?"

I couldn't hold any tighter than I already was. Good thing, because Griffen picked us both up and carried us to the kitchen. Setting me on the counter, he turned me so my feet were over the empty sink.

Smiling gently at Petra, he said, "Are you hungry, honey? Do you want to eat a cookie in your chair while I fix Alice's feet?"

Petra looked up at me, a question in her eyes. I curved my lips in what I hoped was a comforting smile. "A cookie would be nice, wouldn't it? I'll be right here. You'll be right next to me."

Petra turned serious eyes to Griffen and gave him a solemn nod. He wheeled her high chair beside the sink and got her strapped in, placing two big, round chocolate chip cookies on the tray in front of her.

Leaving us for a second, he unlocked the front door, snagging the first aid kit from the pantry on his way back. I didn't want to think about why Griffen knew where Cooper kept his first aid kit. That thought was almost as scary as the first aid kit itself.

An oversized tackle box, this was no collection of antiseptic spray and band-aids. I was pretty sure I saw needles, glass bottles, and a suture kit in there. Not going to ask.

Turning on the water, Griffen said, "One of the guys will let the paramedics in. I want them to take a look at your feet, but I think you're okay. Lift the right one up and let me see."

I did as he asked, only wincing a little as he shone a thin penlight at the bottom of my foot, pressing and probing. I was more worried about Lacey than my feet.

I had to ask. "Did I kill her?"

Griffen shook his head, his attention on my foot. A painfully long squeeze of the ball of my foot and he held up a sliver of glass, pink with blood. It clicked as he dropped it in the sink and went back for more.

"Don't worry about Lacey."

"Griffen. Tell me." *Don't worry about Lacey? Was he nuts? What if I'd killed her?*

He shook his head again. "She's bleeding more than she should be—probably the alcohol. Paramedics will be here soon. Did she try to brain you with that lamp on the floor?"

"Yeah. Got me in the arm but—" I didn't want to replay how I'd swung the lamp at her, the way she'd flown off her feet and crashed through the glass. I'd be seeing that in my nightmares for the rest of my life.

"It'll be okay, Alice." Griffen sounded distracted as he probed my other foot for more glass. "I don't think you

302

need any stitches. I'm going to wait to bandage these until the paramedics take a look, just in case."

He poked at my shin. "That looks like it hurts."

I looked down to see a long gash a few inches below my knee, my shin stained red with blood. Damn. I knew it hurt when I'd slammed into the coffee table, but I hadn't realized— I winced as Griffen cleaned it, the antiseptic burn almost as bad as the injury itself.

The front door swung open with no warning and chaos streamed in. Two men holding a gurney. A few of our guys who'd been working downstairs. Cooper, followed by Evers, Knox, and Axel.

Cooper met my eyes in a brief, flat glance I couldn't read. Didn't want to read.

He was angry with me.

Of course, he was. Why wouldn't he be?

His mother was bleeding all over the floor, unconscious, because I'd almost killed her. Might still have killed her. Griffen said not to worry about her, but he hadn't said she'd be okay. Maybe she'd bled out. Maybe—

I wanted to lift my chin and pretend I didn't care. I couldn't pull it off. I couldn't pull anything off. Everything hurt. Lacey had tried to kill us. I might have killed her. There'd been so much blood. Everywhere.

I couldn't pretend it was okay. I couldn't pretend anything.

To my utter shame, a tear rolled down my cheek as I watched Cooper and his brothers cross the room to where Lacey lay splayed in the middle of the shattered glass table.

Another tear streaked down my cheek. Then another. Hot and salty, they were a tangible sign of my guilt, of how badly I'd messed up. What if I'd killed Cooper's mother?

I'd hated Lacey at times over the years, pitied her at others, but never in a million years would I have guessed that I might kill her.

An arm wrapped around my shoulder. Griffen, drawing my tear-streaked face into his chest. I sobbed, shame and sorrow pulling me under. I couldn't look at anyone. I couldn't look at Cooper. The one time I managed to lift my head he was staring at us, his face so completely blank I might have been a stranger.

It was over. Everything between us was over. He'd never be able to forget this. He'd never be able to love the woman who'd murdered his mother.

Griffen raised a hand to get the attention of a paramedic. The next thing I knew, someone was moving my left arm, poking at my feet, studying them using the pen light, then pronouncing me ready for bandages.

I sat there like a doll, still and silent, while Griffen applied antibiotic goo and wrapped them up. I watched the scene in the apartment with hollow detachment as if it were a television show, blank-faced as the paramedics loaded Lacey on a stretcher and rolled her out, followed by Evers and Axel. My breath shallow, my head felt like a balloon floating on a long string, high above everything happening around me.

Knox and Cooper came into the kitchen, silent as ghosts. Someone said something that ended in "...dilated. Lay down ...back soon." I didn't catch most of the words. The world was whirring by me, my ears buzzing with static. I was freezing cold, heart pounding, sounds coming from a distance as if I sat alone at the end of a long tunnel.

Cooper was saying something, but I couldn't hear. His hand came up, reaching for my face. That was all I saw as my vision went grey at the edges. Everything wavered as if I was watching through heat waves coming off pavement.

I was falling, pitching forward into nothing as the world went black.

I opened my eyes to see the ceiling of Cooper's bedroom, his tall, navy-blue headboard rising above me.

How did I get in here?

"You fainted," said a familiar, amused voice.

Had I said that out loud? I never fainted. Ever.

"Yep, you said it out loud. And you definitely fainted. The paramedic said it was an Acute Stress Response."

"No." I struggled to sit up only to find myself pinned to the bed by Petra and bunny. She was curled into my side, her head on my stomach, eyes closed, a smear of chocolate on her chin.

Giving up, I lay back, rolling my head to meet Griffen's laughing green gaze. "I did not faint."

"You totally did. I took a picture and everything."

I swatted his arm with my free hand. "Asshole."

"I'm kidding about the picture. I wouldn't do that to you. The paramedic said you'd be fine, just the stress and the adrenaline crash catching up to you. Don't worry about it. If anyone had a right to faint, it's you."

"Lacey?"

"Cooper and the guys are still with her. She's alive. Probably already berating the hospital staff."

I didn't know what to say to that. I hadn't killed Cooper's mother. That was good. I'd killed once protecting a child. I didn't want to make it twice.

How could I explain what had happened to Cooper? What if he didn't believe me?

I couldn't forget his face, so flat and cold. She'd been about to kill me. Hadn't she? Had I been wrong?

Interrupting my thoughts, Griffen said, "We have another problem."

"I don't want any more problems. I'm tapped out."

"Well, get back on your feet, champ, because I need you on full alert. While Lacey was up here trying to bash your head in and kidnap your girl, Maxwell disappeared."

Chapter Thirty-Eight

COOPER

I OPENED MY FRONT DOOR TO DARKNESS, THE only source of light a single bulb over the breakfast counter, illuminating Griffen. He sat there alone, drinking from one of my oversize mugs, scrolling through something on his phone.

Without looking up he asked, "Everything okay?"

"Not even close. Alice and Petra?"

"Asleep. They're fine."

I swung through the kitchen to get myself a beer from the fridge. "Want one?"

"Nah. Doesn't go with half a pot of coffee," Griffen said, saluting me with his mug.

"I appreciate you staying with Alice. And getting here so fast."

He waved off my thanks. "Did you figure out how Lacey got in? Were the cameras on?"

I twisted open my beer, delaying the moment I had to admit the truth. They'd played me. Both of them. Leaning against the kitchen island, I drank from my beer before I answered.

"Maxwell had a back door programmed into the system way back when. It's a good thing he didn't know about the cameras I put in up here or he might have turned them off. He let Lacey in—" After what she'd done to Alice, I couldn't bring myself to refer to her as my mother. "—after she gave him a phone. While she headed up here, he deactivated the cameras on the back entrance and took off."

"Shit." Griffen took a long sip of coffee. "Lucas pissed?"

"I hope for Agent Holley's sake he finds Maxwell first because Lucas is ready to strangle him. He does not like the idea that there are holes in his system."

"Internal security was in place long before he got here," Griffen pointed out.

"He doesn't care. Thinks he should have caught it. He's going through every line of code until he finds it."

Griffen nodded, unsurprised. "I made Alice take one of those pain pills from when she had that bump on the head. She wanted to wait up for you, but she was hurting and freaked out. Thinks you hate her for killing Lacey."

I froze with the beer bottle halfway to my mouth. *Alice thinks I hate her?*

I'd reviewed the security footage, watching over and over as Lacey raised the lamp over her head ready to crack open Alice's skull.

She'd tried to kill Alice. How could I make up for that? There were no words I could say, no recompense big enough to fix this.

Alice was supposed to be safe with me.

Instead, I'd practically served her up to be murdered by my own family.

Me hate Alice? I couldn't imagine how *Alice* didn't hate

me. At the very least she had to be having serious second thoughts about staying with me. First, I'd put her in the middle of an explosion, then decided we should take on a toddler, and if that weren't enough, I'd let Lacey try to kill her.

All these years wanting Alice, and now it seemed like all I could do was fuck up the whole thing.

I set the bottle of beer down on the counter. I had to talk to her, to tell her how wrong she was. I could never hate Alice. Not in this lifetime or any other.

I started out of the kitchen when Griffen said something that halted me in my tracks.

"You didn't call."

I turned to see his eyes narrowed in something that looked like accusation.

"What?"

"You didn't call. She sat here all afternoon and half the night brooding, afraid you were going to come back and end things, kick her out, and you never even called."

"I— We— We were with Lacey, and then trying to find Maxwell—"

And I was hiding out because I couldn't face Alice. Wasn't ready for her to walk away.

"I've never known you to hide from your problems, Cooper." His eyes steady on mine, Griffen took a slow sip of coffee.

I wanted to deck him. I picked up my beer instead. He was right. I was being a coward. I should have pushed Griffen out of the way when Alice had been crying on his shoulder, should have let my brothers follow Lacey to the hospital.

I could have argued my case, told Griffen it was touch and go there for a while with Lacey, the high levels of alcohol in her blood causing problems with bleeding, the doctors worried about blood on her brain.

I could have told him that Alice wouldn't be safe until we caught Maxwell and used him to get Tsepov off the street. All of that was true. True, but still excuses.

I'd been jealous at the way Alice had cried in Griffen's arms. Guilty and heartbroken that I'd let Lacey hurt her.

I should have stayed with her. Instead, I'd done what I did best. I focused on solving the problems right in front of me. Lacey. Maxwell. And the disaster my parents had caused between them.

Griffen was right. I should have called. I should have been here, should have let my brothers deal with the rest of it.

"I love her," I said.

"I'm not the one you need to tell."

"No shit. But she's doped up on pain meds and sleeping. You want me to wake her up?" If I sounded surly it's because I felt surly. Surly and frustrated and sick with love for Alice.

"No. Let them both sleep. It's been a hell of a day."

"Thanks for staying with her and Petra. I was an ass for being gone all day, but I wouldn't have been able to focus for shit if you hadn't been here with them."

"Anything for Alice, man. You know that."

I gave a wry laugh that was a touch too raw, remembering the way he'd held Alice as she'd sobbed. "What is it with you and Alice? Do I need to kick your ass? Because I'm not giving her up. Not for you, not for anyone."

Griffen was one of my best friends, one of the few people I trusted completely. He was as close as a brother, but I'd level him if he thought he was going to go after Alice.

"Fuck, no, Coop. Jesus. You're like a brother," he said, echoing my own thoughts. "I don't poach."

His eyes went dark as he said the last. Griffen would never go after another man's woman. He'd learned about betrayal the hard way.

"I know. So, what then? You've always been a little protective. Axel bitched about you when he was trying to get Emma back, but with Alice, you're—different."

A grin spread across Griffen's face. "Axel deserved it. He was an ass and Emma was in a tight spot. I did them a favor. She needed to know she had a way out. She needed to *choose* Axel, not end up backed into a corner because he was a dick and a dumbass."

"Agreed. But that doesn't answer my question."

Griffen stared into his coffee mug for a long moment before turning his eyes on me and saying quietly, "She reminds me of someone, okay? Someone I haven't seen in a long time."

An uneasy feeling spiraled through me. "Your ex-fiancée?"

Griffen's face twisted into a bitter smirk. "You mean my sister-in-law? That viper? Fuck, no. She's nothing like Alice."

His eyes drifted to the mug again. I waited, wishing I hadn't brought up the fiancée who'd dropped him for his brother the day the ink was dry on yet another new copy of his father's will, this one transferring a fortune from Griffen's future to his brother's.

I only knew about the ex-fiancée courtesy of a bottle of tequila nearly ten years before. Griffen never talked about her. Or his brother. About any of the Sawyers. He'd walked away and never looked back. I couldn't say I blamed him. It sounded like the ex-fiancée wasn't the only viper in that nest.

The corner of his mouth quirked in a wry smile and he gave a single shake of his head before he said, "Not

311

someone I was with. Not a girlfriend. A friend. One of my best friends. Until she wasn't."

"What was her name?" I asked, ready for him to shut me down.

"Hope. Her name was Hope." He shook his head as if trying to shake off a clinging memory. "Hope is nothing like Alice. She doesn't have her spunk, for one. But the spine of steel? That determination? Yeah. Hope is quiet, unlike Alice. But Hope has a quirky sense of style. Not the same as Alice's, but it still reminds me of her. The way she'd always dress in her boring school uniform, but there'd be something—ladybug earrings or socks with melting clocks on them. Something that was quirky and offbeat and so exactly her.

"She was taller than Alice—I mean, everyone is taller than Alice—but slender. She looked so breakable I used to worry for her, but she was like a reed. She'd bend, but she never broke." He trailed off, his tone wistful, eyes staring at nothing.

"You never dated her?" I had a number of platonic female friends, but I don't think I've ever described one the way Griffen described his Hope.

His eyes came back to mine, dark with remembered pain. "No. I was too caught up with the Viper back then, and she was too young. Never occurred to me, to be honest. And then she fucking stabbed me in the back along with the rest of them, so I guess it's a good thing I didn't."

I didn't know what to say to that.

"Anyway, Alice is a friend. I swear, that's it. I've never once thought of her as anything more. But I'll look out for her. Even if that means I have to go head-to-head with you."

"Fair enough."

"Anyway, I'm bunking on the cot in the holding room tonight. With Maxwell out there and Lacey saying she was going to give Petra to Andrei—"

"What?" What the fuck was wrong with her? Give a child to Tsepov? I buried the instinctive swell of rage. There was no point. Not now. Petra was safe and she was going to stay that way.

Griffen set down his coffee cup and gave me a curious look. "You didn't know? I thought you saw the feeds?"

"I didn't have them wired for sound, just video. I was only trying to keep an eye on Alice when she was injured. You know how she is, she won't sit still."

"Shit. I didn't realize. Lacey didn't say anything?"

"She refused to speak to any of us." She'd laid in that bed, covered in bandages, her head turned resolutely to the wall, lips pressed firmly together, not even acknowledging her sons. "What do you mean she was going to give Petra to Tsepov? What the fuck?"

"She told Alice that if she got rid of Petra, everything could go back to normal. Your mother is deluded, man. She needs treatment."

Good luck with that.

I couldn't bring myself to say it out loud. I'd long ago given up on the idea of my mother seeking help for her drinking. Wasn't going to happen.

I settled for, "I have extra security on the building. Teams out looking for Maxwell. Holley is pissed, but he has guys on it. We should be okay for the night."

"Probably. I'm staying anyway."

Griffen pushed himself off the stool at the breakfast counter, unwinding his body slowly as if weighed down by memories he wished had stayed buried. I shouldn't have brought up the fiancée.

I'd been an asshole all day. To my best friend. To the woman I love. I'd make it up to them tomorrow.

Tomorrow had to be a better day than today, didn't it?

I was an asshole and an idiot.

It turned out tomorrow would be even worse.

Chapter Thirty-Nine

COOPER

*B*ANG.

Bang.

A fist pounding on my door.

I woke from a dead sleep to wonder if I'd been catapulted back in time.

Alice was in my arms just like she'd been two nights ago.

I blinked away sleep.

This time Alice wasn't naked. She slept beside me wearing one of my old Army T-shirts and a pair of cut-off sweats. I wore a loose pair of athletic shorts. And beside us, curled into Alice's side, was a peacefully sleeping toddler.

Petra.

I'd locked the door behind Griffen only hours before. Paranoid after what happened with Lacey, I'd triple-checked my security before coming to bed, unable to bring myself to wake Alice. Griffen said she thought I was angry with her.

She had to be crazy. If anyone had the right to be pissed, it was Alice, not me. For fuck's sake, my own mother had almost killed her. The fact that she'd left my mother cling-ing to life was irrelevant.

Maybe it shouldn't have been, but Alice had been the only thing between a crazed Lacey and the little girl who slept beside us. What else was she supposed to do? Step aside because Lacey was my mother?

Fuck, no. Alice did what she had to do. I would never be anything but proud of her for that.

Bang.

Bang.

Bang.

Fuck. I'd been hoping that was a dream. But no. There it came again.

My gut knotted. There was no good reason anyone would be banging on my door at this hour.

Lacey was in the hospital, under surveillance and attached to tubes and wires. She wasn't going anywhere.

Griffen or another of my people would have called rather than waste time coming to my door.

My father and Tsepov were still on the loose.

I'd secured the building as well as I could, but Lacey's attack on Alice and Petra proved that Maxwell had built back doors into my security. I had no idea how many.

Rolling to my feet, I pulled on clothes, grabbed my weapon, and strode from the room, closing the bedroom door behind me. I pulled up the hall surveillance on my phone as I went.

What I saw made my blood run cold.

Fucking hell. Just when everything had turned to shit, only Maxwell could make it worse. He had a gift. I wished I could send it back.

I opened the door to my apartment, stepping to the side as Maxwell fell at my feet. Blood covered the front of his torso centering around a slice in his shirt just below his ribs. Stabbed. Fuck.

"Get in here."

I reached down, hooking my hands under his armpits, and dragged him inside. I should have been scared at the sight of my father bleeding from a stab wound. Maybe I would have been a week ago. Not now.

Whatever he'd done to earn that wound, he was no innocent victim. I already knew that.

I dragged him far enough to clear the door, slammed it shut and locked it, setting the security in the hallway to alert at any movement. I hadn't bothered before since my guys were doing regular sweeps, but if Maxwell had made it up here I wasn't taking any more chances.

My father dragged himself to a sitting position, leaning against the wall by the front door.

"Talk," I ordered. "What the fuck did you do?"

Maxwell's eyes slid away from mine, then back, defiant and apologetic at the same time. I was pissed as hell, but I couldn't deny my stomach twisted as he drew in a shallow breath and the stain of red over his stomach darkened.

Fuck. I needed to call the paramedics. I had a bad feeling that wasn't an option. I resisted the urge to order him to talk again and waited.

Sucking in another shallow breath, he managed, "Went after Tsepov. Needed to take him down before Holley—"

Maxwell shook his head, cutting off the line of explanation. I didn't need to hear it.

He didn't want to go to jail, and he couldn't leave Tsepov out there, so he thought he'd take care of the problem and then disappear.

A part of me couldn't even blame him. I wouldn't want to go to jail either. Who did? I'd give him the tiniest bit of credit for not bailing on us again knowing that Tsepov would come for his family if he took off.

Forcing himself to sit up further, he took another breath and got to his feet slowly, laboriously.

"I need a weapon. He's coming. I set up a meet, trying to lure him out in the open. Worked too well." Maxwell gave a wry laugh that ended in a cough. "He has more men in town than I thought. Sent them ahead. Flanked me."

Maxwell was on his feet, wavering but steadier. He walked to the kitchen and got himself a glass, filled it with water from the sink and drank.

"Get some gauze or tear up a sheet or something. Gotta bandage this. Can't be bleeding all over the place."

Glad Alice and Petra hadn't woken up when Maxwell banged on the door, I grabbed the first-aid kit from the counter where Griffen had left it after tending to Alice's cut feet only hours ago. It felt like a lifetime.

"Pull up your shirt."

Maxwell did, and I got a first-hand view of the neat slit of the stab wound right into his gut. Fuck. No question he had internal bleeding. He was running on adrenaline, but I had to get him to a hospital soon or he'd be fucked.

Pulling out packages of gauze, I held them to the knife wound with one hand and opened up the roll of bandages with the other. Maxwell stood still, breath held as I wrapped him up tightly enough to keep him mobile just a little longer.

"What happened to the guy who did this?" I asked, not wanting the answer.

"I took down both of Andrei's men. But there are more. He's coming."

"What the fuck does that mean? *He's coming.* As in coming inside the building?"

Another guilty slide of his eyes away from mine. Fucking hell.

"You want to explain how he's going to get inside, Dad?"

Like a sullen teenager, he muttered, "I had a fucking plan."

"Yeah, I can see that. Get Mom liquored up and sic her on Alice and Petra, then bring the mob boss who wants to murder you into my home. Great plan."

Maxwell wasn't entirely immune to sarcasm. "You boys had me locked down so tight it was the best I could do."

"No, Dad, the best you could do was work with the fucking FBI to put fucking Andrei Tsepov in jail and not egg Mom on until she tried to murder Alice and sell your goddamn daughter to a trafficker. I don't even know who you are anymore. The dad who raised me wasn't a great guy, but he wasn't evil."

"I knew Alice wouldn't let her take Petra," Maxwell said, sending an affronted look my way. Where he got the gall to look affronted, I couldn't imagine.

"You're right, there was no way Alice was going to let Mom take Petra." I tied off the bandage. "She almost died trying to save Petra from Mom, and now Mom is in the hospital. What the fuck were you thinking?"

I didn't wait for him to answer.

"Stay here. I'll be back with supplies."

"A weapon?" he asked hopefully.

I thought about taking a swing at him, then decided I might need him, assuming he planned to aim that weapon at Tsepov and not me. Given the way the rest of this bullshit had gone, I wasn't sure I could count on anything.

I left him in the kitchen and strode down the hall. First order of business—secure Alice and Petra. I didn't have a safe room in my apartment. Not exactly. Between the holding room on the company floor and the safe house apartment that Lacey and Maxwell had been using, it seemed like overkill.

The closest I came was a spare room where I stored equipment and files too sensitive to keep in the main office space. While it wasn't a full-fledged safe room, it did have reinforced walls and a steel door that would be almost impossible to break down. It was the best I could do on short notice.

While Maxwell was out of earshot, I made two calls. Agent Holley was coldly furious but ready to move on Tsepov. Hanging up on him, I called Griffen and filled him in, glad he'd decided to stay on-site for the night. He could coordinate the team I had on watch while I took care of Alice and Petra.

Alice and Petra were still asleep when I went back into the bedroom. I sat on the side of the bed and ran one finger across Alice's cheek, tucking a strand of her dark hair behind her ear.

I wished I'd woken her earlier. Wished I'd told her I loved her. That I believed in her. That she'd done the right thing. That, in my eyes, she'd always do the right thing.

I wished I'd woken her so I could have told her how sorry I was about Lacey. About Maxwell.

Sorry that I'd waited so fucking long to claim her.

I wished a lot of things, and I didn't have time for any of them.

Chapter Forty

COOPER

ALICE'S EYES FLUTTERED OPEN, DAZED with sleep, a slow smile spreading across her face. She was reaching for me when her brain clicked online and shutters fell over her eyes. Her hand dropped to her side as her mouth drew tight.

I cupped her cheek in my palm, turning her face up to mine. "We have trouble. Maxwell is here. He's been stabbed. Tsepov may already be in the building. I don't have time to get you and Petra somewhere safe. I need you to come with me."

Alice didn't ask questions. She pushed the covers off and rolled to her side, ready to scoop up Petra.

"I've got her. Let's go."

Alice followed me out of the bedroom and down the hall. When I opened the door to my makeshift safe room, she said, "I was wondering what was in here."

"Nothing interesting, but the door would keep out a tank. I need you to stay in here until I get this sorted out."

Her hand closed over my wrist. "Stay with us. Don't go back out there."

"I have to, Alice. He's my dad."

She slumped for a heartbeat of time, her head pressed to my chest as she shuddered against me. Before I could comfort her, Alice pulled herself together, spine straightening, lungs expanding as she drew in a fortifying breath.

"Okay. I know. I can help. I can—"

"I know you can." I ushered Alice into the room. There wasn't any furniture, just stacked boxes and two gun safes bracketed between tall metal shelves.

"I don't have time to argue, baby. Sit down and let me give you Petra."

Alice sat, leaning against the wall facing the door. I knelt, transferring the still-sleeping toddler from my arms to hers.

Alice watched me with wary eyes. For just a second, I was tempted to stay there with her, to lock the door and let my father deal with Andrei Tsepov on his own.

To forget the world and tell Alice everything in my heart.

There were so many reasons I couldn't do that. I couldn't leave Tsepov to my father. It wasn't just that I didn't trust Maxwell to do the job right. Tsepov would kill him and then come after us.

Time with Alice was all I wanted.

In that moment, it was the one thing I didn't have.

Turning my back on her was like cutting out a part of my soul, but I had to get back to Maxwell. I ransacked the gun safe and the shelves. A bulletproof vest for me. Another for Maxwell. Extra clips for my Walther. A weapon for my father.

I strapped a knife to my ankle, a backup weapon on the other side.

Taking the time to drop a brief kiss on Alice's mouth, I said, "Don't come out for anyone. Not until I get back."

Stopping in the doorway for a second I didn't have, I couldn't resist adding, "I love you, Alice. Stay safe."

The surprised flare of her eyes struck me right in the heart. I held it close as I locked the door, securing Alice and Petra behind four inches of steel.

When I returned, Maxwell was leaning against the island in the kitchen, feet steady, his face ashen. He was bleeding internally from the stab wound, but there wasn't much I could do about that until he got to the hospital.

"How close is he? Where did they get you?"

"Two blocks east. I don't know how far behind them Andrei was, but I'm guessing not far."

My phone rang, and I stabbed a finger at the screen, putting Griffen on speakerphone. "Status."

"Incoming. All over the fucking place." His words were breathless, loud and then distant as if he was running while holding the phone. "Everyone stationed on the perimeter is down. I have two of Tsepov's men on the cameras in the garage, headed for the elevator. Another in the stairwell. The two who got in from the street entrance are on their way up to you. I can't tell what they're carrying, but it's big, Cooper. Stay away from the fucking door. If it weren't for Alice and Petra I'd tell you to leave Maxwell and get the fuck out. I'm on my way."

Griffen disconnected. I tossed the bulletproof vest at Maxwell. It wasn't great protection, but it was better than nothing. He managed to get it on, wincing as the movement pulled at the open wound in his stomach.

The FBI was on the way. Tsepov's men incoming. Nothing to do but wait until someone made a move.

323

We didn't have to wait long. Griffen had been right, Tsepov's men were carrying something big. A fucking acetylene torch. They'd used the same thing at Knox's house. Andrei's boys liked their toys. I could only hope this crew was as badly trained as the ones who'd gone after Knox in Maine.

At the spark of the torch, Maxwell and I ducked, using the kitchen island as a shield. I couldn't let them get past the kitchen. If they did, it would take time for that torch to breach my safe room door, but eventually, it would. If they took us down they'd have all the time they needed to get to Alice and Petra.

The torch cut through the steel of my door in minutes. It slammed open, Tsepov's goons pouring through in a hail of gunfire, every bullet aimed straight ahead. They never looked to the side, never saw us crouching in the kitchen.

I raised my weapon. One shot from me, one from my father, and the first two dropped.

Too bad the guys after them weren't as stupid.

The clink of metal and a dark cylinder rolled across the floor. I dove for the back of the kitchen, expecting a flash-bang grenade. No sound, no light, but smoke filled the room, leaving me blind.

My father hadn't been able to dodge with that knife wound in his gut. I thought I heard the rasp of his breathing beneath the pound of feet filling the room. I hoped I heard it.

The sound of footsteps died away. So much for stopping them here. I had no idea how many were inside or where that fucking torch was.

At the end of the island, through the haze of smoke, my father struggled to his feet, weapon in his right hand, held loosely behind his back.

A figure emerged through the smoke, tall and slender, elegant in a dark suit. Andrei Tsepov. He stood in the foyer flanked by two goons carrying AR-15's, surveying the smoky chaos with the arrogance of a king.

Fuck. I didn't want to see those AR-15's

The lightweight semi-automatic rifles were overkill in these close quarters. Overkill and deadly as hell. Our protective equipment was the best available outside of the military, but it couldn't stop a bullet from an AR-15.

If I did nothing else, I had to take down those two men.

Andrei stopped less than ten feet from my father. In his cultured, lightly accented voice, he said, "Maxwell. You think to betray me to your FBI? I never would've guessed you'd be so foolish."

Dismissing Maxwell with a lift of his chin, he called to the men I couldn't see through the smoke, "Search the place. Bring anyone you find to me."

At least he hadn't told them to shoot on sight. I'd take whatever favors I could get.

Moving in a low crouch, weapon raised, I made my way around the kitchen island, staying out of sight. The island wouldn't protect me from the AR-15's any more than my vest would, but right now all eyes were on Maxwell. The further I got from him, the better. I couldn't fire if I was caught in the crossfire.

"I fucked up," my father said, bracing his free hand on the counter.

"You certainly did," Andrei agreed. "Too many times, Maxwell. You stole from me. First the girl, then my money."

"I can make it right, Andrei. Take your men and leave. I'll come with you. Give you back the money. Give you more. As soon as we're out of here. But we have to go. Now."

What the fuck was Maxwell talking about? The FBI was on the way. We had to stall, not get rid of Tsepov and his men. Maxwell didn't want to go to jail, but at this point, Agent Holley was his best bet.

I had no doubt that if he gave Andrei the money Maxwell wouldn't live a moment longer than it took to transfer the funds.

In the end, it didn't matter. Andrei Tsepov wasn't buying my father's promises.

"You think I'm that stupid, Maxwell? If you were going to give me back my money, you would have offered it when I killed the whore."

"She wasn't a whore," Maxwell ground out.

Andrei's flat, cold eyes betrayed nothing as he raised his hand and fired a single bullet. Maxwell staggered, the arm he'd braced on the counter folding as he tilted sideways.

My finger itched to squeeze the trigger of my own weapon. It took everything I had to hold my fire. I couldn't take out both of the men with AR-15's, and my first shot would give away my position. My father might let anger drive him into a deadly mistake.

I wouldn't do the same. I couldn't. Alice and Petra were depending on me.

"I assume you mean Mila," Andrei continued conversationally as if he hadn't just put a bullet in Maxwell's arm. "She was a whore. Born and bred. First, she was mine. Then she was yours. Even in your hands, she remained my property. Which, as we both know, makes your pretty little girl my property as well."

I clamped my teeth together to hold back the growl. Petra. He wasn't just here for Maxwell, the sick fucker was here for Petra. She wasn't fucking property. She was a child. A human being.

Petra was my baby sister. Mine to protect. To keep safe. I'd die before I let Andrei Tsepov lay eyes on her, much less take her away from us.

Never in my life had I genuinely wanted to end a life. Not until that moment. Andrei Tsepov deserved death. I wanted to be the one to deliver it.

It didn't matter. Petra and Alice's safety came first. There was still a chance to get out of this, but it had to be done right. One mistake and we'd all be dead.

Chapter Forty-One

COOPER

*Y*OU'RE TOO LATE," MAXWELL BLUFFED. "Cooper took the girl away after Lacey tried to kidnap her. They're long gone by now."

Another negligent flick of Tsepov's wrist. Another shot to the arm that sent my father staggering before he slumped over the kitchen island.

"Lie. It's a shame Lacey couldn't get me the girl." A lazy shrug. "It was worth a try. Your wife could be very accommodating when she wanted to be. If she wasn't an addict I might have had more use for her."

Maxwell's breathing was ragged, but he kept his mouth shut.

"My men have been watching the building, Maxwell. I know the girl is here. They'll find her and her pretty little keeper. Then we leave. All of us. You'll give me the money and I'll keep the woman and child as interest."

"Not going to happen," my father hissed.

"Or," Andrei said, raising his weapon slowly and aiming it at Maxwell's chest, "I kill you now, take the woman and child, and kill every one of your sons, their women, and your wife. Choose."

I couldn't let it register that he was talking about taking Alice. Couldn't allow the threat to sink in. I had one job. To stop these men. If I could do that, I could save all of us.

I drew in a slow, deep breath. Alice. I wouldn't lose Alice.

I'd wait for my opening, and I'd take it.

I'd get us out of this.

Get us out or die trying.

Maxwell forced himself mostly upright, the hand holding his weapon still tucked behind his back. He wasn't fooling anyone, but at least he was still armed.

Don't move, I silently warned. *Don't shoot. Hold the fucking line.*

Maybe he heard my furious thoughts. Maybe it took everything he had to stay upright. Whatever the reason was, Maxwell didn't move.

Tsepov waggled his gun at Maxwell. "Choose, or I choose for you."

Maxwell cleared his throat. I shifted position, sliding an inch to the side, losing my cover just enough to put all three figures in the foyer in my sights.

A flash of movement at the door caught my eye.

Griffen. Coming in low, weapon raised, he took in the scene in an instant. His eyes met mine.

After over a decade of friendship and way too many hours together in the field, I didn't have to say a word.

I drew a bead on the goon to Tsepov's right. Griffen took the goon on the left. As one, we fired.

The goons dropped like stones and the world erupted in gunfire.

Tsepov pulled the trigger of his weapon over and over.

Shots from my left—Maxwell returning fire.

Pounding feet came down the hall, and a flood of goons erupted into the open space between the kitchen and foyer shooting at anything that moved.

A thud on the other side of the kitchen. A hammer blow to my chest. I fell back, sucking in a choked breath.

Relief as I realized my lungs were working. A regular bullet then. If one of the AR's had hit me, I'd be drowning in my own blood by now.

I rolled, coming to my knees and looking through the kitchen and the foyer. Griffen was the only one on his feet, leaning against the wall on the far side of the foyer, a blossom of red spreading across his right shoulder.

Fuck. *Fuck.* The blood was spreading too fast. In the movies, a shoulder wound is no big deal. That's bullshit. The shoulder has more than one major artery. A bullet in the wrong place can cause bleed-out in minutes.

Griffen sagged, sliding down the wall, a tide of blood staining his arm.

Fucking fuck.

I had to get an ambulance or he was going to die. My father was probably already gone.

More footsteps coming from the back of my apartment. On my feet, I raised my weapon, ready to make my last stand. I thought of Alice, prayed she was still locked in the safe room, that she'd be okay until the FBI could get her out.

I had time for the fleeting wish that I hadn't waited so long to make her mine.

I love you, I thought, holding that love close as I aimed my Walther at the end of the hall and prepared to pull the trigger.

331

I fired once. Twice. Tsepov's goons dropped, one after the other. Pounding footsteps from the hall outside. My heart sank. I was trapped in between, couldn't take them all.

This was it. I was done.

Backing up, I retreated into the kitchen until I could see both the shattered front door and the rest of Tsepov's men coming down the hall. My arms were steady as I kept my weapon raised, but my heart was hollow. It wasn't supposed to end this way.

The remains of the front door flew back. I swung my weapon to the foyer, finger tightening on the trigger. What I saw froze me in place. At least a dozen bodies flooded through the door, fanning out the cover the room. More feet thundered in the hall.

"Drop your weapon and get your hands up."

I'd never been so glad to see those familiar navy-blue vests, those bright yellow letters emblazoned on the front. *FBI.*

About fucking time. Dizzy with relief, I lay my weapon on the floor in front of my feet and raised my hands over my head.

Agent Holley entered just behind his initial team. With a disgusted look at me, he said, "How many?"

"I don't know. They tossed a smoke bomb. I couldn't count how many got past me before the air cleared."

Agent Holley gave a brusque nod and sent half of his men to clear the rest of the apartment. Surveying the bodies on the floor, he shook his head. "Paramedics are downstairs."

"You going to shoot me if I move? I need to check Griffen. I think that shot to his shoulder nicked an artery."

Crouching beside Tsepov, Holley felt for a pulse, shaking his head again. "Fine. Go."

I had a fleeting thought for my father. A better son would have checked him first. I wasn't that man. My father had brought this on himself. Between the stab wound and the shots to his arm, he was beyond my help. Griffen was here out of loyalty. Out of friendship. I wouldn't pay that back with death.

I eased him down to lay flat on the floor. There was too much blood. It had soaked into his shirt, his vest, so much that I couldn't tell if he was bleeding heavily or bleeding out. I yanked off my vest and pulled my shirt over my head, folding it into a pad and pressing it into his shoulder. His eyes opened, clouded with pain and shock.

"Got hit, Coop."

"Yeah, you did. Paramedics are coming up. Hold on for me."

"You okay? Alice?"

"I'm fine. I'll get Alice as soon as the paramedics get here."

His breath coming fast, skin pale, he struggled to speak.

"Shut the fuck up. Just stay still and hold on."

His head dropped back to the floor, eyes sliding shut, but he breathed, "Status?"

"Don't fucking know. Looks like my dad is down. Tsepov and most of his guys are down."

"Dead?" the word came out on a whisper.

"Maybe. Probably."

I'd think about that in a minute. In this moment, for this breath and the next and the next, my only thought was to keep pressure on Griffen's shoulder. To slow the flow of blood. To buy him another minute of life. Then another.

It was an eternity until I was pushed aside by the paramedics. They swarmed Griffen, stabilizing the wound with a pressure dressing before loading him on a gurney and racing for the door.

He disappeared from sight before I got to my feet. Turning, I saw a team leaning over Tsepov, another around my father. The team working on my father moved with urgency. The one by Tsepov, not so much.

Tsepov was dead.

Agent Holley had lost his target. He'd be pissed, but all I felt was relief. It was over, the cost of ending it far too high.

The paramedics with my father pushed his gurney through the door as quickly as they'd moved with Griffen. He was alive. For now. I wanted to follow them to the hospital. I couldn't go. Not yet. Alice and Petra were here, along with the people I'd put on the perimeter. I had to secure the building and my people, get Alice and Petra out before I could go to the hospital. Time to call in the cavalry.

Agent Holley hung up the phone as I approached. "I sent two men to follow your father. You on your way?"

"As soon as I settle things here. Griffen said I have people down outside."

Holley gave a sober nod. "My team is securing the building, called more paramedics. So far, no fatalities, but two are critical."

No fatalities was good. Better than I'd expected. "Alice and Petra—my little sister—are here. I need to get them somewhere safe."

"Since when do you have a sister?" Holley asked, surprise chasing the somber expression from his face.

"Since my father showed up at my door with her tagging along. I'll fill you in later. She'll stay with Alice and me. I don't want either of them to see this."

"You have a safe room in here somewhere?" Holley asked. "I know it's not at the end of the hall since the door Tsepov's idiot men were cutting open leads to the back stairwell."

Relief flooded through me. They'd had that torch back there for too long.

"Thank God. It's more of a storage room than a safe room, but it was the best I could do on short notice. Of all the things I planned for, my father letting Tsepov in wasn't on the list."

Holley shook his head. With my father's life hanging by a thin thread, neither of us wanted to say what we were thinking. He was a liar and a criminal, but he was still my father.

"I can free up two men if you can add one of yours," Holley said. "Put Alice and the girl with your brother's families. If they're all in one place they'll be easier to secure until we're sure we got all of Tsepov's people. We're not out of the woods yet."

"I'd appreciate the extra men. Until we know about Griffen and my father—"

"I know. Make your calls, we'll get Alice and the girl out of here, and then you and your brothers can get to the hospital." I was thinking about who to wake up first when he said, "I think Sawyer will pull through."

"But not my father?" I couldn't help asking.

Holley's face was expressionless as he said, "He should have taken his chances with prison."

My throat closed, I nodded in agreement. Fucking Maxwell. So determined not to spend a minute in jail, he'd almost killed us all. Raising my phone, I turned and headed for my bedroom. We weren't coming back here for a while. Alice and Petra would need clothes. I grabbed one of Alice's duffel bags and started to fill it from her side of the closet as I made my calls.

First on my list was Knox. After Tsepov's attack weeks ago he'd upgraded every aspect of his security. No one was getting near his place without him knowing. Everyone was safest there.

Knox's voice was as clear and abrupt as if he'd been wide awake.

"I'm sending Alice and Petra to you," I said, without pre-amble. I filled him in on the rest and hung up. Knox would take care of calling Axel and Evers.

Done with packing for Alice, I moved to Petra's room. She was more complicated, and I didn't have time to con-sider everything she'd need. Some clothes and pull-ups would get her through the next few days. Whatever I forgot we'd get later.

Next on my list was Riley Flynn. I needed him here to coordinate what remained of the team, then at Knox's house watching the women and kids. My last call was to Lucas Jackson. He might be our resident hacker, but he was a one-man army, six feet, seven inches of deadly force.

"Forget Knox's place," he said the second I laid out my plan. "Take them to Winters House. I'll call Aiden. He'll want to know about your father and Griffen anyway. Tsepov's men won't think to look for them there, and Aiden never downgraded the added security we put in back when Annal-ise came home. Motion sensors, floodlights, it's all still up."

I was rattled or I would have thought of it myself. The Winters were as good as family, but they were also one of the wealthiest families in the country.

Winters House was less a house than an estate. The place was huge, in the center of ten acres, almost impossible for any of Tsepov's men to sneak up on, especially after the way we'd jacked up their security when Annalise Winters had come home with her stalker on her heels.

On top of the location and the security, Gage Winters was former special forces. If he hadn't gone to work for the family corporation I would have recruited him for my own team.

"Good idea. Call Aiden and set it up. Update Riley. We'll meet you there."

I sent a quick text to fill my brothers in on the change in plans and shoved my phone in my pocket, heading down the hall for Alice.

I opened the door to the storage room and froze, looking straight into the barrel of a Walther PK identical to the one I'd left on the floor of the kitchen.

Alice stood in a perfect stance, legs spread, arms raised, the weapon steady as a rock. Petra was curled up on the carpet behind her, fast asleep. I was so relieved to see my girls in one piece my chest hurt.

Without lowering her gun, Alice asked, "Everything okay?"

"Okay? No. But we're safe. Agent Holley's here. I need to get to the hospital."

Alice lowered her weapon as her eyes turned dark. "Who?"

"My father and Griffen."

She swore under her breath.

"The FBI will take you and Petra to Winters House. Summer, Emma, and Lily will meet you there. I got your stuff together."

I held up the duffel and she took it, face clouded with worry.

Taking the Walther, I set it in the gun safe before I cupped her face in my hands and kissed her. Just once, the briefest meeting of lips. There was never any time.

Later. I hoped there would be all the time in the world later. Time to tell her how I felt. What I needed. What I wanted. Time for everything.

Griffen and my father might already be dead.

I had to get to the hospital.

I let her go, cold settling around me as I moved away.

I said the only thing I could, the thing I'd said only once before.

"I love you, Alice."

Then I turned and raced for my car.

Chapter Forty-Two

ALICE

Y LIPS WERE STILL WARM FROM COOPER'S AS he took off down the hall. I stood there holding the duffel bag, staring after him like an idiot. I couldn't catch up.

I love you, Alice.

He *loved* me? He'd said it when he locked us in, but I'd been so scared it hadn't registered.

He *loved* me?

Even after I'd put Lacey in the hospital?

I'd think about that later. He'd said he loved me, but he hadn't said anything about Griffen or Maxwell. They were injured, on their way to the hospital, but I had no clue what that meant. At that moment, I couldn't make myself care about Maxwell.

Griffen was another story. I couldn't stand the thought that he was seriously hurt. If anything happened to him, Maxwell had better hope he died because if he survived and Griffen didn't, I'd murder Maxwell myself.

I'd worry about that later, too. Trying to distract myself with something I could control, I dropped to my knees and unzipped the duffel, checking everything Cooper had packed. He'd done a pretty good job.

Petra could show up at Winters House in her jammies, but there was no way in hell I was walking through the door of the grand estate for the first time in Cooper's cut-off sweats and a threadbare T-shirt.

I didn't want to leave the safe room, unsure what I would find in the rest of the apartment and unwilling to leave the sleeping Petra alone even for a few minutes. Making do, I pulled out a Kelly green dress Cooper had packed, a white crinoline, and my hairbrush, along with a pair of wedge flip-flops.

I had the dress over my head and zipped up in a blink, the crinoline beneath a second later. Good thing, because a quick double-knock hit the door just as I was pulling the brush through my hair.

Agent Holley pushed open the door without waiting for a response, his face strained and somber. A dark-haired man wearing a navy-blue FBI vest followed behind.

Angling his chin at the floor where Petra still slept, Agent Holley asked in a low voice, "This the sister?"

"This is Petra." I smoothed my skirts and asked the question I wasn't sure I wanted the answer to. "Griffen? Cooper didn't say—"

"I think he'll pull through. He took one in the shoulder. Looked like it nicked an artery, but Cooper got to him fast. He has a good chance."

My stomach filled with lead. *A good chance* wasn't *He'll be fine*. I didn't even bother to ask about Maxwell. I don't think I cared. Griffen had been my friend since my first day at Sinclair Security. I refused to think we might lose him.

340

"Are you ready to go?"

"I just need my purse and phone from the kitchen."

Holley nodded to the other agent who disappeared down the hall. "Agent Williams will get you to Winters House. Lucas Jackson is on the way there."

I knelt by Petra and scooped her up, ignoring the pain in my bruised arm. She raised her head and blinked at me with bleary eyes before settling her cheek on my shoulder, bunny clutched in her hand.

A few minutes later we were whisked to the garage and off to Winters House in an FBI van. Winters House was deep in the heart of Buckhead, not far from the Sinclair Security offices. I'd seen pictures, both in the media and our own files as we updated security on the vast property.

I thought I was ready for Winters House.

I was wrong.

We turned off the main road onto a smooth, wide, asphalt drive, coming to a stop behind a Sinclair Security SUV, parked so it blocked the imposing black iron gate.

Lucas Jackson jumped out of the driver's seat and came to the van. "ID," he said brusquely before sending a concerned look my way. "You okay, Alice?"

"I'm fine." I wanted to ask if he'd heard anything about Griffen, but it was too soon.

After calling in the agent's badge number, he returned to his SUV and opened the gate. We followed him up the long, winding drive to the house. Lined by live oaks arching over us, every other tree lit with spotlights, even the drive-way to Winters House was a little intimidating.

Winters House emerged out of the dark, the exterior lit by more spotlights. Built in a Mediterranean style, the mansion was all creamy stucco, tall arched windows, and a distinctive red-tiled roof. Imposing and yet welcoming, it was a gorgeous home, even in the dark of night.

We came to a stop at a second gate, this one also black iron but more delicate, blocking the entrance to a porte-cochère. The gate swung open in front of Lucas' vehicle and we rolled slowly into a spacious courtyard with a lit fountain at the center.

Designed in a square, Winters House surrounded the courtyard on all four sides. The section we'd driven through and those to my left and right were all one level, their arched windows looking out into the courtyard.

I got out of the FBI van slowly, taking it all in, and turned to face the largest section of Winters House. Two stories high, this part of the house loomed over me as we climbed the steps to the enormous, carved wooden double-door.

Aiden Winters swung open the door, exchanging low words with Lucas before nodding at the FBI agent as he stepped back to allow them to enter.

I got a warm smile. "Alice. Sorry to see you under these circumstances."

"Me too. Thank you for opening your home in the middle of the night." Aiden closed the door behind us and led me in through the foyer. I'd never seen him dressed in anything other than a business suit.

I've been head over heels for Cooper for more years than I'd like to admit, but I have eyes. With his auburn hair, warm brown eyes and gorgeous smile, Aiden Winters is hot in a suit. But like this? Sleep rumpled, his broad shoulders stretching an old Emory t-shirt? Wow. Hot doesn't cover it.

Aiden gave a hint of that smile as he shook his head. "Cooper and his brothers are family. You know that." With a gentle hand, he reached up to tuck a strand of hair off Petra's cheek. She looked up at him with serious eyes. "This the new addition? With those eyes, she looks just like Cooper and Axel when they were kids."

Petra looked to me. "Coop?"

I cuddled her closer. Already she was asking for Cooper instead of her father. Her father who was probably already dead. Aiden must have been thinking the same thing.

"Cooper will be here soon, honey," he said. "In the meantime, Violet is in the library with coffee and tea. And cookies."

He smiled as Petra's eyes popped wide. "Cookies?"

"Cookies," he confirmed. To me, he said, "I'm going to talk to Lucas and the FBI. We won't let anyone get to you."

"Thanks, Aiden. If you hear anything about Griffen?"

"I'll let you know," he promised.

I followed him to the library where a stunning woman sat in front of a loaded tea tray. She looked up with a cool smile, her eyes warming as they landed on Aiden. Her pale-blond hair was caught in a loose ponytail, and she wore shorts and a t-shirt, but despite the casual look, she was every inch the queen.

This must be Violet Westbrook, Aiden's soon-to-be fiancée. According to the Sinclairs, he hadn't proposed yet, but he would.

"Alice?" she asked. Not waiting for me to confirm, she rose and held out her hand. "I'm Violet. I've been dying to meet you. You're a legend around here."

Aiden withdrew, an affectionate smile curving his lips, and headed out to secure Winters House against any possible invasion.

"A legend? I like that, but I'm not sure what I've done to earn the title." I sat on the leather couch opposite Violet, leaning forward to snag a cookie off the tray for Petra.

343

"Definitely a legend," she said, her eyes twinkling, their color somewhere between lavender and periwinkle. They were arresting, especially combined with her poise and her ice-blond hair. This was a woman I could see with Aiden Winters.

Her queenly reserve melted under the warmth of her amusement. "An office full of bossy alpha guys and you run herd on all of them. Lucas and Riley say the place would fall apart without you."

"Oh, that," I said, reaching for my own cookie. "I *am* a legend for that," I admitted. "They can be a handful. And the women on the team are just as bad. The job does not attract laid back people."

"I bet," Violet said with a smile. "Coffee? Tea? I'm not Mrs. W," she said, referencing the family housekeeper, "but I threw together what we had. Fortunately, she keeps us stocked in shortbread. Charlie is in the kitchen making sandwiches. Aiden said Emma, Summer, and Lily are on the way. Sophie and Lise are still asleep. Gage and Riley didn't want to wake them."

Lise was Annalise, Aiden's younger cousin. She was married to Riley. I'd met her a few times when she'd stopped by the office. I didn't know Sophie, Gage's wife, though I did know she'd come to Winters House as an employee. A nurse they'd hired to take care of their great-aunt Amelia, apparently, Gage had taken one look at her and swept her off her feet.

Charlie was a different story. We weren't BFFs, but we hung out now and then. Younger than me, Charlie never sat still and didn't take any shit. A girl after my own heart. She'd married Lucas Jackson a few years before, not long after he joined the company. The first time she'd strolled into the office I'd known we'd be friends.

On the surface, she and Lucas were an odd pair: The billionaire princess of the Winters clan and a scary, former black-ops hacker. They might have been odd, but they were one of my favorite couples.

Charlie was a spitfire and Lucas adored her just as much as he enjoyed watching her wreak havoc. Deep down, where it counted, they were a match made in heaven.

"I can get Petra juice," Violet offered, proving gossip moved like wildfire between the Sinclairs and the Winters. She'd probably known about Petra only hours after the little girl had ended up at our door. Before I could answer, Charlie strode in with a second tray, this one piled with small sandwiches.

"I tried to channel Mrs. W, but I can't promise these are any good," she said, setting the tray beside the other and sitting next to me. Bumping my shoulder with hers, she said, "Why did I have to find out from Lucas that you moved in with Cooper?"

"Because it happened yesterday?" I asked, bumping her shoulder back.

"Aiden said it was about time," Violet added, pouring a cup of coffee and setting it in front of me.

I slid Petra to the corner of the couch and handed her another piece of the buttery shortbread, quietly asking, "Do you want juice? Or just a cookie and a snuggle?"

"Cookie," she whispered, hugging bunny to her chest and curling into the couch, her eyes already starting to droop.

"Okay, gumdrop," I said, pressing a kiss to her forehead. I'd worry about sugar and proper nutrition later. Tonight, she needed cookies.

I was just grateful she hadn't witnessed any of the violence that had erupted in our home. My heart squeezed. *Cooper.* She'd seen nothing because Cooper had protected us, been willing to die for us. Griffen still might. My heart squeezed again, and I rechecked my phone. Nothing.

"*Everyone* said it was about time," Charlie agreed, bringing me back to the conversation. "Cooper's been moping over Alice for years."

"He has not," I protested, still not used to the idea that Cooper had wanted me for so long.

"He totally has," Charlie insisted. "Just ask Aiden. It was killing me to keep my mouth shut. Killing me! When you got divorced, Aiden was sure Cooper would pounce. Damn, that man is patient." She leaned around me to wink at Petra. "Sorry. I should be used to watching my language with Rosie and Adam around."

"I think she's heard worse," I said dryly, brushing her hair off her forehead. "Anyway, Cooper doesn't pounce."

"Really?" Violet raised one sleek, platinum eyebrow and took a sip of her coffee. "I saw him throw you over his shoulder at Evers' engagement party. That's close enough."

Okay, she had a point. Then there was the time he'd tossed me on the bed...

Charlie laughed, a bold, happy sound that was welcome after the night we'd had. "Look at Alice blushing! Maybe Cooper didn't pounce before, but he does now." More quietly, bumping my shoulder again, she said, "It's nice to see him happy. He—"

Her mouth slammed shut as we all thought about what Charlie had said. It had been nice to see him happy, but with his mother in the hospital, his father probably dead, and his best friend clinging to life, *happy* wasn't the best description of his current circumstances.

"I wish we knew what was going on with Griffen," I said, annoyed at my fretful tone. "I know he's in surgery, but I hate the waiting. I hate that he got hurt trying to protect us."

Charlie closed her hand around mine and squeezed. "There was no way he would have been anywhere else. Griffen loves you guys. Cooper is like a brother to him."

"This isn't the first time one of the team has gotten hurt," I said, trying to convince myself this was all business as usual. "It's just that—"

"This isn't work," Violet finished gently. "This isn't Griffen on a case, this is Griffen being your friend."

"Poor Cooper," I whispered, unable to stop myself. If it weren't for Petra I would have followed him to the hospital. Would have been there for him. But I couldn't leave the little girl curled into my side, devouring cookie after cookie. She needed me, and Cooper had his brothers. Considering I was responsible for putting their mother in the same hospital where their father was, I might not be welcome.

I would never have hurt Lacey if she hadn't come after Petra. She'd been about to kill me. I'd done the right thing. Surely, they would understand that. I could only hope. I took a sip of coffee and another piece of shortbread, trying to chase the dark thoughts from my mind.

Breaking the mood, I pinned Charlie with a steely look. "So, you knew about Cooper? All this time?"

Chapter Forty-Three

ALICE

ROWN MEN SQUIRM WHEN I USE THAT LOOK, but Charlie only gave a sheepish squint. "I did," she admitted. "He's a lot older than me, but I've known him since birth. And I asked Aiden a while ago why he didn't have a girlfriend. Aiden said he was interested in someone who wasn't available, and the first time I saw you two together I knew it was you."

I smacked her arm before snagging another cookie and splitting it with Petra. "Why didn't you say anything?"

Charlie rolled her eyes. "I wanted to. But you were still married, and you wouldn't hear anything negative about Steve. And then Lucas and Aiden both made me promise to stay out of it. Lucas said Cooper would pull his head out of his ass soon enough."

I let out a gust of breath and confessed, "Hearing about you leaving Winters, Inc. and starting your own business is part of what made me get serious about divorce."

Charlie stared at me, her jaw dropped, shocked speechless. I didn't think it was possible to shock Charlie speechless. "How? What did I have to do with it?"

"Well, don't take this the wrong way, but you're so young." Charlie was not quite twenty-six, though the life she'd lived had given her a maturity far beyond her years. "And you changed your whole life because you weren't happy."

Violet made a discrete humming sound in the back of her throat. Charlie shook her head. "I didn't do anything. Aiden fired me, threw me out of Winters, Inc. on my ass. I would have spent another decade being miserable if it weren't for him."

"He wouldn't have let that happen," Violet murmured.

"That's why he's the best, even if he is a controlling jerk sometimes," Charlie said.

"I didn't know the part about Aiden," I said, trying to explain. "But I was miserable with Steve, watching my life pass me by, and then I met you, and you'd had the courage to reinvent yourself. You'd changed everything, had your whole life in front of you, and I was watching mine pass me by. So, I asked Knox to look into Steve, discovered what a cheating rat he'd been, found a lawyer, and then I was free, too."

"I'm glad that disaster with Aiden was good for something." Charlie rolled her eyes.

"Other than landing you next door to Lucas?" Violet asked with another raise of her eyebrow.

"Other than that," Charlie said with a satisfied grin.

My phone beeped and I checked the screen, my heart lurching in my chest. A weather alert. Damn. I couldn't call Cooper, didn't want to distract him, but despite the good company and our relative safety, I couldn't relax until I knew Griffen would be okay.

350

A clatter of shoes echoed in the hall as Lily, Adam, Emma, and Summer all piled in. Adam was sleepy-eyed and stumbling, barely awake.

Lily took one look at Petra and said, "I'm going to tuck Adam into bed down the hall. Aiden said it's Charlie's old room. It's just a few doors down. Do you want to come with us, Petra? I'm going to read a story."

Petra slid off the couch, her hand clasped around mine, giving the other women a wary look. She followed Lily and Adam, tugging me along with them. She allowed us to tuck her in bed alongside Adam, curling up, her back against his side, as he drifted off. It took longer for Petra's eyes to shut, but when they did, she was out.

I tiptoed after Lily back to the library. My seat on the couch was taken, which was fine with me. Now that Petra was settled, I needed to pace.

"Any word from the hospital?"

A room full of head shakes. "Not yet," Emma said. "No texts, no calls. I don't want to bug them but—"

Griffen had saved Emma's life. They had a bond, and I knew she was as worried sick as I was.

"I know," I said.

I needed to hear from Cooper.

I love you, Alice.

He loved me. With a sickening realization, it hit me that I hadn't said it back. He hadn't given me a chance. I'd been so convinced he hated me for almost killing his mother, and then he hit me with *I love you* and disappeared. I was such a jerk.

I pulled up my phone and stared at the locked screen. He was busy. He had his brothers. He didn't need to hear from me right now.

Before I could talk myself out of it, I unlocked the screen and typed *I love you, too. In case you didn't know.*

No answer. I resumed pacing, trying not to think of all the ways things could go wrong. Tsepov's men might still be out there. Griffen might not make it through surgery. Maxwell was surely dead.

I checked my phone again. Not even a read notice on my text. I wasn't going to make it until morning. The waiting was killing me.

I was wearing a groove in the carpet in front of the fireplace when a hand closed around my arm, pulling me into a hug. I looked up into Charlie's familiar ocean-blue eyes, the color of her chin-length auburn hair identical to Aiden's.

"Sit, Alice. You're just winding yourself up with the pacing."

I stayed where I was, not pacing but not sitting either. I didn't think I could sit. "I didn't tell him I love him," I whispered, the confession physically painful.

"He knows," Charlie said, simply.

"What if he doesn't?" I pressed, my worry for Cooper and Griffen and everyone I loved mixed up in a tight, ugly ball of fear.

"He knows because if you didn't love him you would have brained him by now." Charlie gave me a little shake. "He knows, Alice. And so do you. Griffen is going to be okay. Lucas thinks Tsepov's men will scatter as soon as they know he's dead. You'll be out of the woods in no time."

"I want to be out of the woods now," I complained mulishly.

"Sit," Charlie said again, not acknowledging my whine.

She was right, I was just way to stressed out to think clearly. I let her push me to an armchair and hand me a cup of herbal tea with an impish twinkle in her eye. I handed it back. "Coffee."

"It was worth a try," she said, taking the tea and replacing it with a cup of coffee.

I sipped and tried to participate in the conversation, only checking my phone every thirty seconds or so. I was with friends, safe, Petra was sleeping, but I couldn't relax. Not until Griffen was stable and Cooper was back. Conversation moved from Summer's disaster of an engagement party to their plans for a wedding to Knox's renovations and speculation on when Aiden would propose. Violet didn't seem worried about the latter.

"I told him we needed to slow down and date like normal people—" she said.

"—and then he moved you into Winters House," Charlie finished. "He would have married you months ago if he wasn't worried he'd scare you off."

Violet's lips curved. "This is only temporary."

"Yeah, right," was Charlie's response. "I'd love to see you try to move back out. If you do, let me know so I can make some popcorn and call everyone else. Now that everyone is settled down, we need the entertainment."

Violet rolled her eyes, somehow managing to look elegant and not like a recalcitrant teenager.

Two cups of coffee later, I was on my feet again, holding up a hand when the entire room scowled at me. "I'm going to pace. Don't try to stop me."

They all settled back, clearly recognizing a woman on the edge. How long could surgery take? It had been hours. The sun was cresting the horizon, daylight spilling into the library. I jumped and whirled at the sound of footsteps coming down the hall, even as I registered that they were too light to be Cooper or one of the guys.

A small woman with silvery-blond hair poked her head into the room. "Hi." She gave a little wave. "I'm Sophie.

Mrs. W said to tell you breakfast is ready. She is not happy you didn't wake her up. Aunt Amelia is also not happy. I told her it was Violet's fault."

I expected Violet to be annoyed at being thrown under the bus, but she only gave a serene smile. "Good, Amelia needs something to get worked up about or she'll get bored." She stood, and everyone else did the same, following her down the hall to the dining room.

I barely noticed the grandeur of the Winters House dining room. I ate mechanically, only half-tasting the delicious breakfast set in front of me, obsessively checking my phone. I caught Charlie watching me with worried eyes, but she let me stew.

Finally, as I was finishing my millionth cup of coffee, Lily's phone beeped with a text. "They're on their way."

"And?" Emma prompted, her eyebrows arched in impatient query.

Lily gave a frustrated shrug. "That's all. Just *On our way*. I guess they'll tell us when they get here."

The next twenty minutes were among the longest in my life. I was exhausted with worry. I just wanted to see Cooper, to know Griffen would be alright. To tell Cooper I loved him. To hear him say the words when the world wasn't falling down around our ears.

The front door opened, and we flooded from the dining room to meet them. As soon as I saw their faces, I knew. Maxwell was gone. I wanted to ask about Griffen, but I waited.

Cooper put us out of our misery. "Griffen came through surgery. He's in recovery now. He'll have some mobility loss in the shoulder, but otherwise, he'll be fine. No other serious injuries from the team in the building when Tsepov's men hit."

"Maxwell?" Summer whispered.

Evers crossed the hall to take her in his arms. "He didn't make it, baby. He never regained consciousness."

My heart sank. I knew, but I'd hoped. For Cooper, for Petra, I'd hoped. Tears blurred my eyes as I vaguely took in Knox holding Lily, Axel embracing Emma.

A hand closed over my elbow. I looked up to see Cooper, his face somber, eyes guarded. "Will you come with me?"

Heart heavy with dread, I nodded. He'd said he loved me, but that was before his father died. I'd said it back, and he hadn't responded. Maybe it was all too much. Maybe he'd said it in the heat of the moment but he hadn't meant it.

I followed him back down the hall to the library, where someone had already cleared the trays from last night, leaving the room immaculate as if we'd never been there.

Turning, I faced Cooper. I wasn't ready for this, but I was no coward.

"I'm sorry about Maxwell."

"Me too." Cooper had that same oddly hesitant look I'd seen in the cabin. "Are you okay?"

I didn't know how to answer that. No, I was nowhere close to okay. I lied. "I'm fine."

"Petra?"

"Still asleep down the hall with Adam. She didn't see anything. Neither of us did. Thank you for—" My throat locked. He'd said he loved me and walked out, knowing he might not come back. He got us to safety and then he left us. "—thank you for—" I couldn't get the words out.

Everything burst at once, and I strode across the room, punching him in the shoulder, tears pouring down my cheeks. "You could have died, you idiot! You left us. You kept us safe and then you left us. You could have died, Cooper! What am I supposed to do if you die?"

I sobbed as his arms closed around me, holding me tight against the strong length of his body. I knew what I was saying was all wrong. Cooper would never have hidden in that safe room with us when his father and Griffen were in danger.

He'd done what he had to. He'd done the right thing. I knew that. I loved him for always doing the right thing. I'd been so scared, huddled in that room with Petra, hearing the muffled gunshots and not knowing.

"I'm sorry, baby. I'm so sorry. For everything."

He rubbed his palm over my back, soothing me as my tears ran their course. I should be letting Cooper cry instead of bawling all over him. It was his father who'd died. I was being a selfish jerk. Again. And still, I cried, cried until my eyes ran dry.

When I stopped, I stayed where I was, pressed against him, breathing in the salt and man scent of him. Cooper. In one piece. With me. Cooper.

He held me, but he didn't say anything. He'd said he was sorry. What was he sorry for? None of this was his fault.

I pushed away, wiping under my eyes. I was probably all blotchy and puffy. Great. Still, he was silent, taking me in with guarded eyes. The agony of waiting was too much. I couldn't take it a second longer.

"Cooper—"

"Do you remember your promise?" he interrupted.

Promise? What promise?

"At the cabin. You promised you'd never walk out on me again. I'm holding you to that, Alice."

"What?" I wasn't going anywhere. If anyone was going to walk, I figured it would be Cooper.

"If you try to go, I'll follow you. You love me. I know you do."

"Cooper, I—"

"I can make it up to you. Make up for Lacey, for Maxwell, for everything that's gone wrong. Just give me a chance."

"Cooper," I cut in, "what the hell are you talking about? I'm not going anywhere."

Cooper stared at me, face blank. Slowly, he said, "Alice, my mother tried to kill you. My father brought the mob into our home."

"I know. I was there." Reaching up, I lay my palm against the side of his face. I couldn't blame Cooper for being a little spun, for getting all of this backward. He'd just watched his father die. "I put your mother in the hospital, Cooper."

He gave a quick shake of his head, and I dropped my hand, confused. I couldn't forget Lacey, bleeding and unconscious, lying in the midst of all that broken glass. If I couldn't forget, how could Cooper?

Catching my hands in his, he said, "I need to know if you can forgive me."

"Forgive you for what?" *Cooper* felt guilty? God, we were idiots. I started to laugh. Cooper's eyebrows knit together in confusion.

"Griffen is right," I said through giggles that bordered on hysterical. "We *are* dumbasses. This isn't your fault, Cooper."

"It's not yours, either."

"I *did* almost kill your mother."

Cooper shook his head. "As much as I hate to say this, she had it coming. And you didn't almost kill her. Didn't Griffen tell you?" He shook his head again. "Never mind. He didn't know. She's fine. She'd lost a lot of blood and she hit her head, but she's fine. Not speaking to us at the

357

moment, but I can't say I'm sorry about that. She's lucky I'm not pressing charges for breaking and entering, trying to murder you and kidnap Petra."

"I love you, Cooper. You said it twice, and I was so surprised I never got to say it back. I love you."

"Why were you surprised?" he asked, stroking a finger down the side of my face. "What was all of this about if not love? Of course, I love you. I've loved you forever."

"Good, because I'm not going anywhere. Except home. With you."

Cooper pulled me against him, looking down into my face, the blank shock finally erased from his eyes, replaced by a heat I knew would warm me for the rest of my life.

"Home," he agreed. "But not yet. We're staying here for a while. Our place is a crime scene. And we don't have a door."

"What?" What had happened to the door?

"Don't ask. You don't want to know."

Normally, I didn't like to be shut out of information, but this time Cooper was right. I didn't want to know. He was safe, Petra and I were safe, Griffen was going to recover, and Cooper loved me. That was all I needed to know.

Out of nowhere, the world turned upside down and I was over Cooper's shoulder, moving through the room and into the hall.

"Cooper! What are you doing? Put me down."

He didn't answer, opening a door not far from the library and flicking on a light. A lock turned, a metal bar *snicking* into place. My hair flipped back over my head as he set me on some kind of counter. I looked around. Wine everywhere.

With that wicked grin I loved, Cooper said, "The Winters House wine room. I happen to know it's the only room on this floor with a deadbolt. I want you to myself, just for a minute."

His lips stroked over mine and the rest of the world fell away. His family waiting outside. Petra, soon to wake up. We'd be there for all of them. In a minute.

For now, Cooper was all mine, and I was his. I fell into his kiss, my body wrapped around his, my heart full of Cooper.

He was everything I'd ever wanted. Everything I'd dreamed of.

I'd keep my promise. I'd never leave him, never give up on him. We belonged to each other. Now and forever.

Epilogue One

ALICE

COOPER DUMPED ME ON MY ASS, A BRIGHT SPARK of glee in his ice-blue eyes. My tailbone smacked the mat, but I wasn't even mad. It had been too long since I'd seen him so carefree. So happy. If it took tossing me on my butt in the sparring room to put that look on his face, he could do it all day as far as I was concerned.

Let's be honest, I never want to get in a fight again. I'm no pushover, but fisticuffs are not my thing. Even so, after everything that had happened with Lacey, Maxwell, the invasion of the Russian mob—I'd realized that Cooper's training wasn't a joke. I wanted more.

I didn't need to be on his team of scary operatives. I just wanted to know I could protect myself. Protect Petra. If anyone ever tried to put a hand on me again, I wanted to know I could put them on the ground long enough to get away.

As I'd guessed weeks before, sparring with Cooper never stayed all business. Even when we had the best of intentions, once we were sweating, his hands on me, my hands on him—things happened. Good things. Hot things. Naked things.

I wasn't complaining. For the first time in what felt like forever, life was approaching normal, and it was better than I'd ever imagined normal could be.

Lacey, after finding out Maxwell was dead, had gone completely silent for a full day before quietly asking Cooper to find her a residential treatment center. No one was expecting a miracle, but it was a start.

We were still trading off at the office, Cooper working mornings and me afternoons so Petra had time to adjust, though days like today we took advantage of her nap time and left the office to Cooper's brothers.

Axel had gone back to Las Vegas, but Evers and Knox could handle things for a while. Lily had been coming by each day for an hour or two and Petra had taken to her right away. She wasn't attached to Lily the way she was to Cooper and me, but when Lily was at the door Petra ran to her, laughing, arms raised for a hug. Soon enough she'd be ready to spend half days with Lily, then full days, and we'd transition to the next stage of normal.

The first two weeks after that awful night were anything *but* normal. It took a while for the FBI to finish with our place, then for the doors to be repaired. We'd spent that time as guests of Winters House.

Cooper had practically grown up in Winters House and took the move in stride. I think after losing his father it was comforting to re-live the best parts of his childhood surrounded by friends who were as close as family.

I won't deny it was pretty sweet, a lot like living in a luxury hotel except without any strangers around. Gourmet meals, housekeeping, a pool and tennis court. Sophie and

Aunt Amelia taught us to play croquet. The Winters house-hold welcomed me as if they'd known me all their lives.

Once he was released from the hospital, Griffen joined us at Winters House, though he wasn't quite a ray of sunshine. In pain, refusing to take his meds, and frustrated at the extent of the damage to the ligaments in his shoulder, he growled as often as he used to smile.

He had reason. Griffen had been lucky, considering all the ways a bullet to the shoulder could go wrong, but he'd never regain full use of his arm. If he were a normal guy, he'd never notice the lack. For someone who depended on split-second reaction times, the loss of function was devastating.

Sophie Winters—one of the kindest, most patient people I'd ever met—had offered to oversee his recovery. Gage's wife and Amelia Winters' nurse, she was qualified and didn't mind putting up with Griffen's crankiness. Griffen said he was sick of the hospital, sick of being treated like an invalid, but I think what he wanted most was to hole up in his house and brood. None of us were willing to let him.

Sophie kept reminding us that acting like a prickly bear was par for the course when a big strong guy had his shoulder blown open and refused to take his pain meds. We knew she was right, but it was still hard seeing the normally sunny Griffen so far off his game.

He was better now that we'd all moved home. Mostly. We all knew that unless a miracle happened, his shoulder would disqualify him from most field work. For now, everyone was tiptoeing around the topic.

Griffen's arm was still in a sling. We had time before anything was official, but Griffen knew what was coming. I couldn't blame him for being a miserable grouch. If it were me, I'd probably be worse.

The two weeks at Winters House were fun, but the second the FBI said we could go home, Cooper wrangled a bunch of the guys and they moved me into his place for good. Since the furniture stayed with the apartment, it took only a few hours.

Before I knew it, I was fully ensconced in Cooper's apartment, now *our* home, and my old place had been converted back to the secondary safe room. Cooper had taken advantage of the re-construction of the doors to have the crew create a secret access from the back stairwell to my old apartment so that if anything ever happened again we wouldn't be stuck with the storage room as our only bolthole.

Personally, I thought it was overkill. With Tsepov out of the picture, it was unlikely we'd face another invasion, but if being overprotective helped Cooper sleep at night, I wouldn't argue. Cooper had lost his father, had almost lost his mother. Anything that eased him through it all was okay in my book.

It didn't take the FBI long to determine that Tsepov's remaining men had scattered to the winds, all looking for a better payday now that Tsepov was gone. We weren't in any danger. Agent Holley had rounded up everyone he could get his hands on and was making a case against the remaining players, none of whom had the slightest interest in the Sinclairs.

In the ultimate irony, the ballistics report confirmed that while the bullets that killed Maxwell came from Tsepov's weapon, Tsepov had been killed by his own men. In the end, Andrei Tsepov had enough money and ego to wreak havoc in all of our lives but not enough skill to hold onto the top-notch men his uncle had commanded.

The second-rate team of goons backing him up had been a disaster and ultimately, his demise. I felt badly for

Agent Holley—all that time building a case and all of his witnesses ended up dead—but the Tsepov empire was dust. This time, the good guys won.

Cooper hovered over Petra and me even more than usual those first few weeks after Maxwell and Tsepov died. We both hovered over Petra, bizarrely relieved the first time she shoved her dinner off the high chair tray and pitched a fit, demanding cookies. If she did that every day it would get old, but it was reassuringly normal to see a three-year-old turn up her nose at vegetables.

Petra asked for Maxwell every day. We'd followed the guidance of the company therapist and told her Maxwell was dead and she would be staying with Cooper and me. I'm not sure exactly how much she understood about Maxwell, but her eyes had lit up at the news that she was staying with us.

It was a lot of change—for all of us—but the good far outweighed the bad. The good was better than just good, it was the best. Our nap-time sparring sessions case in point.

I got to my feet on the mat, dusting off my rear end, and threw my shoulders back, lifting my chin in Cooper's direction with a cocky toss of my hair. "You're not going to do that again."

"You want to bet, pixie?"

"I'm not a pixie," I said without heat. I'd never admit it, but I secretly liked it when Cooper called me *pixie*. Next to him, I felt like a pixie.

We squared off against one another, balanced on the balls of our feet as we waited for my signal. This time, I remembered a move he'd showed me the day before and somehow managed to execute it perfectly. I stepped into him, pressing my knee into the side of his, gripping his forearm and counterbalancing exactly right until he fell on his back and I landed on top of him.

Straddling his waist, I shook my hands in the air, wiggling my hips and singing *Another One Bites the Dust*. Silly, considering it was the first time I'd taken him down, but I was celebrating anyway. Who knew when I'd manage it again? Probably never.

Cooper's grin stretched wide, his hands closing over my hips as he flipped me on my back, settling between my thighs and rising over me. I had a feeling the sparring part of our session was over. Fine by me.

Raising my legs, I hooked my ankles behind his back and settled into the mat. I could stay like this all day, Cooper's body covering me, damp with sweat, strong, and vital, and mine.

There was a part of me that still couldn't believe it was Cooper between my legs. Cooper looking down at me.

Cooper. I'd never imagined I could be this happy. I was holding onto it with everything I had.

Cooper's eyes were blue flame as he lowered his head, his lips brushing mine, raising to skate across my cheekbone, the hollow of my neck, butterfly kisses so light they set a fire everywhere they touched. Teasing, building the need inside me until I was squirming beneath him, my mouth seeking his.

I reached for him, letting out a growl of frustration when he caught my wrists and held them over my head, pinning me motionless beneath him.

"Cooper," I breathed, "stop teasing."

"Never," he rumbled, balancing his weight on an elbow as he reached with his free hand and pulled something from his pocket. He settled himself back between my legs, his weight comfortable against me, never too heavy. Just enough that I felt connected to him, like I was exactly where I belonged.

A black velvet box loomed in front of my eyes.

He'd had that in his pocket? Sneaky, sneaky man.

I saw the box, should have known, but I still wasn't expecting it when he flipped it open and the icy fire of diamonds hit my eyes.

The ring held my gaze like a magnet.

"Are you serious?"

He pulled the ring out of the box and pressed his lips to mine in a hard kiss. "I've never been more serious, Alice. I told you, this is forever. I want to make it official. I want you to be my wife."

"Are you sure?" I didn't really need to ask. This was Cooper. I'd stopped wondering if he meant it when he said he loved me. I knew he did, knew that this man meant what he said, and he would love me forever.

"I've been ready to make you mine for ten years, Alice. I don't want to wait any longer."

"I don't want to wait either, Cooper. Let's get married."

I held up my hand and he slid the ring on my finger. Of course, it was a perfect fit. This was Cooper. He knew everything about me right down to my ring size. The ring was gorgeous, sparking fire on my finger. Not small, but not so big it would overwhelm my pixie-sized hands. "You have good taste, Cooper Sinclair."

"Obviously. I fell in love with you, didn't I?"

Tears pricked my eyes. This man. How could he be so arrogant and so sweet at the same time? Because he was Cooper, and he was all mine.

"Soon, Alice," he ordered. "No June wedding. We can do it at Thanksgiving when everyone is here."

My family would be in Atlanta for the holiday along with his and the entire Winters clan.

Perfect.

"Whatever you want, boss," I said, and sank my fingers into his thick, silky hair, pulling him down for a kiss.

The first kiss of the rest of our lives.

The first kiss of our forever.

Epilogue Two

GRIFFEN

I HATED MY DESK. THIS OFFICE HAD BEEN MINE for the better part of a decade. It should have felt like home, but I'd never been a desk kind of guy. Any excuse to get in the field. I did my job, didn't slack on the paperwork, but I never felt truly alive sitting behind a desk. Now it looked like I'd be stuck here for the rest of my life.

Fucking Andrei Tsepov and his fucking idiot goons. I should be glad it was just a bullet to the shoulder. More than a few men had died that night. I could have been mowed down by one of the AR-15s they were using. If a bullet from an AR-15 had hit my shoulder I would have lost my arm.

One shot from a handgun and I'd been down. Shoulder wounds are a lot more complicated than people think. The bullet had nicked an artery and torn through ligaments and tendons, breaking bones along the way. Hours of surgery, weeks in a sling, followed by months of physical therapy. I was almost as good as new. *Almost.*

For a guy with a regular job, *almost* would have been good enough. For me, *almost* meant the end of my career. It had to be my right fucking arm, didn't it? My brain might have the reaction time I needed, but my right arm would always be a fraction too slow.

No matter how much I wanted to be in the field, wanted the adrenaline and the danger, I wouldn't risk a client's life to soothe my ego.

I was grounded. I'd have to find a way to live with that.

I'm not a brooder. I grew up in a family of volatile personalities, surrounded by rage and betrayal, malice and grudges. I'd walked away when I was twenty-two, resentful and angry, but once I'd tasted the freedom of life away from my family I'd made a decision.

I wasn't going to let the bullshit get me down.

There's always a bright side, always a reason to laugh. I'd never give in to hate. I'd seen what happened to people who did that, seen the way it sucked the life from them, leaving them dried up, bitter husks.

That wouldn't be me. That would never be me.

For fourteen years, I'd managed to hold on to that, always ready with a smile, always looking for the silver lining. And now this. Holed up in my office during the day, hiding in my house at night. Grumbling, growling, and snapping at my friends, the friends who'd become my family.

I knew I was being an asshole. I tried to smile, to laugh, tried to pretend everything was great, but we all knew it was a lie.

Everything wasn't fucking great. Everything was all fucked up.

A buzz sounded on my phone. Alice at the front desk. I picked up the handset and winced as I heard myself bark, "What?"

I was being a bastard. Alice was like a sister, now married to my best friend. She was family. She deserved better than me being a dick.

Before I could apologize, she let out her sparkling pixie's laugh and said, "Hello to you, too, sunshine. You have a visitor. Says her name is Hope Daniels. Should I bring her back?"

Hope Daniels?

Not possible.

What were the chances the name could be a coincidence?

None. No chance.

I cursed the universe. Kick a man while he's down, why don't you? Whatever dark force had brought fucking Hope Daniels to Atlanta, it could just take her back.

Twenty-year-old Griffen would have welcomed her with open arms. The Griffen of six months ago would have at least been curious. Me now? With this fucking bum shoulder aching like a rotten tooth, I wanted to tell Hope to fuck off and get out.

No good could come of Hope Daniels walking back into my life.

"Griffen? You want me to just leave her standing here until she gathers dust?"

I couldn't help the tiny smile that spread across my face. I shut it down. Might as well get this over with. I'd find out what Hope wanted and get rid of her. No big deal.

"Bring her back."

"Righty-ho!" Alice hung up.

Hope fucking Daniels.

Alice was going to want to know who she was. Cooper, Evers, Knox, everyone would want to know who she was. When was the last time a woman had walked into the office and asked for me? Never. I kept my personal life separate from work. Always.

Hope wasn't personal. Not like that.

She wasn't a woman, she was a sign of the fucking apocalypse.

All too soon, Alice swung open the door of my office. My first thought was that she must have made a mistake. The woman standing beside her was not Hope Daniels.

She was tall and slender like Hope, with the same sandy brown hair and cognac colored eyes, but this was not my Hope.

With her hair scraped back into a tight knot at the base of her skull, her face pale and eyes flat, she looked more like a scarecrow than a woman. Hope had always been slender, slight of build despite her height, but this woman was scrawny. Brittle. Her face was devoid of makeup. She lacked all ornamentation outside of a simple set of gold studs in her ears.

The woman who called herself Hope Daniels stood in front of me wearing a beige suit that fit her as if it had been purchased for someone else, the jacket and skirt boxy, overwhelming her frame and hiding any hint of the body beneath.

Her matching pumps were dull and serviceable. She was neat and clean, but utterly and completely bland. Forgettable. I studied her, searching for any hint of the Hope I'd known so well.

My Hope had reminded me of Alice. She'd been far quieter than our outspoken office manager, but Hope had the same core of steel and, like Alice, a funky, quirky style all her own. I'd loved keeping an eye out for the secrets she'd hide in her school uniform.

A headband embroidered with skeletons. Socks with mermaids woven into the pattern. She'd spent her allowance looking for ways to be different despite her guardian's demand that she fit in. My Hope wouldn't have been caught dead in beige.

Alice waited at the door, expectant, her eyes ping-ponging between me and Hope. When neither of us said a word, she raised an eyebrow and offered, "Coffee? Tea?"

"No, thanks, Alice. Hope won't be here long enough for that."

Narrowing her eyes at my rudeness, Alice shrugged a shoulder and excused herself. I had no doubt her next stop was Cooper's office. Whatever. They were my friends, and this absolutely qualified as gossip. If the tables had been turned, I would have done the same.

Not only was a female visitor unusual, I was never rude. Well, lately, yeah, but it was only to the friends I knew would put up with my bullshit. Not in the office with a stranger. But then, Hope Daniels was no stranger.

In a low voice that held no inflection, Hope said, "May I take a seat?"

I leaned back in my chair. "Suit yourself."

No reaction from Hope. There'd been a day when an unkind comment from me would make her eyes fill with tears—not that she'd ever been subject to an unkind comment from me. Not until the end. In the end, there'd been tears all around.

She sat, smoothing her ugly skirt over her legs and crossing her feet at the ankle. It was like the Hope I'd known had been wiped clean, an automaton substituted in her place. This new Hope grated against every nerve.

Hope had been a girl when I'd walked away from Sawyers Bend. Only a girl, but she'd been the spark that set the fire, the one who'd turned the gears that ended in heartbreak and loss, in a grudge that would last the rest of my life.

"What do you want?"

Showing her first sign of weakness, Hope drew in a long breath and looked down at the purse she'd stowed neatly on her lap. When she looked back at me, her eyes held the faintest glimmer of emotion.

The last words she'd spoken to me had shattered my life. This time was no different.

"Your father's dead. Ford is in jail for his murder. All the assets, corporate and personal, are frozen until the will is read."

I swallowed, fighting the burn of her words. Those people meant nothing to me. Not anymore. Hardening my heart, I forced myself to say, "Then read the will and leave me out of it."

"We can't. Your father stipulated the will couldn't be read without you."

Her words lanced through me, cauterizing the wound as they went, leaving me numb and hollow.

My father was dead.

I hadn't seen him in fourteen years. I'd hated him far longer than that.

I wasn't alone in hating my father. Prentiss Sawyer was one of the most hated men in our patch of North Carolina. Hell, he was probably one of the most hated men in the country. Stalling, I said, "How? What happened?"

"Sterling found him in his office at Heartstone Manor. He was shot. He'd been dead a while."

Sterling. My little sister. Half-sister. Most of my siblings were halves. Prentiss collected wives, but he was shit at keeping them. I resisted the urge to ask if Sterling was okay. Sterling wasn't my problem. None of them were.

"Where?"

"His office," Hope repeated more slowly, as if I were hard of hearing.

"No, where on his body was he shot?"

"His forehead."

Execution style. A crime of passion I could see. An angry husband or a betrayed lover, sure. Not an assassination. And Ford was in jail for killing him? No way.

I had a lot of reasons to hate my brother, but there was no way he could have killed our father with a single shot to the forehead. Ford didn't have it in him. He knew his way around a gun, all the Sawyer kids did, but that kind of cold-blooded murder? No.

How much had changed since I'd left?

I pushed Ford from my mind. *Not your problem*, I reminded myself. "The bastard changed his will after I left. Again."

My father was famous for changing his will. He used that thing like a weapon, setting my siblings and me against one another in a constant play for dominance.

It wasn't enough that the Sawyers practically owned the town of Sawyers Bend, owned hundreds of millions of dollars in real estate and industry in North Carolina and the surrounding states.

Prentiss Sawyer wasn't happy unless the rest of us were dancing to his tune like puppets on strings. That will had been changed so many times the fees he paid to the family estate attorney had bought the man a second home.

I'd walked away from Sawyers Bend, turned my back on my family after they'd betrayed me in the worst way. My father's will was not my problem.

"He kicked me out fourteen years ago," I reminded her. "I have my own life now. Solve your own problems. "

A ghost of emotion flitted across Hope's face. Fear? Worry? Desperation? It was gone so fast I couldn't tell.

She leaned forward a scant inch. "Griffen, you need to understand—everything is frozen. Everything. Personal funds. Business funds. Everything. People won't get paid. Businesses will go under. The *town* will go under. You don't have to stay. Please, just come home so Harvey can read the will. As soon as it's done you can leave, and you never have to see any of us again."

Fucking hell. My goddamned father. He always knew how to twist the knife.

He wanted me back in Sawyers Bend for some godforsaken reason, and he was the expert at getting his way, even from beyond the grave.

He knew I wouldn't come back if he asked. I didn't need the Sawyer fortune. I'd been raised to take the helm, groomed to follow in my father's footsteps, but I'd walked away. I'd made my own money. I didn't need my father's fortune, and I didn't owe those people a fucking thing.

My family was poison, but the town of Sawyers Bend was a different story.

Sawyers Bend was filled with people just trying to live their lives. Good people. People dependent on the various Sawyer enterprises for their livelihood. Without the free flow of Sawyer cash, Sawyers Bend would grind to a halt, and it was the people of the town who would suffer first.

I wanted nothing to do with my family, but I wouldn't destroy the town.

"When is the reading of the will?"

"Tomorrow afternoon. Harvey's office."

"I'll be there. And then I'm leaving."

I watched Hope walk out of my office, her back straight, posture perfect, the girl I'd known nowhere in sight.

Noon. I'd be back on the road to Atlanta by five, finally done with Sawyers Bend.

Nothing on this earth could convince me to stay a second longer.

ARE YOU READY FOR GRIFFEN'S STORY?

Visit IvyLayne.com/Griffen
to see what happens next!

Never Miss a New

Release:

Join Ivy's Reader's Group

@ ivylayne.com/readers

&

Get two books for free!

Don't miss
the series that started
it all.
The Alpha Billionaire
Club Trilogy.

Also By Ivy Layne

THE UNTANGLED SERIES

Unraveled
Undone
Uncovered

SCANDALS OF THE BAD BOY BILLIONAIRES

The Billionaire's Secret Heart (Novella)
The Billionaire's Secret Love (Novella)
The Billionaire's Pet
The Billionaire's Promise
The Rebel Billionaire
The Billionaire's Secret Kiss (Novella)
The Billionaire's Angel
Engaging the Billionaire
Compromising the Billionaire
The Counterfeit Billionaire
Series Extras: ivylayne.com/extras

THE ALPHA BILLIONAIRE CLUB

The Wedding Rescue
The Courtship Maneuver
The Temptation Trap

About Ivy Layne

Ivy Layne has had her nose stuck in a book since she first learned to decipher the English language. Sometime in her early teens, she stumbled across her first Romance, and the die was cast. Though she pretended to pay attention to her creative writing professors, she dreamed of writing steamy romance instead of literary fiction. These days, she's neck deep in alpha heroes and the smart, sexy women who love them.

Married to her very own alpha hero (who rubs her back after a long day of typing, but also leaves his socks on the floor). Ivy lives in the mountains of North Carolina where she and her other half are having a blast raising two energetic little boys. Aside from her family, Ivy's greatest loves are coffee and chocolate, preferably together.

Visit Ivy

Facebook.com/AuthorIvyLayne
Instagram.com/authorivylayne/
www.ivylayne.com
books@ivylayne.com

Made in the USA
Middletown, DE
03 November 2023